Last night my whole world came tumbling down. Now I'm running scared.

Have you ever been going along, living your life, living in your reality, and then suddenly something happens that rips your world right in two? You see something or hear something, and suddenly everything you are, everything you're doing, shatters into a thousand shards of sharp, bitter realization.

It happened to me last night.

About the Author

Cate Tiernan was born in New Orleans, LA. She loves the idea of magick, and tries to write worlds that she would prefer to live in. She currently lives in North Carolina with her husband, four children, and a bunch of pets.

IMMORTAL BELOVED

Cate Tiernan

HODDER

First published in America by Little, Brown and Company,
a division of Hachette Book Group, Inc.
First published in Great Britain in 2011 by Hodder & Stoughton
An Hachette UK company

First published in paperback in 2011

1

A CIP catalogue record for this title is available from the British Library.

B format paperback: 9781444707014
A format paperback: 9781444707069
Ebook: 9781848949904

Typeset in MT Sabon by Hewer Text UK Ltd, Edinburgh

Printed and bound in the UK by Clays Ltd, St Ives plc

Hodder & Stoughton policy is to use papers that are natural, renewable
and recyclable products and made from wood grown in sustainable forests.
The logging and manufacturing processes are expected to conform
to the environmental regulations of the country of origin.

Hodder & Stoughton Ltd
338 Euston Road
London NW1 3BH

www.hodder.co.uk

With love to my husband, Paul —
the bearer of unconditional things.
Your love and support make it all possible.

With appreciation and affection to Erin Murphy,
for your hand-holding, cheerleading,
and savvy instincts.

Thank you.

Chapter 1

Last night my whole world came tumbling down. Now I'm running scared.

Have you ever been going along, living your life, living in your reality, and then suddenly something happens that rips your world right in two? You see something or hear something, and suddenly everything you *are*, everything you're *doing*, shatters into a thousand shards of sharp, bitter realization.

It happened to me last night.

I was in London. With friends, as usual. We were going out, as usual.

'No, no, turn here!' Boz leaned forward and jabbed the cabbie on the shoulder. 'Here!'

The cabbie, his huge, broad shoulders barely encased in a sweatshirt and plaid vest, turned around and gave Boz a look that would have made a normal person sit back and be very quiet.

But Boz was by no means a normal person: He was prettier than most, louder than most, funner than most, and, God knew, dumber than most. We'd just come from a dance club where a knife fight had suddenly broken out. These two crazy girls had been pulling hair and screaming like fishwives, and then one of them had pulled out a knife. My gang had wanted to stay and watch – they loved stuff like that – but, you know, if you've seen one knife fight, you've seen them all. I'd dragged them all away, and we'd stumbled out into the night, luckily grabbing a cab before the cold made us sober up.

'Here! Right here in the middle of the block, my good man!' Boz said, earning himself a murderous look that made me feel grateful all over again for gun control in Merrie Olde England.

'My good man?' Cicely snickered next to me. The six of us were packed into the back of this big black cab. There could have been more, but we'd found that six wasted immortals were all the back of a London cab could hold, and that was only if no one puked.

'Yes, Jeeves,' Cicely went on brightly. 'Stop here.'

The cabbie slammed his foot on the brakes, and we all shot forward. Boz and Katy hit their heads on the glass partition between us and the driver. Stratton, Innocencio, and I all catapulted off our seats, landing in an ungraceful, giggling heap on the dirty cab floor.

'Hey!' Boz said, rubbing his forehead.

Innocencio found me under the tangle of arms and legs. 'You okay, Nas?'

I nodded, still laughing.

'Get t' hell outta my cab!' our driver spat. He lurched out of the front seat, came around, and yanked our door open. My back was against the door, and I immediately fell out into the gutter, hitting my head on the stone curb.

'Ow! Ow!' The gutter was wet – it'd been raining, of course. The pain, the cold, and the wet barely penetrated my consciousness – knife fight aside, the evening of heavy festivities had wrapped me in a warm cocoon of hazy well-being.

'Out!' the cabbie said again, grabbing my shoulders and hauling me out of the way. He dumped me on the sidewalk and reached in for Incy.

Okay, hello, anger and a trickle of consciousness. I frowned, rubbing my shoulders, sitting up. We were a block away from the Dungeon, yet another horribly seedy underground bar where we hung out. And only this short block away, the street was dark and deserted, empty lots alternating with burned-out crack houses, giving the street a missing-tooth appearance.

'All right, hands off!' Innocencio said, landing on the sidewalk next to me. His face was cold with fury, and he looked more awake than I'd thought.

'You lot!' the cabbie snarled. 'I don't want your kind in my cab! Rich kids, think you're better than everyone else!' He leaned into the cab, grabbing Katy's coat collar while Boz scrambled out on his own.

'Uh – gonna be sick,' Katy said, half in, half out of the cab. Boz jumped out of the way just as Katy's system purged itself of an evening's worth of Jameson whiskey – right on the cabbie's shoes.

'Goddamn it!' the cabbie roared, shaking his feet in disgust.

Boz and I giggled – we couldn't help it. Mean Mr Taxi Driver.

The cabbie grabbed Katy's arms, intending to haul her to the sidewalk, and suddenly Incy muttered something and snapped his hand open.

I had a split second to think, Huh, and then the cab driver staggered as if struck with an axe. Katy went slack in his hands and he crumpled, his spine curving almost in half. He pitched backward, landing heavily on the sidewalk, his face white, eyes wide open.

A wave of nausea and fatigue overcame me – maybe I'd had more to drink than I thought. 'Incy, what'd you do?' I asked, bemused, as I got to my feet. 'Did you use *magick* on him?' I gave a little laugh – the idea was kind of ridiculous. I leaned against the lamppost, holding my face up to the chilly mist. A few deep breaths and I felt better.

Katy blinked blearily, and Boz chuckled.

Innocencio stood up, frowning at his new D & G boots, now flecked with rain.

Stratton and Cicely got out of the other side of the cab and joined us. They looked down at the cabbie, lying frozen on the wet pavement, and shook their heads.

'Very nice,' Stratton said to Incy. 'Very impressive, Mr Magician. You can let the poor sod up now.'

We were all looking at each other and at the cabbie. I couldn't remember the last time I'd seen anyone use magick like this. Yeah, maybe to get a good table at a restaurant or to catch that last train on the Underground . . .

'I don't think so, Strat,' said Innocencio, his face still tight. 'I don't think he's a very nice man.'

Stratton and I met eyes. I tapped Innocencio on the shoulder. He and I had been partners in crime for almost a century, and we knew each other very, very well, but this cold rage was something I hadn't seen too much of. 'Right, leave him, then. He'll be fine in a few minutes, yeah? Let's go – I'm thirsty. And I guess Katy is now, too.'

Katy made a face. 'Ugh.'

'Yeah, let's go,' said Cicely. 'They have a band tonight, and I want to dance.'

'By the time he comes to, we'll be long gone.' I tugged on Incy's sleeve.

'Hang on,' said Incy.

'Leave him,' I repeated. I felt a little bad about just leaving the cabbie in the chilly, sprinkling rain, but he'd be okay once the spell wore off.

Innocencio shrugged off my hand, surprising me. As I watched, he snapped both of his hands open at the cabbie, his lips moving. I didn't hear what he said.

With a loud, horrible cracking sound, the cabbie bucked upward, once, his mouth opening in a scream he was unable to voice.

Again I felt a wave of nausea, saw a gray film pass

over my eyes. I blinked several times, reaching out for Cicely's arm. She chuckled as I staggered, obviously blaming drink. A few moments later my vision cleared, and I straightened up, staring at Incy, at the cabbie. 'Now what? What'd you *do*?'

'Oh, Incy,' Stratton said, shaking his head. 'Tsk, tsk. Bit unnecessary, surely? Well, let's get going, then.' He set off down the sidewalk toward the Dungeon, closing his warm coat against the chill.

'Incy – what'd you do?' I repeated.

Incy shrugged. 'Sod deserved it.'

Katy, still a little green around the gills, stared dully at the cab driver, then at Innocencio. She coughed and shook her head, then headed off with Stratton. I let go of Cicely and she shrugged, taking Boz's arm. They followed the others, and soon their footsteps faded into the darkness.

'Incy,' I said, taken aback that the others were just leaving. 'Incy – did you – break his back, with magick? Where'd you learn how to do something like that? No – you didn't. Right?'

Incy looked at me then, a half-amused expression on his unearthly, darkly handsome face. His black curls were flecked with tiny diamonds of rain, glittering in the lamplight.

'Darling. You saw what he was like,' he said.

I looked at him, then at the cabbie, still motionless, his face a rictus of pain and terror. 'You broke his *back*?'

I repeated, suddenly quite sober and horribly present. My brain skittered around the thought as if it were a hot spark to avoid. 'You used magick to – good lord. Okay, well, go ahead and fix him, then,' I said. 'I want a drink, but I'll wait.' I couldn't help the cabbie myself. I had no idea where Incy had learned a spell like that, and no idea how to counteract it, undo it, whatever. For the most part, I shied away from magick, the magick immortals are born with, that comes naturally to us. It was too much trouble, and it usually made me physically ill. The last time I'd dabbled in it, I'd at most made someone walk into a door or spill coffee on herself. And that had been ages ago. Nothing like this.

Innocencio ignored me and looked down at the cab driver. 'Right, mate,' he said in a low voice. The cab driver's eyes, now wild with shock and pain, focused on his with difficulty.

'That's what happens when you're rude to my friends, see? I hope you've learned your lesson.'

The cab driver couldn't even grunt, and I realized he was under a nul-vox spell. An actual nul-vox spell – I'd only maybe seen that just once or twice before, in hundreds of years. Much less –

'Come on, undo it,' I said impatiently. I'd never seen Incy like this, do something like this. 'You taught him a lesson. The others are waiting for us. Just undo it so we can go.'

Incy rolled his shoulders, shrugged, and took my hand

in a hard, painful grip. 'Can't undo it, my love,' he said, and raised my hand to his lips to kiss. He pulled me with him toward the Dungeon, and I looked back at the cabbie over my shoulder.

'Can't undo it? You broke his back for *good*?' I stared at Incy, my best friend for the past century. He grinned down at me, his beautiful angel's face haloed by the streetlamp.

'In for a penny, in for a pound,' he said gaily.

I gaped. 'What next, putting Stratton through a wood chipper?' My voice was rising as the increasing mist wet my face. Incy laughed, kissed my hair, and marched me forward. In those moments I'd seen something different in his eyes – more than just uncaring indifference, more than a casual need for revenge. Incy had enjoyed breaking that man's back, had enjoyed seeing someone writhing in pain and fear. It had been *exciting* for him.

My brain whirled. Should I call 999? Was it already too late for that cabbie? Was he going to die, already dying? I leaned away from Incy, turning back, but within seconds I felt the vibrations of the deep bass drums of some band, throbbing up through the ground, through my shoes. The Dungeon seemed like another world, another reality, beckoning me to it, lulling me with its noise, letting me leave the appalling shock of the paralyzed cabbie outside. I wanted so badly just to succumb to it.

'Incy – but – you have to —'

Incy just shot me an amused look, and a minute later we were going down a steep flight of stairs slick with rain. I was split by indecision as Incy raised his fist and pounded on the red-painted door. I suddenly felt as though we'd gone down the steps to hell and were waiting for admittance. A small slit in the door opened, and Guvnor, the bouncer, nodded at us. The door opened and an enormous swell of music throbbed out at us and drew us in, into the darkness lit by burning cigarette tips, the hundreds of voices competing with the screaming band, the smell of liquor coiling sweetly into every breath I took.

The cabbie, outside – this felt like my last chance. My last chance to take action, to act like a person who gave a crap, like a normal person.

'Nasty!' I was enveloped in a huge, slightly unbalanced hug. 'I love your hair!' my friend Mal shouted as loud as she could into my ear. 'Come dance!' She put her arm around my shoulders and pulled me into the dark, low-ceilinged room.

I hesitated only a second.

And just like that, I let myself leave the outside world behind, let myself disappear into the noise and the smoke. I was horrified, and if you knew the usual high jinks I myself was often up to, those words would have more weight for you. I split away from Incy, not sure what to think. He'd just done what I thought was probably the very worst thing I'd ever seen him do. Worse than that incident with that mayor's horse, back in the forties. Worse than that poor girl who'd actually wanted to marry him, in the 1970s. That had been such a disaster. I'd managed to explain away those situations to myself, made them make sense. This one I was having a harder time with.

With a last, beautiful grin at me, Incy headed off to prowl the crowd that was already sending out tendrils of interest, from both males and females. Incy was irresistible, a seductive magnet, and most people, human and immortal alike, were helpless under the charm that hid a side that was, suddenly, so much darker than I'd realized.

Twenty minutes later, I was making out heavily on a sticky couch with Mal's friend Jase, who was cheerful and drunk and adorable. I wanted to sink into him, be someone else, be the person Jase was seeing on the outside. He wasn't immortal, didn't know I was, but he was a welcome distraction that I threw myself into with nervous urgency. People talked and smoked and drank all around us while I ran my hands under his shirt and he wound his legs around me. His fingers pushed into my short black hair, and with a sudden shock I felt an unexpected warm breeze on my neck.

I was already reeling back, grabbing for my scarf, quickly rewinding it around me when I heard Incy say, 'Nas? What's that on the back of your neck?'

I looked over my shoulder at Incy standing by the end of the couch, a drink in one hand, a long cigarette glowing in the other. His eyes were black holes, glittering at me in the darkness.

My heart was beating hard. *Don't overreact, Nasty.* 'Nothing.' I shrugged and collapsed on Jase, and he reached up for me again.

'Nas?' Incy's voice was quiet but determined. 'You know, I don't remember ever seeing the back of your neck, come to think of it.'

I forced a small laugh and looked up even as Jase tried to kiss me again. 'Don't be daft, of course you have. Now clear off. Busy here.'

'Is it a tattoo?'

I tugged my scarf tighter around my neck. 'Yes. It says, *If you can read this sign, you're too bloody close.* Now clear off!'

Incy laughed, to my relief, and moved away. The last I saw of him, a beautiful, slinky girl in satin was coiling around him like a snake.

And I just didn't let myself think about the cab driver again. When the thought, the vision, intruded, I squeezed my eyes shut and had another drink. But the next morning it all came back to me: the cabbie's face, the agony written there. He would never walk, never drive again, because Innocencio had snapped his spine and left him on a rainy London street, worse than dead.

And I had done nothing, *nothing.* I had *walked away.*

The good thing about being immortal is that you can't literally drink yourself to death, as frat boys can. The bad thing about being immortal is that you can't literally drink yourself to death, so you wake up the next morning, or maybe the day after that, and you feel everything you would be spared feeling if only you'd been lucky enough to die.

It was sort of light outside when I finally pried my eyes open for more than a few seconds. I blearily scanned the room and saw a window. The light coming in was pale and pink-tinged, which meant dusk or dawn. One or the other. Or perhaps the neighborhood was on fire. Always a possibility.

I knew it would be bad, trying to sit up, so I took it slowly, moving one small part of me at a time. Last was my head, which I raised cautiously a few inches off the mattress. The washed-out yellow roses of the bare mattress slowly clarified and resolved. Mattress, no sheet. Window with light. Dark painted brick walls, like a factory or something.

I turned my head slowly to see another sleeping body, a guy with spiky green hair, a thick silver chain around his neck, a writhing dragon tattoo covering most of his back. Um, Jeff? Jason? Jack? Something with a *J*, I was almost certain.

I achieved a semi-upright state several minutes later, then immediately hurled my guts up as my body attempted to rid itself of the toxins I'd ingested the night before.

I didn't make it to the toilet. Sorry, Jeff.

Feeling hollow and shaky and wishing immortality

wasn't so incredibly literal, I saw I was still wearing all my clothes, which meant either the J-man or I, or both, had been too wasted to further our . . . acquaintance last night. Just as well. Reflexively I felt for my scarf and found it still knotted tight around my throat. I relaxed a bit, then remembered Incy standing over me, asking me about the mark on the back of my neck. I couldn't believe that had happened on the same night as the cabbie. I swallowed, grimacing, and decided to think about that later.

My leather jacket and one of my beautiful green lizard-skin ankle boots were inexplicably missing, so I took the boot I could find and crept out, not that an earthquake would have woken Jay up then. I was pretty sure he was still alive – his chest seemed to be going up and down. I vaguely remembered having two drinks to each one of his.

I stepped over a couple more sleeping bodies on my way out. This was a big, bare warehouselike building, probably on the outskirts of town. My shoulder and butt felt bruised, and all of my muscles were sore as I limped down the industrial brick steps. Outside it was really cold, the wind whipping bits of trash up the deserted street.

At least it wasn't raining, I thought, and then it all flowed back into my brain, against my will: the night before, everything we'd done, the rain, the knife fight, falling on the sidewalk, Incy breaking that cabbie's spine, me almost losing my scarf in that club, in front of everyone. My stomach roiled again and I stopped for a moment, sucking in a cold breath as I ran through the details, dismay creeping over me anew. Where had Innocencio learned that magick? As far as I knew, he hadn't made a point of knowing any, and in the last century of our hanging out, I'd never seen him do much, certainly not anything that big, that dark. No friends in our immediate circle had honed their skills with magick. I leaned against the graffitied cinder-block wall of the warehouse while I pushed my bare foot into my one boot.

The cold air filled my nose and made it start running, and suddenly the morning was horribly bright, horribly clear. Incy had done something awful last night with powerful magick, out of the blue. And I had done something just as awful, though not with magick. I'd watched Incy break that guy's spine, and then I had just . . . walked away. I'd walked away and *gone dancing in a club*. What was wrong with me? How could I have done that? Had someone found the cabbie during the night? Someone had, surely. Even though that neighborhood was mostly deserted. Even though it had been very late. And raining. Still, someone must have happened on him, taken him to the hospital. Right?

And on top of that, Incy had actually seen the mark on the back of my neck. And might well remember it. How ironic. I'd been obsessive about keeping my neck covered at all times for the last 449 years, and all at once, one night, that effort had been shot. Would Incy know the significance of what he'd seen? How could he? No one did. No one who was still alive. So why did I feel so afraid?

And all of these horrible, fevered thoughts bring us back to the beginning:

Last night my whole world came tumbling down. Now I'm running scared.

Chapter 2

After some of the events I've witnessed, the Incy/
cabbie/magick/neck night should seem like a
party. I've raced away in the night, clinging to a horse's
mane, with nothing but the clothes on my back, while
a city behind me burned to the ground. I've seen bodies
covered with the oozing sores of the bubonic plague, piled
high in city streets like logs because there weren't enough
people alive to bury them. I was in Paris on July 14, 1789.
You never forget the sight of a human head on a pike.

But we weren't at war now. We were living an ordinary life, or as ordinary a life as an immortal can have. I
mean, there's always a bit of a surreal quality. If you live
long enough, through enough wars and invasions and
attacks by northern raiders, you end up defending yourself, sometimes to an extreme point. If someone's coming
at you with a sword, and you have a dagger tucked in the
back of your skirt, well . . .

But that was different. It didn't matter that your
attacker probably wouldn't kill you – how often does
someone actually cut your head clean off? – it still *felt*

like a life-or-death situation, and you reacted as if it were. But last night had been . . . just a regular night. No war, no berserkers, no life or death. Just a pissed-off cabbie.

Where had Incy gotten that spell? Yes, we're immortal, we have magick running through our veins, but one has to learn on purpose how to use it. Over the years, I'd known some people who were all about studying magick, learning spells, learning whatever they needed to learn to wield it. But I'd figured out a long time ago that I didn't want to. I'd seen the death and destruction that magick could cause, I'd seen what people were willing to do to pursue it, and I didn't want to have anything to do with it. I wanted to pretend it didn't exist. And I'd found some like-minded aefrelyffen (an old word for immortals), and we hung out.

Okay, maybe I'd use magick to get a cab when it's raining and there's none to be found. To make the person in front of me not want that last *pain au chocolat*. That kind of thing. But to snap someone's spine, for fun?

I'd seen Incy use people, break girls' and boys' hearts, steal, be callous — and it was just part of his charm. He was reckless and selfish and a user — but not to me. To me he was sweet and generous and funny and fun, willing to go anywhere, do anything. He was the one who would call me to go to Morocco at a moment's notice. The one I'd call to get me out of a jam. If some guy wouldn't take no for an answer, Incy was there, smiling his wolfish smile. If some woman made a snide remark, Incy's wit would skewer her in front of everyone. He helped me pick out what to wear, brought me fabulous stuff from wherever he went, never criticized me, never made me feel bad.

And I'd done the same for him—once breaking a bottle over a woman's head after she went after Incy with a long metal nail file. I'd paid off doormen, lied to bobbies and gendarmes, and pretended to be his wife or his sister or his enraged lover, whatever the situation demanded. We would howl about it afterward, falling together, laughing until tears came out of our eyes. The fact that we'd never been lovers, never had that awkwardness between us, only made it more perfect.

He was my best friend—the best friend I'd ever had. We'd been tight for almost a century, so it was amazing that he'd managed to shock me last night. And amazing that our other friends hadn't been shocked. And amazing that I'd managed to reach a new low, even for me. The low of indifference. The low of cowardice. And, to top it all off, Incy had seen my neck. Better and better.

When I got back to my London flat, I took a shower, sitting on the marble floor and letting the hot water rain down on my head for a long time, trying to wash the alcohol and the warehouse off my skin. I couldn't even name what I was feeling. Fear? Shame? It was as if I'd woken up into a different life from the one I'd woken up into yesterday, and I was a different person. And this life and I were both suddenly much darker and grosser and more dangerous than I'd realized.

I soaped up all over, practically feeling the alcohol oozing out of my pores. I washed my hair, automatically avoiding my . . . it's not a tattoo. Immortals get tattoos, of course, and they last a long time, maybe about ninety years or so. Other scars heal, fade, and disappear much more quickly and completely than on regular people. A couple of years later, you can't tell where you were injured or burned.

Except for me. The mark on the back of my neck was a burn, and I'd had it since I was ten years old. It had never faded, never changed, and the skin was slightly indented, patterned. It was round, about two inches across. It had been caused by a red-hot amulet pressed against my skin 449 years ago. Sure, despite my paranoia, the occasional person had seen it, now and again, over the last four and a half centuries. But as far as I knew, no one *now living* had ever seen it. Except for Incy, last night.

Finally I got out, all prune-y. I wrapped myself up in a thick robe I'd taken from some hotel, avoiding looking at myself in the mirror. Feeling like a ghost, a wraith, I wandered into the living room and saw the *London Times* on the floor in front of my door, where I'd kicked it. I carried it into the kitchenette, where all I found were an ancient packet of McVitie's and a bottle of vodka in the freezer. So I sat on my sofa and ate the stale crackers, skimming the *Times*. It was buried way in the back, before the obits but after, like, Girl Guide meeting announcements. It said: *Trevor Hollis, 48, an independent taxicab driver, was attacked last night by one of his fares and suffered a broken spine. He is in the ICU of St James's Hospital, undergoing tests. Doctors have said he will likely be paralyzed from the shoulders down. He has been unable to name or describe his attacker. His wife and children have been at his side.*

Paralyzed below the shoulders. If I had called an ambulance, gotten him help sooner, would it have made a difference? How long had he lain on the sidewalk, rigid with pain, unable to scream?

Why hadn't I called 999? What was wrong with me? He could have died. Maybe he would have preferred to. He wouldn't be driving a cab any longer. He had a wife and children. What kind of a husband could he be now? What kind of a father? My eyes got blurry, and the stale crackers turned to dust in my throat.

I had been part of that. I hadn't helped. I'd probably made it worse.

What had I become? What had Incy turned into?

The phone rang and I ignored it. My buzzer sounded three times, and I let the doorman handle it. I'd lost my mobile a couple of days ago and hadn't gotten around to replacing it, so I didn't have to worry about that. Finally, at about eight, I got up and went to my bedroom and pulled out my biggest suitcase, the one that could hold a dead pony. (Before you go there, I'll clarify that it never has.)

Quickly, with a sense of abrupt urgency, I grabbed armfuls of clothes and whatever and shoved them in, and when it was full, I zipped it up, found a jacket, and headed out. Gopala, the doorman, got me a cab.

'Mr Bawz and Mr Innosaunce were looking for you, Miss Nastalya,' he told me. I'd always been amused at how he butchered all of our names. Of course, he was doing a damn sight better here than what I could do if you plunked me down in the middle of Bangalore and expected me to hold a job.

'I'll be back soon,' I told Gopala as the cabdriver hefted my suitcase into the boot.

'Ah, are you off to see your parents, Miss Nastalya?'

As usual, I'd invented mythical parents for myself, to explain why a teenager would be living on her own with an unlimited income.

'Oh, no – they're still in . . .' I thought quickly – 'Tasmania. I'm just going to Paris, do some shopping.' Maybe I was having a nervous breakdown. I felt afraid, anxious, ashamed, and cautious, as if every cabdriver in London now carried my picture on his sun visor, with a big red WANTED stamped across my face. I felt as if Innocencio would spring out at me from behind a big planter, and didn't know what I'd do if he did. I remembered his expression as he looked down at me from the end of the couch. He'd looked . . . intrigued. Calculating? Even if he had no idea of the significance of my scar, I *hated* the fact that he knew about it. I felt like I'd never be able to bear to see him again, and he was my best friend. My best friend who'd crippled someone last night, whom I was now – afraid of? This was my life. This was the situation I had created for myself.

I scrambled into the backseat of the cab, giving Gopala a big tip. 'Just off to Paris. Back soon!'

Gopala smiled and nodded, touching the bill of his doorman's cap.

'So, you want St Pancras?' the cabbie asked, marking his log. 'Catch the train through the Chunnel?'

'No,' I said as I sank down into the seat. 'Take me to Heathrow.'

The next morning I was in Boston, in America, renting a car at some dinky little company that would rent to someone under twenty-five.

'Here you are, Ms Douglas,' said the clerk, handing over a set of keys. 'And how do you say your first name?'

'Phillipa,' I answered. Like every immortal, I have a bunch of different passports and IDs and driver's licenses. Someone always has a friend who knows someone who can get what we need. For years I'd used this one little man in Frankfurt. He'd been a genius, had forged a thousand different identity papers during World War II. My passports list different names, ages (in my case, a range between eighteen and twenty-one), places of origin. It had been so much easier before governments started tracking people. I mean, birth certificates? Social Security numbers? What a freaking headache. 'Phil-ip-pah.'

'What a pretty name,' the clerk said, giving me a cheer-leader smile.

'Uh-huh. Is the car out this way?'

As soon as I was out of Boston, I pulled over and unfolded my map of Massachusetts. The rental-car people could have plotted the course to West Lowing for me, but then they might remember doing it, if anyone asked them later. And right now I just wanted to disappear. I felt like – like the devil was after me. Like I was being swallowed up in a disaster or something and just had to get . . . far away.

I'd had seven hours to think about things on the flight from London to Boston. Seven hours isn't long enough to fully contemplate four hundred years of mounting dark-ness and stupidity, but it's plenty of time to remember enough bad things to make you feel like a slug beneath a rock. Worse than a slug. Like slime mold.

I found West Lowing. It was smack dab in the middle of Massachusetts, near Lowing Lake and right on Lowing River. I'm guessing someone named Lowing was a big shot a couple hundred years ago and felt a need to splash his name all over the place.

It would take only about two hours to drive there. In Ireland, two hours of driving could take you three-quarters of the way across the country, horizontally. You could drive straight through Luxembourg in about five minutes. America is a big, big place. Big enough to get lost in? I hoped so.

* * *

So, the whole immortal thing. You must have questions. I don't have all the answers. I don't know how many of us there are. I've met hundreds over the years, and simple math says our numbers must be increasing all the time, right? New ones are born, old ones only very rarely check out. You've probably run into quite a few yourself, without realizing it. Basically, immortals are humans who just don't die when we're supposed to.

Most of us believe that there have simply always been immortals, just as people who believe in vampires think there have always been vampires. (In fact, if you look into old vampire myths, you'll see some overlap with the 'living forever' theme.) I don't know how we began, or where, or why, but I've met immortals of most races and ethnicities. It does take two immortals to make new little immortals, so when an immortal hooks up with a regular person, their offspring won't be immortal – but in a lot of cases, those are the people who live weirdly long lives, like over a hundred years. There was that woman in France – and there's a town in Georgia (the country, not the state), where an odd proportion of people live to be over a hundred years old. They attribute it to their healthy living and yogurt-heavy diet. Ha! It just means there was an immortal there who really got around.

We do age, but in a different pattern than humans. Most of the time, until you're about sixteen, it's a year = a year. After that, it's usually about a year = a hundred human years. I've seen immortals who have aged a lot faster or slower, but I have no idea why. The oldest person I've ever met was about eight hundred. He'd been awful, so full of himself, mean and evil. What's odd is meeting an immortal who's still only about forty or fifty – it hasn't really sunk in for them, the reality, and they feel like adults but still look like teenagers. It leaves them in a weird limbo, and they kind of don't know what to do with themselves.

For myself, I was born in 1551, a nice symmetrical number. Almost 460 years later, I still get carded in bars. Before you think *Oh, awesome!* let me tell you what a pain in the ass that is. I'm an adult. I've been a grown-up for*ever*. But I'm locked in an eternal twilight of adolescence, and I just can't move past how I look. But then, many teens seem to feel immortal, as though nothing can touch them. The concept of danger or death is completely foreign, without weight or reality. So maybe I *am* still a teenager. Okay, I know: Cry me a river.

We don't get cancer or diabetes or things like that. We do get colds and flu and the plague, but we recover. For your info, smallpox scars take about fifteen years to fade. We can get burned, have limbs cut off, have horrible wounds – but they heal, as I explained earlier. It takes time, but they all heal. Limbs grow back, a process both disgusting and fascinating. It takes several years. Despite our name, we can be killed. But it takes some doing, so don't knock yourself out trying.

What do we do with all of our time? Lots of the same

stuff regular people do. We live on the same planet, we have the same resources available to us. Some of us are wastrel partiers. (Not naming any names – okay, me.) Some immortals use their time more wisely: to study, learn, hone artistic talents or crafts, travel. Some people neither party nor improve themselves. They live in a perpetual state of dissatisfaction, not liking anything, always finding something to complain about, hating other immortals, hating humans. I've met people like that, and I've always wanted to put them on an ice floe and push them off into the ocean.

Do we get married, have kids? Sometimes. I've been married. It's a conundrum – if you marry a regular person, no matter how much you love him, he gets old and dies and you don't. So at some point, you either have to tell him about yourself, or you let him stew and wonder. Either one of you has a secret, or both of you do. And if you marry another immortal, well, you're going to be married a looong time. Worse, if you're married to a non-aefrelyffen and you have kids, seeing those kids age and die is even worse than seeing your spouse age and die. But more on all that later.

Four hours, three espressos, and a bag of Chips Ahoy! later, I hit West Lowing. I drove straight through the town in less than ten minutes. Not a major metropolis. I turned around and drove back into it, cruising the neighborhoods, following the winding roads around the town's outskirts. I didn't even know what I was looking for. A sign? Either a literal sign, like RIVER'S EDGE, TURN LEFT, or a metaphorical sign, like a burning bush or something, a bolt of lightning pointing me in the right direction.

Two minutes later I was out of the town again. I pulled over, leaned my head on the steering wheel, and slammed my palms against the dashboard.

'Nastasya, you are an idiot. You are a stupid effing idiot, and you deserve this.' Actually, I deserved so much worse, but then, I'm pretty easy on myself.

After several minutes of thought and consideration, I got out of the car and walked into the woods by the side of the road. No cars had passed me in a while. About twenty feet in, hidden from the road, I knelt on the ground, putting my hands flat. I said a bunch of words, words so old that they sounded like a string of unrelated syllables. Words that had already been ancient by the time I was born.

Words that reveal hidden things.

One of the few spells I knew. I couldn't remember the last time I'd used it. Maybe to find my keys, back in the nineties?

I closed my eyes, and after a minute, images floated into focus. I saw a road, a turn, the shape of a maple tree, its leaves sprayed with autumn's colors. I saw where I needed to go.

Taking a deep breath, I stood up. Where my hands had been, the leaves and twigs were powdered, dry, disintegrating. Bits of late clover were withered and dying, their cells sucked dry of life so I could work my baby spell. Two handprints of destruction marked where I'd gotten my power. Because that's how immortals do it – to make magick, we rip the power away from something else. Most of us do it that way, at least.

I got back in the car and drove again down winding roads that led through and around the small town. I started looking carefully, trying to feel where I was. I knew I had been down this road just ten minutes before, but this time I examined every tree, every unpaved turnoff.

There it was: An unmarked road, a maple tree aflame with color, its wide branches forked into a V, as if hit by lightning years ago. I turned. My tiny rental bumped over the unpaved drive – I bet it would be almost impassable in a heavy snowfall. I was starting to feel chilled, so I cranked the car's heater. I felt hyped up on caffeine and sugar and was suddenly overcome by the supreme ridiculousness of what I was doing.

I was insane. This was the stupidest thing I'd ever thought up. Part and parcel of my panic, my nervous breakdown, I supposed.

Abruptly, I stopped the rental and rested my head on my hands on the steering wheel. I'd come all this way to look for a woman named River. This was so incredibly asinine. What had I been thinking? I needed to turn around, return the car, and go home. Wherever I decided home was going to be, this time.

When had I met her, River? Like, 1920? 1930? All I remembered was her face, smooth and tan, and her hands, strong and slender. Her hair had been gray, very unusual for an immortal. Innocencio had wrecked his first car — and I do mean *first*. As in *just invented*.

Had it been . . . 1929? That sounded right. Innocencio had bought himself a truly beautiful Model A, sort of a dusty blue. It was one of the first Model A's that Ford shipped to France. Incy had it a couple weeks, and then he crashed it into a ditch on a road near Reims. Another car stopped to help us. It was night. I'd been thrown through the glass windshield and had landed in the ditch. My face was shredded — this was before safety glass, before seat belts. It was freezing.

Innocencio and Rebecca had been thrown out of the car. Rebecca had a bunch of broken bones. She was a regular human and probably ended up in the hospital. Imogen was dead — her neck had broken when she hit a tree. Innocencio and I were messed up but could walk away. We'd met Imogen and Rebecca only the day before, at a party. They were both pretty, rich, and ready for fun. Unfortunately, they'd met us.

A car had stopped. A woman and two men ran over to help us. The men carefully loaded Rebecca into the back-seat of their car, and they discovered that Imogen was dead. The woman checked Innocencio, who was already starting to shake it off, mourning the loss of his beautiful car. Leaving him, she came and knelt by me, where I was climbing out of the icy ditch water. In French, she told me that everything would be fine, that I should lie still, and she tried to check my pulse. I brushed my sodden hair out of my eyes, pulled my fox-fur collar closer around my neck, and asked her what time it was – we were on our way to a New Year's Eve party. Imogen was dead, and it was too bad, a shame, really, but it hardly registered on me. Depraved indifference. Incy hadn't killed her on purpose, after all. Humans seemed so . . . fragile sometimes.

That was when the woman looked at me. She held my chin in her hands and really looked into my eyes. I looked back into hers, and we recognized each other as immortal. There isn't a distinguishing characteristic. It's not like we have a big *I* painted on the backs of our retinas. But we can recognize each other.

She sat back, looking at the scene: the ruined car, the dead girl, Innocencio and I already starting to pull ourselves together.

'It doesn't have to be like this,' she said in French.

'What?' I asked.

She shook her head, her warm brown eyes sad. 'You can have so much more, be so much more.'

That was when I started to get belligerent, wiping blood out of my eyes and standing up.

'My name is River,' she said, getting up also. 'I have a place, in America. In Massachusetts, up north. A town called West Lowing. You should come there.' She gestured at the ruined and smoking car, at the men gently carrying Imogen's body to their own car. She gave Incy a glance that seemed to sum him up in an instant as a wastrel, a good-time guy, the proverbial rock that seeds of wisdom would die upon.

'I've been to Massachusetts,' I said. 'It was straitlaced. Snooty. And cold.'

She gave a brief, sad smile. 'Not West Lowing,' she said. 'You should come, when you get tired of this.' Again she looked at the car, at Incy. 'What's your name?' Her eyes were sharp, intelligent – they seemed to memorize the planes of my face, the curve of my ear. I drew my fur closer around me.

'Christiane.'

'Christiane.' She nodded. 'When you get tired, when you want to be more, come to West Lowing. Massachusetts. My house is called River's Edge. You'll be able to find it.'

The woman named River got into the car with the two men, with Rebecca and Imogen's body, and they drove off, leaving me and Incy and his ruined, beautiful blue car. Eventually someone came along and we hitched a ride, then took the train to Paris, and then down to Marseilles, where it was warmer. It was a beautiful spring in Marseilles, and I put River – and Imogen – completely out of my mind.

Until two days ago. Now, eighty years later, I was deciding to take River up on her offer. Eighty freaking years later, as if she would still be here, her invitation still good.

As you might imagine, immortals move around a lot. To live in the same village for fifty years, your looks not changing – well, it would arouse suspicion. So we rarely stay in one place too long. Why would I assume that River would still be here? It was just . . . she had seemed so timeless. A pointless cliché for an immortal, I know. But she had seemed – unusually rock solid. Like if she said she'd be there, that I could come anytime, well then, by God, she would be there, and I could come any freaking time.

The espresso and sugar made my hands shake, my insides churn. What to do, what to do?

There was a tap on the window of my car, and I jumped, barely able to stifle a scream.

My frantic eyes focused, and the man leaned down to look at me.

Almost-hysterical laughter tickled my throat, and I had to swallow it. A Viking god had tapped on my window, was looking at me with concern – or suspicion. His golden handsomeness was breathtaking, as if a mythical figure had come to life, had warm blood flowing through his veins.

In the next moment, I squinted at him – his face was familiar. Was he a male model? Had I seen him in an underwear ad, forty feet across, in Times Square? Was he an actor? On a daytime soap? I couldn't quite place him as I rolled down my window. Please, please be some sex-starved nutcase who wants to kidnap me and make me your love slave, I begged silently.

'Yes?' My voice sounded dry, cracked.

'This is a private road,' the god said, looking at me disapprovingly. He was, maybe, twenty-two? Younger? Did he like teenage girls? I blinked at him, feeling again, at the edge of my consciousness, as if I'd seen him somewhere before.

'Ah . . . um, I was looking for River? River's Edge?'

His topaz-colored eyes flared in surprise. It occurred to me she might have cloaked her place from neighbors. If she was still there at all.

'Do you know anyone like that?' I pressed.

'You know River?' he asked slowly. 'Where did you meet her?'

Who was he, her personal guard? 'I met her a long time ago. She said I could come visit her,' I said firmly. 'Do you know if her place, River's Edge, is around here?'

Too fast for me to react, one strong hand reached through the car window and touched my cheek. His hand was warm, hard and gentle at the same time, and I knew that my skin felt icy under his touch.

He was immortal, and he now recognized that I was, too.

I tilted my head to one side. 'Do I know you? Have I met you somewhere?' If I'd met him, surely I would remember him with much more clarity, much more intensity. No one would forget that face, that voice. Still, I'd pretty much crisscrossed every continent too many times to count. Maybe he wasn't that old. Or—

He was one of them, the other kind of immortals. The kind I had nothing to do with, nothing in common with, avoided like the plague, mocked with my friends. The kind I disdained almost as much as they disdained me.

The kind I was hoping would . . . save me. Protect me. The Tähti.

'No,' he said, drawing his hand away. I shivered, feeling colder than ever.

'It's down this road here,' he said, sounding reluctant. 'Down this road. It curves to the left. Take the first left fork. You'll come to the house.'

'So River is still here, then?'

I couldn't read anything in his expression. His face was closed.

'Yes.'

Chapter 3

I watched him in the rearview mirror as he walked down the road. He was tall and broad-shouldered, and the way his jeans hugged his butt was a rare treat. As I looked at his back, that feeling of recognition lingered, and I frowned, racking my memory. Then I caught a glimpse of myself and groaned out loud – my skin had an unhealthy nightclub pallor, my lips were practically as pale as my skin, my eyes looked weird because of my blue contacts, my spiky black hair was lopsided and stiff. I was his antithesis: He was the perfect man, while I was the least perfect of women. Strung out, unhealthy. Well, what did I care? I didn't care.

Four minutes of rutted road later, I finally pulled up in front of a long two-story building that looked more like a school or a dormitory than someone's home. It was large and rectangular, painted a severe, pristine white, with dark green shutters on each precise window. There were at least three more outbuildings off to the sides, and a stone fence that might enclose a large garden.

I parked my car on autumn-dry grass next to a beat-up

red truck. It felt like the next few minutes were monumental, as if they would decide my whole future. Getting out of this car would be admitting that my life was a waste. That *I* was a waste. It would be admitting that I was scared of my friends, scared of myself, my own darkness, my history. Everything in me wanted to stay in this car with the windows rolled up and the doors locked, forever. If I'd been a human, and *forever* meant only another sixty years, I might have actually done it. However, in my case, forever truly would have been unbearably long. There was no way.

I'd come here for a reason. I'd left my friends and disappeared to a different continent. On the plane coming over, I'd realized that besides Incy crippling the cabbie, despite my disgust at my lack of action, despite my paranoia about Incy's seeing my scar, it had been a hundred, a thousand other things leading up to that, chipping away at my insides until I felt like a shell with nothing alive left in me. I hadn't been going around killing people and setting villages on fire, but I'd been cutting a destructive path through my existence, and I'd realized, with nauseating honesty, that everything I touched was harmed. People were hurt, homes broken, cars wrecked, careers destroyed – the memories just kept trickling in like rivulets of fresh acid dripping into my brain until I wanted to scream.

It was in my blood, I knew. A darkness. *The* darkness. I had inherited it, along with my immortality and my black eyes. I had resisted it when I was younger. Had pretended it wasn't there. But somewhere along the way, I'd stopped fighting, given in to it. For a long time, I'd run with it. But that last night, the darkness that had been following me for more than four hundred years had come crashing down on me with a suffocating weight, and now I hated the horrible thing I'd become.

If I were a regular person, I'd be tempted to kill myself. Being me, I had almost collapsed with hysterical laughter when I realized that even if I managed to cut off my own head, I wouldn't be able to make sure it was far enough away from my body for long enough to actually kill me. And what was my other option? Throwing myself headfirst into a wood chipper? What if it jammed when only half my head was through? Can you imagine the regrowth process of *that* stunt? Jesus.

My life suddenly felt like I'd fallen off a cliff and would fall forever toward ever-increasing despair, never to be happy again. I couldn't remember the last time I'd felt truly happy. Amused? Yes. Diverted? Yes. Happy? Not so much. Couldn't even remember what it felt like.

The only person who had ever offered to help me, who had ever seemed to understand, was River. She had invited me here so many decades ago. And here I was.

I glanced around again, and this time I saw her, standing on the wide wooden steps of the house. She looked just the same as I remembered, which was unusual. We tend to alter our appearances frequently, drastically. I certainly had, probably twenty times since I'd met her. I didn't see how she could possibly recognize me. But she was watching me, and it was clear that she intended for me to make the first move.

I let out a deep breath, hoping the house was toasty warm inside, that I could get some hot tea or a drink or take a hot bath. Would she even remember me? Was her offer still good? I knew how ridiculous it was to hold her to something she'd said more than eighty years ago. But what else could I do?

Well, I'd done more pathetic things. I got out of the car and hunched into my leather jacket – my old one, not the one I'd lost two nights ago. I scuffled across the fallen leaves on the ground, already making plans for what to do when she turned me away. Go hide someplace warm, definitely. Fiji or something. Stay there till I felt better, felt like less of a waste. It was bound to happen sometime. Eventually Incy would probably seem less scary. Eventually I would forget all about the cabbie, as I'd forgotten about Imogen until yesterday.

'Hello,' she said when I was close enough. She wore a long paisley skirt and a woolen shawl around her shoulders. Her gray hair was straight, the sides pulled back by a clip. 'Welcome.'

'Hi,' I said. 'River?'

'Yes.' She searched my face for remembrance. 'What's your name, child?'

I gave a short laugh at being called a child, at my age. 'Nastasya. Currently.'

'We've met.' It was a statement, not a question.

I nodded, crunching leaves under my boots. 'A long time ago. You said — if I ever wanted to do something more, to come to West Lowing.' I looked casually off into the distance, saw clouds rolling in from the southwest.

'Nastasya,' she repeated. She looked at my straggly black hair, the contacts that made my eyes match the description on my American passport. I tried to remember what I had looked like when we met, but I couldn't.

'Christiane,' I said, recalling. One of a very long line of names. Not the one I was born with. 'My name was Christiane then. We met in France, after a car wreck. Like, in the late 1920s?'

'Ah, yes,' she said after a moment, nodding. 'That was a bad night. But I'm glad I met you. And I'm glad you're here.'

'Well,' I said awkwardly, looking anywhere but her face. 'I know that was a long time ago, but I thought, you know, if—'

'I'm glad you're here, Chr— Nastasya,' she repeated. 'You're welcome. Do you have anything with you?'

I nodded, thinking of my huge suitcase. And, of course, all my emotional baggage.

'Good. Let me show you to your room, and then you can get settled in.'

I got a room? 'Is this like a hotel or something?' I asked, following her through the door into a foyer. A round table held a vase full of dried maple branches. A beautiful, wide curving staircase led to the second floor. Everything was white, simple, elegant. It was weird, but as soon as I stepped across her threshold, I felt – less scared? Less, I don't know – vulnerable? Maybe I was imagining it.

'It used to be a Quaker meetinghouse,' River explained, heading upstairs. I could feel that there were other people in the building, but it felt calm and peaceful. 'In the eighteen hundreds, about forty Friends lived here, working a farm. I've owned it, in various guises, since 1904.' The various guises meant that she, like all of us, had assumed different personas to explain her continuing existence. She started off as one person, then pretended to die, then showed up again as that person's long-lost daughter to inherit the house, and so on. I think there was a *Star Trek* episode that dealt with this.

'What is it now?'

River led me along the wide hallway, then took a right, which led to another long hallway with windows on one side and regularly spaced doors on the other. She gave a slight grin that made her look younger. 'It's a home for wayward immortals, of course.'

'What do the locals think it is?' I asked.

'A small, family-owned organic farm, where people come to learn organic farming techniques. Which is true also.' She stopped in front of a door that was just opposite a window. Amber autumn sunlight slanted across the door, and River opened it.

I looked inside. 'Like, organic farming for monks?'

River laughed.

The room was small, plain, and basically empty except for a narrow bed, a tiny wardrobe, a wooden desk, and a chair. The last time I was away from my flat in London, I had stayed at the George V in Paris. The time before that, at the St Regis in New York. I tend to go with extreme, over-the-top comfort.

'No, not for monks,' River said, going into the room. 'Just for people, immortals, who want to focus on other things at this point in their lives. But you're welcome to put your own belongings around, make it homier.'

I thought about my typical home furnishings of discarded clothes, empty liquor bottles, overflowing ashtrays, books, magazines, and pizza boxes and thought, *Maybe not.*

'So there are more of us here?' I asked, sitting on the bed experimentally. It did not have a comfort pillow top.

'Right now we have four teachers and eight students,' River said. She closed the door and leaned back on it, her face serious. 'You can take a week to decide if you want to stay, Nastasya. I hope you do. I think you'll get a lot out of it and that you'll be able to find happiness here if you're open to it. But just to be clear, this isn't a spa or a hotel. It's sort of a combination kibbutz and rehab.

There's work to be done, and we all do it. There's stuff, hard and painful, that you'll have to learn. Over the years we've come up with systems that work for us, and we're not interested in someone coming here and insisting our rules don't apply to them.'

'Uh-huh.' Maybe I would stay for a few days, figure out Plan B, and head off again.

River smiled and seemed so genuinely warm and welcoming that I wished I could be a better subject for her. But already that seemed impossible. 'If this doesn't work for you, no one will force you to stay. No one's going to convince you to save your own life. If you're not a big girl after – what, two hundred years?'

'Four hundred,' I said. 'Four hundred and fifty-nine.'

Surprise flickered in her eyes, and I had the uncomfortable feeling that it was my behavior rather than my looks that had made her think I was younger. 'Okay, four hundred and fifty-nine. But if you're not a big girl by now, we have no interest in dragging you there. We'll help you as much as we can, in any way we can, as long as you're doing your share. If you want to skate through, this place isn't for you.'

'Uh-huh,' I said.

River laughed, and then she came over and hugged me, leaning down to where I sat on the bed. She felt warm, solid, and comforting. I couldn't remember the last time a hug had felt like that. Awkwardly, I hugged her back, patting a little with one hand.

'I don't mean to scare you off,' she said. 'I want you to stay. But I don't want you to work out immature bullshit here, either. You know?'

I nodded. 'Uh-huh.' No scintillating words were popping into my brain. Now, more than ever, I had no idea what I was doing here. Maybe I had been overreacting to everything. This had all been a laughable mistake. At least, I was sure I would laugh about it someday. Decades from now. *The time I tried to escape, ha ha ha.* I mean, maybe I wasn't so bad, after all. Then I remembered the cabbie, his face starkly outlined by the streetlight, and how I had just walked away, and something inside me crumpled.

'How old are you?' I asked, without meaning to.

She paused in the doorway. 'Well, older than you,' she said ruefully, brushing some strands of hair off her face.

'Like, how old?' I don't know why I cared – maybe I didn't want someone younger than me acting like she had it all together.

Her eyes met mine. 'I was born in 718 in Genoa, in the kingdom of Italy.' She smiled. 'It hasn't changed all that much.'

'Oh.' I nodded, and then she smiled one last time and left, closing the door behind her. I was glad I hadn't blurted out my first reaction, which was, 'God*damn*, you're old.'

I fell back on my bed, incredibly tired. I so didn't belong here. This place radiated calm, peace, patterns of life and change and sameness, all at once. I was a whirling Japanese throwing star, careening through the world. I was trouble. An icy despair seemed to seize my chest – this had been such a laughably ridiculous plan, and yet it was the *only thing I could think of*. Oh, God, I was so screwed.

My room was warm. There was a small metal radiator against one wall, and it was working. I pulled off my worn leather jacket and my heavy motorcycle boots, feeling free and weightless and so comfortable. I was wearing a man's velour pullover, and I tucked it around my neck, reflexively making sure my neck was covered, very cozy.

My eyes were drifting heavily shut when there was a tap on the door.

'It's open,' I said, thinking longingly of room service. I'd already noticed that none of the doors had locks. How quaint.

The door opened, and the Viking god stood there. I peered at his face from beneath lowered lashes, searching, again troubled by a dim recognition that faded as soon as I tried to pin it down. In one hand he carried my suitcase, which easily weighed more than I did. He set it down in my room. 'Here.'

'I was going to get it in a minute.' I sat up, feeling self-conscious, knowing what I looked like. There have been times in my life when I've been truly beautiful. I have symmetrical features, pretty eyes, a full mouth, high cheekbones, and so on. On the occasions when I have my act together, I know I can look really good. I just hadn't had my act together, looks-wise, in about forty years. Or so. Now I was acutely, painfully aware that I was junkie-skinny, with rats'-nest hair dyed a garish, fake-looking black. I probably looked as if I'd been embalmed, or had just recovered from cholera. My clothes were whatever items I'd found that didn't actually have stuff caked on them. In short, I couldn't have looked much worse.

Viking God Person was so striking, with glowy golden skin, and short, perfectly mussed tawny hair, and golden eyes the color of a sherry wine that I'd tasted once in Georgia (again, the country, not the state). He was tall but not pointlessly tall, strong and muscular without it looking like compensation for something else, with masculine features neither too rough nor too pretty. His nose had a slight bump and was a tiny bit crooked, as if it had been broken once, and of course that completed his perfection, in the Japanese *wabi sabi* view of perfection. Where had I seen his face before? But whatever – he took my breath away.

He looked like he just couldn't be bothered with helping me, which, sadly, only increased his appeal.

'What's your name?' I asked, trying to look unrattled.

'Reyn.'

Rain? Reign? Rane? 'I'm Nastasya.'

'I know.'

He was unfriendly, unwelcoming. I wondered why he

was here. Was everyone here a lost cause, like me? Was anyone else in hiding? I wanted to know this guy's story. With any luck, it would be worse than my own.

'Okay, thanks,' I said shortly, unnerved by his attitude.

'River asked me to tell you that dinner is at seven.'

He stepped backward and almost silently closed my door. I wanted to ask where one ate dinner but figured he'd probably just tell me to follow my nose.

I fell back on the bed, wide-awake again. My heart constricted as I accepted that this wasn't going to work out. If I'd needed further proof, which I hadn't, this Reyn guy had provided it. These people were probably all about good works and making the most of their endless lives. I was just trying to escape the darkness that was oozing over everything I touched. I was trying to hide – from Incy, from myself, from my past and my present and even my future.

Incy. I shivered again and rubbed my arms up and down my fuzzy sleeves. By now he would be wondering where I was. We rarely went a day without seeing each other, talking to each other. Was he worried? What was everyone thinking? Would they try to find me?

I couldn't go back. That much I felt sure about. And I couldn't stay here. Okay. A couple of meals, a couple of nights' sleep, and I'd be gone, baby, gone. It wasn't like there was that much left of me to save, anyway.

Chapter 4

San Francisco, California, 1967

Come on, *I want a* picture of me and you,' Jennifer said, tugging on the sleeve of my caftan.

I flicked my long honey-blonde hair over my shoulder. 'Of course you do.'

Together, Jennifer and I posed on the wide staircase and smiled at Roger's Polaroid camera. In the sunken living room below, people were shrieking with laughter. 'Eight Miles High' was playing on the expensive turntable. There were candles and incense burning, and the new light machine was casting psychedelic patterns on the walls.

I looked incredible, I knew: My heavily lined Egyptian-look eyes, the palest lipstick, the silk, Nehru-collared caftan I'd gotten in India covered with rioting swirls of bright color. To be safe, I had a Peter Max silk scarf knotted around my throat. I was *loving* the sixties. The forties had been so depressing, everything gray and drab and self-sacrificing. And I'd hated the fifties, when everyone was buying into the anally rigid American dream and rocket-fender automobiles the size of elephants.

But the sixties were perfect for us immortals, my friends and me. Anything went, everyone was crazy, anyone who didn't agree or approve was dismissed as an uptight square. And the parties. The last time I'd been immersed in such a pervasive party atmosphere had been on Long Island, New York, right before the big crash of 1929.

'Hope!' Someone pressed a glass of champagne in my hand and kissed both cheeks. Then he was gone again, his purple velvet jacket weaving through the crowd.

'Hmm.' I took a long sip of champagne as Roger's camera continued to flash. At one point he changed the flash bar, throwing the used one over his shoulder. It landed in the fountain trickling in the foyer, and we laughed.

'Hope.'

'Hi, Max,' I said, grinning. I was feeling bubbly and floaty and beautiful and delicious.

'Are you old enough to be drinking that?' There was almost, *almost* a serious intent behind his words. Max produced movies in Los Angeles – he was a big star. Not immortal. There were only a couple of us at this party.

'Afraid of a cop raid, busted for serving alcohol to minors?' I asked cheekily. I blinked, feeling my eyelids suddenly become very heavy. In the next moment, this situation became the funniest thing I'd ever experienced, hysterically funny, so, so, so funny, and I was the happiest person in the world. This was the best party *ever*.

'Something like that,' Max said, adjusting his glasses on his face, looking down at me.

'Oh, gosh,' I breathed, looking at the champagne bubbles floating very, very slowly to the top of the golden wine. 'Gosh, I can see every bubble. It's beautiful.' Had Max said something that I needed to answer? I didn't know. Right now it was vitally important that I watch every bubble of champagne until it burst on the surface. If I could truly, totally immerse myself in that, it would unlock the secrets of the universe. Of this I was certain.

'Oh, damn it,' Max muttered. 'Roger? Rog! Did someone lace the champagne?'

Roger giggled, snatching my attention away from the champagne. He continued to click away on his camera, which kept spitting white-framed gray squares out to litter the floor. The gray squares slowly assumed faces and smiles and colors. It was *magic*. 'Yeah, man!' Roger said. 'Some of Berkeley's finest!'

Max groaned. He took my champagne away, making me panic.

'No!' I shouted. 'I need to watch the bubbles!' My world would collapse if I didn't perform my bubble mission. 'Give it back!'

Max held the glass above my head. 'Hope, no. You're too young for this. You shouldn't even be here. Jesus, if we get busted—'

'Give it back!' I said, trying to lunge for it but instead

swaying like a willow in a hurricane. 'Oh. Oh. Look, I can see all my hands.' When I moved my hand, it left shadow images of hands behind, as if it had been filmed in slow motion. I was *amazing*.

'Hope, you're amazing,' Jennifer said, suddenly next to me again, putting her arm around my waist.

'I know!' I said. 'Look at my hands!'

'Hope! Hope! Over here!' Someone waved to me from the orange suede sectional sofa. My shoes were too much for me to deal with, so I kicked them off and wiggled my toes in the white alpaca rug.

The touch of the wool was much too intense on the bottoms of my feet. 'No, I need my shoes,' I decided out loud. I sat down to put my shoes on again, apparently pulling Jennifer down with me. Then we were lying on the white rug, smiling at the ceiling together.

'Hope, you're so beautiful,' Jennifer said.

'Hope, why are you on the ground? You're so silly.' Incy smiled down at me, then lay on the rug on my other side. The three of us stared at Max's crystal chandelier overhead.

'Hi, Michael,' I said, proud I'd remembered his current name.

'Hope is so beautiful,' Jennifer told him. Incy grinned, and Jennifer looked mesmerized, drawing in a breath.

'Hope? How about I give you and some of the others a ride home,' Max said. His eyes were kind behind his horn-rimmed glasses, but he still looked uptight and establishment, with his maroon turtleneck sweater and straight-legged suit pants. 'Okay? It was stupid of Roger to invite you. Maybe in a couple years, huh?'

'Hope always has to come!' Jennifer insisted. 'There's no party without Hope!'

I smiled up at Max. It was like looking up a long, long tunnel. 'There's no party without me,' I reminded him.

'Yeah!' said Incy. 'We need Hope!'

Someone a few feet away heard this and repeated it, as if it was her newest mantra. In another minute, everyone in the whole downstairs of Max's huge home on the hill was chanting: 'We need Hope! We need Hope!'

The fact that they were talking about me, the double meaning the chant had, how beautiful I felt, how loved, how in demand, how popular – it was so fun, so happy, so lovely. I wanted it to last – forever.

'It's all right, Max,' I said dreamily. 'I'm four hundred and . . .' – I did the math fuzzily – 'and sixteen. Per-fectly legal.'

Incy cracked up next to me, Jennifer grinned in cheerful confusion, and Max sighed and rolled his eyes.

I don't remember how I got home from that party.

Max died two years ago; I saw it on the news. He'd been seventy-four years old.

I still look seventeen.

And, yeah, come to think of it, that was probably the last time I felt happy.

A bell clanging in the distance made me open my eyes. I half expected to see the young Max leaning over me with concern, expected to feel thin Indian silk gliding across my body, was already starting to wonder whose party I would go to tonight.

Instead, I saw a plain white ceiling with a thin, spidery crack starting in one corner. I was chilly, lying on a hard, narrow bed.

Oh, God. It was fifty years later. I was at River's Edge. Still here. And the bell clanging must be the dinner notice.

I rolled over on my side, tucking my velour shirt around me. I couldn't deal with dinner. My stomach gave a fierce, hungry growl then, disagreeing with me and telling me to get my ass in gear. I hadn't eaten since the coffee and Chips Ahoy! this morning.

I got creakily to my feet and picked up one of my heavy motorcycle boots. I glanced at the unlocked door and listened but heard nothing out in the hallway, no one walking nearby. Quickly, I slid a thin metal pin out of the boot's tongue and inserted it into an almost invisible hole in the heel. Then I held the heel in my hand and pushed, glancing again at the door. The top swung sideways, revealing a cavity. Heavy, ancient gold gleamed dimly at me. Unable to help myself, I drew a finger across its surface, feeling the runes, the other symbols that I didn't know the names of, the purpose of.

I snapped the heel shut again and slid the pin back into the leather. I shoved my feet into the boots and stood up. It was still safe, still hidden – my amulet. Half of it, anyway. The only half I had, the half that matched the burn on the back of my neck.

Out in the hall, I couldn't remember which way I'd come in, so I started off, circled back, and then found some stairs. A food smell wafted up from below, and my stomach growled again.

My memory of San Francisco had been so cheering. I'd gone down a wide wooden staircase, not too unlike this one. But the silk caftan and gold sandals were a glaring contrast to the man's pullover, raggedy black pants, and heavy boots I wore now.

Sniffing like a truffle pig, I followed the warm scent of food until I reached the dining room: A long, plain room with a wood floor; a really long wooden table that could have seated twenty; high, uncurtained windows showing blackness outside; a big, old, gilt-framed mirror over the fireplace; and twelve people looking at me with surprise, curiosity, and, on River's face, welcome.

'Hello, Nastasya,' River said with a smile. She unfolded a cloth napkin and put it in her lap. 'I'm glad you didn't sleep through dinner! You must be hungry. Here, take a seat next to Nell, right there.' She pointed to a gap between two people on a, yes, wooden bench.

Feeling like a clumsy schoolchild *in the eighteen hundreds*, I clambered over the bench, trying not to whack anyone with a motorcycle boot.

'Everyone, this is Nastasya,' said River, reaching for a

white tureen filled with something steaming. 'She's going to be with us for a while.' Her eyes met mine. 'As long as she wants.'

'Hi, Nastasya,' a girl said, across the table. She looked dark and serious, with wire-rimmed glasses, a no-nonsense pageboy, and olive skin. 'I'm Rachel. Where are you from?'

Did she mean originally? I glanced at River for guidance as someone passed me a large bowl of . . . looked like sautéed greens. Oh, joy. I scooped some onto my plate and passed the bowl to Nell, on my right.

'Either most recently,' River clarified, 'or originally. Up to you.'

I wouldn't be here long. I didn't need to spill my guts. 'The north. Originally. England, most recently.'

'I'm from Mexico,' said Rachel. 'Originally.'

'Cool,' I said, taking the next bowl, which held orange chunks. Yams.

'Let's all introduce ourselves,' River suggested. 'By the way, Nastasya, what we're eating was all grown right here, on our farm. We're very proud of our gardens. You'll see them tomorrow. Everything is organic, and balanced in terms of energy.'

Whatever the eff that meant.

I nodded and looked down at the small mounds of food on my plate. There was a bean/some kind of grain mixture (possibly quinoa?), the orange yams, and the limp, dark greens that made me feel like I'd be chewing my cud later.

What I really felt like was some sushi. With a nice bottle of hot sake. I glanced around hopefully for some wine bottles but didn't see any. Please, please let there be wine somewhere.

'I'm Solis,' said a lifeguardish-looking man sitting next to River. I almost snorted, thinking that naming oneself Solace was a bit much, but later I found out that it was a family name and not spelled the same way. He was tan, with short, dark blond hair and a full beard that was almost reddish. Oddly pretty hazel eyes were framed by long lashes.

As River had told me, there were four teachers: River, Solis, Asher (who was River's partner), and Anne. Then there were the students. It wasn't like most school setups, where you can easily tell the teachers from the students, mostly by age. River looked the oldest of the teachers, but one of the students, Jess, actually looked older than her. He was a withered, wasted old man who looked as though he'd packed more hard living into his life, however long, than I'd done in four centuries.

The teacher Anne looked about twenty, with fair skin, fine, straight dark hair, a round face, and blue eyes that examined me with friendly curiosity.

Most names went over my head as I tried to choke down the greens. Would it have killed them to throw some cream and butter in there? Ha ha ha. No.

The Viking lord nodded stiffly at me and said, 'Reyn.'

'Like, rain-Rain?' I asked, my mouth full of yam.

The girl next to me gave a charming smile. She was a portrait of an English maid, with glowing, healthy skin, shining blue eyes, and softly curling pale brown hair that hung halfway down her back. With a little laugh, she said, 'Reyn's a German name.' She spelled it.

'Ah, *German*,' I said, making it sound as if I held him responsible for World War II. His jaw set – he was such a stuffed shirt, it was impossible not to bait him. Now, looking at him, I was actually pretty sure I'd never met him. Maybe he was reminiscent of someone I'd once caught a glimpse of, or something.

'I'm Dutch,' he said tersely. 'Originally.'

'Umm,' I said, trying to get the bean/grain mixture down. I took a couple of big gulps of water. Plain water. Some Dr Pepper would have gone a long way just then.

'And I'm Nell,' said the British lass next to me. 'Welcome, Nastasya. I hope you'll be happy here. Do let me know if I can help you settle in.'

'Okay,' I said. 'Uh, thanks.' I felt unclean, uncouth, uncultured, and a bunch of other *un*s. As soon as it was light in the morning, I was hitting the road. I could deal with my problems on my own, I thought, even as my brain whispered, Can*not*. But what did it know?

The names washed over me; the faces, male and female, white and Asian and black and Hispanic, sort of melded together. I didn't try to keep them straight; I wouldn't be here long enough for it to matter. I did fleetingly wonder what had brought them here – had their lives been miserable? Or were they just here to learn whatever River was teaching? What was she teaching, anyway? Magick? How to be immortal without losing your mind? Or just . . . organic farming? River had called this a home for wayward immortals. *Wayward* suggested people who had gone astray. But looking around, really, only Jess seemed like he was either now or had formerly been astray. The others looked pretty healthy, happy, not tortured. How did I look to them?

Let's sum up: Here I was, in a chilly, sparsely furnished dining hall, eating bland food with a bunch of immortals who were trying to be extra good. I so did not belong. And I didn't belong back in London anymore, either, with Boz and Incy and the rest of them — the thought of it made me feel ill, like I was choking. If anything, I belonged back in the beautiful, colorful sixties, when everyone loved me and I looked fabulous. I gazed at my plate glumly, no longer even hoping for dessert, absolutely certain that the chance of this food being laced with any kind of fun drugs was completely nil.

Why had I done this to myself? Such a good question. One I'd asked myself a thousand times over the years, in various situations. It seemed to be a constant theme in my life.

Chapter 5

At last dinner was over. I was about to sprint up to 'my' room so I could huddle in a fetal position on my bed and feel sorry for myself, but one of the students asked if I was going on the evening walk.

My face must have shown my lack of enthusiasm, because she laughed as she pulled on a down vest and wrapped a fleece scarf around her neck.

'We go on a walk almost every evening after dinner,' River told me in her beautifully modulated voice. She tugged a red beret over her silver hair and smiled at me. 'It's part of paying attention to the world – we look at the stars, the moon, the shadows of the trees.'

'There are different birds out at night,' said one of the guy students, the handsome Italian-looking guy – Lorenz? 'We learn their different calls and habits.'

I nodded gravely, thinking, You must be kidding.

'This time of year, trees have mostly finished losing their leaves,' Nell said, looking beautiful and outdoorsy in a Burberry trench coat. 'You'll learn the patterns of which one loses its leaves first, and whether it's fast or slow.'

Over my dead body, I thought. Yes, even immortals use that phrase. It has extra oomph for us.

'When there's a full moon, the outside is lit up like daytime,' said Solis. His hazel eyes seemed to watch me intently, as if he was trying to figure out why I was really here. 'Tonight there's a gibbous moon, which has its own beauty.'

I'll take your word for it.

'Would you like to grab a jacket and come with us?' River asked. Her eyes were sparkling with humor. Was this a test? If so, I would happily fail.

'No, thank you,' I said politely.

'Oh, lovely,' River said, sounding relieved. 'People who are staying home help with the cleanup. The kitchen is right through there.' She pointed.

I looked at her.

She was practically chuckling as they went out through the wide green-painted front door.

Score? River 1, Nasty 0.

Given my advanced age, it's only natural that I quit trying to please people about 440 years ago. It would have been no skin off my nose to merely stalk upstairs, assume the fetal position on my bed as planned, and let whatever happened, happen.

And yet.

It really did feel like she had scored one off me. I bet she'd been certain that I wouldn't go for a nighttime stroll with her and the rest of the campers. She'd known

I'd weasel out, and known that scullery duty awaited me when I did. How annoying. Now she was, no doubt, *expecting* me to merely stalk upstairs and assume a fetal position on my bed – as if she knew me way down deep. It was totally galling.

I clenched my teeth and stalked to the kitchen instead. I'm here by choice, I reminded myself. I'm here because I can't bear to be not-here anymore. I'm here because I can't tell right from wrong, light from dark. I'm here because I can't stand being me. I'm here because I don't want anyone to know where I am.

The kitchen was large and poorly lit. It had been the height of efficient convenience back in 1935 or so. There was no restaurant dishwasher whipping through loads every two minutes, no granite countertops or etched-glass doors on the cupboards. There were tall, open wooden shelves, stacked with the heavy white stoneware we'd used at dinner. Glass jars of pasta, rice, grains, beans, and cereal lined another shelf. Large windows showed blackness outside and reflected the inadequate ceiling light.

And the best part? My buddy Reyn, standing at the soapstone farm sink, looking at me. He literally sighed and looked at the ceiling, then held out a soapy plate.

'You can rinse,' he said, pointing to the other sink full of clean water.

Proving that maturity doesn't necessarily come with age, I saluted and goose-stepped to the sink. 'Yes, Herr

Kommandant!' I flipped my scarf over my shoulder, shoved my sleeves up, swished the plate in the clean water, then put it on the drainboard.

He handed me another one. Rinse, swish, stack.

I was doing my best to look nonchalant, way too cool for him and completely unaware of him as a person. As if he were a tall, forbidding machine handing me soapy plates. The humiliating truth of the situation was that this guy was truly a knockout, and I was, uncharacteristically, about to hyperventilate, being close to him.

I don't really have a type of guy that I find attractive – they don't have to be tall or short or muscular or thin or bulky; color of hair or skin doesn't matter. I don't actually get interested in guys that often. For me, hooking up with someone is like a convenience, a time killer, like Warehouse Jase, scratching an infrequent itch. The last time I'd been in love, he ended up dying in India when the British finally succeeded in annexing the Maratha territory. Um, 1818, I believe. Which was the beginning of the British rule of an enormous, non-English country and the end of my allowing myself to fall for humans. I hadn't truly been in love since, even with immortals. Falling for an immortal had an awful ring of permanence that I just couldn't deal with. Think about breaking up with someone and then having to risk seeing him, maybe happy with someone else, for *hundreds* of years. I mean, no thanks.

But standing here next to Reyn, I felt the heat of his

body, smelled the clean-laundry scent of his clothes, and he seemed – unique, and like he could handle anything, you know? Something in me wanted to wrap my arms around his waist and lean my cheek against his chest, right over his heart. My face flamed at the thought. But overwhelmingly I felt that anything could happen right then – meteor, government collapse, stampede – and Reyn would just step up and handle it and protect . . . whomever he was with. For all of his standoffishness, even dislike, he still felt like . . . safety. Like he would always make the right choice, do the right thing, even if he didn't want to.

He seemed to be the opposite of Incy, whose skills lay purely in getting what he wanted, charming people, skirting around rules, laws, and social mores.

Reyn, whom I didn't know a single thing about, gave off an impression of solidity, of strength and resolve, and it struck me that I didn't know anyone else who did. Not in my life.

Of course, he also gave off an impression of being a snob, stuck-up and full of lip-curling disdain, so I guess it's true what they say: No one's perfect! Just swish and rinse, I told myself. Face it, he's an irresistible jerk who doesn't care whether he's hot or not, and doesn't care whether *you're* hot or not, and has zero interest in pursuing you because his mind's on loftier, more important things.

I hate guys like that. There was a stunning priest back in Malta in the thirties – but that's another story.

Now my cheeks were burning, and I had to slow down my breathing. Rinse, swish, stack. When I had a nice pile, Mr Personality handed me a clean dishcloth. I started drying, making another stack. I was feeling anxious again, a twitchy nervousness that was unfamiliar and unwelcome. My crowd was used to me; they accepted me as is, without comment or question. Among my group, I was *fine*. Here, I stuck out so much; I was realizing that I had drifted so far away from regular societal norms that I seemed almost freakish next to these people. It was weird and unbalancing and underscored my desire to flee. And of course my nervousness increased my obnoxiousness quotient.

'I guess this is really Zen and stuff,' I said, my tone insinuating that I wanted to be Zen about as much as I wanted to be a plague victim.

Reyn glanced down at me for a second and didn't respond.

I'm five-three, which had been *really tall* for a woman back in my time. I had been an *Amazon* compared to other women, even in Iceland, with our hardy, northern marauder stock. As recently as a hundred years ago, I was a good height for a female in virtually any country except the Netherlands, where they grow them unusually tall. Now, given improved nutrition and better prenatal care, everyone is shooting up all around me, and I'm not even *average* anymore. It's so incredibly unfair, because clearly I'm done growing. I've *been* done growing.

So it was infuriating that Reyn got to be tall. It was infuriating that he got to be tall and golden and the most gorgeous person I'd ever seen, male or female, and that I should even be aware of him at all, much less so intensely, unexpectedly, unwelcomely aware of him.

'Here.'

I blinked in the middle of my internal rant to see Reyn holding a plate in front of me, as he had apparently been doing for some moments without my noticing.

I took it and swished it sourly, wishing I were a countess and he were a peasant coachman, and I could just have my way with him with no repercussions. Ah, the good old days.

Not that I'd ever been a countess.

'The weather tomorrow is supposed to be cold and clear,' Reyn startled me by saying. Now that I listened for it, there was a faint, faint crispness to his consonants that bespoke his Dutch heritage. It was, of course, intensely attractive. One more thing to hold against him.

'Thank you for sharing that,' I said. I dried another plate, put it on the stack, and then carried the stack over to an open wooden shelf where all of its little plate friends were waiting.

'So you won't have any trouble with the roads, when you leave,' he went on, and the light clicked in my head. Oh.

'It's clear that you don't belong here,' he said with Teutonic stolidness, and handed me another plate. 'I know you've come to the same conclusion. Obviously, you're horrified by our life here.' He shrugged. 'It's not for everyone. Most people, in fact, wouldn't be able to hack it. It doesn't mean you're – *weak*, or anything.' He handed me another plate with a bit more force, while I seethed.

'Let me guess,' I said, rinsing the plate. 'You're using reverse psychology on me, trying to piss me off and make me feel unwelcome so I'll be determined to stay and prove you wrong. Right?'

'Oh, no.' His golden eyes, bewitchingly slanted a bit at the ends, looked down at me. 'No, I'm really not,' he said with an insulting definitiveness. 'I really do think you should leave. We've got a good life here, with our lessons and work, and we don't need some screwed-up tornado whipping through here, tearing it to pieces.'

My jaw clenched, and the fact that he was pretty much right on the money about everything only made me angrier.

'Everyone will understand.' He handed me the last plate and dunked his hands in the clean water. 'River will understand. You're not the first lost soul hoping for a cheap and easy fix – River collects them like stray dogs.' He rolled his shirtsleeves down powerful forearms dusted with dark blond hair. 'New York or Rome or Paris is a better place for you. Bright lights, big city.' He gave a brief, sardonic smile. 'Not the wilds of Massachusetts, with nothing to do except work, and breathe, and pay attention to the night stars and the gibbous moon and the way leaves fall off trees. Just forget we even exist.' He looked at me intently, as if he was literally willing me to forget they existed. As if he was using magick, maybe. Maybe these people used magick all the time. There was a small potted herb plant on the windowsill above the sink, and I shot a glance at it to see if it was withering, crumpling in death as he took power from it. But it stayed perky and green, and when I looked over at Reyn, he raised his eyebrows slightly.

It was a mark of personal growth for me that I didn't slam a heavy stoneware plate down on his head to wipe that supercilious smile right off his face.

I was furious, and it was strange, because usually I can't muster up more than annoyance or boredom. I'd long ago given up on more extreme emotions as taking too much energy. But Reyn had pierced my thick hide with his beauty and open disdain, and in my head I was shrieking hysterically. At least, I really hoped it was in my head.

I breathed tightly in and out, searching for just the right scathing comment to leave him deflated and defeated in this asinine kitchen. And . . .

'You're – you're really not that good-looking,' I finally snapped. His eyes opened slightly – he had probably expected a comeback of somewhat higher quality. 'Your nose is too pointy.' I was mortified to see my chest heave as I sucked in breath. 'Your lips are too thin, you're too tall, and your hair is really more brownish, not gold. Your eyes are small and squinty!'

Now he was looking at me as if he'd never seen someone having a psychotic break before and found it fascinating.

I flung down my dish towel, humiliated to be doing something so – clichéd. 'Plus,' I hissed, 'you're such an asshole!'

I whirled away and rushed through the heavy wooden swinging door, out into the dining room. If I were Scarlett O'Hara, he'd rush after me, seize me in his manly arms, and sweep me upstairs to make a woman out of me. Instead, the door behind me stayed shut, I still looked like a complete and utter idiot, and I heard the laughter and footsteps of happy, well-adjusted people approaching the front door.

I took the stairs two at a time, became panicky when I couldn't find my room right away, then threw myself through the door, slammed it, and leaned against it, panting, just like in the movies.

This, this is why I go to great lengths to numb all emotion.

Because it *hurts*.

Chapter 6

The one thing this place had going for it was tons of hot, hot water. I was dealing with the fact that this hot, hot water was in the women's *communal* bathroom *halfway down the hall* from my room. There was one deep, claw-footed tub in its own little compartment, and then separate stalls for toilets and a couple of showers. A boarding-school row of five sinks lined one wall, each with its own small mirror over it. No makeup lights, no full-length mirror – nothing to indulge vanity here!

Which is a good thing when you haven't paid much attention to personal grooming in, say, several decades. I sank into the deep bathtub, suddenly transported to another fabulous deep tub I'd once known, in a somewhat ramshackle but gracious house I'd lived in for a while in New Orleans. That tub could have held a polar bear. The real estate agent had told me it had been made for a judge back in the thirties – he'd had two regular tubs sawed in half and then welded together, creating one mammoth, claw-footed behemoth of a bathtub that I could lie down flat in.

But this tub was not bad, despite the inadequate fluorescent lightbulbs that cast a cold, cadaverous gleam on everything. The water was steaming hot, the soap was homemade and rough with dried lavender, and there was a small wooden box filled with dried herbs. What the hey – I grabbed a handful and sprinkled them under the water gushing from the faucet. Herb-scented steam filled my nose and throat as I lay back and closed my eyes.

The steam reminded me of being in Taiwan, back in 1890, one of the times it was being colonized by Japan. I'd had tuberculosis for a while, and the coughing was making me crazy. I'd tried any number of remedies, and finally someone recommended I take the healing waters in Taiwan, on the mountain Yangmingshan. On one side of the mountain, the air was full of egg-scented steam, wreathing the green mountain like a fine, fog-colored silk scarf. The rotten-egg smell was disgusting at first, but within just a couple of days I didn't even notice it. Twice a day, every day, I would sit in an invalid chair at the edge of a natural hot spring and breathe in the warm steam for an hour. Many other people were there for different health reasons – mostly lung- or skin-related. I watched as locals crouched at the shallow edge of the spring, where water bubbled up gently through the sandy bottom. They would take wooden chopsticks and make little fences out of them, sticking them into the sand in a circle. Then they would put a couple of eggs inside the circle, where they would be cooked by the hot geothermal spring. Eating eggs cooked like this was considered extra healthy. I stayed there two months, enjoying the lush beauty of Taiwan and breathing in sulfurous air. My TB was cured.

Now I breathed in unsulfurous steam, more than a hundred years later. I was jolted back to the present. Was it just two days ago that I'd been in London? Yesterday? Unexpectedly, tears stung my eyes beneath my closed lids as, once again, the cabdriver's face loomed before me. Was he still alive? What was his family thinking, feeling, doing?

I sat up, guilt sticking to me like soapy film, and grabbed the shampoo. I hadn't done it – it had been Incy. All I'd done was . . . walk away.

I washed my hair and dunked underwater to rinse it. The water was starting to cool a bit, and I took a sea sponge off a hook, soaped it up, and scrubbed all over my body, feeling as if I were taking off the top layer of skin. Everywhere I scrubbed turned pink and tingly, and I felt weirdly clearheaded, breathing clearly, seeing the water start to swirl down the drain. I felt clean and smooth-skinned and alive.

Stupid, huh?

Luckily, I got back to my room without seeing anyone else. I found my bed turned down and a cup of hot tea on the small table beside it.

'No chocolate?' I murmured, and rooted around in my suitcase. I hadn't packed any sleepwear but found an old

T-shirt that didn't seem too bad. I couldn't find a comb, either, but raked my fingers through my short black hair, getting out most of the snarls. Then I wrapped my wool scarf around my neck, climbed into bed, and sniffed the tea. It smelled herbal, of course. These people were all about herbs. Herbs coming and going, every time you turned around.

The tea tasted kind of minty and a touch licoricey. My room was chilly, my hair was still wet, and the warmth felt good going down. I turned off the light and snuggled under the blankets and down comforter, surprisingly cozy and comfortable. The bed was tiny and hard, but I've slept in boat bunks, the backseats of cars, and a million train compartments, so it was no problem. I hated the fact that there was no lock on the door, but before I had time to worry about it, I was asleep.

I'm not a great sleeper. My brain usually doesn't turn off. I'll be almost asleep, almost there, and then I'll start thinking about going somewhere, or refurbishing a farm-house in France, or where I left a pair of shoes, or if I can find a particular food in this particular city.

Then, when I'm asleep, I usually have bad dreams. Not dreams, actually, like where I'm talking to a pretzel and then a squirrel is laughing at me and it's all about my subconscious working through weird crap. More like memories. Bad memories. Memories of people, human and immortal, whom I've known and who have died, of really horrible years I've had (I was literally in a Turkish prison. In the 1770s. Not a picnic.), of plagues and world wars and car accidents and horse-and-carriage accidents and train wrecks and . . . It's like a heavy weight of bad things, and when I close my eyes at night, when I'm so exhausted that I can't help letting my eyelids sink down – that's when the memories come calling, insisting that I look at them all over again, like they want me to feel more emotion this go-round.

Usually I self-medicate to the point where even if I dream, I can't remember nothin' in the morning. It works pretty well, to a point, but the side effects can be kind of brutal.

When I woke in the morning, keeping my eyes squeezed shut against the pinkish light swelling through the window, I immediately shied away from any memory of the night before. I waited for the physical wretchedness to overwhelm me, and tried to calculate how many steps away the bathroom was and if it would be better to just hurl out the window.

But I . . . felt okay. I opened one eye. A clock on the bedside table said 6:17. AM? Gee, that was . . . early. Last night – I winced, but actually the worst thing that had happened last night was my acting incredibly stupid in front of the Viking lord. In the grand scheme of things, not so bad. I took a couple of breaths and didn't feel at all sick. In fact, I felt pretty good. I felt like I'd actually slept. I sat up slowly and remembered that I hadn't drunk any liquor, hadn't had anything except the most boring food known to man or beast. Huh. The room was chilly, the radiator just starting to hiss slightly, and I pawed through my suitcase, finding 'clean' clothes – and I use that term in a relative sense. I shimmied into them quickly, seeing my breath making fog in the cold air. Then I tossed all my stuff back into my suitcase and zipped it up. I would lug it downstairs – right after I mooched a cup of coffee.

I set it by my door and pulled on my motorcycle boots, my fingers skimming one heel. I was probably imagining it, but I thought I could feel the amulet's energy. As if someone could hide it inside a book in a huge library, and I could run my fingers over all the spines and immediately know when I found it. I'm so sure.

My car keys were in my pocket; the map was still in the car. I could easily find my way back to Boston, or maybe there was a closer airport, like for commuters. I paused, my hand on the doorknob. The thought of going back to London was a dark cloud looming in front of my face. I felt – dread. It was the same feeling that had made me lie to Gopala, to use a passport Incy didn't know about. Why? I was acting on instinct, but *what* instinct? Incy had never harmed me. Annoyed? Yes. Exasperated? Frequently. But hurt me? Scared me? Never.

I didn't know where to go, what I was doing, or why.

And that was such a familiar feeling, but in a completely different way.

I let out a breath and opened my door. I would decide where to go when I got to the airport. But first, coffee, that precious life-giving fluid that would unstick my eyes and lubricate my brain cells. Oh, God, please, please have coffee, real coffee, here.

No one was in the dining room, and I wandered back into the kitchen, my nose twitching. Slowly I pushed open the heavy door, and in stark contrast to the silent, empty gray dining room, the kitchen was full of heat and bustle. The lights were on, people were talking and laughing, and the air was full of smells.

'Nastasya!'

My head whipped sideways to see River smiling at me.

'I thought I'd just grab some coffee,' I began.

'Breakfast isn't quite ready – most of the others are still doing chores,' said River.

'I never eat breakfast,' I said. 'But coffee—'

'Come here,' River commanded and, oddly, my feet obeyed her. 'Let me see your hands.'

A fingernail check? I held them out, relieved to see they were clean, thanks to my scrubby bath the night before. Was she going to read my palm? It seemed all too possible.

'You have incredible hands,' River said, sounding pleased. 'Strong. Here, do this.'

'Huh?'

River pushed my sleeves up past my elbows. I flinched when she swung my wool scarf over my shoulder so it hung down in back of me. Then she grabbed my hands and literally stuck them into a huge mound of warm dough lying on the wooden worktable like a great big larva.

'Uh . . .' I felt frozen, like my hands were stuck fast into this tar baby of dough.

River's eyes, a clear, tanned-leather brown, looked deeply into mine. 'I know you know how to knead bread.' Her voice was soft. My cheeks flushed; she was referring to the fact that many immortals had been born before there were bread factories. Many immortals (the women, at least) had probably made their own bread thousands of times – unless they'd been born rich and had somehow stayed rich all their lives.

I'd been born rich but had been as poor as a peasant by the time I was ten. I'd lived on farms, several different farms, until I figured out that I liked cities better.

I knew how to knead bread.

'It's been a while,' I said, still not moving. Like, hundreds of years.

'Yes,' River said, more softly. 'Yes. But one never forgets how.' She put her hands on top of mine and scooped them together. Together we pushed the larval dough away from us, then brought in the sides, then pushed down again.

Across the room, someone – Charles, with the bright

red hair? – started frying bacon in an iron skillet on the big old-fashioned stove. The black girl – possibly Brynne? – took a couple of loaf pans out of the oven, flipped them onto a clean dishcloth on the table, and thumped them firmly. Fresh-baked, steaming bread popped out of the pans and gleamed golden in the dawn light.

Yes! I smelled coffee! Yes! Thank you, God, Brahma, Saint Francis, whoever. There was coffee in my future!

I realized River had left me to start pouring pitchers of apple cider. Still I kneaded the bread, my hands and arms moving automatically.

Once I glanced up to see Brynne smiling at me. 'You do that well,' she said, and wiped some sweat from her forehead.

I muttered something unintelligible, and it occurred to me that I couldn't remember the last time anyone had told me I did anything well. Actually, there wasn't much that I did do well. Not anymore.

'Here,' said River. She held a heavy stoneware mug up to my lips, and without taking my hands out of the dough, I sipped some hot coffee, cut half and half with boiled milk and already sugared just a bit. It was the most perfect freaking coffee I'd ever had.

I think I made a pathetic whimpering sound of pleasure, because River laughed then, and she looked so pretty, her tanned face flushed from the warm kitchen, her silver hair pulled back in a practical knot, little wisps escaping. I took another sip while she held the mug, and I thought, *She's almost thirteen hundred years old.* Which was such an incredibly bizarre thought, even for an immortal, and I would have pondered it more, but there was this intensely good coffee sliding down my throat, and I felt awake and clear-headed and not ill, and then the Viking lord came through the back door, breathing steam, wearing a heavy plaid shirt like a lumberjack in a Monty Python skit.

He glanced around the room, taking off leather work gloves, and there I was, the scum of the earth, kneading dough like a pro and drinking coffee made by the head honcho of the whole shebang. The fun of whacking and kneading warm, yeasty dough? Say twenty dollars. This perfect coffee? I'd gladly pay seventy-five dollars for it. The expression on Reyn's face when he saw me working in the kitchen at barely daybreak? Priceless. I smirked at him when no one could see, and a muscle in his jaw twitched. He went to the coffeepot and poured himself a mug while I divided the dough into two equal parts, draped a dishcloth over one of them, and started to roll the other one out on the table. I got it to about half an inch thick, then started at the top, using my fingertips to roll it into a long snake, very tightly. When it was all rolled up, I pinched the seam shut and bent the two long ends beneath it. Then I popped it, seamside down, in a buttered loaf pan and made a shallow slash in the top. And that was one loaf, ready for the oven.

Reyn looked so disappointed that I couldn't help

snickering. My stomach growled; the air was full of good bacon smells, baking bread smells, cider smells, and it had been so, so long since I'd gone anywhere close to a breakfast. I usually couldn't stomach breakfast, was never hungry before noon, if then. But I was hungry now.

Maybe I could stay another day. No one knew where I was, and I could see how my bread came out.

Chapter 7

At breakfast several people smiled or said hello, and the ones who didn't just seemed like they weren't morning people, not like they totally hated my guts already. I didn't eat much, felt uncomfortably full really fast, but the toasted bread with butter was surprisingly satisfying, and the bacon had much more flavor than bacon usually did – salty and chewy and crisp with fried fat.

After I'd dutifully carried my empty plate into the kitchen, River said, 'Come with me.' I grabbed my beat-up black leather coat and trotted after her into the chilly autumn air. She led me past a stand of maple trees, dropping their scarlet leaves to the ground like blood. Several dogs ran up to us, and I watched them warily until River patted their heads. 'Yes, Jasper, yes, Molly, there's a good dog.'

A long, narrow barn was kitty-corner to the house, and its large double doors were closed. River took me through a regular-sized door in the side of the building, and once we were in, I saw there were no animals, no hay, no tractors. Instead, high windows let sunshine flood the whole building. It was divided into large rooms that opened out onto a middle hallway. Already people were filing in, lighting gas heaters, moving chairs into place. This was the schoolhouse portion of River's Edge.

River took me into the third room on the left. Solis was there, sitting on a flat pillow on the worn, unvarnished floor. He looked up, and a glance passed between him and River that I couldn't read. Then River gave me one last smile and left, making no sound.

A few people – Jess, the old man; Daisuke, the smiley Japanese guy; and Brynne, who was black and pretty and had her hair twisted in tight rolls against her head – came in and hung their coats on some hooks on one wall. They looked at me curiously but took their places around the edge of the room, opening worn books. Blimey, I'm at Hogwarts, I thought, then Solis motioned me to sit down next to him. I did, keeping my coat on, my scarf snug around my neck.

'Nastasya,' he began, speaking low so only I could hear him. 'River wants me to teach you – she's asked me to. But I can't take you as a student. I won't.'

This was unexpected, and I sat in silence. I'd been halfway out the door, anyway. But—

'Yeah? How come?' I tried to keep my voice down, but it came out as belligerent. My cheeks were heating as Solis's words sank into me.

Solis looked sad and kind, like a thoughtful California

lifeguard, and I felt like throttling him. 'You're not committed,' he said simply, no bullshit. 'Maybe you had a crisis. Maybe you thought you needed a change. You remembered River and thought this would be a good halfway house. But you're not really here, not to stay. Your heart isn't here. You've already got one foot out the door. I don't – I don't want to waste my time.'

A bunch of sentences jammed together in my brain, all trying to get out at the same time. Shockingly, what came out was: 'How do you know where my heart is?' I sounded like a street punk.

Solis blinked, the overhead sunlight highlighting his short curls of dark blond hair. 'Well, I *know*,' he said, as if I'd asked how he knew the sun would come up tomorrow. 'I can feel it.'

I felt embarrassed, humiliated in front of the other students. I sneered. 'Yeah, right,' I said in disgust, getting to my feet. 'Whatever. You're right, I don't want to be here. I won't waste your time – and mine.' I pulled open the classroom door, aware of the curious looks boring into my back. 'Whatever,' I said again, over my shoulder. Then I closed the door way too hard and stomped down the hallway, my boots shaking the floor. I slammed out the barn door and practically plowed right into His Holiness, who threw out his hands to catch me.

'Get off, you stupid git,' I snarled, regaining my balance. 'You win. You can have your little Xanadu all to yourself again. I'm gone.'

Reyn gave me a narrow-eyed look. I had managed to surprise him again. Bully for me. I ripped my arms out of his grasp and spun away. Solis hadn't kicked me out of the place – no doubt River would let me stay anyway. But he'd refused to teach me. I mean, who needs that? Five minutes later I had hauled my dead-pony suitcase down the stairs and out to my rental car. I was practically weeping with rage and frustration trying to get the goddamn thing into the boot, but I'd bust my gut before I asked anyone for help.

At last I slung myself into the driver's seat, popped it into gear, and peeled out, spewing rocks behind me like the tacky adolescent I was.

To hell with them.

Chapter 8

ould not find the effing map. Could not remember how the hell to get back on the highway to Boston. My breakfast now sat like acid-laced lead in my stomach as I pulled too fast into the parking lot in front of MacIntyre's Drugs on the main street of this town. Literally, on Main Street. There was one main street, and this was it. God, get me out of here.

To add to my jangled nerves, my feeling of unease, almost panic, for lack of a better word, was seeming to increase the farther I got from River's Edge. What was going on? What was hanging over me? For the past twenty-four hours, my nervous breakdown had seemed to tamp down a little. It was back in full force now – a howling in my brain that told me to hide. My fingers brushed the back of my neck, made sure my scarf was there.

A couple of local kids, dressed in goth black and smoking cigarettes, sat with their backs against the building in a wide alley between the drugstore and the next store over, Early's Feed and Farmware. One of the kids, a girl with green-streaked hair and a silver hoop in her nose, decided to mess with an outsider. She called, 'You can't park there. Handicapped spot.' The other kids giggled.

I shot her the bird without replying and strode into the store, hearing them laughing again outside. A quick glance around showed cheap sunglasses, a stand of fishing lures, and an ancient chest freezer with LIVE BAIT written on the side. A tall, slender girl stood behind the counter, straightening boxes of old-fashioned alarm clocks on a shelf. A feather duster was stuck in her apron tie. She turned around, already smiling, but faltered when she saw me. 'Can I help you?'

'Do you have any maps?' I said brusquely. 'Like for Massachusetts or the Northeast?'

'We sure do,' she said, coming from behind the counter. From outside we heard more laughter and then the sound of breaking glass. The girl started, glancing outside, then bit her lip, not wanting to take on the local JDs. 'Um, right over here.' She led me to a crooked wire stand, its yellow paint chipping off to show rust underneath. 'Here's one for Massachusetts. And here's one for the Northern Atlantic Region.'

The girl seemed colorless, her pale ash-brown hair almost the same shade as her skin and eyes.

'Meriwether!' The loud, harsh voice made the girl jump.

'I'm here, Dad.'

'Why aren't you behind the counter?' the man barked, coming into view. He was red-faced, with thick black hair and long, unhip sideburns. Big hairy arms stuck out from his turned-up sleeves, and he wore actual red suspenders.

'I'm just showing this . . . girl the maps,' the girl, Meriwether, said. Clearly she was cautious of her father, if not afraid. Maybe afraid.

Her father looked me up and down, then seemed to dismiss me as the same kind of lowlifes who were loitering outside. 'What do you want?'

Staring him down, I held up the two maps Meriwether had given me, then put them on the counter. Meriwether scurried around to the other side and started ringing them up, punching in the prices by hand. My gaze fell on some high-octane energy drinks, and I added a four-pack of those. And then some candy bars.

'Okay,' Meriwether said breathlessly. 'Is that everything you need?'

'Yes. Thanks very much for your help,' I said deliberately. 'You were very helpful.'

'Oh,' said Meriwether, blinking. 'Thank you.'

Her father snorted and headed toward the back of the store.

Blushing, Meriwether gave me my change and banged the register drawer shut. 'Thank you, come again,' she said by rote. I thought, No way in hell am I coming here again.

Outside, the morning seemed too bright and still chilly, a brisk wind whipping right through my black leather coat.

'Better move your car,' the goth girl called again, and I shot her a lethal glare that seemed to take her aback. She laughed nervously and turned to her friends.

'Get a life,' I snarled, slamming into my car and throwing it into gear. She looked at me in surprise, then shook her head angrily, shrugging.

It occurred to me that I should take my own advice. But I never do.

Every big city has immortal hangouts. It seems to go through trends – for decades, many of us will prefer Milan, and it will be full of clubs and immortals with apartments or houses – always lots to do, lots of people to hang out with. Then Milan will slowly fall out of favor – maybe the political climate will change, or the economy, or a war will break out, and another city, like San Francisco, will become popular. But all major cities, and of course many smaller cities, keep a fairly consistent, if smallish, population of immortals.

Some people fall in love with a city and stay there for centuries. They usually hate the inevitable modernization and talk fondly of the old days, before there were streetlights, etc. Forgetting the fact that the roads were horrible before streetlights, and people got robbed all the time, and it took forever to get from one place to another. I mean, hello? Indoor plumbing? A huge plus.

But most of us have favorite places, favorite time periods. I don't. Right now the hip happening place was London. But I knew I could find old friends in Boston, knew where to go to look for them. It was stupid, this feeling of dread, like I had to hunker down somewhere with my head low. It was stupid and irrational and I was going to ignore it. In Boston I would chill with people I knew and hang out while I decided where to go next. I cranked the rental's radio up loud and flew down Route 9 until it hooked up with I-90.

It felt like about twenty years ago that I had been slugging down gin at the Dungeon. How could I have been so – unaware – just, what, four days ago? It was another lifetime, another Nastasya. Maybe it was time to change my name again, reinvent myself, move to another city. I'd been Nastasya for about thirty years. I was past due for becoming someone else. Someone who didn't hang out with Incy and Boz.

That's what you'd been trying to do at River's Edge.

I'm an old hand at ignoring the voice inside my head, so I simply pushed back farther on my barstool and motioned to the bartender for another screwdriver. She'd asked for ID, of course – they almost always did. I knew better than to exaggerate too much – my American license showed me to be just a few months past twenty-one.

It had been better when the drinking age was eighteen – closer to how I look. But I could pass as a young-looking twenty-one.

I'd gotten to Boston in the late morning, checked into a hotel, and crashed until about ten PM – time to go out. I'd decided to go to Clancy's, finding it right where it had been about ten years earlier. They'd updated it, and I didn't like it. I remembered it as dark, grungy, with repulsive olive-green carpet surrounding a twelve-by-twelve wood-tile dance floor. A tiny closet had held a cheesy DJ who would play your request if you sat on his lap. It had been homey, cozy, and packed with immortals.

Now it had better lighting, faux-distressed wooden floors, and a real DJ stand, raised above the dance floor, with some pink-pigtailed kid spinning vinyl records. The clientele seemed to be about half and half, human/immortal. I recognized some faces, but no one was running up to me and giving me air kisses.

Of course, you know, immortals are human. We're not aliens, put here to infiltrate the earth and take over everything. We're completely human, but we just don't . . . die so much. When I was little, my father had told us fairy tales about a princess who was so good, she was given the gift of immortality. I've wondered if he had really believed that. There are different myths and theories in different immortal cultures, but when you analyze them, it always comes down to, boom! It just happened! It was a gift or a curse or they drank magick water or ate a magick plant. I thought maybe it had been a weird spontaneous genetic mutation. Like cancer or color blindness.

Want to hear something funny? I didn't even realize I was immortal until I was in my twenties. I knew I still looked really young, but I remembered my mother also looking very young. Anyway, I was a servant in a house in Reykjavik. The mistress of the house, Helgar, recognized me as immortal and then slowly had to convince me.

She became my best friend and taught me more than I had learned in the twenty-one years up till then.

One day we'd been sitting in the front parlor, the one that overlooked the cobbled street. It was winter but not snowing, and the fire in the big carved fireplace was crackling and leaping. Helgar sat in her chair doing the needlework of a cultured lady, embroidering flowers and rabbits onto what would become the cover of a kneeler in the family's church. I'd learned how to do that as a child, when I'd lived in my family's *hrókur*. Like a castle, but medieval, rough – not fancy, like Versailles or something.

But now I was a servant, so I sat on a wooden stool, carding wool.

'I don't know when we started,' Helgar said. She had a strong, deep voice and spoke well. 'My own mother was born in 1380 in England. She still calls it Aengland. She said she knew people in her village who'd been born around the year of our Lord 1000.'

My eyes had widened.

'Anyway, Sunna, it stands to reason that there must

have always been immortals,' Helgar had gone on. She came to the end of her thread and bit it off, then knotted a new strand. 'After all, there's always been evil.' She sounded complacent. 'I would guess the first immortals, the aefrelyffen, came out of Eden itself, right after Eve and Adam. First came the light, then the dark.'

'I don't understand,' I'd said. 'What do you mean, *evil*?'

'Terävä,' Helgar had said. 'Didn't your parents tell you?'

'My parents died when I was small.' I kept my head down, feeling familiar pain.

Helgar looked nonplussed, her embroidery forgotten in her lap. 'Died! Died? Both of them?'

I bit my lip, feeling a new shame, for having immortal parents who had managed to die.

Helgar was astonished, no doubt running through what it would have taken to kill my parents. Clearly they had both been immortal, since I was. But yes, they were dead. I was quite sure. Quite, quite sure.

'But what about – Terävä?' I asked.

After several moments, Helgar blinked and said, 'Terävä. The dark. Immortals are born in darkness and live in darkness. We can't help it. There's evil within us.' Seeming shaken, she picked up her embroidery again, not looking at me. Knowing about my parents had changed me in her eyes, made me something different. I pretended not to notice.

'What do you mean, *evil*?' I asked again.

'Our magick,' Helgar told me, but seemed unwilling to say more.

'Nastasya!'

I swallowed and blinked a couple times, seeing that I was still in Clancy's, though four hundred years later.

Someone leaned in and kissed my cheeks, left, then right, then left again. She pulled back, and I saw sleek brown hair, brown eyes, a wide smile.

'Alanna,' I said, trying to inject enthusiasm. I flipped my scarf over my shoulder and smiled.

'Darling! Actually, it's Beatrice now.' She slid onto the next stool and clinked her glass against mine. Alanna/ Beatrice was relatively young, barely ninety, and filled with the energy and enthusiasm of youth. Her hair was chic, her pearls real, and she wore a leopard-print cashmere sweater and skinny black pants. She looked fabulous.

'Nasty – still Nastasya?' I nodded. 'Nasty, I haven't seen you in *ages*.' She smiled her thanks to the bartender and pushed a tip over to her. 'Now, you,' she said to me. 'You look—' She faltered and took another good look at me.

I waited.

'Are you okay?' she asked finally.

'I'm fine.' I took several big gulps of my drink, citrusy and fresh, overlaid with the cold medicinal vodka after-taste. 'What have you been up to?'

'Appreciating the longevity of stocks,' she said, and giggled, obviously deciding to let my appearance go. 'I spent last summer in Venice, and it was so lovely, except for the tourists. I think I'll go back next summer.'

I just didn't have the energy to ask her questions about it, get recommendations about restaurants, hotels. I liked Al— Beatrice. She was always cheerful, always happy about something. And she looooved being immortal. She thought it was the best thing since the invention of air-conditioning. I'd never minded hanging out with her.

'You know, it's funny I've run into you,' Beatrice said, signaling the bartender. 'People have been asking about you.'

'What do you mean?' I asked, feeling a sudden pang of alarm.

'A couple of people have asked me if I'd seen you, and I said no. Oh, could I please have a sidecar?' Beatrice asked the bartender, then turned back to me. 'How funny! What a coincidence. It was Incy, of course. I think Incy and Boz have been calling around, looking for you, asking everyone. What's going on? Where are they? You guys are always together.'

My mind raced. 'Oh, it's stupid,' I said with an embarrassed smile. 'We were arguing one night, about how everyone knows everyone, and Incy said that no one in our group could really disappear, you know?'

Bea sipped her drink and nodded, looking intrigued.

I let out a theatrical sigh. 'So I bet him that I could

disappear, successfully, so he couldn't find me. It's stupid, I know. I have to stay lost for at least two months.'

Beatrice laughed. 'That sounds like Incy. But two months! What did you bet?'

I grimaced. 'If he finds me, I have to get his name tattooed on my ass.'

Beatrice roared with laughter, throwing her head back. She smacked the bar lightly with one hand. She positively whooped. Yep, Incy was a scamp, all right.

'Oh, my God!' She wheezed, trying to catch her breath. 'And does he have to get yours tattooed on his if he can't find you?'

I nodded. 'Inside a heart. You know how long tattoos last on us.'

Beatrice laughed again. 'Oh, God, too funny! You guys are crazy! So I guess you want me to keep seeing you a secret?'

I tried to make puppy eyes at her and probably ended up with more of a rabid squirrel vibe. 'Unless you want his name on my ass on your conscience.'

Beatrice whooped again. 'Oh, God, no! I can't have that! I won't say a word!'

I grinned at her gratefully but inside felt almost panicky. Incy had been calling around, asking people about me, already. And he wasn't even close to Bea – she was probably way down on his list. I really would have to get lost, and good.

'So will you stay in Boston long?' Bea asked. 'You'll

probably run into other people if you do. I think I'll stay through Christmas. It's so pretty in the winter, with the snow.'

'No,' I replied. 'I'm just stopping here tonight.' I forced another grin. 'I'm going to join a mountain-trekking tour in Peru. Like to see him find me there!'

Actually, that wasn't a bad idea . . . I asked the bartender for another drink, feeling a pleasant warmth in my stomach, a gentle relaxation in all my muscles.

'Perfect!' Bea said delightedly, and mimed zipping her mouth shut.

'Bea!' Someone called her name from across the bar, and Beatrice swiveled excitedly.

'Kim!' Kiss kiss kiss.

Kim was cool and sophisticated, a beautiful blonde who had been a top model in the seventies, under a different name, of course. It had killed her to finally have to pretend to age and disappear from the scene. But it was either that or endure all the plastic surgery rumors, which had become increasingly catty and resentful.

'Hey, Kim,' I said, smiling.

'Nastasya,' she said. Kiss, kiss. 'I barely recognized you. When did you cut your hair?'

'Oh, I don't know,' I said truthfully.

'And the black.' She looked at me with a critical eye. 'So . . . *striking* with your skin tone.'

'Yeah. I'm really more of a spring,' I said flippantly.

'No,' Kim said, shaking her head. 'No, you're not.

You're a winter, with that pale skin, those oddly dark eyes. Have I ever seen your real hair color?' Kim loved this stuff, hair and clothes and makeup.

'Uh, I don't know,' I said again. 'Anyway. What's new with you?'

Bea quickly filled Kim in on my crazy bet with Incy, and Kim smiled and agreed to play along. It had been a *brilliant* idea, I must say. Then she launched into what she'd been doing lately, which, as it turned out, was quite a bit.

This was what I had wanted, right? Lights and noise and drinks and people all around to talk to. Of course, I hadn't imagined the long tendrils of Incy's influence closing in on me here. But at least this was better than that chilly, empty house in West Lowing. And yet the memory of it, the smell of the kitchen, the laughter, the crunch of fall leaves underfoot, the scent of Reyn's flannel shirt as he stood next to me – it pierced me sharply, and I inhaled.

' – so I thought I'd check Clancy's out,' Kim finished.

'Ah.' I nodded, opened my eyes wider, and finished my drink.

The bartender wordlessly slid another one toward me, and I nodded my thanks and pushed a ten her way.

'Kim!' Bea said, struck by a thought. 'Show Nastasya your thing!'

Whuh-huh? I thought.

'Oh, that.' Kim looked modestly unsure. 'It's just a party trick, really.'

'No, no, do it,' Bea said, sipping from the tiny straw in her drink. 'It's so cool.' She turned to me. 'Kim has created this thing, and it's divine. Kim, you have to show her. And look – there's Leo, and Justin. And Susie. They'd love to see it!'

'Oh, well, if you insist.' Kim blushed beautifully and slid off her stool. Bea ran over and started gathering people, only immortals, none of whom I knew.

'Come on!' said Bea, motioning us toward the back of the bar.

She led about nine of us through a dark back hall to a rickety staircase that led up. And up. And up. We climbed four flights of stairs, and then Bea pushed open a black metal door that led outside to the roof of the building, smelling of cold tar and wood smoke and cooking scents from the restaurant next door.

Most of the buildings in this area were six stories or less, since that had been the limit of how high a roof cistern could pump water by gravity, back when they were being built. There were still some cisterns to be seen, rusted metal standing primly on three supports, their small, broken ladders hanging to one side.

'Okay, now,' said Bea. 'This is so cool. But all of you have to put down your drinks and smokes. Is nine people enough?' she asked Kim.

'Should be. Can we get into a circle and hold hands?' Kim held out her hands.

We were going to make magick. I felt a tingle of mingled

dread and excitement. I hadn't been in a circle for – about two hundred years? I avoided 'big' magick, and most of my friends were too lazy to learn all the stuff necessary to make it work. The few times I'd tried anything more than a minor spell, I'd almost always had a bad reaction, including barfing, headaches, and fainting . . . That reveal spell I'd done to find River's Edge had been the first even tiny one I'd done in ages. I was reluctant to try again, but everyone around me seemed to have no hesitation, and I'd feel stupid if I backed out now. Maybe I should get over my anti-big-magick prejudice. Maybe it would be better this time. Maybe I would be better at it now. I nodded, feeling reckless and determined, and I cheered up. This was just what I needed. This was exactly what I couldn't get at River's Edge.

I stepped up and took one of Bea's hands and one of Susie's. We all grinned at each other, and Bea squeezed my hand. I felt interested and excited and lucky to be there.

'Okay, you all know how to lend me your power,' Kim said, and we nodded. 'Wait till I ask for it, then say the words. But first I have to set things up.'

She took several deep breaths and closed her eyes. For a minute everything was quiet, the only sounds being people talking and shouting, five storeys down. Cars honking in the distance. Faint music. A couple yelling in the next building over. But up here it was still, serene. I slowed my breathing and closed my eyes. Helgar, when she'd gotten over the mystery of my parents, had described our magick as having a black snake coiled up inside you, and when you say the right words, its power is released through your mouth. Gross imagery aside, that was still how I thought of it.

Now I concentrated on gathering my power. It wasn't simple, like clenching muscles. It was more a focused concentration, like in yoga or meditation. Both of which had always bored me to tears.

I heard Kim start to sing, and her words were as ancient and dark as the few I knew, but from a different root language, maybe a Romance language. I felt a prickling in my chest and focused on breathing in slowly and out slowly, one, two, three, four. Kim sang, and her spell began to weave itself around us, interlacing through our hands, joining us together. My hands grew warm from Bea's magick on one side and Susie's on the other, and my chest began to feel tight. I always hated this part, when I felt I couldn't draw enough breath, and my head felt as if it might explode, and I was afraid if I screamed for help, nothing would come out. But it always passed, so I kept a short rein on my panic and focused on breathing. I felt our power growing, felt the magick coming to us the way insects come out of wood to escape fire.

I recognized Kim's words now: She was calling on our power. Quietly I sang, 'Gefta, ala, minn karovter. Pav minn gefta, hilgora silder.' I sang the words several times, not knowing their actual translation. They had been taught to me long ago as a way to give my power to a spell-maker. I'd used them only a few times, but once learned they were impossible to forget.

Minutes later I heard someone gasp. My eyes popped open. There, silhouetted against the night sky, was Kim, smiling grandly, her arms outstretched.

Susie laughed and clapped her hands, dropping mine, which felt burning hot.

There were other whispered words of praise and admiration. Kim's party trick was truly stunning: Her neck and shoulders were covered with songbirds, arranged according to color. Goldfinches made a bright yellow outline, soft gray titmice lined her arms, wrens made a feathery brown cape along her shoulders. The air was crackling and alive with magick, the birds holding perfectly still, blinking slowly, warblers, kingbirds, orioles – they made an intricate, precious pattern, full of energy and life and small, quickly beating hearts.

It was one of the most beautiful things I'd ever seen, but I couldn't help wondering what on earth had possessed her to even try this. To think of it. What was the point? Yeah, we all have a lot of time on our hands, but . . .

'Isn't it incredible?' Bea whispered, putting her hand on my shoulder. 'I just think it's amazing.'

'Yes, it's something, all right.' I couldn't look away – so many pairs of black, shiny eyes looking dully off into the distance, as if they were drugged. My stomach twisted, and I was suddenly so sorry that I was here, that I had agreed to be part of this. Another stupid wrong turn.

'Thank you, thank you,' said Kim, making a tiny curtsey. 'But I can't keep it up any longer, so—' She breathed out and said a few words that released the birds from her spell. I waited for them to shake their heads, come to themselves, and fly off, bewildered, into the night.

But as the first few of us headed for the stairs, I saw the birds close their eyes, leaning their small, smooth heads to one side. Then one by one, they toppled off of Kim's back, falling silently to the roof. Dead.

'Whoa,' said Leo 'They're kind of single-use birds, eh?'

People laughed, and Kim shrugged gracefully. 'It does do a number on them.' They headed to the door, and soon I was left alone on the roof of this Boston bar, with a splitting headache, a bad taste in my mouth, and my feet surrounded by a hundred vibrant, lovely songbirds, their soft feathered bodies already growing cold.

Chapter 9

That night the dreams came again.

I left Clancy's right after Kim's spell. I was the only one who'd minded it, the only one whose drinks curdled in her stomach at the thought of the tarred roof upstairs littered with bright bits of dead fluff. Plus, what with the shocking headache and the usual nausea, I'd begged off, leaving Beatrice, Kim, and the others looking at me with bemused expressions. It had been about midnight, and I'd gone back to my hotel, feeling unclean.

I'd worried about not being able to sleep, but exhaustion and worry hammered me into a deep unconsciousness that sucked me down, down into the black horror of my childhood, back to the night my life first changed.

A big shaking feeling woke me, and I glanced across at my older sister, Eydís, asleep in the bed we shared. Had it been a peal of thunder? I loved storms. I looked at the narrow window, sealed with small, thick panes of real glass. Light flickered outside. Lightning? More like fire?

The sound came again, a huge, hollow boom that shook our bed. I saw Eydís blink sleepily, and in the next moment, the door to our room flung open. Our mother stood there, her eyes wide, long golden hair flowing down her back from beneath the small linen cap she slept in.

'Móðir?' I said.

'Quick!' she said, throwing shawls at us. 'Get up! Put on your shoes! Fast, now!'

'What's happening, Móðir?' Eydís asked.

'No time for questions! Hurry!'

I felt the next boom in my ears as I pushed my feet into my winter slippers, made of elk hide and lined with rabbit fur. It was freezing in our room; the fire had died down, and the stone walls were skimmed with lacy frost.

In the corridor we met my older brother, Sigmundur, who at fifteen was as tall as my father. He held my little brother, Háakon, by one hand. Tinna, my oldest sister, was already wrapped in a heavy woolen shawl, her long yellow braids falling over her shoulders.

'Come, children, quick!' My mother whirled and flew down the wide main staircase with us so close behind her that her hair whipped into our faces.

Shouting and pounding footsteps greeted us as we reached the first floor, and there we saw Faðir's men, armed with swords and bows, wearing heavy leather armor. We pressed back against a stone wall as they ran past, shouting orders. In a single column, they rushed down the narrow back stairs, which curved downward in a counterclockwise spiral. Sigmundur had demonstrated to me and Háakon the brilliance of its design – if you were heading downstairs, defending the castle, your right arm with its sword had plenty of room to cut down invaders. If you were an invader heading up, your sword arm had no room, and you were forced into an unnatural fighting stance.

And again the huge boom, the shaking. Dust from the stones above our heads trickled down, making me sneeze.

'Móðir, what's happening?' Seven-year-old Háakon had been ill for the last two weeks with chills and fever. It had left him thin and pale, with blue circles under his eyes.

'The outer wall has been breached,' my mother said tightly, herding us to my father's study. 'Northern raiders.'

Eydís and I looked at each other, eyes wide. The thundering noise came again, and Tinna grasped my hand. 'A battering ram,' she said under her breath.

As we raced down the hallway, my mother knocked the torches from their iron wall sconces. The sticks hit the ground and sputtered out in a shower of sparks, leaving darkness behind us.

We reached my father's study. Inside, my mother turned the large brass key in the door's lock, and then she and Sigmundur put the heavy wooden beam across the door, resting it in its brackets. My sisters and Háakon and I huddled by the fireplace as our mother went to Faðir's big wooden cupboard and unlocked it with quick, trembling fingers. As soon as the doors were open, Sigmundur strode forward and plucked the largest sword from its stand. It was several inches taller than I was, straight and sharpened on both edges, with a simple wooden stock wrapped in thin strips of leather.

My mother looked at the weapons for a moment, then grabbed one for Tinna. My sister's arms bent under its weight. Eydís was next – at twelve, she'd had six years of weapons classes, but usually we used smaller daggers that we pretended were swords. I was ten, and I held out my hands. After a moment of hesitation, my mother gave me a short sword, maybe sixteen inches long. I grasped it in both hands, unable to comprehend what was happening. Even Háakon got a dagger, which he regarded with round eyes.

'Where's Faðir?' Sigmundur asked, hurrying to the window and peering out its narrow slit.

'Downstairs with the men.'

'Will you have a sword, Móðir?' Háakon asked, still admiring his dagger.

'I have something more powerful.'

Móðir felt beneath the neck of her nightgown and pulled out her heavy amulet, the one I loved to look at. I'd sat on her lap and held it in my hands, studying it, but she never took it off, never let me try it on. It was round, almost as wide as the back of my hand, with a flat, translucent, milky stone in the middle, about two inches wide. All around the stone were carved symbols. Some were our alphabet, runes, that I recognized, but some I didn't know. I'd asked her what it was made of, and she'd said, 'Gold. Gold and power.'

Now she took the amulet in her two hands, closing them around it. As another boom shook the room, she closed her eyes and started to sing.

I woke up gasping, icy sweat running down my face. The back of my neck burned, and I tore off the thin scarf I slept in, running my fingers over the puckered skin.

I hadn't had that dream in a long time. I shook my head, still panting, then stood on trembling legs and went to the bathroom, where I turned on the tap and splashed water on my face. It hadn't been a dream, of course, but a memory. The memory of my mother trying to save our lives that night. She hadn't known, there'd been no way for her to tell that in gathering us all into my father's study, she'd actually herded us toward our own deaths.

Except me.

Still breathing hard, I patted some cold water on my neck, then retied my scarf. In the room I drew the heavy hotel curtains and saw that the sun was coming up – I'd slept about six hours. Once I was breathing more normally, I got dressed and used the hotel's computer to find used-car lots.

❋ ❋ ❋

Three hours later, I crossed my arms over my chest, feeling the chilly fingers of autumn creeping into the car – the used, beat-up brown hatchback that I'd bought this morning in an anonymous lot outside Boston. The engine was off, and so was the heater, and a deep shiver started in my stomach and made my entire body tense. Though the sun was shining through high, wispy clouds, it was still barely forty degrees.

I didn't want to get out of the car.

I'd hated what Kim had done with magick last night. Magick meant death and pain. Pursuing magick was pursuing power, and if you have power, someone will want to take it from you. Someone will go to great lengths to take it from you. I hated that Incy had called about a million people, looking for me, telling them to look out for me. More than ever, I wanted to be away from him, from all of them.

Then I'd had the memory. I tried hard never to think of that night, and for the most part I was surprisingly successful. I hadn't dreamed about it in decades. A week ago, all my feelings and memories had been safely wrapped in layers of cotton wool, insulated from inspection. Now my shell had cracked, and pain was leaking out. I laughed drily – was this how Eve had felt when she tasted the apple? That she suddenly saw things she didn't want to see?

I swallowed, my throat feeling tight. Here I was. I had nowhere else to go. Being around my kind in Boston had been a disaster. The thought of going back to England filled me with revulsion. Worse than revulsion. Fear again. Dread.

Really, what choice did I have? I'd hit a wall. After more than four hundred years of drifting along, I suddenly had no idea who I was or what to do with myself. I'd changed names countless times but had always felt like the me I was presenting on the outside. Now I was feeling like the me I'd left behind so long ago, and the thought was making hysteria rise in my throat. Now I felt like a brittle casing around something dried up, blackened, and dead.

Ten years ago – five years ago – I would have been envious of Kim's spell, impressed, almost wishing I knew enough magick to do it myself. What had changed in me? Who was I becoming?

I jumped at Solis's gentle tap on my window. I was ashamed, humiliated to come crawling back, such a loser that I had nowhere to go, such a mess that I had to ask for help from strangers. I tried to swallow again and opened the door, feeling extremely old as I climbed out of the car. It was much worse now than the first time I'd come. It was mortifying to be back here, and so quickly. But I just . . . didn't know what else to do.

Solis nodded at me, his eyes watching as I scowled at the ground, scraping dried leaves around with the toe of my boot. He nodded again and touched my arm. 'This way,' he said, and started walking.

I followed him to a vine-covered stone wall behind the

big barn. A wooden door, taller than me, was almost hidden beneath the ivy, and Solis opened it and gestured me inside. I almost groaned when I saw the neat rows of raised vegetable beds, the cold frames, the greenhouse. I re-examined my wood-chipper suicide idea and again reluctantly dismissed it.

Several people were working in the garden. I refused to look at them, afraid of seeing the Viking lord or, worse, Nell, all friendly, insincere treacle. I was also not looking forward to running into River – no doubt she would be understanding and generous, which would make me practically hate her.

Solis leaned down and tugged on some thick green leaves. A turnip popped out of the dark earth, and I almost gagged. I hate, hate, *hate* turnips. Once you've gone through a couple of famines where all there is to eat are turnips and lentils, you never want to see either one again.

'Plants get their nourishment from the earth,' said Solis, as though he were speaking to a simpleton. I was silent, the only response coming to me being *No freaking duh*.

'They take what minerals they need,' he went on, 'extracting and processing them with their roots and leaves so they can grow and seed and repeat the cycle. But they can't grow in darkness, yes? They need sunlight, the energy of the sun also.'

I bit the inside of my cheek to keep from screaming.

Now he would talk about recycling and composting and taking care of Mother Earth. I really, truly, no kidding this time, wanted to die.

'Terävä are like plants,' he said, surprising me. My eyes opened and I glanced quickly at him. Most immortals avoided talking about Terävä, the dark and the light. Helgar had been one of the few I'd ever heard say the name out loud. 'They make their magick by taking energy, life, from things around them. Just like plants, which can deplete the soil they grow in, making it barren and unable to support life, Terävä deplete the life force of everything around them. That's why things die when Terävä make magick. As I'm sure you've noticed.'

I thought about Kim's little birds, and my throat ached. 'Hmm,' I said. 'So . . . you guys don't make magick?' I could easily give it up without regret. I didn't use spells that often, didn't want to make my magick stronger. Yes, there were a few times that I'd felt that rush of excitement, that burst of beauty, but the aftereffects were so bad. I didn't think I would miss it.

'Oh, no,' Solis said with a hint of a smile. 'We make magick all the time. It's our lifeblood. Living without magick would be like . . . like being mortal.'

Back in my little nun cell, *eons* later, I tried to get the dirt out from under my fingernails. At least we had sinks in our rooms, even though we still had to go down the hall for everything else. I was tired, my shoulders aching.

My face felt windburned, possibly sunburned. Every finger-nail I'd had was shredded, and I'd cut them all very short.

A knock on my door made my heart start. Maybe . . . Reyn? I allowed myself the fantasy of thinking he'd secretly – *way* secretly – be glad to see me back.

'It's open,' I called. 'Of *course*.'

River opened the door and came to stand behind me at the sink. She put her hands on my shoulders, smiling at me in the mirror. 'Welcome back,' she said lightly. 'I dig your car.'

Her antiquated word was supposed to make me smile. I held up my ruined hands. 'I dig your garden,' I retaliated, and she laughed. I tried not to enjoy it.

'So Solis says. You picked your weight in turnips, beets, and kale, I hear. I know you'll be excited to see them at dinner.'

My eyelids fluttered, and I couldn't help a moan of dismay. River laughed again. 'I know. I've been through my share of famines, of course. Once, in southern England, all the cows were ripe and overflowing with milk, but most of the food crops failed. We drank milk, made cheese, ate cheese, fed cheese to the animals – the stink! It was enough to put me off dairy for about sixty years.'

I flipped my scarf around my neck again and sat down on the bed. Outside, it had suddenly gotten dark. I prayed that people had started to whip up some dinner, then remembered it would be turnips and beets and kale. Despite everything, being depressed here still felt better than being not here. Being in the outside world. Getting lost in my memories. Again I wondered what my friends had thought of my disappearance. Were they looking for me? Was I truly hidden here?

'I don't understand why I have to work in the gardens,' I said. 'I just – want to be, I don't know. Like, saved or something. Tell me what to do and I'll do it. But I don't see what gardening has to do with it.' I scrubbed my clean hands against my pants, the itchy feeling of dry dirt impossible to get rid of.

River thought for several moments, her elegant profile outlined against the darkness outside. I got up and pulled the heavy winter curtains closed, cold emanating from the window's glass.

'For immortals, time passes by very quickly,' she said at last. 'Do you remember how, when you were a child, every day took forever to get through, and each year until your birthday seemed to take a lifetime? Then, once you were older, time seemed to pass more quickly. Do you remember that?'

I avoid thinking about my childhood as much as possible. 'No.'

'Well, it's an almost universal feeling,' River said, undeterred. 'That's because, when you're a ten-year-old child, one year is a whopping ten percent of your entire existence in the world. And if you don't remember the first two or three years, then one year is an even bigger percentage. Do you see that?'

'I guess. But the garden—'

'When you're forty, one year is only one-fortieth of your entire existence. So each individual year seems to pass more quickly, to not carry as much weight. Is this making sense?'

'Um, well, okay,' I said.

River was patient, as a 1,300-year-old person must be. Her eyes were clear and warm, looking intently into mine. 'When you're aefrelyffen, immortal, it feels like you're looking ahead into – oblivion. Or worse, you realize you'll probably be alive in the year 2250 or something, and it's terrifying because you have no idea what it will be like. When you're immortal, years themselves quickly lose all meaning. Years, decades, and eventually centuries seem to whiz by in the blink of an eye, until, say, the seventeen hundreds feel only like a bad party you went to once.'

I fiddled with the ends of my scarf and didn't say anything.

'Because of the relative lengths of our lives, so many things lose importance or become lost themselves, against such a huge backdrop,' River continued. 'How many lovers have you had? How many children? How many friends have you loved who are dead now? For regular people, these events are tremendous and shape or change their entire lives. For us, it's just a wink in time. But they do affect us. Little by little, bit by bit, loss by loss, we ourselves become diminished. We've lost so much for so long that most things, most people, most *experiences* lose their value for us, their weight. We forget *how* to value things, how to *feel* things. We forget how to love.'

Well, okay, food for thought. Some of this was sounding uncomfortably familiar.

'What we start off doing here,' River said, 'is to give you a crash course in relearning the significance of moments, of minutes. You'll learn the skill of being fully aware, fully present, in the now. You'll relearn how to feel things, how to value things. And you will feel happier and more complete afterward.'

I bit my lip, fearing that she was speaking the truth, and hating it.

'Working in the garden, preparing a meal, cleaning up – these tasks are repetitive and boring. For an immortal, they're almost unbearable. We're generally in search of the next *huge* emotion, *huge* event, *huge* physical sensation, because after a while that's all we can feel.'

Oh. Hello. Ouch.

'Our gift to you, and to all immortals who come here, is to teach you how to value and feel every moment that your hands are immersed in suds. To really see and smell every weed you pull. To feel the hard smoothness of a turnip, to really taste the earthy greenness of its leaves. To be within your own skin without wanting to run around screaming. To enjoy yourself, value yourself, know yourself. And once you do that' – she stopped and smiled again – 'then you'll be able to love, to really love, someone else.'

I didn't say anything. My throat felt tight again, and my eyes were hot. Running around screaming felt like all I could bear to do right now. Oh, God, she might actually know what she's talking about. It was a horrible realization. She might actually know *me*, how I feel. And how wretched and mortifying would that be? My insides were so ugly, so miserable, so drenched in pain and horror that the thought of someone truly knowing them was terrifying and torturous. I felt like a caged rat, and my cage was slowly being lowered into boiling oil. I felt the level creeping up, felt it searing my skin—

'And of course,' she said calmly, ignoring the growing panic in my eyes, 'you'll also be able to make magick without killing anything. You'll be Tähti.'

I almost gasped, hearing the word spoken aloud. As much as people only rarely talked about Terävä, no one *ever* talked about Tähti. None of my friends had ever met one, and some people insisted they were just a myth. I'd come here hoping they weren't.

'You're born one way or the other,' I said faintly. 'You can't change.'

'One can. One does.' River seemed quite sure and calm. 'I'm Tähti – now. We make magick without darkness, without destruction. You can learn how to.'

It was as if she were telling me I could learn how not to be human, to be an alien instead, or a tiger. Just incomprehensible.

'What do you mean, now?' I asked.

'I wasn't always sweetness and light,' River said, standing up. 'There was a time when I was . . . very dark indeed.' She looked away, as if wondering if she'd said too much. 'And now the turnips are calling our names.' She gave a little smile and gestured toward the door.

I looked at her, unable to process everything she had just told me. In the last ten minutes she had unraveled my very persona, split my chest open and laid bare the rotting corpse inside me. I was completely freaking out.

Freaking out and, uh, also hungry. Working for hours in the cold, the sun, and the wind had sharpened my appetite, and I was starving.

'Come on,' River said, holding out her hand. 'You can freak out while you eat. I hear there's apple pie for dessert. For those of us who finish our turnips.'

Oh, God, oh, God, she knew me. *She knew me.*

Chapter 10

'Oh, Nastasya, *help*!'

I whirled at the sound of River's voice and saw her coming from behind the battered red farm truck. It was early morning, and I'd been virtuously bringing kindling to the house for the big fireplaces in the main sitting room and the dining room. I didn't know how this was going to save my soul, but it was better than pulling up beets. Now I set down the handle of the firewood cart and headed toward her – she was bent over, holding one of the farm dogs by the collar.

'Nastasya – you have to take Jasper,' said River. Her fine silver hair was escaping its braid, framing her face in wisps.

'Uh, okay,' I said, reaching for him. 'Oh. Ew. Is that *skunk*?'

'Yes. I'm sorry, but I have to get these cabbages to the farmers' market before eight. Jasper usually goes with me, but he obviously had a run-in with the local wildlife. Can you please take him and give him a bath?'

I looked at her. Jasper panted happily by my feet, reeking to the sky.

'With tomato juice,' River said. 'Put him in the big stable sink and dump tomato juice all over him. I've already asked Reyn to bring it out to you and to help you.'

'Huh,' I said.

River started to see the humor in giving me this heinous job and tried to suppress a giggle. 'I'm sorry, Nastasya. You're my last hope. A bunch of tomato juice and then a good shampoo, and he should be fine. Right, Jasper, sweetie?'

Jasper looked cheerful and pleased with himself.

'Sorry – have to run. Thanks so much!' She patted my shoulder briefly, then hurried back to the truck. I watched her back up and then head down the long unpaved drive that led to the main road.

I looked down at Jasper. He smiled up at me. He smelled so, so awful. If any of my friends could see me now . . . they would find me just as inexplicable and wretched as I found them.

'Okay, come on, then, you,' I said, leading Jasper to the horse stable.

There was the big barn, where classes were held, and then a couple of other outbuildings. River kept six horses, though this stable had stalls for ten. In one corner was the tack room, and opposite that was the big tin sink. Reyn stood next to it, already punching holes in several huge cans of tomato juice. He glanced at me with a lack of enthusiasm.

'We're supposed to give him a bath,' I said unnecessarily.

'Yes.' Reyn put the stopper in, then bent down and lifted Jasper easily into the sink. I tried not to appreciate how strong he was, how capable and unruffled he was. Jasper scrabbled uncertainly, then stood still.

'Good boy,' I said, trying not to breathe in. 'Oh, jeez. Let's hope this juice thing works.'

'Hold him,' said Reyn, and tipped a can of tomato juice over Jasper's back. It was probably cold, and Jasper quit smiling, looking affronted.

'Get that cup and dump more over him,' said Reyn.

I did. I became aware that Reyn and I were alone in this warm, hay-smelling stable. The morning was still new; slanted beams of early light streaked through the few windows. Around us horses huffed quietly, their velvety noses twitching as they caught scent of our boy Jasper.

I was uncomfortable. I hated being in stables, being around horses. I'd had horses that I had loved terribly, and losing them had hurt so much. Now I tried hard to avoid being near them.

Reyn's strong arms tipped can after can of tomato juice over Jasper, who was now distinctly unhappy, his head hanging down. Jasper was a corgi, with short legs and big bat ears, and he was up to his elbows in tomato juice. I scooped up cup after cup and continued to pour it on him, working it into his fur with my free hand.

'Let's talk about choices, Jasper,' I said. 'Let's talk about making the right decisions.'

Next to me, Reyn was so solid, like he could stand up to a tidal wave. He smelled like crisp autumn air tinged with wood smoke, unbearably good. His plaid flannel work shirt was open at the throat, and I wanted to press my face against the smooth skin of his chest and breathe him in. Then he could put his arms around me, and I would be so warm and safe . . . Despite his seemingly one-speed emotional range, I could imagine him laughing hard, really guffawing. I could picture him drunk, though not an atom of his person seemed like he would ever indulge. I could see him furious, raging . . . I faltered, my hand still in Jasper's thick fur.

I looked up at Reyn, examining his face.

He looked down at me, then poured more juice.

Reyn furious, raging . . .

I shook my head, blinking, the image slipping away from my brain like fog. What was it? It had been . . . I didn't know. It was gone. I decided to grab the bull by the horns. 'You don't like me. Are you sure we've never met?'

Reyn's eyes flickered. He dumped the last big can of juice over Jasper, and I rubbed it in, trying to cover every inch of whiffy dog. 'I don't . . . have any feelings about you one way or another,' he said, his voice as distant as his manner. 'Let the juice sit a minute.'

From the corner of my eye, I saw the vee of skin in the neck of his shirt, his chin showing the slightest bit of beard. 'How long have you been here?'

He slanted a glance at me, then said, 'Rinse him off and then you can shampoo him. I've got work to do.'

'Can you help me? He might jump out.' I didn't think Jasper was going anywhere – he was totally demoralized now, just awaiting his fate. He'd even sat down in the tomato juice. A tiny muscle twitched in Reyn's jaw, but he stayed. I rinsed Jasper off and pulled the stopper up, then went at him with some horse shampoo.

'Oh, Reyn, there you are!' Nell's voice made me turn, and I saw her walking up the aisle, looking fresh-faced and suitably outdoorsy in a hand-knit woolen sweater and corduroys tucked into proper wellies. I looked like I'd been out clubbing all night and then washed a skunked dog. Not in a good way.

'I've been looking for you,' she told Reyn. He didn't have a big response to this, and Nell turned and looked me up and down, cheerful and friendly as always. I tried not to care that my black sweatshirt had a skull picked out in rhinestones, or that my high-waisted purple harem pants would have looked at home at Cirque du Soleil. I mean, *whatever*.

'Nastasya, maybe you've found a new calling!' She smiled at me, and my back stiffened.

'Meaning what?' I asked.

'As a dog groomer!' She gave a little laugh. 'You look like a professional.'

I decided not to spray her down with the sink's hose, but sighed to myself.

'Reyn, I was wondering if you could come help me.' Nell gave him one of her English-maid smiles, practically coiling a curl around one finger. 'I've got to sow some early spinach.' I'd noticed her doing this before – trying to be with him, near him, getting him to help her do whatever. He seemed clueless.

I expected Reyn to leap at this reprieve, but he shook his head. 'I'm going to finish this up, and then Solis asked me to look at Titus's shoe.'

'Is Titus one of the horses?' I asked, without any real interest. Nell gave me a condescending smile.

'Yes. Reyn is our resident horse master. He has an excellent seat.'

I grinned. 'I've noticed.'

Reyn's face tightened and Nell flushed, looking embarrassed. 'It's an equestrian term.'

'Really? I thought you were talking about his ass.' Now they both seemed discomfited, and I gave myself extra points. They were two of the most irritating people I'd ever met. They deserved each other, though the thought of them together made bile rise in my throat as I rinsed Jasper off again. I leaned over and sniffed the dog's back experimentally. Just the slightest touch of eau de skunk. Acceptable.

'Okay, boy, do not do that again,' I said, hefting him out of the sink. Despite his solid bulk, he probably weighed only about thirty pounds. I set him on the ground, and waited . . .

'Oh!' Nell jumped back as Jasper shook mightily, spraying us all with water.

I dried my hands on the rough towel and grinned at Reyn as Nell turned and almost stomped down the aisle.

'Thanks for your help,' I cooed at him.

He looked at me for a second, then headed out past me in the opposite direction of Nell.

They both gave me a royal pain.

River and Solis apparently decided I was light-years away from being able to handle formal classes of any kind, and so instead he simply put me to work. My name was written into the job chart, and for the past several days, I'd struggled against the omnipresent weights of both mind-numbing boredom and white-knuckled, finger-nail-screeching desperation. I mean, I had *avoided*, on purpose, every single thing I was doing. For *decades*, if not centuries.

At last, however, I'd found a job I liked: Whacking the hell out of things with a hammer. Today Brynne, Jess, and I were repairing some of the weatherboard siding on the big barn where classes were held. I thought about how different this activity was from whatever I'd be doing with Incy and Boz, back in London. Would we be planning a fabulous vacation? Going to the inevitable parties? Recovering from a wild night out? Crippling cabbies? It all seemed so pointless. Whereas, looka here, I was fixin' up a barn! Useful, eh?

'So tell me about yourself, Brynne,' I said, wiping my nose on the sleeve of my shirt. 'What brings you here?'

Brynne held up a board so Jess could pin it in place with a few quickly placed nails. Then we would nail it in more completely.

'I come here every decade or so, stay a year or so,' said Brynne. Today the tight rolls of her hair were covered by a brightly colored cloth. She was elegantly beautiful, like a teenage model, like a cheetah. A cheetah wearing overalls and a raggedy green sweater. She grinned at me, lighting the dull gray afternoon sky. 'Usually after a horrible breakup. River takes me in, cheers me up, I brush up on some skills, and then when I feel okay again, I'm off.'

I remembered Reyn's stray dog comment and tried not to flinch. 'Huh. What kind of skills?'

Brynne shrugged. 'Watch it, Jess – there's a splinter there. Oh, anything. Magick, cooking, gardening, whatever. One year I helped River repaint a bunch of rooms. One year I focused on baking. One year I did nothing but study gem and crystal magick. One year – oh, do you remember, Jess? I came here and taught everyone how to dance hip-hop.' She laughed, throwing her head back, the line of her brown throat silhouetted against the sky.

Jess grunted, nails in his mouth. Apparently not into hip-hop.

'How old are you? I mean, if you don't mind my asking.'

Brynne thought a moment. 'Ooh. Two hundred and thirty-four. Whoa.' She smiled again. She looked maybe eighteen.

'How did you meet River?' Was it tacky to grill her? I didn't know.

'Okay.' Jess nodded at me and gestured to the board. I held a nail in place and slammed it with the hammer. Best. Chore. Ever.

Brynne quit smiling. 'I got mad at someone and set them on fire.'

I blinked, running the words through my head again. Had she said that? Jess didn't even look up. I decided to let my jaw drop open.

'Say what?' Funny, she didn't seem like a psychopath . . . I thought back uncomfortably on some of the things I had done, remembered Incy's cabbie, and picked up another nail.

'It wasn't real fire,' Brynne said, leaning against the board to hold it in place. 'It didn't really burn them. But I wanted to scare the hell out of them, and I did. Anyway, River was walking by the alley – this was in Italy, maybe in, what, 1910? 1915? Before the First World War. She saw that *clearly* I was misusing magick, and came up to me, gave me a little pep talk.'

'And then you just came here?'

'Oh, no. I punched her.'

Jess snickered and handed me another nail.

'But eventually I came around. I first came here in 1923. After the war.'

'Where are you from?'

'Louisiana. My mother was a slave, from Africa. Angola. My father was a white landowner. Ha! Try being an immortal slave! God.'

I finished with that board and held one up for Brynne to nail.

'What happened?' This was great stuff.

'My father realized my mom was immortal, of course. They waited it out, waited for his wife to die, and then they ran away together. He sold the plantation, set everyone free.' She laughed. 'They're still together. I've got ten siblings. You might meet some of them – they drop by sometimes.'

I handed her a nail, thinking about this. I hadn't known many happy immortal couples, but clearly here was one. And they had added eleven more immortals to the world. It seemed weird, to have children for years and years, so you had siblings who were a hundred years older than you. I'd met a couple. All of my own siblings had been just a year or two apart, for whatever reason.

'How about you?' I finally said to Jess.

'I'm not going to talk about it,' he said in his gravelly voice, and fit another board into place.

All righty, then.

'Do you know other people's stories?' I asked casually. 'Like Lorenz or Nell? Or Reyn?' Oh yes, I'm subtle. Soooo subtle.

Brynne shrugged easily. 'They can tell their own stories,' she said. 'I know that Lorenz is about a hundred, and he's from Italy, obviously. I got the impression that his family was friendly with River's family. Nell is English, and only about eighty or so. Reyn I don't know much about. I think he said he was about two-sixty-something? And Dutch. Other than that, you'll have to talk to them.'

I nodded, thinking.

'What about you?' Jess asked. His voice was like shaking a can of rusty nails.

My first instinct was to give him his own line back – I'm not going to talk about it. But I was here to grow and to learn to *love* myself, right?

'I'm older.'

Brynne grinned. 'Okay. How old? Where are you from? What's your story?'

And just like that, the darkness of my past came crashing down on me again, and I couldn't go there, couldn't share anything, couldn't do the normal give-and-take of conversation.

I looked at Brynne, and I guess she saw something in my eyes, because her face softened and she patted my arm. 'It's okay,' she said. 'Some roads are longer and harder than others.'

I nodded mutely, thinking that some roads seemed to lead straight to hell.

*　*　*

Different teams of people, usually two, sometimes three, made dinner each night. Other people cleaned up. People went for walks almost every night after dinner, even if it was raining or bitter out. I was forced to go sometimes, though I hated being out in nature in the dark. Surrounded by everyone else, though, it felt less threatening, and I stayed in the middle of the group so if something attacked us, it'd have to go through a bunch of people to get to me.

Hey, if I were totally rational, I wouldn't be here.

'Wasn't there a movie about this?' I asked a couple of days later, as I peeled a mountain of potatoes. I'd dug these effing potatoes out of the ground two days ago, and the crawly feel of dry dirt still clung to my hands. Sadly, not every chore was as satisfying as pounding nails. 'And all of a sudden I'll turn into a karate expert?'

Asher, washing kale next to me, smiled. 'Yes. It's been our secret plan all along.'

'You're a teacher here,' I said. 'So how come you're still doing grunt work? Haven't you achieved nirvana yet? Are you not appreciating every minute you wash kale?'

Asher smiled again. '*Au contraire, mon petit chou.* I *am* appreciating every minute. But it's important that you truly comprehend that you don't just do x, y, and z, and then you're happy and can relax for the rest of your loooong life.'

His sense of humor surprised me, and I realized that River shared it. In fact, it seemed I was often overhearing a joke, hearing laughter drifting to me across the garden, or the yard, or down the hall. Of course, I'd yet to see Reyn crack a smile except in my imagination, but I wasn't holding my breath on that.

'What do you mean?' I asked. 'Like, I'm not ever going to be . . . better?'

'No, no, don't misunderstand,' said Asher. He put another pile of clean kale on the counter and dunked more in the sink. 'It's just that it's not like climbing a mountain, and you're done, and you've climbed the mountain, and you never have to climb it again.'

Shit. 'I have to climb the mountain *again*?'

'No.' He turned off the water, dried his hands on a dish towel, and looked at me. 'It's just that once you climb the mountain, you realize the view is so spectacular that you want to keep going toward it.'

I shook my head. 'I'm lost. Drop the climbing metaphor. Give it to me straight.'

'None of us here just decided one day to embrace good, or light, and leave darkness behind forever,' Asher said patiently. 'It's not a decision you make once. Being Terävä is how we're born, but not how we have to stay. Being Tähti can be achieved, but once it's achieved, it's easily lost again.'

I was still shocked at how easily people talked about this here.

'Being "good" – and by good I mean not dark, not evil – but not like a Goody Two-shoes, you understand?'

I nodded.

'Being good is something that one must choose over and over again, every day, throughout the day, for the rest of one's life,' Asher said. 'A day is made of a thousand decisions, most small, some huge. With each decision, you have the chance to work toward light or sink toward darkness.'

'Oh, God,' I moaned. 'I don't even want to be that good!'

His smile lit his face. 'I'll tell you a secret: None of us makes every single decision all the time on the right side. Not even River, and she's the most genuinely good person I've ever met.'

'Then what's the point of trying if you can't even win?'

'You win in lots of different ways,' Asher said. 'Lots of little wins. The point of this life is not to be good all the time. It's to be as good as you *can*. No one is perfect. No one does it right all the time. That's not what life is.'

The kitchen door opened, and several people came in: Lorenz, Nell, Anne, and . . . the Viking god. I saw Reyn every day, of course. After our mutual dog-washing episode, I'd had the misfortune of working next to him, or close by, on a couple of other occasions. He spoke only when spoken to, never smiled, never laughed – in short, he was forbidding and chilly and a pain in the ass.

I continued to find him familiar without knowing why. The more I looked at him, the more irritating he was, the more forbidding – and with true karmic irony, my psyche had chosen to find him more attractive than every other person I'd ever met. It had surprised me. And Reyn had given me *nothing* to work with, no sign whatsoever of interest. But I was drawn to him as if we knew each other, had a past together. For a fevered minute I had wondered if we'd had a past life together, like, reincarnated, and then realized that the idea of more than one life as an immortal was, like, please, no.

And yet I couldn't stand him – he didn't have a single admirable trait except his total, boring devotion to goodness. Okay, let's just say he didn't have a single admirable trait. He was the most annoying, restrained, stuck-up, gooder-than-thou, stick-in-the-mud jerk I'd ever met. And yet every night in my hard little single bed, I . . . *missed* him, as if I'd once had him and now wanted him back. I burned for him, longed for him to come to me, for his touch, ached to kiss him, to make that facade break, to make him lose his cool, make his breath come fast.

I mean, I don't like most men in general and have only very limited, short-term uses for them. But Reyn had gotten under my skin, and I had a visceral, intense attraction to him, whether I wanted it or not.

'Nastasya?' Asher was looking at me. Everyone was looking at me.

I took a breath, picked up a potato, and started peeling it viciously. 'Okay, explain the whole good/evil thing again.'

The others laughed (except Reyn) and turned to leave,

all smiles and rosy-cheeked wholesomeness. At the door Nell paused.

'Oh, Reyn? My door is sticking. Do you think you could take a look at it?' She gave one of her smiles, looking all peaches and cream.

Reyn nodded and started to follow her.

'Reyn?' Asher said, stopping him in his tracks.

'Yes?' Reyn's tone was deferential – not warm, exactly, but not the disdainful tone he used with me. Nell paused, but Asher gestured that she could go. After a moment's hesitation, she smiled and left.

'I've described our quest as being a continuous series of decisions throughout the day, throughout our lives,' Asher said. 'And tried to explain how none of us is perfect, how no one can actually choose to act for goodness every single time without fail. I've said that's not what life is. Can you put it a different way, to help Nastasya get what I mean?'

Oh, God, yes, please put it to Nastasya, I thought evilly, then mentally slapped myself upside the head. There I go: Making a choice not for good, right here, right now. I was hopeless.

Reyn looked appalled, which made me feel a little better. He didn't like being around me any more than I liked being around him.

'How's *your* quest going?' I asked flippantly, sending potato peels flying into the sink. He looked . . . just unbelievable, hair tousled by the wind, bright-eyed, face slightly flushed. It was all I could do to not knock him down right there in front of Asher and climb on him. If I stunned him with a frying pan first, he might not struggle too much . . .

'It's hard,' Reyn said. 'It's the hardest thing I've ever done. It's a constant battle. It's life or death.'

Asher looked taken aback.

Reyn usually didn't give up that much, and I looked at him. I understood about the life-or-death part, but you'd think he'd be more cheerful, fighting the good fight.

'And why do you try?' I wasn't trying to be a smart-ass – I genuinely wanted to know.

Reyn was quiet, and I thought he'd leave without answering me. But he said, 'Because to not try is to admit the other side has won. To not try is to embrace death and eternal darkness. And in that way lies madness and despair and unending pain.'

Both Asher and I were wide-eyed.

'Oh, huh,' I said.

Reyn's gaze was unreadable. He walked out of the kitchen without another word.

I glanced at Asher, who looked thoughtful and maybe concerned.

'He's a fun guy,' I said.

Asher just stroked his beard and left me and the potatoes alone to struggle together.

Chapter 11

'Are you going to stay?' River's gentle question made me pause in the middle of folding clean dishcloths.

I opened my mouth to say, *No, just can't*, but it didn't come out.

It was not a total holiday, being here, but when I thought about it, I didn't feel like I was in searing pain all the time, either. And it *had* felt painful being in Boston, being in London. I'd felt like I was dying, already dead.

I didn't feel like that here.

I still wondered, of course, what Incy and the others were doing now, if they missed me, if they were concerned. I'd never just up and disappeared before, not this completely. I mean, I'd skipped town, leaving notes like *Meet me in Constantinople* or whatnot, but this time I'd tried to drop off the face of the earth. How had they reacted to that? I shivered with a sudden chill.

My life had changed completely, in every facet. Wasn't that what I had wanted? I woke each morning in time to see the first chilly fringes of dawn creep over a distant hill.

I made my bed (at least pulled the blanket up), got dressed, and went downstairs. Sometimes my name was on the roster to help make breakfast. Sometimes I had to do something else, like collect eggs, or sweep the porches, or set the table.

My mornings were filled with work, usually with a teacher or one of the more advanced students: Daisuke, Charles, or Rachel. Sometimes they asked me questions, which I tried to answer; sometimes they talked about random stuff, and it was only later that I realized they had imparted Important Life Lesson #47 or something.

I now knew everyone, their names, where they were from, where their rooms were, how long they'd been here. Jess was in fact only 173. But he was coming off a worse bender than I was, and this was his fifth attempt at being here. I'd never seen someone so young who looked so old – gray, grizzled hair, lined face, nose covered with broken blood vessels. His last time out, he'd gotten drunk and accidentally hit someone riding a bicycle. The cyclist hadn't died, but Jess said the guilt weighed about a thousand pounds on his shoulders. He had a lot to reconcile in his life. As I did.

Rachel was usually pretty serious but could, on occasion, be wickedly funny. Her stories of what she had done during the twenties were hilarious and made us all laugh.

Anne, the other teacher besides River, Solis, and Asher, was cheerful, smiling, and always in a hurry. And she was physical, touching my arm, putting her hand on someone's shoulder, rubbing River's back. I had gotten to where I no longer flinched. She was 304 and ascribed her youthful appearance to 'all this clean living,' which caused the other teachers to snort, making her crack up.

Yes, they were a merry bunch.

Lorenz and Charles – they were nice enough, interesting enough. I hadn't invested a lot of energy getting to know them, since I probably wouldn't be here long, but they didn't piss me off or anything. Lorenz was in fact Italian, with a striking black hair/blue eyes combination and a lovely Roman profile right off an ancient mosaic. He was kind of loud, with big, expressive emotions. Charles was originally from Ireland and still had a very slight accent, as most of us did, but he had lived in the American South for the last two hundred years. He was gay, with bright red hair, green eyes, and freckles. He managed to look trim and dapper even while hoeing weeds or milking cows. Brynne, as I said, looked like a model – tall, slender, and graceful, with a beautifully symmetrical face. Like Lorenz, she was incredibly vibrant, a hothouse flower. She seemed to have it all together – when the fryer had caught on fire, she'd simply doused it with salt, not even missing a word in the story she was telling.

Reyn was himself. Nell still went out of her way to be friendly and helpful, but it took only about a minute to see how fake it was, just a show for other people.

Especially Reyn. I had figured out that Nell was a wolf in preppy clothing, but no one else seemed to notice it. No one seemed to notice how wrapped up she was in Reyn, either. She was subtle, but not so subtle that I couldn't see it. Outwardly, she was the sweetest little thing: All smiles and helpful offers, hardworking, serious about her studies, and kind to everyone.

But underneath I saw her quiet desperation over Reyn, who treated her like an indulged lapdog. He thought they were friends, coworkers, because he was a dense, oblivious schmuck. She wanted to ride off with him into a Tähti sunset and have him all to herself literally for*ever*. Again and again I had seen her work things so the two of them would be assigned to the same chore, working side by side. She asked him for help with her studies and did all sorts of little thoughtful things for him that he hardly noticed.

People usually either really adore me or really hate me, and Nell seemed to fall into the latter camp. I didn't know if she actually hated me, but if she saw Reyn and me working together, she got this look in her eyes, as if she'd turn me to stone if she could. Then I'd blink, and it would be gone.

It added interest to my days.

I realized that River was waiting for an answer.

I wished I could say, 'Yes! I am loving this! Bring it on! My heart and soul are here, and I am ready for a change!' But I couldn't.

'Uh, I might be able to stomach another week,' was all I could manage, and tensed in anticipation of River asking me to leave.

'That's good enough,' River said, and kissed my cheek.

I was floored. I couldn't help raising my fingers to touch where she'd kissed it.

'One final thing,' she said, and I raised my eyebrows. 'You need different clothes.' She looked around my room with open curiosity. 'Like regular jeans and cords. Long underwear. Socks. Heavy shirts, wool sweaters, thick gloves. Lighter boots or work shoes. Sneakers. Slippers. Something warm to sleep in.' She nudged my wardrobe with her shoe. 'Got any of that in there?'

I thought of the ragtag, mismatched, mostly black clothes I'd stuffed in there, expensive designer items I hadn't taken proper care of, cheap punk tees and ratty dresses.

'Yeah, I guess you're right,' I said glumly. 'Since I'm apparently going to be working outside *a lot*.'

River grinned. 'Yes. I'm sure someone will be going into town soon and can take you shopping.'

The next day, late in the morning (and by late I mean, like, freaking nine AM) I was sweeping the long front staircase and trying to remember how the song in the Disney movie version of 'Cinderella' had gone. And I was thinking about how the story of Cinderella – really, of most fairy tales – had changed throughout the years, gotten cleaned up, less scary, with more happy endings. There was the whole glass-slipper thing, and the translation mistake. I'd first heard it with her slipper being made of *vair*, which is fur, animal hide. It was translated into English as *verre*, glass. So there you go. Now I was sweeping and humming the mice's song from the movie. And let's all ponder just how far my life had fallen, in terms of excitement and chicness, shall we? Yes. Pretty damn far.

'I'll drive,' Nell's voice said gaily from below, in the front hall. Her light brown head appeared by the stair banister, and next to her Reyn said, 'I can drive.' I had decided he was the Viking god Odin, god of odiousness.

Nell gave a pretty pout, and the devil grabbed me by the tail. I called down, 'By all means, let him drive, Nell. He has a weenie. It makes a huge difference.'

Her blue eyes widened and she stared up at me, first as if wondering at my audacity, then in irritation as she realized Reyn was also looking up at me.

I was bored. Time to stir the pot a little. Sweeping busily, I said, 'I mean, not with driving, it doesn't make a difference. Of course. But in other stuff. Peeing standing up and all.'

Reyn's voice was tight. 'Your point?'

'No real point. Just lobbying for your right to drive. I mean, you're old enough, right? How old are you? Like, thirty?' Most of him looked barely twenty, twenty-two, except his amazing eyes. His eyes looked hundreds of years old.

He didn't say anything, and Nell frowned. 'He's two hundred and sixty-seven. I'm eighty-three. And how old are you?' Her British accent was crisp.

'Older.' I went down a step and continued sweeping. I'd gotten it down to an art: One broad stroke across, then two quick vertical strokes to get each corner. How was this saving my soul, exactly? Like, was I sweeping my way to salvation, or what?

'Oh, good, I caught you before you left,' said River, coming down the hall from the kitchen. 'You two are going to town, aren't you?'

'Yes,' said Reyn.

'And Reyn's going to drive,' I said. 'Because he's a booooyyyy.'

River's eyebrows raised.

'I'm driving because Nell has clipped both fenders of the truck,' Reyn said, taking his jacket off the long row of hooks by the front door. 'And scraped the side of the Toyota. And popped a tire on the van.'

Nell shot me her usual poisonous glance before she defended herself. 'I was getting used to driving on the wrong side of the road! Everything is backwards here!'

'You've been here for two years,' Reyn said, picking up some car keys. Nell looked like she was going to explode, and I got the feeling that if River and Reyn hadn't been there, she would have spewed venom at me. Instead she snatched her own coat from the row of hooks and shoved her arms into its sleeves.

'Yes, well,' said River, looking bemused, 'Reyn – and Nell, whoever's driving – I'd like you to take Nastasya into town with you this morning. She needs more practical clothes. Can you take her to Early's?'

If Nell had made any sound right then, it would have been a high, spitting shriek. Instead she just turned and headed out the front door without a word.

'I have a car,' I pointed out. 'I can take myself.'

'This saves gas,' River said comfortably. 'We try to combine errands as much as possible.'

Reyn and I looked identically reluctant. Then I realized the fun in being an obnoxious third wheel on this outing that Nell had no doubt finagled in order to be alone with Reyn. I'm ashamed to admit that I made another wrong choice on the road to goodness just then, and trotted down the stairs, ready to make Nell's day miserable.

Okay, not ashamed, exactly. More like, triumphant. But at least I recognized that it was wrong, so that's progress, right?

Early's was the general store right next to MacIntyre's Drugs. It sold farm supplies, gardening stuff, clothes, toys, old-fashioned candy, and kitchen gadgets. It had a wooden floor, a pressed-tin maroon-painted ceiling, and tall, fluted metal columns holding up the roof. It was basic and unpretentious.

'Clothes are over there.' Reyn pointed to one section of

the store. 'I have to get some feed. I'll come get you when I'm done.' He couldn't have sounded less interested.

I gave him a warm, come-hither smile. 'Thank you,' I said sweetly, and saw his pupils flare. 'You are such a darling.'

Nell's face set like marble, and she walked off in the direction of the kitchen supplies.

Reyn looked at me for another moment, then he too turned and headed off.

I snickered after they left. I found myself facing racks of women's clothes, piles of neatly folded jeans on tables, stacks of sweaters – and I felt a little overwhelmed. I couldn't remember buying practical clothing before. When I was poor, hundreds of years ago, I'd made my clothes – hey, rough-spun linen, anyone? Homespun wool? Woohoo!

By the time I'd had money, I didn't need practical clothes. A long time ago, everything had been made for me, by people who'd come to the house. Nowadays, as much as I was thrilled to pieces over the death of corsets and hoopskirts, I still didn't have much approach to fashion. When I ran out of stuff to wear, I called up a personal shopper to send over whatever I needed. It had been decades since I'd worried about what went with what or having the right outfit for different occasions. I never worried if I looked pretty in something or if it was flattering.

'Shit. Okay, I can do this,' I muttered to myself.

What kind of moron doesn't know how to buy regular clothes? Nell obviously did.

'Huh? You talkin' to me?'

I started, looking up to see a goth teenager, a pair of black jeans in her hands. She looked vaguely familiar, and in a couple of seconds I recognized her as the JD who'd been hanging out in front of that old drugstore the day I'd bought the map. Her heavily lined eyes were narrowed at me, her hair dyed in wide swaths of brown and green.

'Nah,' I said, pondering the sea of clothes. 'Sorry. Talking to myself.'

'Way to make sure of your audience,' she said under her breath, and held the jeans up against her waist.

'So . . . you're just . . . seeing what fits?' I asked conversationally. I picked up a pair of corduroys and held them up to my waist. They seemed big. Should I try them on? 'Then what?'

'Then. I. Buy. It.' Her face was sharp, wary.

I slung the cords over my arm and picked up a sweater. It was navy blue. 'Navy goes with everything, right?'

'What the hell is wrong with you?' she demanded, and tossed down the jeans. Thirty seconds later, the doorbell over the entrance jangled as she left. I couldn't help laughing, but it was an uncomfortable laugh, one that announced I was out of my element.

'You ready?' Odin was impassive, holding a hundred-pound sack of something farm-y on one shoulder. I glanced around for Nell but didn't see her.

'Uh—' Oh, crap, it was going to be one of those days, chock-full of personal growth. I could see that now. It was all I could do to not scuttle out of here and find a nice bar somewhere. 'I'm having trouble . . . deciding what to get.'

He blinked and let out a breath, then looked me up and down. I was wearing chalk-striped Lacroix satin trousers that were, of course, now shredded around the knees. A man's blue velour pullover – God knew where I'd gotten it from – draped around me like a shroud. My scarf, green-and-white-striped, was looped several times around my neck. My delightful motorcycle boots completed the ensemble. It had been either these or a pair of leopard-print Manolos, which seemed to be the only two pairs of shoes I'd brought in my exodus.

'I haven't worked like this in . . . a couple of centuries.' I gave a little laugh, but inside I felt amazingly lame and stupid. 'I'm just glad petticoats aren't in the picture.'

Reyn set down his heavy sack, as well as a smaller shopping bag. 'What size are you?'

'Um, size thirty-six shoe?' I offered. 'And . . . maybe small, other things?' I was still stick-thin, no curves to speak of. I just – hadn't paid attention to all this stuff in so long.

'Okay.' Reyn let out a long-suffering sigh for my benefit. He gave me another appraising look, then turned to the table of jeans. His long fingers skimmed through the piles until he found what he was looking for and pulled them out. 'Try these. You'll have to roll up the bottoms.' He pointed to a dressing room, curtained off from the main room.

I tried them on. They fit. He'd guessed an accurate size by looking at me – clearly, despite his monklike reserve, he had a bit of experience gauging women's bodies. Who was he? Where was he from? What was his story? I was quite . . . fascinated.

'They fit,' I said, coming out in my own clothes again.

'Get two more pairs of jeans and two pairs of corduroys in that size,' he ordered. He was flipping through shirts and had already made a small pile of wool sweaters.

Soon I had a bunch of new clothes in a shopping cart. Reyn surprised me by showing me how things went together, T-shirts and flannel shirts, button-downs under sweaters. None of the clothes were designer, or fashionable, or even cute, but they fit, were sturdy, and would be so much more comfortable and warm at River's Edge. Of course, I could never appear in real society dressed like this, but I was actively avoiding real society right now, anyway.

'Did you used to be someone's dresser?' I asked. 'A valet?'

Reyn threw some packages of socks into the cart and picked up his sack again, heaving it onto his shoulder with little visible effort. 'No. I assume you have, like, underwear and all that.'

'Uh . . . I keep meaning to get some,' I hedged, and saw his jaw tighten.

'It's over there.' He pointed. 'Get simple stuff that will wash well. You're not out to seduce or impress anyone here. I'll be at the register. Waiting.'

'Aye, aye, *sir*!'

There were no La Perla satin undies with handmade lace. I got some cotton ones with pictures of little animals on them, frogs and monkeys. In bras I picked up the second-smallest ones I could find. I didn't want to try them on, probably wouldn't wear them anyway. I found a down vest and a puffy coat that was warm and light and washable, unlike my Roberto Cavalli leather coat, which, surprisingly, had proved inappropriate for yard work. And since scarves are a huge part of my fashion identity, I threw a couple into the shopping cart.

Nell arrived just as I was unloading underwear, bras, camisoles, and long underwear onto the counter. Words quivered on my lips, provocative things that would make Nell think that Reyn had helped me pick out my underwear, but I held them in. Which made, what? Evil 2, good 1. Or was evil ahead 3–0 by now? It was almost noon. Evil was probably winning by three points, at least.

I paid for all my stuff, amazed at how little it had all cost. I'd regularly spent two or three times that amount on a single pair of shoes. They had been fabulous shoes, but still.

'Where were you?' Reyn asked Nell.

She smiled, either acting or having truly regained her sunny outlook. 'I didn't need anything here, so I went down to the yarn shop.' She gave me one of her friendly grins. 'They have a great yarn and craft shop here, a few stores down. Do you knit? Did you make that scarf?'

'No, don't knit, I'm afraid,' I said, loading full shopping bags into the cart.

We all trooped out to the truck and loaded our stuff into the back. Reyn looped a couple of bungee cords over everything, and we climbed into the cab. Nell had been careful again to be in between us, pressed up against Reyn on one side, which he seemed not to notice. God, he was dense.

'I love knitting,' Nell said once we were on the road. We passed by MacIntyre's Drugs, where poor Meriwether was no doubt being berated by her thug father. I made a mental note to stop in if I was in town again.

'It's very calming,' Nell pressed on. 'And it gives your hands something to do. And then at the end, you have something beautiful and useful.'

I nodded. 'Hmm.'

'What kinds of things do you like to do?' Nell's face was open, her tone deliberately innocent. She was banking on the fact that I hadn't been specializing in Girl Scout skills.

I started to say something flippant, like 'drinking and whoring,' but then was caught by the idea that I didn't actually *know* what I liked to do. Hobbies, skills? *Does* drinking count? Holding my liquor? I used to know how to sew – not well, but enough so I wasn't wearing a potato sack. I'd cooked, off and on, but that had been a long time ago. I liked going to museums and to movies, but that was hardly a skill. I knew how to ride. Had I ever done anything well? Was I proud of any skill?

Not really. Not consistently. The only thing I had consistently done was survive. And obviously I didn't even do *that* very well. I was struck by the thought that I'd had all this time, so many years, and I hadn't developed . . . myself. When I'd finally had enough money to not work, I'd truly *not worked*, at anything. And neither had my friends. For the first time, I felt ashamed of that fact. I remembered the art openings of sculptors who had been liberating the life from within marble for a century or more, learning all the time with different teachers. Composers, musicians, who'd had more than one human lifetime to hone their gifts. Scientists who'd made an 'overnight' discovery after decades of experiments and study. You think that guy really invented Velcro because he suddenly looked at his dog? No. There were artists working today, museums buying their current work, and those same museums, unknowingly, had other examples of their work from the last three centuries. Those people had evolved, grown, changed.

I hadn't.

Things that don't evolve and grow are not alive.

I became aware of Nell's pert interest, her wide

blue eyes. Reyn was waiting, too, though his eyes were on the road, his strong hands on the steering wheel.

'I don't know,' I said slowly, with uncharacteristic honesty. 'I'm not good at very much. I've done different things at different times, but I haven't really kept up with anything. But . . . I can learn. I think I'm learning here. Maybe.'

Reyn flicked a glance at me, those golden, lionlike eyes.

'Well,' Nell said. 'Yes, this is a good place to learn. But it takes commitment. And time. You haven't even started taking real classes yet, have you?'

I quoted Solis: 'There are lessons to be learned in everything,' I said piously. 'I'm learning to appreciate every moment, to pause and feel every minute, being fully here in the now.'

Nell was nonplussed, and Reyn snorted a laugh that he turned into a cough. At least I thought it was a laugh.

'You really need to have the right attitude,' Nell said, implying that I so did not.

'Hmm,' I said again, and looked out my window.

Chapter 12

I had landed on a different plane of existence: The River dimension. I had to relearn so many habits and patterns – to pick up after myself because there was no maid, to clear my plate after a meal, to leave my shoes by the door so I didn't track in mud or worse.

My new clothes survived the laundry much better than my Jean Paul Gaultier jumpsuit and cashmere sweater, which I had thrown through the washer and dryer. The sweater had come out small enough to fit Jasper, who now wore it proudly, flouncing around in hot pink Chanel. I hoped he wouldn't skunk it up.

There was no cable TV, only a handful of fuzzy local stations. River did have a computer in her office, and one could sign up on a sheet to use it. I didn't need it for anything. We got the local paper every day, and out of extreme boredom I found myself poring over the latest crop reports, reading about whose cow got loose, whose barn got struck by lightning, and what grade-school teacher was going to run for city council. The *London Times* had been full of wars, government scandals, celebrity arrests, society weddings, race reports. It had all seemed like a blur – prime ministers came and went, the people rose up in protest and then settled back down. Here, the smallest inconsequential blip on the screen was treated like stunning breaking news.

People were starting to teach me things that I'd never wanted to know: The names of the stars, patterns of the sun's movements, names of trees and plants and birds and animals. How to gather herbs and hang them to dry. How to focus your attention on a candle flame. Yoga. Meditation, which I hated. But every time my inner spirit rebelled, which was, like, eighty times a day, I was always struck by the fact that I couldn't bear the thought of doing anything else, being anywhere else. So I just sucked it up and kept doing whatever needed doing, until I could find a reason to leave. Until it didn't feel scary to leave.

One morning my job was to gather eggs from the henhouse. River kept about thirty hens. They ran free in the yard, pecking up insects and being annoying. At night they roosted in their boxes, locked in to protect them from weasels, foxes, hawks, stray dogs, and so on. Our own dogs held them in contempt, naturally, but never attacked them.

Anyway, every morning some poor sap (today, me) had to muck through the low henhouse, always warm, humid, and smelling of feathers and straw and chicken poop. Not even I could stand up in it, and by the time I'd stuck my hand into every nest, sometimes under a determined hen who wouldn't leave her roost, my back was killing me.

'You, shoo!' I said to one brown hen. These chickens were big and fat, with glossy feathers and bright eyes. They looked healthy and happy, like the other animals. But this hen was a pecker. She really, really wanted to sit on her eggs and not have them stolen out from under her. She tended to attack whoever came near, and this morning I had forgotten my leather gloves, just like every other morning. Which was why my unmanicured hands looked like they belonged to Jess.

'Look, if it were up to me, you could keep your stinking eggs,' I told her. 'But up at the big house, they have different ideas. They have a total hard-on for your freaking eggs. So get out of my way.' I flicked my fingers at her several times, but she just *bawk*ed indignantly and started to get a wild, pre-peck look in her eyes.

'Goddamn it.' I looked down at my basket. It was pretty full. No one would notice, probably, if I was a couple of eggs short. And then whoever gathered eggs tomorrow would do a better job of it and surely get this hen's holdout stash.

The chicken looked at me, like, *Yeah, run.*

Maybe I should try just once more, very slow and easy . . .

'Hello?'

I jumped several inches at the unexpected voice, hitting my head on a low rafter. My sudden movement panicked the brown hen, so she sank her hard, sharp beak into the back of my hand, causing me to shriek and swear, stamping one foot up and down while I rubbed the rapidly swelling knot on my head.

'Goddamn it!' I roared again.

'Uh, sorry – are you okay?' An ash-brown head looked into the henhouse and saw me thrashing around in the semidarkness.

'Goddamn chicken!'

'I'm sorry,' the voice said again. 'River said to come out here. I usually get our eggs from here? Usually they're up at the house.'

I was apparently running late.

I gave the brown chicken the evilest eye I could, then ducked out of the henhouse. To hell with her eggs.

Outside, Meriwether stood waiting, tall and gangly, a recycled egg carton in one hand. She looked at me, probably trying to remember why I seemed familiar.

'Oh,' she said. 'You were passing through, weren't you?'

'Yeah. I bought some maps at your store. How many eggs you want?'

'A dozen.' She fished a dozen still-warm eggs out of my basket, placing them carefully in her carton. Suddenly I felt like it was two hundred years ago and this was a totally normal, everyday scene. I didn't like it.

Meriwether straightened up, closed her carton, then handed me two dollars. I sighed heavily and pushed them into my jeans pocket. Not exactly high commerce. I remembered the day I had bet my third of the Trans-Siberian Railroad so I could stay in a high-stakes poker game. Now I was in mud-stained jeans selling eggs for two bucks.

'Thanks,' said Meriwether. Again she seemed washed out, kind of dull and lifeless. Well, who could blame her, with that jerk father? She turned to go, and I said, 'How's your store doing?'

She turned back, startled. 'Um, it's doing okay. I guess. Things are harder all over town since the textile mill closed, over in Heatherton.'

'Oh.'

'They used to make sheets and pillowcases,' Meriwether said, brushing some hair out of her eyes. 'We were the only drugstore around, and we did a great business.'

'Is that why your dad's such a putz?' I asked as we walked to her car. ''Cause business is bad?'

Meriwether swallowed uncomfortably, seeming unwilling to admit her dad was a putz. 'Um, well, he's not happy,' she mumbled, fishing her keys out of a pocket. 'My mom . . . died four years ago, and he's just . . . he never got over it.' She got into the front seat and popped the parking brake.

'Oh.' Many immortals become attached to humans, of course, myself included. Fall in love or befriend them. After my Robert-the-Soldier had died in India, the inevitable bad conclusion had prevented me from getting close to anyone else. And among my friends, we tended not to dwell on problems or pain – just pretended they didn't exist, and found something to distract ourselves or dull our perceptions. So I was unused to someone confiding in me about painful personal issues, and I had nothing intelligent or helpful to say. It was too bad, is all. But I guessed she was pretty used to it.

'Thanks again,' said Meriwether, putting the little car in reverse.

'No prob. See you.'

'Nastasya? Come with me,' said Anne. 'Meditation class. Your first time with a group.'

I stood, my spine slowly uncoiling from hours of bending over. Here I was, picking up walnuts off the ground. A line of about ten large walnut trees bordered the front yard, and harvesting the nuts was an ongoing fall chore. It was cold, tedious, backbreaking work, and because I'd once again forgotten my gloves, my fingers were now stained brown from the shells. It would take weeks for the color to fade. My knees were muddy and wet from kneeling on the damp ground, my nose was running, and I felt chilled through.

'Rock and a hard place,' I complained, and Anne grinned. So far meditation had seemed to be nothing but soul-crushing, endless sitting still, coupled with the fun of reliving past horrors. No, thanks. Last week I'd done it alone, with just one other person guiding me. Now it was time for the full group experience. Oh, joy.

'Come,' she said again, pointing to the house. 'At least you'll be warm.'

I looked at my burlap sack – it was about three-quarters full. Sighing heavily, I got up and went with Anne.

'Today we're going to use a candle to help us focus,' Anne said soothingly, ten minutes later. I sat cross-legged on a small, hard pillow filled with buckwheat kernels. There were five of us, each sitting at one point of a pentagram drawn on the floor with chalk. We were upstairs at the house, and I could see the slowly dark-ening sky through a wavy-glassed window. I wondered if I could possibly sneak down the hall, back to my own room, once everyone was really under. I didn't want to do this. I especially didn't want to do this with Lorenz and Charles, though they were both perfectly nice. And the dream team of Nell and Reyn.

'Everyone, let's focus on our breathing,' Anne said, her voice low and melodic. She pressed a button on a CD player, and some kind of chime-y, Enya-type whale song chanting started playing softly.

'Pay attention to your breath,' she continued against the backdrop of the music. 'Feel it fill your lungs, feel it leave your body. You're breathing in energy, breathing out that which you no longer need.'

Like carbon dioxide, for example.

'If it helps, you can count to four as you take in a breath and four as you exhale. Then count to six on your next breath, taking six beats to completely fill your lungs. And breathe out to the count of six. You can close your eyes, if you'd like.'

I immediately closed my eyes. Without seeing Nell's tight face and Reyn's stony one, maybe I could just daydream for a while, embellishing my latest romantic fantasy, the one with Reyn, some almond oil, and a hot tub.

'Now, starting with your toes, I want you to relax each muscle, one at a time. Feel your toes, feel them relax. Now your ankles. And your calves. If you're holding any tension there, let it go.' Anne's voice seemed dreamy, floating on the music swirling around us like wood smoke.

My chest felt achy, my stomach hurt, and my nose was still running from being outside in the cold air. Thanksgiving was in a couple of weeks, here in America, and I wondered if River observed it and if I could hope for a non-healthy dessert on that day. I thought back to my town shopping trip and how I had neglected to stock up on contraband junk food. Oh, God, I could use a Ding Dong.

Anne's voice was a low constant in the background of my mind. I settled into my seat, felt some tension leave my shoulders. Stupid walnuts. My hands were going to be stained brown for weeks – it never washed off. That's why people used it to dye fabric, and wool—

*   *   *

I looked up and saw my family's washerwoman, Aoldbjörg Palsdottir, stirring the huge cauldron with her wooden paddle as big as an oar. The day was cold, but not bitter; the fire beneath her pot licked the sides and brought a flush to her weatherworn cheeks. The bitter smell of walnut-shell dye mingled with wood smoke and filled the bailey. It was cozy here, safe. Sometimes my next-oldest sister, Eydís, and I climbed to the top of Faðir's keep. We'd look out past the castle walls and see the wide swaths of black forest all around. Far in the distance were the bare, rocky lands of the mountains, where nothing grew. To the other direction lay the sea. The world outside the castle was dark and forbidding, but here in the bailey, with the goats bleating for straw and the stableboys brushing the horses and Faðir's steward shouting orders, it was full of life.

My younger brother, Háakon, and I were playing a game with pebbles. He was three years younger than me, no longer a baby or skirt-clinger but an actual boy who could run and play games and keep secrets. We sat carefully out of the way of everyone, on a pile of sheep shearings, maybe twenty high, each thick woolly mat in the shape of a stretched-out sheep. The wool was dirty, full of twigs, but still oily and soft and good to sit on.

'I hate that smell,' said Háakon, wrinkling his nose.

'It's not as bad as rock moss,' I said, and he nodded, remembering the smell of boiled lichen gathered from the shore. It had made a deep green dye.

A flash of scarlet made me look up, and I saw my oldest sister, Tinna, and Eydís running through the bailey, laughing, heading for the keep. They held their aprons up in both hands; the fabric pillowed out. I wondered what they were carrying – winterberries? Bark to make tea from? Their fair hair, shades of sun and burnished bronze, flew behind them. Next year, Eydís would have to start wearing her hair up, like a grown-up, as Tinna had started doing last year.

I smiled at Háakon, and he smiled back at me. We had a good life.

Die.

The word popped into my mind like a bubble on a pond surface. I slowly took in a breath, wondering why my butt felt numb. What was I sitting on? For a moment I didn't know where I was, and wondered why I no longer smelled the washtubs in the bailey. Then it came to me: I was a grown-up, and everything I had remembered happened 450 years earlier. None of that, none of them, existed anymore.

I don't know why I didn't open my eyes, why I kept my breathing calm and shallow. I just sat very still, opening my mind to this room, these people, feeling my senses tendril out around me.

That bitch – I hate her.

It was a thought, not a memory, coming from someone here.

No, no, forgive me, I didn't mean it.

Her neck . . . kissing her neck, the heat there . . .

It took everything I had to not react. I was picking up on all kinds of stuff, and suddenly saw the peep-show appeal of group meditation. These thoughts came from males and females but weren't recognizable as voices, per se. Just as distinct personas.

Want her.

Her eyes. Her mouth. Her mouth on my skin, my chest.

Oh, I hate her! I can't help it!

No, no, I can't.

My breaths were coming faster. I was intensely aware of my stiff fingers, curved on my knees, my numb butt on this hard cushion, my dry mouth. Were these thoughts coming from everyone or just two people? And who was thinking what? I knew Charles had a crush on Lorenz, but Lorenz was straight, so that was a bummer. There were obviously Nell and Reyn, of course, the tortured soap opera of her unrequited love. Anne actually had a husband, but he didn't live here, and I didn't know the full story.

It was the most exciting thing that had happened since I'd gotten here. I was waiting breathlessly to hear more, but there was a chime, the music stopped, and my eyes reluctantly opened.

Anne was looking around at all of us, and I thought she seemed more alert, more sharp-eyed, than someone just coming out of deep meditation. The others opened their eyes slowly, some of them looking so relaxed as to be practically asleep.

The thoughts ceased coming to me, and I stretched and wriggled on my cushion.

'Thank you,' Nell said, radiating sweetness. 'That was lovely.'

'Thank you all,' said Anne. 'Goodness, it's almost dinnertime.'

I got to my feet, flexing to get some feeling back in my bottom, and had started for the door when Anne said, 'Nastasya? Please stay a moment.'

I felt like a student caught spitballing, but I waited while Anne shut the door.

'What did you think of it?' she asked me. 'Was the group experience very different?'

'Oh, God, yeah,' I said with enthusiasm. 'I had no idea I'd hear all that stuff. It's better than *Days of Our Lives*.' I didn't mention my childhood memory.

'What do you mean?'

'Those thoughts,' I said. 'Someone hating someone, someone wanting someone, someone who can't do something. It was excellent. I can't wait to hear what happens next!'

Anne stared at me as if I had suddenly turned into a pigeon. 'What?'

Taken aback by her reaction, I said, 'Well, you know, those thoughts. I had no idea that could happen. It was really interesting.'

'You heard thoughts,' Anne said, looking intently at me. 'About someone hating someone, someone wanting someone.'

'Yeah,' I said, feeling unsure of myself. Had I messed this up somehow? Was it not done to mention what one heard? Was I supposed to pretend I hadn't picked up on anything? 'Um, and you know, kissing her neck. Her eyes. Her mouth on his chest. That stuff,' I mumbled. It had been a funny coincidence, given how paranoid I was about my own neck. Mentioning 'the heat there.' Like, from a burn, maybe? Ha ha ha. No. I mean, he hadn't meant my neck, surely. Charles was gay, Reyn couldn't stand me, and Lorenz had never given the slightest indication that he found my drowned-rat appearance a big turn-on.

Anne just blinked.

'Are you . . . okay?' I really, really hoped none of those thoughts had come from her.

'How much meditation have you done? I thought you didn't like it.' She didn't answer my question.

'God, no, I hate it,' I said. 'It sucks. I haven't done much of it.'

Anne sat on the edge of the table, still looking at me.

'Did I do something wrong? Next time I won't say if I hear anything.'

'No, no,' Anne murmured. 'That isn't it. Though I would keep what you heard to yourself. It's just – I picked up on those feelings, but I'm very advanced.

I'm *very* powerful. I'm quite sure that no one else in the room heard or felt anything besides what was in their own heads.'

Huh. Had she heard *my* thoughts? Ugh.

'I felt someone's consciousness but didn't know it was you,' she went on, and I thought, *Whew*. 'I thought it might be Solis – he's next door right now, teaching herbs.'

'So . . . that doesn't usually happen, with anyone else?'

'No.' Anne's gaze was steady and penetrating. 'It never happens, not with students. Never, ever.'

Huh. This episode seemed to suggest that . . . maybe I was really powerful. Right, Nastasya? You would be powerful, right? You're the last powerful one. I felt the automatic shutting down of my thoughts, felt my mind skirting away from those implications like water dancing on a hot skillet.

Just then there was a light tap on the door, and Solis came in. He looked around the room, saw it was Anne and me, and frowned slightly.

'Are you the only two here?' he said.

'Yes,' Anne replied. 'Did you – why did you come in?'

Solis shrugged and smiled. 'Thought I felt something. Seemed odd.'

'You did feel something.' Anne seemed unusually grave. 'You felt *her*.'

Solis paused, as if translating the words in his head. 'What?' he said finally.

'Nastasya sent her consciousness out during group

meditation. I felt her touch my mind, and she picked up on what the others were thinking. She could hear them. Accurately.'

When, *when* am I going to learn to keep my mouth shut? Now I felt like a zoo exhibit, with the two of them studying me.

'I'll try not to do it again,' I offered. I will definitely never say anything again.

Solis actually cocked his head to one side. 'Where did you say you were from?'

Alarms went off inside my head. I was willing to do all sorts of dumb stuff to stay here, but revealing my past was not among them. 'The north.'

The dinner bell clanged then, making me jump.

'Whew! I am *starving*,' I said, putting away my buck-wheat pillow. 'Thanks for the class, Anne. It was great. See you at dinner!'

Clearly I was making a scared-rabbit escape, and they let me, though I felt their eyes follow me down the hall. I went downstairs and headed for the dining room.

Could I still – have power? My inherited power? Could it actually be that strong, after all this time? I should hide it. But even as I had that thought, a new, fierce longing sprang up inside me, wanting to feel the power again, wanting to follow wherever it led, wanting to explore its limits.

I couldn't. I couldn't. I didn't dare. Nothing good would come of it – I had seen that with my own eyes.

One had to be very, very strong to deal with that kind of power. I wasn't strong enough. I would never be strong enough.

I slid into a place on a bench, my mind still reeling. That feeling – it had been . . . magickal.

Chapter 13

What? Get a . . . job? An actual job? Why?' I asked.

The day after the meditation thing, Solis had agreed to teach me actual spellcraft, instead of just the names of the wonderful world around us. I was still pissed about his turning me down before, and I still couldn't say I was one hundred percent committed to this whole thing . . . but it had occurred to me that knowing more about this stuff, my magick, my power, would be better than not knowing. If I knew, then I could control it, protect it, hide it. Not knowing had not worked out that well for me. It was hard to wrap my mind around, because I'd shied away from anything but the most minor spells for centuries. Now I felt the lure, the draw of it, even though it scared me.

But a job?

Solis smiled. 'It's part of the whole picture. The daily grind, so to speak. Showing up every day. Fitting into an environment. Playing well with others. Literally, doing a good job at something outside of here.'

I didn't try to hide my distaste. 'I'm doing tons of stuff around here. I've been a personal slave to you guys since I showed up!'

'And we sure have appreciated it,' Solis said with humor. 'But getting an outside job is an important step to integrating yourself into the real world – not just the world of limitless time and money and friends as shallow and self-centered as you are.'

Ideally, I would have protested vigorously, but in reality, I didn't have a leg to stand on. I gritted my teeth.

'You've had jobs before, haven't you?' Solis asked.

'Yeah, of course,' I said. If you include running that brothel in California in the 1850s. I had made a fortune. Or when I was a model for a French designer in Paris, in the 1930s. But a job-job?

I tried another tack. 'I was really hoping you could just, you know, wave a wand and make me all better.'

Solis chuckled. 'It seems that you have unusually strong abilities, Nastasya. It's very important that you learn what to do with them.'

I thought about saying, 'Oh, pshaw, shucks,' or something, but I was trying to control the rush of mingled anxiety and pride that swarmed through me.

'I'm willing to teach you,' he went on, 'but you have to do it my way. Not because I'm a control freak, but because experience has shown me that this is the best way to teach what you need to learn. So, yes, you have to get an outside job, just like everyone else when they first

arrive. Preferably minimum wage. Something lowly —
work for its own sake, rather than for a big salary or ego
gratification. I hear the library is looking for someone to
help shelve books.'

I stared at him in dismay.

'Go along with you now,' he said. His tone was kind,
but his eyes were shrewd. I might have a weird power
streak, but I was still a pain in the ass, and he still had
major doubts about me. I didn't indulge myself by
thinking that I was suddenly so amazing that he would
put up with a lot of shit from me. Though God knows
that's worked with other people.

Sighing, I left his classroom and headed back to the
house. Asher gave me a shopping list of things I needed
to pick up on my way back home, and I took it and went
out to my car.

Sylvia's Diner on the highway was hiring immediately. I'd managed to get through four-hundred-plus
years without ever being a waitress or bar wench, but
my record was about to end. And how hard could it be?
People ordered the food, you brought them the food.
I didn't have to cook it, I didn't have to work the cash
register. Piece o' cake. The first hour was spent learning
where everything was.

The second hour was a demoralizing, teeth-gritting
docudrama about everything that could go horribly
wrong during rush hour in a greasy spoon.

I quit about two seconds before they fired me, and

without getting a shot at the lemon meringue pie on the counter.

Back in my little car, I pulled in at a Stop & Shop and bought a blue raspberry frozen slushie and a couple of packages of Donettes and Ding Dongs. I pondered my next move as I savored food that was unencumbered by any pretense of nutritive value or organicity or, God forbid, fiber.

It was two o'clock. I had no job.

My mind flashed on Innocencio suddenly – as if I could see him sitting in a dark, smoky, fabulous restaurant. He would order escargots and light a cigarette, already on his second or third Martini. The waiter or waitress would be scurrying to anticipate his every need, as the servers always did. Incy was so elegant, slender and sinuous, dressed in a silk shirt and beautifully cut pants. His hair was such a dark black that it looked almost blue, and his skin was a beautiful light caramel color. His lips were finely shaped, slightly full, but could look hard and cruel. He was so funny, always making scathing comments about other diners. I remembered lying on a bench in Les Deux Magots in Paris, my head in Incy's lap. I was tired and had drunk too much. Incy was feeding me tiny strawberries, the first of the season, his beautiful fingers barely touching my lips. I remembered thinking that I should be happy, that I had everything I needed – but instead I had an awful, howling blankness inside. I hid it from Incy, hid it from everyone.

I remembered not wanting to go to Nice, but Incy had begged and jokingly threatened until I agreed. He'd made me go to St Petersburg, had convinced me to go to Hong Kong. I always enjoyed traveling, loved all of those places. But looking back, I realized I hadn't really wanted to go, but somehow Incy had convinced me. He didn't want to go alone. He didn't want to go without me.

My mind whirled with memories, and a hundred images flew at my consciousness. How many times had I done something on my own in the last thirty years? Incy didn't control my every day – there were a thousand times when I had decided where to go and what to do. But he had almost always gone with me, even when he insisted he didn't want to, even when he complained incessantly. He hadn't wanted me to go by myself. He hadn't wanted to be away from me.

This whole line of thinking was shocking, something that had never occurred to me. I'd simply thought we were best friends. I thought I wanted to be with him – and I had. It wasn't that. It was just that, looking back, I could see that I would have made other choices, done more things on my own or with other people, only Incy was always there. Always, always there. Despite the string of unearthly beautiful girls and boys who revolved through his life, his apartment, his bed, I was the constant in his life. And he in mine. I was just realizing that.

He must be going insane without me. I felt – well,

weird, because I was living this freakishly ordinary life, but I didn't feel like I would die, not being with him. I felt okay. What was he thinking? Feeling? Doing? How strange, that I had never noticed this, his dependency.

Suddenly I felt too alone and quickly started the car to head back through the town, intending to pick up Asher's stuff from the one grocery store, Pitson's. I would have to return to Solis jobless, which embarrassed me, though failure had never bothered me before.

As I passed MacIntyre's Drugs, I thought about color-less Meriwether, and then I saw the sign: HELP WANTED.

Hmm.

I kept going, then quickly did a U-ie in the middle of Main Street. Since Main Street was deader than a door-nail, this wasn't a problem.

I parked outside of MacIntyre's and thought. Had Meriwether's dad fired her? So I would be taking her place in the line of fire?

It was irresistible. I had to know.

Inside, the store was dim and gray. It struck me that it was as lifeless and colorless as Meriwether herself.

'Can I help you?' Mr MacIntyre's voice was gruff and unfriendly. Great! I've always wanted a boss like that.

'I'm here about the job,' I said, holding up the sign.

He looked me up and down – people seemed to do that quite a bit lately. 'You got any experience?'

'Yes. I managed the health-and-beauty section at a SuperTarget back home,' I lied smoothly.

'This isn't no Target,' he said, and I thought, *Oh good, you cleared that up for me.* 'I need someone to stock shelves. Wait on customers. Keep things neat while my girl's in high school.' His girl. Not his daughter. Ugh, what a creep.

'I can do that.'

'You know how to work a cash register?'

I glanced at the one on the counter. 'Um, this one is a little older than the ones we used at Target. I might need a quick refresher course.'

Mr MacIntyre looked like he was trying to come up with a reason not to hire me, only to have his own need for a worker defeat him.

'It's minimum wage.'

'Okay.' Solis would be so proud of me.

'Why aren't you in school? How old are you?'

I've been able to pass for early twenties on occasion, but I knew not to push it. 'Eighteen. I graduated high school early. Taking a year off before college.'

'Huh. Okay. Let me show you around.'

Thus began my career as a glamorous shelf stocker at MacIntyre's Drugs, here in Nowheresville, Massachusetts.

Chapter 14

That evening at dinner I was able to report triumphantly that I had a real minimum-wage job. Nell laughed, then quickly swallowed it at Asher's glance. River gave me a knowing smile, and Solis looked appeased. I had a silly burst of pride that I'd actually done something right. For once.

'Yo, sweetie, load me up,' Brynne said, and I handed her the platter of fish. I was practically wolfing my food, trying to satisfy my ever-growing appetite. When had fish and rice tasted so good? I mean, when I wasn't in the middle of a famine.

Lightning flashed in the dark windows, brightening the dining room for an instant, reflecting in the big mirror over the fireplace. A moment later, thunder rumbled in the distance.

'Very unusual to get a thunderstorm in November,' Asher commented, and River nodded.

'It's too bad,' said River. 'We were going on a star walk tonight.'

I gave silent thanks that there was no star walk in my

immediate future and poured myself more hot tea. The first cold raindrops hit the windows, and I felt oddly cozy here, surrounded by these people I didn't know very well.

'Tonight we would have had a very good view of Zeru-zakur, around eleven,' River continued, and – get this – everyone actually looked up and nodded with interest.

I paused, my fork halfway to my mouth, as my brain scanned for that word. It sounded slightly familiar. What the hey – I would ask. As they say, there are no stupid questions. Only stupid people. 'What's Zeru-zakur?'

A few people raised their heads and looked at me.

Finally Solis said, 'Canis Major.'

Okay, I'd heard of that. A constellation, the 'big dog.' Like the Big Dipper. But what was its significance? I came up with nothing.

'Is Canis Major one of our more interesting clusters, then?' I asked, stirring three sugars into my tea.

Now all twelve heads turned to look at me, and I got the impression that the ignorant newbie had just made an adorable blunder of some kind. But without the adorable part.

'I'll take that as a yes,' I muttered, sipping my too-hot tea.

Even River was looking at me with surprise. To manage to surprise someone almost thirteen hundred years old was quite something, and I stopped drinking and sat up.

'What do you mean?' Nell's laugh sounded a little brittle.

'I know it's a constellation,' I said, starting to feel irritated. I glanced up to see Reyn looking at me, his eyes slightly narrowed, but not meanly. More . . . consideringly.

'It's – Canis Major. Zeru-zakur.' Even Daisuke, who was always very polite and kind, seemed unable to believe that I wasn't all over this thing.

'Yeah, I got that. But what of it?' I asked, setting my tea down. 'Just tell me, and then you can all have a good laugh later.'

After a pause, River said calmly, 'Zeru-zakur is an ancient name for the constellation that many people know today as Canis Major. Its main star is Sirius, the Dog Star, which is the brightest star in the night sky.'

'Okay,' I said. The table was silent, except for Nell's huffing, but River shot her a glance and she shut up.

'We're not sure why – there are many myths and legends, and it's something that many immortal philosophers have studied – but about five hundred years ago, an immortal astronomer realized that for some reason, the stars in the constellation Canis Major correspond almost exactly with the eight *fonts*. Or at least, it's assumed that they did correspond exactly, several thousand years ago.' River broke off a piece of bread, seeming to be deliberately casual. She smiled. 'I wasn't there, so I don't know.'

'*Fonts?*' I repeated. *Font* meant fountain or source. It also meant a style of type, in typesetting.

'Oh, my gosh, you must know—' Nell exclaimed, and

this time the look that River gave her was sharp. Nell drew in a breath and looked down at her hands, plastering a small fake smile on her face.

'The eight *fonts*, or houses, of immortals,' River went on. 'Of our magick. They are in a pattern across the globe that corresponds to the positions of the stars in Canis Major.' She was watching my face for signs of recognition.

'There are . . . *eight* houses?' I asked. The room was as quiet as a tomb.

'You haven't studied this?' River asked. 'Ever? Surely you've heard other aefrelyffen talk about it, even casually?'

I thought back. 'You mean like the immortal capitals? Like in Brazil, or the one in Australia?'

'Yes, so you know about those,' Solis said, his voice gentle. 'Those are two of them. There are, or rather *were*, six others. These eight capitals, or houses, correspond to the eight stars in the constellation Zeru-zakur. So no one has talked to you about the history of immortals?'

I thought back to Helgar, with her Adam-and-Eve theory. 'Not really. Just that – no one knows how we started, or why.'

'I've met people who'd never heard of the eight *fonts*,' Jess offered in his raspy voice. 'People who, for whatever reason, never had it as part of their lives. Hell, I didn't hardly know anything myself, till I came here.'

'Actually, I've met people like that, too,' said Anne.

'It's pretty common knowledge among a lot of immortals, but I could see how someone might not have realized its significance.'

Thank you, Jess and Anne, I thought. It occurred to me that maybe my parents would have taught me about it, about our history, our power. Maybe there had been a rite or something, with a big reveal at the end. Maybe my older brother and my oldest sister had gone through it, before . . . that night. I would never know.

'Okay, Nastasya,' said River. 'I didn't mean to make you uncomfortable. People move in different circles, and the different circles have different traditions and different focuses. Sometimes I forget that.' She smiled at me, and I thought, This is the most sincere woman I've ever met.

'And this means I'll have the pleasure of teaching you,' she said, looking satisfied at that thought. 'Traditionally, these eight *fonts* have been the main – *places* of immortal strength. Immortals seem to have, if not originated from these places, then certainly drawn great power, great magick from them. The main place, with the strongest magick, is in Africa, a place called Mogalakwena Rural, South Africa. It corresponds to the Dog Star. Then, to each side of that, along the line of the Tropic of Capricorn, you have the two you know about, in Coral Bay, Australia, to the east, and in the west at Campinas, Brazil.'

I had been to those places over the years. Because immortals tended to hang out in them. I hadn't really thought about why. I felt a flush heat my face. It was galling, appalling, to realize how much I didn't know, how much was out there to be known, right in front of me, that I somehow had managed to miss and ignore and dismiss all these years. I'd been living in black and white, and now River was showing me that all these other colors had been there all along, but I'd been too stupid to see them.

'Then, moving northeast from Mogalakwena, you had Awaynat, in Libya, right by Egypt,' River continued conversationally, continuing to eat her dinner as if this was no big deal. 'That line died out some two thousand years ago. Two thousand three hundred years. It doesn't exist anymore.'

'Twenty-three hundred years ago?' I said. 'What happened to its power?'

'No one knows,' said River. 'I doubt we'll ever know. And, continuing northeast from Awaynat, one runs into Genoa, Italy.'

I caught the word *Genoa*, and my eyes widened. River grinned. 'I'm from that house,' she acknowledged. 'It's partly why I'm so strong. My four brothers and I are all still alive, and my oldest brother is still the . . . well, the king of that house.'

'King?' Cold recognition was creeping up inside me. My stomach clenched, and I pushed my plate away.

'For lack of a better word,' River said. 'If you ever meet him, for God's sake, don't call him King Ottavio. He eats it up.'

Solis and Asher smiled. I guessed they'd met him. I tried to focus on her words.

'Continuing in sort of a Y shape from Genoa, there's Tarko-Sale, in northern Russia, but that line, too, died out – in 1550. Usurpers stormed the capital and cut off the heads of the house's family.'

I felt the blood leave my face.

Odin the Odious stood up suddenly, shoving his bench back with several people on it. 'Think I left the stove on,' he said, and pushed through the swinging door into the kitchen. Whatever. Guess he'd heard this story a thousand times.

I tried to find my voice. 'And what happened to *their* power?' I asked.

'The usurpers never found that house's tarak-sin, their tool, the focus of their strength. They killed all those people for nothing, and then the magick, the power, was gone forever. So they swept west, looking for another house's power to take.'

Oh, God. My hand gripped my hot mug of tea tightly. 'What's a tarak-sin?' My voice sounded thin and tight.

River sighed sadly, and I realized she had been alive when that happened. I wondered if she had heard about it at the time or had only found out later.

'Each house has a, well, a magickal tool, for lack of a better word. A very old name for it is a tarak-sin. It's usually a secret, though legend tells about the ceremonial knife of Awaynat. Another house might have a special book, or a crystal orb, or even a wand or a ring or some other jewelry as its tarak-sin. And this one ancient thing is imbued with a great deal of magickal power, specific to that house. The head of the house can use it to perform great spells.'

Oh, God. It could even be an amulet. An amulet made of ancient gold and carved with magickal symbols. For example. My head started to spin.

'I saw the tarak-sin of the house in Coral Bay,' said Charles.

'Really?' Brynne looked amazed.

'Yes.' Charles looked very serious. 'It was a barbie. They put magickal shrimp on it.'

For a moment there was silence, then Jess guffawed. Asher cracked up and threw a piece of bread at Charles. River's face lost some of its seriousness, and she put her hand over her mouth and shook her head.

'We always tease my brother that our house tarak-sin is his Oscar, which he won for screenwriting, under his other name,' River admitted. 'He keeps it in the bathroom.'

More laughter, but inside I was screaming.

River cleared her throat and became serious again. 'But back to our story. West along that same line was the house in Iceland, in Heolfdavik. Or rather, a small village close to Heolfdavik. That line, sadly, was also destroyed, in 1561, by raiders. And again, a house's whole power was lost.'

I couldn't say anything, just looked down at my plate and wondered if my face was just as white.

'Truly lost?' Rachel asked. 'I've never understood that.'

'Yes,' River said. 'The raiders killed everyone in the family, then found the house's tarak-sin and tried to use it. But they weren't strong enough, or something went wrong. The story is that they were engulfed in a tower of lightning, leaving nothing behind but ash. And no one knows what the tarak-sin was.'

It was an amulet. Somehow I'd never realized its significance. I knew it was magickal, knew it was my mother's most treasured possession, and had kept it hidden forever because it was the only thing I had from my old life. But it was actually a tarak-sin. I had half, so the raiders must have had the other half. No wonder their magick blew up.

I felt as though I was going to faint. I was trying to keep breathing normally, but my eyes were huge, focused on River's face. She saw my expression, and I thought I saw something flicker in her eyes.

Reyn came back and sat down without a word.

I was looking down, trying to swallow what felt like a golf ball in my throat. I had questions, but I couldn't ask them now.

'Brynne,' said River, abruptly changing the subject, 'is there any dessert?'

Brynne jumped but said, 'Is there dessert? Did *I* make dinner? Do I *ever* make dinner with no dessert? I don't *think* so.' She went to the kitchen and returned a minute later with two apple tarts on a tray.

'Is there any ice cream?' River asked, and Brynne nodded, like, yes, of *course* we have ice cream, we have *tarts*, right? In a moment she brought out a container of organic ice cream made at a dairy a couple of miles away.

I got the feeling that River was giving me time to get a grip on myself, and inside I was frantically clawing at my psyche to get it together, look normal, deflect attention away from myself.

'So no one from those houses still exists?' Rachel asked.

'Not that anyone knows about,' said River. 'Awaynat is a complete mystery. And no one has ever heard of any survivors from Tarko-Sale or Heolfdavik. And somehow, the houses' tarak-sins were lost.' River spoke quietly, scooping ice cream onto her tart.

'We can talk more about that another time,' said Asher, looking at River. 'And I can tell you about the last house, which corresponds to the last star in Canis Major. It's in Salem, Massachusetts.'

'You're kidding me.' I forced a bite of tart into my mouth. 'Of Salem witch trial fame?' My voice sounded like a croak, and the tart lodged in my throat, choking me.

'The very same. Guess how many of those "witches" didn't actually die in their fires?' Solis looked grim.

'Solis is from the Salem house,' River said gently, and

my mind flew to the image of Solis being burned at the stake. For a long time. Without the blessing of death.

'But there weren't any people in America several thousand years ago,' said Charles. 'Except Native Americans. Right?'

'It's a long story,' said Solis, meeting River's eyes. 'At any rate, we're not going for a star walk tonight.' As if to punctuate his words, a huge clap of thunder exploded, seemingly right outside the building. I tried to gag down another bite of dessert as I heard the rain pattering coldly against the windows.

I had a lot to think about.

Later, when I was emerging from a long, hot shower, River was waiting for me outside in the hall. Her eyes were grave but kind.

'Are you okay?' she asked.

'Sure,' I said, rubbing a towel against my wet hair. 'Why wouldn't I be?'

She was quiet for a moment, walking beside me back to my room. 'It was a lot of information to take in,' she said.

'Yeah.' I opened my door and draped my towel over a chair by the radiator. 'It's amazing, these huge gaps in my education. On the other hand, I can swear in eight different languages. At least.'

'Nastasya . . .' she hesitated. 'You were born in 1551. Where?'

My heart seized and thudded to a stop. I said the first thing that came into my head. 'Japan.'

She pursed her lips. 'You'll have to talk about it someday, my dear.'

'Talk about what?' I looked at her blankly, something I've honed to an art.

She nodded, then hugged me and patted my wet hair. 'Get some sleep. You've got work tomorrow.'

My face fell – I had actually forgotten. River smiled at my expression, then left. I had to think. She wouldn't try to pin me down, would she? What would I do if she did? I was amazed that there were *eight* different houses, eight different lines of history. I guessed those were only the main ones, the ones who'd managed to hog a bunch of power. There must be thousands of others. But only eight original tarak-sins? Where had they come from? I pushed my fingers under my thin cotton scarf. What would River think if she knew I had Iceland's tarak-sin burned into the back of my neck?

Unable to stop myself, I listened for footsteps, and hearing nothing, crawled under my bed. A small piece of floor molding behind my bed was cracked, and I dug my short fingernails into the crack and pulled it out. I reached into the hole and felt, once again, the heavy gold ornament that always felt warm, no matter where it was. I reassured myself it was there and replaced the molding, lodging it back in tightly and wafting some dust over it so it would look undisturbed. Then I crawled back out and sat on my bed.

If my amulet *was* the actual tarak-sin of my house,

then it was even more powerful, more valuable, than I had ever known. It was what had gotten my whole family killed. It was what the raiders had come for. It was what they had died for.

Did anyone suspect that half of it still existed? Was only half still worth killing for?

Chapter 15

I don't know if Old MacIntyre was surprised to see me the next morning, on time, but I myself was shocked as hell. It took him about twenty minutes to explain shelf stocking to me, another five minutes to go over the intricacies of the old-but-not-in-a-charming-way cash register, and then another forty-five minutes to put the fear of God into me if I should ever happen to steal anything. He kept the back section, where all the prescriptions were filled, locked, so essentially he was warning me off smuggling Tampax, baby formula, and live bait home in my purse. Whatever.

I rolled up the sleeves of my sexy and provocative plaid flannel shirt, cut open a carton of Garnier Nutrisse hair dye, and starting stocking my little heart out. Focusing intently on this mind-numbing work meant I couldn't think about anything else. I was determined not to think about anything else for as long as I could. I'd gulped down my herb tea last night and had slept surprisingly well – no nightmares, no memories.

But that was as far as I was going to go with the whole eight-houses thing. I mean, how could I come to terms with that? There was so much I didn't know about my own past, my own heritage. I'd never wanted to know. Was afraid of knowing. Look at everything I hadn't known about my amulet. Now that I knew, it gave me a whole new level of paranoia. Fun!

After about an eon of mindless drudgery, it suddenly struck me, the whole point of this, what Solis was hoping I would get out of it: He was hoping that this boredom and pointlessness would so overwhelm me that I would suffer a complete psychotic break, run screaming down the street, and disappear out of his life forever. That *had* to be the thought behind this.

And, oh, baby, I was close. So close. But something in me forced myself to keep going, and all I could grasp was the humiliating, confusing certainty that my life wouldn't be any better if I were anywhere else, doing anything else. Also, as hugely as this sucked – and believe me, it sucked big – this was about as much of a disguise as I could possibly manage. No one I knew would ever believe me capable of being here, doing this. I felt camouflaged, and that nameless fear hanging over me still felt that being camouflaged was important. Why? I didn't know. I was one big mystery, even to myself.

Someone was near me, had been lingering near me for some time, I suddenly realized. As Meriwether had said, the town in general didn't have a lot going on, and

MacIntyre's in particular seemed to be on life support – hardly any customers to speak of. Now I realized that there was someone else here. I felt them, felt their energy, though I hadn't heard the doorbell jangle.

I gathered up some empty cartons and headed toward the back, glancing down each aisle. It was the punk/goth girl, the one I'd seen twice before, the one I kept running into because this podunk town was so tiny you couldn't help running into the same people over and over again.

She glanced at me, trademark defiant look on her face, and I acted as if I didn't recognize her. But I watched her in the round mirror at the end of the aisle and saw her slip some nail polish into her pocket. I sighed and tossed the boxes out back by the trash can.

When I came back in, she was waiting impatiently at the checkout counter. Mr MacIntyre was helping an older woman in back who was getting a prescription, so I muttered a quick prayer that I would remember how to work the stupid cash register and headed over.

Old Mac had given me some tips on customer service, but since he was one of the most hateful men I'd ever met, I'd ignored them.

Now I took the stuff the girl had put on the counter and started punching register buttons, hoping I was doing it right. There was no nail polish.

I dropped the other items into a plastic bag, then said, 'Okay, the polish.'

'What?' The girl was good – semi-convincing unknow-ingness coupled with a hint of belligerence that would make most people back off.

'The nail polish you jacked,' I said matter-of-factly. 'Hand it over.'

Her face turned stormy. 'I didn't jack any nail polish!'

I sighed and shook my head. 'You know, you're doing this all wrong. You jacked two bottles of nail polish that were on sale anyway, two for one. Then you paid full price for this Pixi Lumi Lux Eye Palette of shadows, which isn't much bigger but cost three times as much. Clearly, you should have jacked the eye shadow and paid for the nail polish. Sheesh.'

The goth girl stared at me.

'If you're gonna lift something, lift something that isn't on sale,' I went on. It felt good to be instructing others for a change, instead of being instructed myself. 'I mean, make it worth your while, you know? Now hand over the nail polish – I'm making you pay for it, just as a life lesson. Then maybe next time you'll think ahead.'

I held out my hand and waited.

The girl stared at me, then looked around the store, checking for Old Mac or security cameras. Seeming bewildered, she dug into her jeans pocket and pulled out two bottles of L'Oreal and put them on the counter.

'What now? You turn me in?' Her jaw stuck out a bit; her dark-rimmed eyes were sharp.

'Now I'm charging you for the polish,' I said, ringing it up. 'You already gave me your card, and it just processed.'

'You gonna have me banned from the store?' She grabbed her bag and looked at me in what I assumed was one of her two or three basic expressions: defiance. Geez, who does she remind me of? Let me think.

I snorted. 'Nope. You're the most entertaining thing that's happened all morning.'

'Who *are* you?' She looked as if she hadn't meant to ask.

'Nastasya. Nasty, to my friends.'

After a moment, the girl said, 'Dray, short for Andrea, which sucks, so don't use it,' and tapped her chest. '"Hey, bitch," to my friends.'

'Pleased to meet you, bitch,' I said, holding out my hand. I kind of meant it, too. After all the goodness oozing out of everyone's pores at River's Edge, some good old-fashioned delinquency was refreshing.

After a moment's hesitation, she shook my hand. 'Pleased to meetcha too, Nasty.'

'How did work go?' River's question, innocent enough, caused everyone at my end of the table to look up and quit talking.

I dug into my food and said, 'Guess I'll go back tomorrow.'

I felt surprise and looked up to see Nell looking at me. It was almost like I could hear her voice inside my head, saying snidely, *You mean, they'll actually let you come back tomorrow?*

But she didn't say anything out loud, and I wondered whether I was just imagining things or my own magickal senses, now awakened, were growing stronger. Probably the former.

'Good for you,' said River, and her sincerity was so shining and clear that I felt almost embarrassed. 'Oh, and everyone – it's a new moon tonight, no rain predicted, so if anyone wants to join me for a circle after dinner . . .'

Most people nodded yes. I wanted to hide. I still hadn't recovered from the shocking revelations of the previous night. Somehow, dabbling with magick tonight felt extra threatening. I started to think of a likely excuse, and then the uncomfortable thought came to me: I had spent 450 years avoiding things. Avoiding knowledge. Avoiding magick and power and anything to do with my heritage. Trying to avoid pain. Pretending things weren't true, weren't real.

I was here because I wanted to not be that way anymore, right? The inescapable logical conclusion was that I therefore needed to start facing things.

I hate logic.

But clearly I should perhaps take some risks – the kind that weren't fashion-related. But then again, the few circles I had participated in had made me feel like crap. On the other hand, River was here, and I . . . trusted her. Amazingly enough.

Then I noticed Reyn nodding. And Nell, watching Reyn, quickly nodded, too. That decided it: How could I let that opportunity slip past me? Like Oscar Wilde, I can resist anything except temptation.

'I'm in,' I chimed recklessly, and was rewarded by Nell's laser eyes. I mean, I'm hardly good *yet*.

Chapter 16

'Y ou're coming, then?' River smiled and held her hand out to me. If I weren't so emotionally retarded, I would have taken it, like a friend, and appreciated the warmth and camaraderie. Since I'm me, I ignored it and just tucked my scarf tighter around my neck. So far River hadn't asked me anything more about the eight houses, or my reaction, or my background, and I hadn't offered anything. I didn't know how long she'd let me get away with that.

We crunched through the leaves on the ground, feeling the chilly wind coiling around our ankles. As River had said, there was zero moon, and it was black outside in the way that, nowadays, only the middle of nowhere can be black. Two hundred years ago, stars were so much more obvious, the sky crowded with their pinpoints of light. Nervously, I tucked my scarf tighter around my neck, casting glances all around me. For, like, werewolves. Land sharks. Stuff in the dark.

'Yeah,' I said. 'I mean, I hate circles, but it's probably good for me, you know?' See how virtuous I am? Plus, I got to watch another installment of the Reyn/Nell tragi-comedy playing out before my eyes.

'You hate circles?'

There I went, running my mouth off. 'Yeah. I just hate . . . messing with magick. Big magick. I mean, I like the rush, of course.' I could hear the others in front of us, leading to a clearing, but could barely make out their silhouettes. 'But I hate the whole feeling-sick part, the visions, and so on.'

River stopped, next to me, and it took me a couple of steps before I realized I'd left her behind. 'What?'

I turned back to her. 'What?'

'What did you say?'

'Um, what what? When?'

'Just now – you said you felt sick during a circle? You have visions?'

'Yeah, sure.' I shrugged. 'Sometimes. Usually. I guess I just do it wrong.'

'No, Nastasya.' River's voice was solemn. 'Even if you're Terävä, you shouldn't feel sick during a circle or when working spells. And most people usually don't have visions, unless they're specifically trying to.'

I didn't know what to say. I'd never talked about this with my friends – I guess I'd just assumed that the magick hit us all in different ways, that some people felt ill after-ward and some people didn't. Looking back, I couldn't actually recall anyone else mentioning feeling sick after a circle. But anyway, among my crowd, we thought of immortals who did circles as being kind of . . . Martha Stewart. You know? Quaint, sincere circles. Why bother?

'Feel sick how?' River seemed very intent. The others had gone on without us, and I was glad I wouldn't have to find them on my own – I'd be wandering in the Massachusetts woods for months. A nightmare.

I wasn't sure why River was pressing this, unless it had to do with my background, my personal history. I was pretty sure she had guessed where I was from. Maybe not all the details. Maybe she wasn't sure. Maybe it was just a big deal that I had these reactions. She was acting like Anne and Solis had, when I'd done that meditation thing.

'Um, I guess I'm just really untrained,' I said slowly, wondering if this was actually a good idea. 'I've never really learned how to do all this stuff.' Had avoided learning like the plague, actually. 'You know, so I usually feel – sick. Like I can't breathe, like my head will explode or my heart will burst.' I was self-conscious, as if I was admitting a weakness. 'Afterward I feel hungover. I mean, circles are cool, and that rush of power – but it just makes me feel sick, so I hardly ever do them.'

River was silent. She was so close I could see her looking at me in the darkness.

'Um, at least you'll be here during this circle,' I said with lame politeness. 'You know, I'm willing to try it. If you're here.' I half expected her to send me back to the house to wash dishes or something.

Asher and Solis had realized River wasn't with them, and they came up almost silently and joined us.

'What's going on?' Asher asked, putting his arm around River's waist.

'Nastasya often feels sick when she's in a circle,' River said quietly. 'And she has visions. Asher, tonight you lead the circle, please. I want Nastasya to stand between Solis and me.'

And there was that zoo exhibit feeling again. I felt stupid for calling attention to myself. I was already enough of a freak. I was hoping that River could fix my reactions for me, teach me what to do so I wouldn't feel like death afterward. Even with my background, I couldn't believe I was the only one who felt this way.

We entered the clearing, which was about a hundred feet across, surrounded by tall trees. Dried grass flattened easily as we walked across it and joined the others.

We were all participating, so there were thirteen of us, which I knew was a 'lucky' number for a circle, though they could really be any size – there had been only nine of us at that sucky circle in Boston. Solis knelt in the middle of the circle and made a small stack of dried wood. He murmured a few words, made a gesture, and change-o presto, a bright, lively flame appeared and began to spread eagerly across the kindling wood. Now, there's a useful spell, I thought. I'd love to know how to do that one – conjure fire out of the air.

'We come together this night to celebrate the

appearance of the new moon,' River said clearly. 'Today separates this month from the last, giving us the opportunity to start anew. Today the moon goddess rests, and yet her magick is still around us.'

Superstitious peasants in the old days had sometimes talked about the moon goddess, but I didn't know much about her. The others looked comfortable and expectant: They'd done this before.

As River had requested, I stood between her and Solis. I did feel protected, safer – and, to my surprise, I actually felt a tiny bit of anticipation. Part of the whole 'will never learn' phenomenon, I guessed. Across from me, I could make out Anne's careful gaze. I was bemused by how they were treating me, and I had a moment's anxiety, wondering if I was going to levitate or something. *That* would be new and different.

'Hold out your hands,' said River, 'with both thumbs pointing to the left.'

My left hand was palm-up, and my right hand was palm-down. Then I saw – when we came together, everyone's hands fitted together perfectly, left on right, right on left. Cool.

'You've done circles before, of course,' River said to me. 'But they're different, from group to group. Just follow along, and you'll be fine.'

The circle moved to the right around the fire. People first faced the fire, then on the next step they turned so their left side was toward the fire. Then again face-first, then we all turned so our right side was fireward. It was left, forward, right, forward, left, forward, and so on. A couple of thoughts came to me, and I let them, even though I was supposed to be busy clearing my mind and focusing on the fire, getting ready to feel magick take me over, hallelujah!

One thought was that no one had been gladder than I when court dances had finally fallen out of favor. I'm the biggest klutz in the world, with *no* sense of rhythm, zero ability to keep time, and a complete lack of understanding about where my personal space leaves off and the next person's begins. And oh, my God, the number of humiliating dances I'd endured, fumbling all those gazillion precise steps. I'd been 'the pretty one who dances like a bear.' In several different countries.

But sandwiched between River and Solis, carried along in the circle, I wasn't doing too badly. The fire illuminated each person's face, making all of us look Halloween-y, and the contrast of the warmth of the fire and the cool night breeze around us made me feel like – like there were two of me, one warm, one cold. One light, one dark.

As soon as I had that thought, I shied away from it and instead tried to concentrate on what was happening. People were singing now, but I'd never heard this song. It wasn't at all like the singing Kim had done in Boston, which I'd been able to join. This had a different structure.

As I listened, I realized that each person actually

seemed to be singing something unique. All the voices and melodies blended together, but none of them were the same. Some sounded like words – I thought I heard a bunch of different languages – but some were just sounds, long drawn-out syllables, like they were singing in humpback whale.

It was pretty, though, and more important, I began to feel its power.

No one was paying attention to me – each person was lost in his or her own reverie, focus, sound, and movement. Very quietly I began to hum along.

It felt okay, this humming along, so I increased it. In the few circles I'd been to, even Kim's, the songs that called on power were, well, demanding. Harsh. Orders. Sometimes seductions.

This felt like – a *gift*, not to get all Hallmark-y here. It felt like an offering to the sky, the woods, the new moon, each other. Now I could follow it; I could feel it welling up inside me. I took the leap from humming to opening my mouth and joining in the humpback song, just making sounds that blended with the others' and didn't stick out. Several of the voices sounded extra appealing, and I aligned my voice with those, following along without tripping anyone else up.

And oh, yes, *there*, a few minutes later, I felt the rush, the flow of power filling me up, going through me like warm whiskey, the burst of happiness, the overwhelming feeling of power and joy and excitement. I was happy to give everything I had to whatever we were doing, happy to be a conduit. I would have been happy no matter what our purpose was, whether it was to make corn grow faster, hold off snow, or topple a nation. Anything was fine, everything was possible, and I'd never felt so incredibly hap—

With my next breath, I was inside a small cottage. The walls were made of smoke-blackened boards; the roof beams were carved and painted. Outside I heard screaming, the thundering of horses' hooves, men shouting. Oh, God, oh, God, I thought wildly. My heart was pounding out of my chest; my breath was caught in my throat. I'd done all I could – there was no preparing for something like this. With a shaking hand, I pinched out the single candle – perhaps the cottage would look empty – and crawled behind the straw-tick bed.

The door crashed open. The screams of pain and panic grew louder. I could hear the horses as they squelched through the icy mud outside. Harsh voices. A man strode through the door, stood inside the cottage, looked around. His long gold hair was caught back in braids and spattered with blood, and drying blood arced across his chain mail. He headed for the hearth with its hanging pot, but the pot was empty, and he threw it across the room with a roar. The pot that I could barely lift myself. Our tankards were empty, and there was only a crust of old bread. In a fury, the marauder kicked over the small table and smashed a chair against the chimney, shattering it.

We'd heard of them, of course, the raiders from the north – every village had horror stories. But no one thought they'd cross the steppes in winter; it would be a death march. We'd been wrong.

The man swung to leave, but something stopped him, a small sound. He spun on his heel, hard eyes raking the darkened room. The chaos outside seemed to dim as I held my breath.

He found me in the next second and hauled me up by one arm. He could kill me if he lopped off my head and sent it flying – but he could also come up with many situations that would have me begging for death, praying for death, knowing my prayers were falling on a deaf God's ears.

He roared again, like an animal, and threw me across the bed. He was easily twice my size, covered with the stench of war – blood, sweat, other men's fear – and I covered my face with my hands as he snarled and yanked up my skirt, my tattered underskirt. Just get me through this, get me through this, I repeated over and over in my mind.

He grabbed the front of his pants, and then a small sound again drew his attention. Pinning me down with one hand, he skimmed the room again. We both heard it: A baby's cry. I grabbed his arm as he headed for the noise, trying to remember any barbarian words I'd ever heard. Leaping after him, I grabbed his arm again, and he shook me off as if I were an autumn leaf.

With his mud- and blood-caked boot, he kicked aside the old washtub I'd leaned in the corner. And found my son.

He looked from me to my son, barely three months old, and his eyes narrowed. I broke down, knelt at his feet, ready to promise anything, offer anything, and then a new crashing sound on the door made us both snap our heads around.

Another barbarian, barely recognizable as human, shouted something at my attacker, then shouted again, more urgently, as the raider hesitated.

After endless moments that seemed frozen in time, my attacker hissed curses, knocked me to the ground, and strode out, smashing our clay ale pot on the way.

I crawled over to my son and gathered him up, huddling there in the deepening darkness, as the raiding army marched by. I closed my eyes and sang lullabies, so quietly, and then—

'Nastasya? Nastasya?'

I blinked.

It was dark, and I was on the floor of my – no, I was on the ground. On the damp, leafy ground, blinking up at River, Solis, Anne, and some others who were leaning over me in concern. I blinked and swallowed several times, sniffing the air for the rancid smells of battle and death, of burning homes and flesh and slaughtered cattle, and—

'Nastasya?' River looked very worried.

The air smelled fine. Woodsy. Clean.

The circle came rushing back to me, my feelings of joy, the growing power, and then all hell had broken loose and I'd been thrown back four centuries.

'What's wrong with her?' I heard Nell ask. Someone said, 'Shh,' and Nell said from a distance, 'Everything is such a production with her.'

'Do you know where you are?' Solis asked.

I nodded and tried to sit up.

'No, stay down,' said River. 'Touch as much of your body as you can to the ground.'

I shook my head. 'Gonna hurl.' With that, I lurched to my hands and knees, then stumbled toward some shrubs unlit by the dwindling fire. And I threw my guts up, surprised that I wasn't barfing up the watery porridge and the last of the season's turnips from my memory.

River came over and put her arm around my shoulders, brushing my hair off my forehead, murmuring words. With cool fingers she traced some symbols on my forehead, on my back, on my arm, and slowly I quit heaving.

I stooped there, hands on knees, covered with clammy sweat, and panted, feeling hollowed-out inside.

'Come, let's go back to the house,' said River, helping me stand upright. 'I'll make you some tea, and you can tell me about it.'

I nodded weakly, relieved to see that everyone except the other teachers had already gone. Anne doused the fire, making sure every ember was dead, and we crunched through the leaves toward the warm, lit, welcoming house that looked like a beacon of sanity and strength.

I nodded again, but I knew I wouldn't tell River or anyone else about what I'd seen. It hadn't been a vision – it had been a memory. My son's face – my baby. He hadn't been immortal, and the son I would have done anything for that night had been dead a mere three years later, of influenza. Every time I remembered his round little face, it was a wrenching blow all over again. But that wasn't all. For the first time in centuries, I'd allowed myself to see and recall what my attacker had looked like.

It had been Reyn.

Chapter 17

I ended up going to bed that night, lying awake for a long time, shivering under my blankets. I couldn't stop thinking about Reyn, and the northern raider, and the fact that my door had no lock on it. I wanted to feel my amulet again, to hold it, but somehow I didn't dare take it from its hiding place.

River tried to question me, gently, but I just wasn't going to discuss it. My excuses were so lame and transparent that, in the end, she'd left me alone. I mean, logically, it couldn't have really been Reyn, right? It looked like him, and it would explain his ephemeral familiarity, but it totally contradicted my attraction to him. And he wasn't old enough.

I gulped down my herb tea, and River did a small spell to help me sleep, tracing runes on my forehead with her cool fingers. I fell back on my bed, already half asleep, my fingers nervously pressed against my scarf.

The next morning my eyes flew open a minute before my alarm went off. I did a quick scan of my room, as if I expected to see the northern raider there, from four hundred years ago and four thousand miles away.

I'd suppressed all this stuff for so long. Now it was all escaping through the crack in my shell, like lava. Ugh. I crawled out of bed, noticing that dawn was coming later every day. It was cold in my room – the radiator was just starting to hiss and pop. I threw on jeans, a camisole, a T-shirt, and a flannel shirt over that, put on my sturdy shoes, and headed downstairs warily, afraid that if I saw Reyn I would shriek like a little girl.

'Morning, Nas,' said Lorenz as I pushed through the kitchen door. He threw his arms open wide, holding a spatula in one hand. 'Embrace the day! Embrace another beautiful dawn!' He burst into a bit of opera – something from *La Bohème* – and I smiled at him. Brynne, wearing an apron, laughed and snapped a dish towel at him. This was my new normal, and I had to say, it kicked my old normal's ass.

My name was on the board for egg-gathering, so I took the basket from its hook by the back door and crunched across the frozen grass to the henhouse, looking around me the whole time, as if a thundering horde was going to come up the driveway at any moment. First I opened the small hinged door, and squawking birds started tumbling out. Then I opened the taller, person-sized door and ducked inside.

The only good thing about gathering eggs at dawn was that it was warmish inside the chicken coop, unlike the rest of the world, which was covered with spiky, lacy frost.

Reyn was only 267 years old, Nell had said. He hadn't contradicted her. My memory had been from back in – I don't know – the late fifteen hundreds. Not quite 1600. It had been in Noregr – Norway. Back then it had been the Denmark-Norway kingdom. I used to know those dialects, but they were lost now.

Obviously, if Reyn hadn't even been born then, he couldn't be the marauder from my memory. But I would swear that the raider had looked exactly, *exactly*, like the current Reyn. Except filthy, long-haired, covered with blood and gore, and wearing animal skins and rustic armor. Other than that, an identical twin.

'Here, chickie, chickie,' I murmured, easing my hand under one hen. This one had never pecked me, though I was sure she was pissed that we kept taking her eggs.

'You get lost?'

Whirling, I shrieked and dropped an egg. Reyn filled the low doorway, the dim morning light making him a dead ringer for the raider's silhouette on the threshold of my cottage. He peered in at me while every nerve in my body lit up with adrenaline.

'Get out!' I hissed furiously. 'Get out of here!' I was no longer a helpless villager – this was the twenty-first century, and I would run him down with my car or stab him with a kitchen knife if he threatened me again. Which would . . . definitely slow down an immortal.

'What the hell is the matter with you?' Reyn said with a frown. 'Brynne is asking for the eggs – she only has a few from yesterday.'

I was breathing quickly, wild-eyed, turned from an unpredictable loser to a certifiably crazy person in mere moments.

He cocked his head, looking at me. 'Are you okay?' He sounded curious, as if interested to see what the weirdo would do next.

I swallowed, hating feeling like this. 'How old are you?'

'Two hundred and sixty-seven,' he said evenly. 'Why?'

'Where are you from? Where did you grow up?' I was asking him questions I'd refused to answer myself. Irony, anyone? Irony?

'India, mostly. My parents were Dutch missionaries there. Some of the first.'

It was possible. Why would he lie? *Same reason you lie,* a little voice inside me said. I squashed it, as usual. Slowly, keeping one eye on him, I leaned down and picked up the egg, which had fallen onto a clump of straw and was unbroken. I put it in the basket and glanced around, counting chickens. I'd gotten all of them, I thought, except the mean chicken, and to hell with her.

'Okay,' I said abruptly. 'Here.' I held out the basket, wanting him to take it and get away from me.

He gestured – he was holding two pails of milk.

River kept several dairy cows, but thankfully I hadn't been put on milking duty yet.

Reyn stepped away from the doorway, and I took a deep breath and ducked out into the early morning after him. We walked up to the house in silence, me several feet behind him, the leaves wet underfoot but crackling with ice. Our breaths made little puffs of smoke.

Reyn *looked* Viking-y – much more Cossack/Russian/Norse than, say, Dutch. The Netherlands are closer to England and Germany, after all. His eyes were slanted slightly, more almond-shaped, and his skin was pale but with tan undertones. Not milk and cream, like a lot of Dutch people. His height was Dutch-like, but then the Vikings were tall, too. He was, maybe, six-one? Four hundred years ago he would have seemed like a giant.

I'd been kidding about his being a Viking god, and a couple of days ago that had seemed funny. The fact was he looked really typically northern raider. They all kind of looked alike, ha ha ha. Of course, that didn't mean he was one. It was totally possible that he was 267 and basically Dutch. And it was also possible that my twisted psyche had taken a horribly vivid memory and just cast it with whoever was on my mind nowadays. It hadn't happened before, but all kinds of thoughts and memories were getting stirred up lately, and God knows I spent a lot of fevered minutes thinking about Reyn.

'Nastasya? Hello?'

I realized he must have been speaking to me for a

while, and the hamster wheel of my mind had tuned him out while it spun.

'Huh?'

We paused outside the back door of the house, leading into the kitchen. I could hear people talking, pots and pans clanking, laughter, water running. Out here it was quiet except for some early birdsong, a faint breeze blowing the last few leaves off the trees.

'What happened last night, at the circle?'

I glanced at him quickly, saw his gaze focused on me. I was uncomfortable – not scared anymore, not exactly, but just . . . glad there were lots of people nearby.

'The usual,' I said, striving for lightness. 'Visions, getting sick, barfing. I *love* circles!'

'Why does that happen to you?' he asked. My nerves were frayed and shot, and I desperately wanted to be inside, away from him.

The back door opened, and Nell, looking pink-cheeked and rested, leaned out. I saw her try unsuccessfully to keep suspicion and jealousy out of her face, but I bet that Reyn didn't notice a thing.

'Don't let Nastasya make you late!' Nell admonished Rcyn cheerfully.

It's a measure of my lack of progress and immaturity, coupled with a healthy dose of self-destructiveness, that my first instinct was to say, *Oh, we were hooking up in the chicken coop.* But my nerves were raw, and I couldn't joke about it.

'We're talking,' Reyn said. 'We'll be there in a minute.'

Nell's face faltered. 'Brynne's yelling for the eggs.'

'I got 'em,' I said, and climbed the stairs, leaving Reyn behind. I brushed past Nell, and as I did, she hissed, 'He's mine!'

My head jerked up, and I looked at her. But just like that, her face was bland and normal, and she was smiling at Reyn, holding the door open for him as he climbed the steps with his two buckets.

Yesterday he'd been my hottest fantasy; today he was one of my worst fears and memories. And on top of everything, Nell thought I was trying to take her obsession from her. Great. Karma must be laughing herself sick about now.

And speaking of karma, *I went to work again* that day. Two days in a row! On time! The last time that had happened was ... I couldn't remember a last time. Maybe never. And, gosh, I felt so fulfilled and purposeful and like I was so much farther along the path of healing and wellness and being one with the universe ... nah, not really. I mean, no one could *like* doing this, *no one* could actually find it fulfilling. But mindless work seemed somewhat less depressing than mindless indolence, and I trusted Solis and River to know what they were doing. I wondered how long they wanted me to do this, have an outside job. Two weeks? Would two weeks be enough?

At three thirty, Meriwether MacIntyre showed up and stowed her school backpack behind the counter in front.

'So, you've already graduated from high school, huh?' she asked shyly, putting on the striped apron she wore when she worked here.

'Yeah.'

'Are you going to go to college?'

'Um, sure. I just wanted to work awhile, save some money,' I said. 'What about you? You're a senior, right?' I'd found out that she was in twelfth grade and that basically she went to school and came here and apparently had no other life.

Meriwether nodded.

'College plans?'

She hesitated, looking uncomfortable. 'Not sure I'll be able to leave my dad,' she said in a low voice, as if afraid he would hear her. 'The closest college is only about an hour away – but I don't think he'd want me going there.'

Hmm. My recent brainflash about how Incy had been so clinging and controlling made me extra sensitive about poor Meriwether getting yanked around like a puppet on a string. But what could I say? To hell with him, do what you want?

I knew it wasn't that easy. Which, I guessed, was more than I'd known a month ago, when Meriwether's plight would have been truly incomprehensible to me.

'I guess there are correspondence courses,' I said lamely, knowing she needed so much more than that.

'Yeah,' she said without hope. 'Oh, wow, you got a lot done.' She seemed uncomfortable around me, but I guessed I was pretty different from her normal school chums.

'Yep – busy little beaver, that's me,' I said, recognizing that she wanted to change the subject. I looked at the tidy shelves and tried not to think about walking down the steps of an opera house in Prague in a stunning gown. Heads had swiveled, men had stared, and women had hated my guts. The good old days. Really old, a hundred fifty years ago. 'I have to stay here till four,' I went on, brushing my dusty hands on my jeans. 'You know what I was thinking? Isn't fishing season over? Why don't we move the fishing junk toward the back of the store, and move, like, I don't know, the Kleenex and cold remedies or whatever toward the front of the store?'

Her almost-colorless eyes widened. 'That's what I've been wanting to do for ages! I asked my dad about it, but he said—'

'What are you two gabbing about?' Mr MacIntyre yelled, walking toward us. 'I'm not paying you to stand around and yap!'

Meriwether jumped, but having just relived a nightmare featuring northern raiders, I was unimpressed by a grumpy shopkeeper.

'I was just saying that we should move all the fishing stuff to the back and move wintry things to the front of the store,' I said. 'You want people to walk in, see something, and think, Hey, I need that. Then they think, MacIntyre's has what I need. You know? There's no reason for the sunscreen and fishing lures to be right here when they walk in. It's freaking November.'

Mr MacIntyre stared at me in silence, and I waited to see if literal smoke would come out of his ears.

He turned and looked around the store, almost as if seeing it for the first time – the faded advertising posters, the rust spots on the metal ceiling, the old-fashioned shelves, the worn linoleum tile.

'You've been here, what, two days?' he asked me. 'And now you're an expert?'

I snorted. 'I'm not an expert store owner, but I've got, you know, *eyes*.'

Meriwether hadn't taken a breath since this conversation had started, and I was wondering if she was going to keel over anytime soon.

After another minute of complete silence, during which Old Mac and I stared each other down, he snapped, 'Don't make a huge mess,' and headed back to the pharmacy. 'You better clean up everything you touch!'

I almost laughed at Meriwether's silent OMG expression but instead motioned her to the front of the store.

'I can't believe he agreed,' Meriwether breathed, her gray eyes wide. 'When I suggested it, he bit my head off.'

'Yeah – he doesn't get the warm-and-fuzzy award,' I said. 'Let's make a plan, one that we can do in little chunks, so he won't notice it too much. I can start on it tomorrow, and when you come in, you can take over.'

'Sounds good,' said Meriwether, and gave me a fleeting but real smile. I dutifully clocked out, then got in my battered little car and drove – kind of home.

Chapter 18

So let's see: My previous life of designer clothes; fabulous parties; guys climbing all over me; gorgeous, exciting, fun friends; traveling on a whim; fun fun fun – or my current life of jeans, flannel shirts, and work boots; my menial job at a tiny, run-down drugstore; getting up at dawn; falling into bed at, like, *nine*. There was no reason why this life should feel better, but it did.

Here, for the first time in decades, possibly centuries, my stomach felt – not bad. I've always had a place inside that felt like I'd swallowed a throwing star or a sparkler. A place deep in my gut that was sharp, jangled, painful, tight, tense. Sometimes if I drank enough or whatever, it would fade a little, then come back with a vengeance. It didn't even really bother me – I just noticed it, is all. I lived with it. Sometimes it was worse than others, but mostly I was barely aware of it, this knot of irritation and raw burning, deep inside.

This morning I'd realized that I could hardly feel it. And I hadn't self-medicated in weeks – since I'd come here to River's House of Rehab. It was shocking to realize that I'd been at River's Edge for five weeks. It felt both brand new and like I'd been here for months or years.

Everything was different.

I was taking more real classes now. With Anne, sometimes Asher, Solis, or River herself, I was being taught meditation, astronomy, botany, geology – you name it. If it was dry and incomprehensible, they were throwing it at me. I was learning about plants, and not just the farm plants. There were so many plants and herbs and flowers that had specific properties, either physical or magickal, and these could be used in spells. There are different forms of magick that use plants, or metals, or gems and crystals, or oils, or candles. Different people resonated with different types of magick; like, that kind of magick flowed best with who they were as a person, so their spells would be especially successful using it. I still didn't know what I resonated with. I was learning that basically everything around me, everything in the world, was connected to magick somehow. And therefore connected to me. They'd touched more on the whole eight-houses concept, and I'd tried not to flinch or pass out when they talked about Iceland, about the House of Úlfur.

I was seeing change. Even to my own eyes, I looked less ill. Of course, my natural allure was completely obscured by the calluses on my hands, dust and straw in my hair, butch clothes, and perpetual eau de chicken coop that lingered on me, but my skin and eyes did look healthier.

I was sleeping. Instead of four or five restless hours, I now conked out early and slept like a drugged rock until I had to get up. I was stronger physically; I could easily lift crates and cartons at MacIntyre's, push cows into milking gates, and lift the biggest, heaviest pots in the kitchen. My dreams were not bad. I often couldn't remember them, but I wasn't having constant nightmares and wasn't waking up sick and exhausted.

And yet all this healthy living was starting to feel like it was gonna kill me. Ha ha ha. And even though I was seeing change, I was seeing *difference*; I didn't think I was seeing *progress*.

One Sunday I was in a class with River, working with different metals. Everything (not just my amulet), whether natural or manmade, has an energy, a vibration, kind of. I know – oooh, how New Age-y, how touchy-feely. Hey, I'm just reporting how it is, people. I was learning to become more aware of the vibrations and energy, and how to align mine with them. It was part of the whole Tähti experience – to create power and magick out of working *with* things, rather than just sucking their power out till they die.

It's much easier to just suck the power out of other things and channel it than to actually craft a white spell and work within all the limitations you have to set up – the limitations that we dark immortals never bother with, if we do magick at all. So I was sitting at a table in one of the classrooms, fondling chunks of iron and copper and silver and barely picking up on anything at all, and of course the others, Jess, Daisuke, and Rachel, were all, like, glowing with the rapture of being so in tune with their magick that the metals were practically singing to them, and suddenly it was all too much.

'This sucks!' I said, and slammed down my chunk of copper.

Everyone jumped.

River came to my side and put her hand on my shoulder. 'What's wrong?'

'This!' I waved my hand at the copper, the room, the whole building. 'I'm not getting anything. I don't belong here.' Five weeks ago I would have really meant that – now I was so afraid it might be true, and I didn't want it to be. Not anymore.

River looked at me, and she seemed so – solid. I expected her to try to calm me down, walk me through the process again, maybe give me a little lecture, and I steeled myself.

Instead she seemed to look through my eyes right to my soul, tattered and misused as it was, and she asked, 'What do you want, Nastasya?'

'I want to get the whole metal vibration thing,' I said, thinking, *Obviously*.

She shook her head. 'What do you *want*?'

Was this a trick question? I squinted, thinking quickly.

'I want to – know this stuff?'

'*What* do you want?' River gazed at me unwaveringly, and I was vaguely aware of a roomful of fascinated spectators, none of whom had probably ever acted this way.

Maybe . . . 'I want to – feel better?'

'No. What do you *really* want?'

Okay, now I was getting pissed. I mean, WTF was she getting at? Was this some kind of rehab therapy mumbo-jumbo?

'I want to feel better!'

'No. What do you *really* want?' The words were bitten out.

'I don't know!' I shouted, standing up so quickly my bench toppled over.

River wasn't upset with me – her brown eyes were calm and accepting as she looked at me. She nodded and took her hand away and then sat down at her own table.

I wanted to stomp out of the room and down the hall and go back to the big house. Upstairs, I would fill the big bathtub and soak in it, letting tears roll down my cheeks and mingle with the water.

That was what I wanted to do.

What I did was pick up my bench. My face was burning. I felt like a huge baby. I set my bench down grimly and sat on it. I decided copper was not ringing my bell, so I tried a large piece of raw silver, twisted and smooth and unrefined. Knowing everyone's eyes were on me, I closed my eyes and controlled my breathing. My eyes were hot, and my nose had that pre-crying stuffy feeling, but I kept it all in. Crying in public on top of my scene would be too much.

The silver was heavy and smooth and quickly grew warm in my hand. I concentrated on it as much as I could (not that much) while trying, unsuccessfully, to clear my mind of every other thought. Did I feel vibrations? No, couldn't say that I did. I never wore silver – thought it looked too cold against my skin. My mother had never worn it, either.

Incy wore it.

Incy wore a lot of silver, all the time. Chains, bracelets, an earring, cuffs, belt buckles, buttons – you name it. If it could be made out of silver, he wore it.

I felt River standing close to me. 'Silver is very powerful, magickally,' she murmured in her soothing voice. 'It's associated with the moon, with feminine energy and healing. In the old days, people wore silver to ward off evil spirits.'

'Evil spirits?' I whispered. 'Do those exist?'

River rested her hands on my shoulders. 'What do you think?'

With a sudden clarity, I saw Incy. The room around me faded away, and all I was conscious of were River's hands on my shoulders and the heavy chunk of silver, warm in my hands. I drew in a breath. It was as if a porthole had opened up between my world and his. It was nighttime where he was, and with shock I recognized his apartment, though it had been totally destroyed since I'd last seen it. There were huge holes in the walls, spray-painted words. A chandelier had been torn down . . . furniture was upturned and broken. What had happened?

As I watched, Innocencio heaved a huge Iranian pottery vase – which had cost a fortune – against a wall. It exploded into a million shards as he roared, 'Where is she?' Boz and Cicely were standing miserably by a door, trying to avoid getting hit.

'She's just on vacation, Incy,' said Cicely. 'She went to Paris to do some shopping.'

'She's not in fucking *Paris*!' Incy bellowed, slamming his hand against the wall by Cicely's head. She tried not to flinch. I saw the word spray-painted on the wall by Incy's hand: *Bitch*.

He was talking about me, looking for me. My breath caught in my throat. Dimly, I was aware of River's hands touching me, but I stared in horror at the scene in front of me. 'She's not in Paris! No one's seen her! I can't – *feel* her anywhere! Do you understand? I can't feel where she is!'

He looked like a madman. Incy – suave, sophisticated, handsome Incy, with his beautiful handmade silk shirts and four-hundred-dollar haircuts, looked like a crazy homeless person. He hadn't shaved, his hair was wild, his clothes were torn and dirty. He grabbed Boz's lapels, screaming into his face.

Boz's face went hard, and he gripped Incy's wrists. I saw the skin whitening around his clenching fingers. 'Vestuvio!' he bellowed back, and Incy blinked, shocked. I couldn't breathe. Vestuvio was the name Incy had been born with, almost four hundred years ago.

'Look at yourself!' Boz spat, flinging Incy's hands away. 'You're *ridiculous*! Pathetic! Nas went *shopping*, you fucking idiot! Maybe she ran into someone! Maybe she's hooked up with some French asshole! Maybe she decided to go someplace else! She'll be back!'

Innocencio looked at Boz with wild hope and an almost childish trust. 'She will? Do you think so?'

'She'll be back,' Boz said firmly. 'She always comes back. And what is she going to think of you, of *this*?' He gestured contemptuously at Incy's ruined apartment. The twelve-thousand-dollar-a-month apartment.

Incy looked around, suddenly calm. He frowned at the wreckage around him as if finally seeing it, comprehending it.

'Really, Incy,' said Cicely. 'This is too much. We all miss Nasty, but it's no big deal. You know she'll be back. Her apartment is still there; all her stuff is there. Boz is right – when she comes back, what is she going to think about this?'

Innocencio whirled on Cicely, enraged. 'She won't think *anything* about it! She'll understand! She knows I need her! She needs me, too! She's somewhere going crazy without me!' His eyes became haunted. 'Maybe she's being held against her will. Maybe she's been kidnapped.'

'Oh, please,' said Cicely, and Incy shoved her into the wall.

'You don't know what it's like!' he screamed.

'Fuck you!' Cicely screamed back. She smacked his hand away and headed to the front door. 'Call me when you're done being an asshole!'

'No, Cicely, I'm sorry,' said Incy, contrite. 'I'm sorry! Don't go!'

She shot him the finger and slammed the door on the way out.

'That *bitch*!' Incy raged. 'That hateful *bitch*!'

Boz looked exhausted. He rubbed his hand over his face and slowly sank down against the wall.

Incy opened his mouth to shout something, then saw Boz. His face immediately changed again, and he crouched down by Boz. 'Boz? I'm sorry. I'm sorry. I don't know what's wrong with me. I just – I haven't been away from her in so long. I don't know what's wrong with me. I'm sorry. I . . . just miss her. I want to be with her.'

Boz spoke, sounding very old and very tired. 'You miss her *power*.'

I jumped back, feeling River's fingers digging into my shoulders. I blinked rapidly, and the classroom came back into focus.

My breaths were shallow as I glanced around. I felt like I was waking up from a faint. Jess, Daisuke, and Rachel were all solemn, watching me, their metals untouched in front of them.

My shoulders dropped and my hands opened, spilling the silver chunk onto the table. It was burning hot, practically glowing. I swallowed.

'Unh,' I said.

'Who was that?' River's voice was quiet and hard.

'My . . . friends,' I said, and swallowed again. 'You met Incy that night . . . when you met me. Did you – did you see them? See it?'

River nodded slowly. 'Yes. I'm not sure why – I wasn't trying to.'

My next question was very quiet. 'Could he find me here?'

River shook her head. 'I'll fix it so he can't. We'll fix it. You'll be hidden, as long as you're in West Lowing.'

'Oh, good,' I said lamely.

Of course, I didn't get off that easily. That night after dinner, a solemn Solis, Asher, River, and Anne confronted me in the dining room. After seeing the horrible vision of Incy, seeing Reyn at dinner had hardly registered. Yes, there are different levels of horror, of fear, of pain. Everything is relative. Right now Incy was taking center stage.

'River told us what happened,' Solis said, with no preamble. 'That you had a very real vision during your metalwork class.'

I nodded, wishing, not for the first time, that I wasn't so 'special.'

'These were friends of yours?' Solis asked.

'Yeah. I used to hang out with them.'

'Why would Innocencio be so upset that you're gone?' Anne asked.

'I don't know,' I said truthfully. 'He was – we did almost everything together. But I thought it was . . . normal best-friend stuff. Looking back, I guess he was kind of dependent on me.' The way he was on air, for example.

'Do you think he would harm you? Does he have strong magickal power?' Asher looked concerned.

'I would have said no, to both,' I said, thinking back. 'I never would have thought he would harm me. Now – I don't know. He's pretty . . . upset.'

'Is he strong?' River asked. She meant in terms of his magickal ability.

'Again, I didn't think so,' I said. 'But right before I left, he used a spell that . . . broke someone's spine. Crippled him. Just with magick. I had no idea he could do that.'

'What did the other man mean, that Innocencio missed your power?' River's eyes were grave and kind.

'Boz. I don't know,' I said again. 'I never made big magick – you've seen what it does to me. I don't use much magick at all. I had no idea I had any abilities. I don't know what Boz meant.'

River nodded and patted my back. A tiny noise made me look up, and I saw the kitchen door moving slightly. Nell and Charles had been assigned to clean up after dinner. Had Nell been listening in?

'Let me walk you up to your room,' said River, standing up. 'I'll fix you some tea.'

We walked upstairs together, and the steps felt familiar, the hallway seemed like home. 'What's in that tea?' I asked. 'Something to make me sleep, or not dream?'

River smiled. 'Nothing overtly magickal,' she said as I opened the door to my room. 'Other than the plants' own magickal properties. Mostly it's catnip. It has a relaxing effect on people. Catnip and chamomile and valerian. No spells, no man-made drugs.'

The door three down from mine opened. Reyn's door. He put his head out, saw it was River and me, and nodded stiffly. We heard his door close, and I closed mine.

River made me tea and stayed with me for a few minutes, I guess assuring herself (and me) that I was okay.

As she left, she said, 'Remember – tomorrow is a new day.'

It was a weird, trite thing to say, but I was too tired to wonder what the hell she meant. Sleep claimed me like a tidal wave, and I was out.

Chapter 19

The next morning my nerves still felt jangled and anxious. And to further unbalance my mental state, I was forced to catch a ride to work with the grim Viking. I wanted to protest and just take my own car, but something in River's eyes made me close my mouth and simply climb into the truck. Where I sat as close to my own door as possible, holding on to the handle.

As we drove away, I saw Nell watching us from the front parlor window, and I groaned to myself. Great. She already thought I was horning in on her, and frankly she was starting to seem a few sandwiches short of a picnic. Now I would be self-conscious and paranoid about her all day.

And the sad thing? Despite *everything* – my memory, Reyn's disdain for me, our obvious incompatibility, Nell's increasingly threatening interest – I still thought that he was hot, physically, and I actually appreciated his responsibleness. I mean, right now I didn't trust anyone except River and the other teachers, but let's face it, *no one* would have trusted Boz or Incy with their tractor or their truck or their . . . student. And I'm someone for whom responsibility has never been a selling point. I myself have never been responsible or reliable in any way. Incy, before he apparently went insane, had been amusing, exciting – but reliable? No. If one of my friends said they'd pick me up at four, maybe they would, and maybe they wouldn't. And maybe I'd be there when they got there, and maybe I wouldn't. Everything was much more free flow. But if Reyn said he'd be back to pick me up at four, by gosh, he would be tapping his foot impatiently on the curb outside at exactly four. Weirdly, these days I found that appealing rather than annoying. I found the fact that he wasn't shrieking and spray-painting *bitch* on the walls attractive. My world seemed so topsy-turvy now, my emotions so heightened, that it was like, northern raider, schmorthern raider! He said he's only 267! Whatever!

But I still held on to my door handle all the way to town, ready to leap from the moving truck if Reyn suddenly pulled out a longsword or something. In front of MacIntyre's I quickly opened the door and jumped out, tucking my scarf tighter around my neck. 'Thanks for the ride,' I forced myself to say, not looking at him.

'I'll be back at four,' he said. 'You know—' He stopped, his lips pressed together.

I looked back at him warily. 'What?'

'Nothing.' He shook his head, looking straight ahead.

I turned to go, and he said, 'Your hair. You've got kind of a skunk thing going.'

He'd never made any comment about my appearance, and my impression had been that he tried to look at me as little as possible. My eyes flared, and I looked into the truck's side-view mirror. Oh, geez. My mouth fell open in dismay. Among the other elements of my appearance that I'd let fall by the wayside, there was my hair color. My natural hair color was growing out, and I hadn't redone the black. So, yes, I did indeed have a whitish-blondish stripe down the middle of my head. So attractive.

I shut my eyes and shook my head. 'Just when I think it can't get worse,' I muttered.

'It can always be worse.' Was that bitterness in his voice?

Bastard, I thought, slamming the truck door.

Focus, I told myself. Focus on work. When I entered MacIntyre's Drugs, I saw firsthand that some things actually *can* get better. This drugstore looked better. Meriwether and I had done a lot over the last couple of weeks. Old Mac had refused to spend money on new displays or shelves, and had roared in fury when I'd asked, but we'd still made a big difference. We'd thrown out old, faded displays and come up with new ways to arrange stuff we wanted to highlight. Meriwether had cleared a bunch of crap off the checkout counter, so it now looked clean and accessible. The front windows had practically been blocked by junk, and we'd tossed it out and washed the windows, so the store was filled with light. This place actually looked as though it had made the leap to the twentieth century, if not the twenty-first. Old Mac grumbled and complained, but I had seen his face when customers commented approvingly about the new look, and I'd grinned cheekily at him when he glared at me.

Meriwether, though she had warmed up to me, still seemed faded and worn out herself, and Old Mac still barked at her meanly. I didn't like leaving at four, because it seemed like he saved all his vitriol for her when she came to work after school. I got the feeling that as soon as I left, he started in on her. I didn't know how to effect change there.

I was surprised that I even wanted to.

I hadn't seen Dray in several weeks and didn't know if she was embarrassed about shoplifting or mad that I'd made her pay for the stuff. It was too cold outside now to loiter around, drinking beer on the curb, and I wondered idly where she was hanging.

That day my chest began getting tense at three, and I was quite tightly wound by the time Reyn came to get me at four. I was outside waiting, my nose running in the cold. The pickup pulled in next to the curb, and I got in, remembering the skunk comment all over again. I wasn't going to think about it. I just wanted to go home and drink some hot tea and see what I had to do before dinner. I might even be on the dinner team – I'd forgotten to look. I had to get better about checking in advance, so I'd know what was coming. I shook my head and leaned it against the truck window. This whole train of thought was totally foreign and weird for me.

Reyn glanced at me, but I didn't explain.

I felt anxious around Reyn, though I'd convinced myself he couldn't have been the man in that memory – he was too young. I hated the fact that my screwed-up subconscious had chosen to put a face I was attracted to into one of my worst memories, but I was here to work out all that crap, right? And maybe that explained the vaguely familiar feeling I got from him – maybe he was just reminiscent of a physical type I'd seen before, and not always in a murderous, village-burning marauder way.

I was, in fact, on the make-dinner team, but fortunately not on the clean-up-dinner team, which was worse. So I scrubbed a small mountain of parsnips, cut up ten pounds of pears for a pear crisp, and made like a little kitchen elf while the world got blacker and colder outside.

After dinner, River said, 'Come with me,' and held out her hand.

Oh, God. Please no more magick for a while. Every time I got close to it, some sort of psychological hand grenade went off in my consciousness. I couldn't take any more. River gestured to my coat, and I shoved my arms into it, thinking, No, no, not the wonder of stars! Not tonight. Actually, I was pretty familiar with stars – it was the one class I could sort of hold my own in. I had crossed different oceans on boats more times than I could remember, back when crossing oceans could take weeks or even months. Believe me, when there's nothing to do but stare at the frigging stars, you stare at the frigging stars. I just had never gotten the importance of Canis Major, is all.

She led me out the back door, toward the school barn building. We went into the barn and down the hall, and at the end of the hall was a small, narrow staircase I hadn't even noticed before. It led up into another series of rooms, much smaller than the ones downstairs.

'This used to be the hayloft,' River told me. 'It still smells like straw, especially in the summer.'

'Hmm,' I said, wondering what was up.

River opened the door to a very small room, maybe nine feet square. Its slanted ceiling had a skylight that was chest high, and the highest point of the room was maybe seven feet.

'We use the rooms up here for smaller circles or private work,' she said, lighting a gas lamp and adjusting the wick. 'For one thing, it's warmer up here.' She gave me one of her timeless smiles, then busied herself at a small, roughly made cabinet against one wall. Handing me a piece of ordinary chalk, she said, 'Here. Draw a circle on the floor, big enough for us both to sit in.'

I looked at her. 'Um,' I said. 'I haven't really recovered from the silver disaster, or the awesome, heaving experience of our last circle. What are we doing here?'

'It's not a circle like that,' River said. 'I don't think you'll feel sick afterward. And I can weave some threads into the spell to help you feel fine, if you want. Now go on – draw a big circle, as perfectly round as you can.'

I had a bad feeling about this, but gosh darn it, I'm nothing if not trusting and obedient!

Hunching over, I slowly and carefully drew a chalk circle on the rough boards of the floor. It came out kind of squished and lopsided, but oh well.

'Don't close it,' River reminded me, and I left a two-foot-wide 'door' in it. She came behind me and sprinkled kosher salt, straight from the box, in a circle outside my circle. 'Salt purifies things and offers protection,' she said.

'I knew that!' I said.

She grinned at me, then motioned me to step inside the circle. 'Now we just close it,' she murmured, closing first the salt circle and then the chalk circle. I guessed we were stuck now.

She put four stones at the four compass points, and I started to feel alarmed. It looked like she was getting ready to create lightning or something.

'So, uh, what are we doing here?' I asked again.

'We're going to do a reveal spell,' she said.

Chapter 20

A reveal spell. Well, that clarified nothing. My first instinct was to step right out of the circle and run. Or simply say no and cross my arms over my chest. And I was about to—

'Okay, sit down, facing me.'

And somehow I did. We sat cross-legged, our knees almost touching. River held out her hands, and I hesitantly took them. What were we going to reveal? Buried treasure? A murderer? The place Solis had squirreled away his copper bracelet, which he couldn't remember? Anything, as long as it didn't have anything to do with me, or my past. I was already dreading the inevitable nausea, no matter what River said.

'There won't be nausea,' River assured me, and I started, staring at her.

'You read minds?'

She laughed. 'No. But I can read people's expressions very well. For this spell, I'm going to draw limitations around your power, channeling it and controlling what it does. I suspect usually it just goes all over the place, and your system can't handle it. All the forces warring together would make you sick. That's my theory, anyway.'

'Huh,' I said.

'Now, we both look at the lit candle,' she instructed, nodding at the small taper burning between us.

'What do I need to do?'

'Just follow my lead,' River said in a calm, determined voice.

'What are we going to reveal?'

'You.' Her tone was dreamy now, removed. Her clear brown eyes grew heavy-lidded as she watched the flame flicker and dance. She'd stuck it to a small mirror with its own wax; now white wax ran down its sides and flowed onto the silvered glass.

'No.'

'It will be okay, Nastasya,' River said calmly. 'You just have to . . . trust me.'

Oh, God, I'm gonna die, I thought miserably. *I can't do this.*

'You can do this.' Her quiet strength radiated out from her like heat. Swallowing, despite my fear, I tried to focus on the flame, tried to slow my breathing and release all thoughts, the way I'd been learning in class. I could feel my heart beating hard and fast.

I became aware of River's voice, singing softly. She was singing actual words, none of which I recognized, and I resigned myself to joining in with humpback when it felt right. Letting go of my hands, her slender fingers traced symbols in the air, all of which I recognized: Runes. I knew runes very well. People here used the Elder Futhark, and I saw Eolh, for protection, and Beorc, for new beginnings. That one made me smile – it seemed corny. Eoh confused me for a second – horse? Then I remembered that it signified change of some kind. River's hands moved so quickly that I didn't catch some of what she did, but then she traced the rune Peorth on my forehead. Peorth for hidden things revealed.

She'd said she was going to reveal *me*. I had no idea what the hell that meant, and hated the implications. Like, reveal my whole life to her? That would be very bad. I wanted no part of that. Reveal what I was really thinking? Who would want to do that? I felt her eyes on me and looked up to see her serene face, her tanned, barely lined skin, the silver hair drawn back in a ponytail. Using her hands, she traced the shape of my face in the air, not touching me, and I suddenly felt a wave of . . .

Power.

Oh, God . . . Slowly I drew in a breath, closing my eyes, feeling the power well up right inside me, like light. I felt it swirl around us, felt it discover another power – River's. It was like . . . like two ancient streams suddenly meeting up. I don't know what it felt like. But bathing in light would sort of come close. Feeling awash in joy and life.

Alarms went off inside my head. The few times I'd

done this, this was how I felt right before the inevitable black death of hope, the sudden horrible crashing of happiness, as if a thousand black, scaly insects had swarmed up out of a gutter and completely obscured the sun. Then would come the pain, the barfing, the despair.

River was singing again, her eyes closed now, and she traced other symbols on my forehead, my eyes, my cheeks. She brushed her hands down my shoulders and touched my knees. Gradually the tension left me – I was braced for pain but not feeling it yet. I was a seed, bursting open underground, stretching toward warmth. And I was the warmth, I was the light, and it was . . . glorious.

I basked for a while, then felt the magick gently fading. If I could have grasped it in my hands, I would have held on desperately. But it ebbed away, a low tide rejoining a vast ocean.

I opened my eyes. Slowly, dreamily, River opened hers. She looked at me, and I fancied I saw wonder and perhaps fear in her eyes. Then she looked me over and gave a slow, satisfied smile.

'How do you feel?' she asked.

I did a quick systems check. 'Uh, not bad,' I said in surprise. 'Tired. Relaxed. Sad that it's gone.'

'That's the beauty part,' she said, stretching and breathing deeply. 'It hasn't gone. It's always there. It's inside you, and you tapped it. Which is how Tähti do it, remember? It's a lot harder to tap the power inside you – it takes control, and learning. Much, much learning. Without the spell to harness and control your energy, you'd be your usual sick self, on your knees, vomiting. It doesn't have to be like that, and now you know it.'

I didn't know what to think. A quick elation flooded me – maybe I hadn't made a ridiculous mistake, maybe this was all worth it, maybe I could actually learn this stuff—

Only to be just as quickly snuffed out by my refusal to believe that something this good could happen to me.

River sighed. 'I will get you to believe it,' she said, getting to her feet.

'My face is not that expressive,' I said, standing up. I felt as if I'd just done a bunch of yoga and then run a marathon.

'It really is,' she assured me, and opened our circles.

I helped River gather the stones, then glanced to make sure we hadn't forgotten anything. Suddenly a face was before me, a shocking face, and I gasped and dropped the stones.

Whirling, River took my arm. 'What is it?'

Unable to say anything, I pointed to the strange face, the apparition floating in the darkened skylight. My mouth opened, but no sound came out. Instinctively, I ducked down, crouching on the ground to hide.

River immediately dropped down next to me, her hand on my shoulder. Her face looked both concerned and oddly amused.

'There's someone in the window,' I hissed. 'Like a ghost.'

She nodded solemnly and brushed my hair away from my face. 'Yes, it is like a ghost.'

I stared at her.

There was another small piece of mirror in the cabinet, and River got it out. Watching carefully, she held it up to me.

The ghost. The ghost was me.

I tried to swallow. I slumped onto my butt on the wooden floor, unable to tear my eyes away from the mirror. River again smoothed my hair away from my face. My hair that was now all white-blonde, every trace of black gone. My bangs had grown out far enough to tuck behind my ears, and the spiky layers were flattened because I no longer gelled or fluffed or spiked.

My eyes were dark, the color of a northern sky in winter. My cheeks were fuller and flushed pink. There was no dark eyeliner, no maroon lipstick altering my appearance.

I looked like a teenager. A healthy, normal teenager.

'I don't look like this,' I whispered. 'I never looked like this.'

'Yes, yes, you did,' River said quietly. She knelt next to me, our knees touching. She kept one hand on my shoulder.

I swallowed again, feeling like I was trying to get down one of the rocks I'd dropped.

Oh, yes. Yes, I had. A very long time ago.

*   *   *

'*Sunna, you're marrying Àsmundur Olafson.*' My foster mother looked matter-of-fact as she punched down dough in a big wooden bowl.

I was so surprised I spilled water out of the ladle onto the smooth table. 'What?'

'Your pabbi has made an agreement with Olaf Pallson,' she went on. 'You're marrying come this laugardagur, this Saturday.' I stared at her, but she didn't meet my eyes.

I wiped up the spill with a rag, then finished filling cups with water. Olaf Pallson raised sheep, two farms over. I vaguely remembered seeing Àsmundur Olafson once or twice, on market days. He'd been big and blond, but I couldn't picture his face.

When I didn't say anything, she stopped kneading and looked at me. 'Sunna, you're sixteen. Most maids are wed by now, and some already mothers. Àsmundur is a good lad and will inherit his father's farm – he's the oldest son.'

'I don't want to get married,' I said pointlessly, already knowing there was no choice.

'Sunna.' She wiped her hands on her apron. She was barely thirty-five, already middle-aged. 'Sunna, we have six other mouths to feed.'

I nodded, then took the empty pail outside to the well. It had been hard for them to take me in at all, but I had proved useful in caring for the little ones and helping Momer with the housework. The last six years here had been . . . a respite.

The following laugardagur was bright and clear, following three days of hard spring rain. It was still cold, but the days were slowly getting longer, and two more months would see the warmth of early summer.

My foster parents walked with me to the church. The roads were rutted and muddy. I glanced down into one puddle and thought, 'This is me, on my wedding day.' My long hair was in braids on top of my head. My clothes were clean. Momer had made me a wreath of laurel.

I looked up and saw Àsmundur and his father waiting for us at the church. So that's what he looks like, I thought, studying his broad farmer's face.

That had been in 1567.

I had looked like this.

My young husband had been dead within two years, of smallpox.

Blinking, I stood up.

'Let's go get some tea,' said River, turning off the lamp. 'We'll clean this up tomorrow.'

With the lamp off, there was no ghost me reflected in the window glass. We walked in darkness down the hall, down the narrow staircase. I kept touching my hair. It seemed softer, without the harsh dye in it. I felt bizarre. I knew every time I saw this me in the mirror, I would flinch. I hadn't looked like this in a long, long time.

Outside, River looked up at the sky and said, 'It's later than I thought.'

I looked at the stars, half obscured by clouds. Constellations moved overhead in an arc throughout the night. Looking up, I saw that it wasn't the middle of the night, but it was later than the first hour of night. Say, tennish. The clouds made it more difficult.

'Is it around ten?' I asked.

'Yes.' River looked pleased. 'You're absorbing knowledge against your will.'

I nodded. I felt very unlike me, like I didn't know what to do with myself. As if the reveal spell had erased actual years instead of just the appearance of years. Everything seemed new and different. I just wanted to go to my room and stare at myself in the mirror.

The darkness pressed in all around us, and I kept close to River, keeping my eyes on the lights of the house up ahead. Something weightless and cold landed on my nose, and I looked up to see small, fine snowflakes floating down from the sky.

It was cold and dark and snowing. Just like my childhood, like so many of my earlier years. This is why I preferred warmer places. Even London didn't get cold like this. Between looking like I did way back then, and then suddenly feeling like the weather was similar, I was flooded and overwhelmed with dark thoughts and nameless dread.

We approached the kitchen steps, lit by an angular square of light from the window. I was lunging for the door, wanting to be inside, around other people, when River took my arm, halting me. I looked at her.

'Back then you were here,' she said softly, marking a place in the air with one hand, out to the side. 'Now you're *here*.' She held out her other hand, far away from the first. 'Time moves *forward*. You're not there anymore. Understand?'

'Uh-huh,' I said, though I didn't.

She shook her head. 'You started here, in 1551.' Again she marked a place in the air. Tiny snowflakes drifted onto her hair and disappeared into the silver strands. 'Now you are here. *Here*.' She chopped her other hand downward for emphasis. Reaching out, she pressed several fingers against my chest. 'You. Are. Here. You are *now*. You are this moment.'

I must have still looked lost, because she sighed and pulled open the kitchen door. Immediately warmth and light and the smells of leftover cooking wafted toward us. The kitchen was empty, clean, but still lit. I was hungry, which was weird. I didn't feel sick.

'Pear crisp, I think,' said River, opening the industrial fridge. 'And tea.'

Chapter 21

When you've spent most of your life being a chameleon, changing everything about yourself over and over again, it's shocking, again and again, to see the original you in a mirror. Through the years I'd had every color of hair from white to black, including blue, green, and purple, and every length from crew cut to down past my waist. I'd been rail-thin, pleasantly plump, big and pregnant, starving and skeletal. I'd had the white skin of a northerner, where we went for months without seeing the sun, and I'd been as dark as a walnut, burnished bronze by an equatorial sun that had soaked through my skin to my very bones.

Now I looked like the me that the child me had grown up into. It was freakish, disturbing, and I felt horribly exposed and vulnerable. In the morning I layered several sweaters, wrapped a fuzzy scarf around my neck, and tied a kerchief over my hair, which, ironically, only made me look more like how I used to. Peasant wear. Finally I went reluctantly downstairs. I was on table-setting duty for breakfast.

In the kitchen I muttered a fast hello to Daisuke and Charles, who were making breakfast. I noticed that, typically, the kitchen was neat and tidy, though they were cooking for thirteen people. They were both spare, elegant people who always seemed to be operating from some deep sense of calmness. Brynne made huge messes in the kitchen, and so did Lorenz – and they were both flamboyant, wildly attractive people. Reyn was tidy. Nell was messy. Jess and I were both disorganized, and I'm sure that surprised everyone.

Anyway, I quickly grabbed the flatware tray and escaped into the big dining room, which was still in predawn darkness. Inside I felt jangly, anxious, wound up in a way that I hadn't been in . . . weeks. As soon as I went to work this morning, I planned to disappear into the employees' restroom with a box of hair dye. Auburn, this time, I thought.

The door to the kitchen swung open and Solis came in, carrying an armful of cut twigs. I nodded at him, not meeting his eyes. He set a tall vase in the middle of the table and arranged the long twigs in it, making an arrangement maybe three feet high.

'Forcing blooms,' he said, stroking their bark with gentle fingers. 'Not by magick, but simply by bringing them indoors. Is it wrong to force a thing to go against its nature?'

He almost seemed to be talking to himself, not even looking at me, and I was hoping it wasn't a real question.

There's only so much existential philosophy I can stomach before I've had my first cup of coffee.

I moved quietly around the table, setting River's heavy, beautiful sterling flatware from the early eighteen hundreds at every place.

'What do you think, Nastasya?' he asked, pinning me like a bug collector pins a moth to a velvet tray. 'Do you think it's inherently wrong to force a thing to go against its nature? Is it sometimes all right, like with these branches? And by the way, what plant are they from?'

I paused, looking at the arrangement. First things first, to buy myself some time. They were light colored, not too woody. More like a shrub. It was something that bloomed early, since it was not quite winter and it could already be forced.

I took a stab. 'Forsythia?'

He smiled, and I felt stupidly pleased, like a performing seal.

'Now, the other part of my question. Is it inherently wrong to force a thing against its nature?'

With a sinking feeling I recognized that an Important Learning Moment had crept up on me when my guard was down. The question had been casually asked; the answer couldn't be casually given. Responses crawled through my caffeine-deprived mind.

'Like training dogs?' I tried.

He smiled patiently. There are few things worse than a patient smile. 'The nature of dogs, inherently, is to work.

They've been domesticated for so many thousands of years that it has become their very nature to accept and even need training. Training works *with* their nature, not against it. I'm talking about forcing these buds to bloom out of season, for our enjoyment. Just as one example. Or damming a river. Or keeping a person in solitary confinement. Humans are, by nature, social creatures. Not designed to be alone.'

Daisuke came in quietly and set a basket of biscuits on the table. He glanced at my hair, gave me a slight smile, then pushed through the kitchen door again.

I couldn't concentrate. I was upset and uncomfortable, looking like this, and I just wanted to escape until I could change again. I didn't even have any makeup on. I probably looked like a glass of milk.

I let out a breath. 'I don't know. Maybe.'

I waited for him to tell me to go meditate on it, or to seek out someone's help in finding the answer, but he didn't.

Instead he brushed his fingers lightly along the twigs again and said, 'I don't know, either.' He turned to me. 'Your nature,' he said softly, 'is to look this way. This is who you are, and this is what *you* look like. Please try to embrace it. Remember what Hector Eisenberg said: "A woman's face, naked and unadorned, is as beautiful as the moon, and as mysterious."'

I just looked at him, feeling like bugs were crawling all over my skin. People began to trickle in and sit down, and Charles and Daisuke brought in more platters of food.

'Please don't change again,' Solis said so quietly that only I could hear him. 'Continue to become yourself.' He moved away then and picked up a plate, getting in line for breakfast.

'My face is *not* that expressive,' I muttered, and the corners of his mouth turned up. I wanted to run to my room until it was time to go to town, but forced myself to get in line, behind Lorenz. His dark eyes were barely open – he must have stayed up late last night.

''Giorno, bella,' he murmured, and the patchouli scent of his aftershave wafted down to me.

Behind me, Charles took his own plate.

'Well,' he said, his Irish accent coming through with that one word. With his red hair and freckles, he looked like a travel ad for the Green Isle. 'So you've bleached it, then?'

'No,' I said, just as a huge crash made us all jump. Our heads swiveled to see Reyn standing in the doorway, looking poleaxed. He'd been carrying an armload of firewood, which now lay scattered across the floor.

He was staring at me, looking horrified, his face white, his golden eyes wide. He shook his head and said, 'No. *No.*' Then he realized that we were all gaping at him. He looked down at the firewood, looked up at me again, then turned without a word and pushed through the kitchen door. A moment later we heard the back kitchen door slam.

'What did you do to him?' Nell asked sharply, throwing down her napkin to go after him. River stopped her, taking her arm.

'I'll go,' River said gently.

'No,' Nell said crossly, shaking her hand free. 'We're very close. I know what to do.'

River shook her head slowly. 'Please sit down, Nell. I'll go after Reyn.'

Nell opened her mouth to argue, then caught herself, caught how River was looking at her.

'I can go,' she said, with much less conviction.

'Finish your breakfast,' River directed her, then turned and followed Reyn.

Nell contented herself with glaring at me, shaking her head in disgust. Muttering to herself, she sat down at the table and snapped her napkin open again.

Now people turned to look at me. I shrugged help-lessly, having no idea what just happened. Rachel asked Anne to pass a platter, and slowly people began acting normally. Jess and Brynne quickly picked up the firewood and loaded it neatly in the woodbin by the fireplace. I felt Asher's eyes on me, and Solis's, but I mechanically got some food and sat down on the end of a bench next to Jess, who grunted a good morning. I mumbled some-thing in reply, my brain working quickly.

My kind of white-blonde hair was common in the north, especially among my family and our village. Had Reyn recognized that, understood its significance?

I pondered that for a fevered minute, then realized that duh, he'd been watching my roots growing out for the past five weeks. I'd hardly been painstakingly dyeing an ever-widening stripe of white at my roots.

So what had it been?

As it turned out, I had to go to work before I found out. Reyn and River didn't come back to breakfast, and finally I drove myself in my old battered car to town.

Focus on work. Be in the present, live in the now. Worry about Reyn later.

Old Man MacIntyre gave my hair a sharp look but didn't say anything. 'A new shipment of – ladies' products came in,' he barked. 'Go ahead and put them in your *special aisle*.' He scowled at me, then turned and stomped away. I laughed wryly to myself. One of the changes Meriwether and I had made was that we'd grouped all the 'ladies' products' in one place. During the process we had learned that a surefire way of getting Old Mac to leave us alone was to hold up a box of Kotex and ask him about pricing.

I hauled the big plastic bins to our *special aisle*, already looking forward to relating the story to Meriwether.

Close to lunchtime, I felt someone standing next to me, and looked up.

I gave Dray a mock frown. 'Why aren't you in school?'

She made a face back. 'Already graduated.'

Standing up, I stretched and dumped an empty cardboard box back into the bin. 'Did not, you big liar. You can't be more than sixteen.'

'Seventeen. What do you care? You're not in school either, and you're what, maybe seventeen, too? Eighteen?' Her frown this time was real, and then I glanced down and saw she was holding a pregnancy test.

She saw my look and stuck her chin out. 'Which one of these is the cheapest?'

Solemnly I checked all the prices. 'This one,' I said. Then I had a thought. 'Bathroom's over there.' I pointed. 'Go do it.'

She drew back, ready to refuse, but she hesitated.

'Go on,' I said. 'Do it now, while I'm here, instead of at home by yourself.'

For a split second, I saw a crack in her tough-girl facade, saw the scared teenager beneath. Her fear won out, and she grabbed the test and headed to the public restroom that we were required to have but that no one ever used. Guess who got to keep it spick-and-span? Yes.

Finally Dray returned. 'Are these reliable?'

I nodded. 'Afraid so.'

She let out a huge breath and pulled out the stick. It was negative. 'How much do I owe you?'

'Eight seventy-nine, plus tax,' I said, starting to head to the front. 'Hey! I have an idea! Why don't you buy some condoms? Then we won't have to go through this again. Not that it hasn't been *fun*.'

She narrowed her eyes. 'No, thank you.'

What an idiot. 'They come in different colors,' I coaxed. She shook her head.

At the front counter, I took the opened box and rang it up, then threw it in the trash. 'Isn't there, like, a women's clinic, on the road that intersects Route Twenty-seven? I've passed it.'

Dray shrugged. She was hugely relieved but didn't want to show it. 'I don't know.'

The register popped open. I took her ten and started to make change. 'Well, there is,' I said. 'It's a women's clinic. They could put you on the Pill, for cheap, I bet. Or check you out, make sure there's nothing wrong, 'cause I'm sure you *associate* with only the highest-quality guys.' I rolled my eyes.

I could see her process the information.

'It's within walking distance,' I said in a bored tone, looking at my fingernails. 'If they're gonna give away stuff cheap, might as well get it.'

Dray shrugged again, but the idea had definitely taken up residence in her brain. She pushed her way out the door, then leaned back and said, 'Rockin' hair, BTW. Wicked!' She flared her eyes to make sure I got the sarcasm, and I stuck my tongue out at her. She was smirking as she went past the store window.

And there you have it: my mitzvah for the day. Nastasya Doe: Savior of teenage girls.

It was late when I got back that afternoon, already dark. I was rising before dawn and getting home after sunset, seeing the day only through MacIntyre's windows. It sucked. I had a few minutes before dinner, and miraculously, wasn't signed up for any chores, so I trudged upstairs in my stocking feet. Or sock feet, I guess.

I headed down the long hallway, passing one dark window after another, returning to my room as surely and as mindlessly as our cows came in at milking time.

I automatically turned at my door and reached for the doorknob. Then stopped. Why? I looked up and down the hallway. No one was near. Something felt weird, off. My door was shut – there wasn't a bucket of water on top of it, for example. Everything looked fine, reason told me that everything must be fine . . . and yet it felt strange, forbidding, and I was reluctant to go in.

I went and got River.

Chapter 22

Hmm.' River looked at my doorframe.

Downstairs, dinner was almost ready. My stomach was growling. I felt like a big sissy whiner. 'It's nothing, I'm sure,' I said. 'I was imagining things.'

'No,' said River. 'You weren't.'

'I don't see anything,' I said.

She looked at me. 'But you felt something. Something made you not go in.'

It sounded stupid. I nodded. I didn't know if I was now afraid of so many things (Incy, Reyn, the dark, myself, my history) that I was seeing danger everywhere.

River reached in her pocket and took out a small, beautiful silver box, its top embossed with a hunting scene. I thought she'd been squirreling away silver for centuries. Inside the box was a fine, gray-green powder. A small silver spoon rested inside the box.

'Coke gone bad?' I guessed.

She shook her head, taking the small spoon and scooping up the powder. She murmured a few words over it, then held up the spoon and blew hard. The powder flew through the air toward the door, and I stepped back quickly, almost gasping. There were symbols all over the doorframe. The powder had illuminated them, and now they glowed with a faint silvery sheen. A few were runes, but I didn't know most of them.

'What is all that?' I asked.

River was examining them. 'Sigils. Spells.' She crouched down, following them with her finger.

'For what?'

'They're not very powerful,' she said, standing up straight. 'And they're not deadly. They're mostly designed to draw bad luck to you – so you'll trip and break your ankle, or lose your keys, or burn something in the kitchen. Have a fender-bender.' She cocked her head to one side, thinking. 'Hmm.'

'So that's what I felt? These . . . spells? And they would have worked on me if I'd gone in?' Who had done this? River had said she'd spell the place so Incy couldn't find me. I still found it hard to believe that he would know this kind of magick anyway. So, Reyn? Who else? Nell? She was pissed this morning, when Reyn freaked out.

River nodded. 'They would have worked on the first person who went through the door. It's hard to believe that you picked up on them – they're pretty weak.' She paused, looking thoughtful. 'I wonder . . . could probably use Asher here.'

As if on cue, we heard steps on the stairs, and moments later Asher came into view.

'Need me?' he asked.

River quickly explained the situation. Asher frowned when he saw the sigils, seeming surprised, and then looked more surprised when River told him I'd felt them.

He stood there silently for a minute, his dark brown eyes thoughtful. He stroked his short beard. Finally he looked up. 'There's something inside. That's what she felt.'

'Something inside?' I echoed. 'Like, a tiger? What's inside? That's my room!'

'All right, then, let's null them.' River seemed brisk and no-nonsense.

'What's inside?' I almost shrieked. My amulet was in there.

'More spells,' said Asher. 'Much darker. Stronger.'

I'm not a rocket surgeon. I'm pretty bright and have a kind of street savvy that's served me well. But I'm not a genius. All the same, I'm embarrassed to admit that it was *only then* that I truly realized that someone had actually done this to *me*, deliberately. Not just the door spells. Something worse inside. Someone here had wanted to hurt *me*. I felt that frisson of fear that had haunted me, off and on, since I'd left London. Had some stranger snuck in? I didn't see how they could. Which left someone here, in the house. Maybe Nell? I seemed to be getting in the way of her beeline to Reyn. Someone else? Great.

River and Asher checked the other doors nearby. They were clean.

'We'll do a comprehensive sweep later,' said River. 'But right now let's get these off.'

'Magickal Windex?' I asked faintly.

River grinned, looking blissfully normal. 'Sort of.'

Anne came up to get us for dinner, and her eyes bugged out of her head when Asher told her what they were doing. She looked from them to me in shock.

All she said was, 'Hmm.' Then she headed back downstairs.

River and Asher did the spell to nullify whatever spells had been placed on or in my room. They stood forehead to forehead, eyes closed, murmuring words. Sometimes together, sometimes only one of them. It took a couple of minutes. It occurred to me that they had probably been making magick together for years, even decades. I didn't know how long they'd been together. River was probably older than Asher, but I didn't know by how much. River was the oldest immortal I'd ever known or heard of. I wondered if she was the only one. No, of course not – she'd said her oldest brother was the king of their house. And there would have to be others.

River and Asher's tuneful chanting ceased, and they slowly opened their eyes and pulled away from each other.

'That should do it,' said Asher. 'It was some ugly stuff.'

'Like what?' I asked, as River reached out to open the door.

Asher shrugged, then followed River into my room.

I confess I hesitated, waiting to see if a bear trap snapped around their ankles, or spiders fell on them, or they burst into flames. I poked my head around the door.

'It's okay,' said Asher. 'You can come in.'

'You sure?' When had I turned into such a sissy? When I began caring about what happened to me, a small voice answered inside my head. I told it to shut up, like always.

Inside my room, River had blown more powder onto my door. It too was covered with rapidly fading spells. Asher was running his hands under my mattress, turning over my pillow, even getting on his hands and knees to look under my bed. When had I last swept under there? Oh. Never. Oops.

'Ah,' he said, and reached under my bed. He pulled out a small leather bag as River and I crowded around.

'Any signatures?' asked a voice from the door. Solis stood there, his hazel eyes sharp in his youthful face.

River frowned. 'I don't know.'

Solis came in then. 'You don't know?'

'Signatures like what?' I asked, but everyone was ignoring me.

Asher opened the leather bag and carefully dumped it out onto the bed. It was a jumble of pins and needles, a tiny glass vial full of dark, reddish-brown liquid, and a dark, shiny stone that looked like metal. Hematite, I remembered, patting myself on the back.

'Is it, like, a joke?' I asked, peering over Solis's shoulder.

'No,' said Asher. 'Not a joke.'

'What is going *on*?' I said, raising my voice slightly.

Solis looked at me, then went back and shut the door to my room. He opened his hand at it and murmured a few words that I didn't recognize. Then the three of them, as if choreographed, looked at me.

'What?' I said. 'I didn't do this.'

'We know,' said River. 'Tell me, did you know anyone here, before you came here? Besides me, I mean. Is anyone else familiar to you?'

'No.' Yes, I'd had those flashes where Reyn seemed familiar to me, and I'd also had that vision of berserker Reyn. But I really hadn't met him before I came here, I was sure of it. I ran through the others' faces again, trying to picture them in different guises, and couldn't remember ever seeing anyone here before. 'No, I don't think so. Why?'

River looked into my eyes solemnly. 'Someone here wants you dead.'

I dunked my bread into the leftover stew broth in my bowl. The four teachers and I were all sitting at the dining-room table, having a late dinner. In the kitchen we could hear Jess, Nell, and Lorenz doing the cleanup. Lorenz was singing an aria from *Tosca* – he had a beautiful voice.

'So what happened with Reyn this morning?' He hadn't been at dinner, either, and I wondered if he had any connection to my spelled room. Despite everything,

I didn't think so, but something about me had definitely spooked him this morning.

'You suddenly looked familiar to him,' River said frankly. 'Something about the color of your hair, the way you looked standing there – he had a painful flashback.' She grinned wryly. 'Like you do. Are you sure you don't know him?'

'No, I really don't think so,' I said again. 'I've mostly been . . . hanging out with more or less the same crowd for a long time. I don't think I've met anyone here before. There was . . .'

'What?' River asked.

I hesitated. 'Well . . . during that circle – I had a, not a vision, but a memory. I remembered something that had happened to me a long time ago. A really long time ago, like before 1600. In that memory, I saw someone who looked just like Reyn. As being the one who . . . almost hurt me. A raider. One of the raiders who came in the winters back then.' Ugh. I had never actually told anyone about that whole episode. I'd been burying it for four hundred years, along with a bunch of other awful memories that were bubbling up to the surface of my consciousness.

River's eyes looked into mine, and I dropped my gaze and busily dunked my bread into my bowl again.

'But I mean, Reyn's only two hundred sixty-seven,' I said. 'So it wasn't him. Just someone who looked, you know, exactly like him. Or my mind playing tricks on me, just inserting Reyn's face into that memory. It was . . . weird.'

The teachers were silent for a while, and I got the impression they were all looking at each other over my head.

'Has anyone here expressed anything negative to you? Have you pissed off anyone?' Solis's youthful face was concerned.

'As likely as that is, no, I don't think so,' I said. 'I mean, not really, not to that extent. I think Nell definitely dislikes me, but it's more schoolgirl stuff, you know?' Another thought occurred to me. 'Although Reyn did tell me to leave, my first day here.'

'He told you to leave?' River's dark eyebrows arched gracefully.

I wished I'd kept my mouth shut. Now I felt like a sissy, whiner *snitch*. It kept getting better and better. 'It was just my first day. No one thought I would stay. I didn't have an aura of probable success all around me, you know?'

River gave a small smile.

'And the jury's still out,' I felt compelled to add. I didn't want them to be too disappointed or surprised when I eventually flunked out and went down in flames.

'Anyway – Reyn's all about choosing good, over and over, and flogging his soul and whatnot. He wouldn't lose karmic progress by doing something like this. Right?' I looked at River, then the others. They all nodded slowly, thoughtfully. 'Um, what did you mean by *signatures*?' I asked.

'Magick is a very personal, intimate thing,' said Anne. 'Each person makes magick in his or her own way. As we've discussed, what spells you use, what sigils and runes, what elements you work with, whether you use moon spells or sun spells or wind spells or water spells – people develop patterns of what they like to use, what's successful for them. After working magick with someone a couple of times, you can often identify the person's kind of spell. It's imprinted with their persona, their vibrations.'

'Some people actually weave signatures into their spells,' said Asher. 'They're proud of their craft, or they want to send a warning. So their name is built into part of the spell.'

'And no one left their name on this? It would be stupid of them to,' I realized.

'No one left an outright signature,' said Solis. 'But the spells seemed deliberately – disguised. Created by one person but crafted as if they were done by someone else. And then the whole thing obscured, fudged.'

I stared at him. 'Can someone actually do that?' Oh, God, this was all so much more complicated than I could have imagined. I would never get a handle on it.

'Yes,' said River.

'But they were spells to make me . . . die?'

'Yes, pretty much,' said River. 'Which is actually silly,

given the immortal thing. Not outright, like murder. More like, get pneumonia and die. Have a fatal accident. Be killed during a robbery. Not anything actually premeditated, someone coming to kill you. On a regular person, they would be deadly indeed. For you, for us . . . they were spells to draw a great darkness to you. It wouldn't have killed you – you know how hard that is – but you would have attracted a terrible darkness. Something that could immobilize you with fear, for example, or an unshakable depression. I haven't seen anything like it since – well, a really, really long time.'

'And the talisman under your bed,' said Asher. 'Dark stuff.'

'The sewing kit?'

Asher tried to smile but couldn't. 'It would have been working on you strongly, every moment you lay in that bed.'

My stomach was in knots again. I remembered what it had felt like, reaching for my door, then hesitating. It had felt like a cold, dark shadow had been waiting for me in my room. A shadow that would snatch me up, envelop me, so no one would ever see me again. *Could* it have been Reyn? No – despite everything, I couldn't imagine him doing it. But then who? Nell? Yes, she was a beeyotch, but did she hate me this much? Was she this good at magick? One of the others? My head started to hurt.

'Maybe I shouldn't be here,' I said faintly. 'I mean, we all know I shouldn't. This is just proof.'

'On the contrary,' said River. 'To me, this means you should be here more than ever.'

Solis, Asher, and Anne nodded, though I saw Solis shoot a glance at River.

Anne nodded. 'I agree. This is what we were talking about,' she said to the other teachers. 'She has an unnaturally strong power, something ancient and powerful. She must learn to harness it, understand it, use it for good. Or she'll be vulnerable forever.'

'The question is, does someone else know about her power? Is it threatening to someone?' Asher asked.

River shook her head, looking at me, while I tried to act casual and not hyperventilate. My skin had gone cold with the phrase *ancient and powerful*. 'Besides her friend Innocencio? And I guess Boz, since he mentioned it. Other than that, I don't think so. She's too unknown, too untaught. Yes, she has power, but she's incapable of doing anything with it. She just doesn't know enough.'

'I'm sitting *right here*,' I said.

With no warning, River put out her hand, touching her fingers to my temple. What was she doing? And then I felt – her.

I felt River's mind. For a moment I sat there marveling at the sensation, then I realized everything it could mean, and I slammed my own mind shut, dropping every wall that I had into place. She was right, I was untrained, I didn't know how to do anything, but I still sent screaming signals of *Protect* through my brain.

Her eyes widened slightly, and she took her hand away.

I tried to act as if nothing had happened. 'Do I have a fever?' I managed to ask.

She shook her head.

That night, all four teachers put sigils of protection on me, actually tracing them onto my forehead, my arms, my back, over my heart. Solis and Anne walked with me back to my room, and they drew more spells onto my doorframe, my door, the inside of my door, over my bed.

'How about the bathroom?' I asked cheekily. 'I could fall off the john, break my neck.'

They did not think that was amusing.

'Do you know how to do a lock-door spell?' Anne asked me.

I stared at her. 'Those exist?? Jesus Christ! You could have told me a month ago!'

Anne and Solis cracked up. Then she taught me an elementary spell that wouldn't stop a buffalo, say, but would stop anyone who tried to come in without my permission. It was a simple spell, and I recognized the basic structure from the spellcrafting-for-dummies class that Asher taught. But even a simple spell has to be limited to time, place, person, effect . . . It was those kinds of details that made me want to scream, that I had no patience for.

Still, I'd *hated* not having a lock on my door. If this would keep people out, then I would learn it. Anne went over it twice with me, and I finally nodded. Then she left my room and waited in the hall. Very slowly and painstakingly, feeling like a dropout from Stupid School, I made the spell, including words, hand gestures, the whole shebang.

'Okay,' I finally called, feeling like I had run across the Brooklyn Bridge.

Anne tried to come in. I saw the doorknob turn.

'I can't,' she said, sounding satisfied. 'The harder I try, the less I can. Good job!'

I was amazingly pleased with myself, until I remembered that I was only doing this because someone here, someone close to me, hated my guts.

That sucked some of the thrill out of it.

Chapter 23

That day seemed to mark a new chapter in my career at River's Edge. Because of the teachers' reactions and concern, it made me slow down and do everything with more awareness, trying to pay attention to any malevolent feelings around me.

I watched both Nell and Reyn at mealtimes or when we were working near each other. Reyn was literally trying not to look at me and acted as if I were invisible. He no longer gave me rides to town, and we were never assigned to work together. Nell seemed to have gotten a grip on her hostility and had resumed being pleasant and friendly in a fake, vacuous way.

I picked up on nothing, and no one found any evidence of more dark spells anywhere else. We were all on guard, but it started to seem as if it could have been a one-time thing – like a warning shot across a bow, without much intent to follow through.

That's what I was telling myself, anyway.

A couple of days later, Old Mac told me that the store would be closed for five days. Apparently, once or twice a year he went off with his man friends and fished. I pictured a bunch of grumpy old men, griping at each other, standing glumly in icy water, flicking their rods. But maybe for him it was therapy, a reprieve.

It sure was for me. At first I was thrilled – five days off! – and then panic set in: What would I do with myself? Right now, every moment of every day was occupied, and even when it was a two-hour stretch of something heinous and soul-crushing, I was still focused on trying to be aware of who and what was around me.

With five days off, I pictured myself getting bored and thinking of dumb-ass things to do to entertain myself. Like messing with the locals, showing up in a flashy car, taking up smoking, leaving.

Was this when I would start to go downhill, when any gains I'd made would be stripped away from me in a couple of singularly bad choices? I knew it was coming. I always, *always* ruined a good thing.

As it turned out, this time, at least, my fears were ungrounded. I should have known the power-hungry slave drivers at River's Edge would see my five days of freedom only as a challenge to be filled.

'Yule is coming,' River told me cheerfully, piling my arms high with quilts and other bedding. 'It's a wonderful time to clean house. Then, on the solstice, when the longest night of the year finally cedes to the shortest day, and we know every day after will be a little longer, a little brighter – well, it's a wonderful feeling to have everything scrubbed clean and fresh.'

I looked at her over the tops of the linens. 'You have *got* to be kidding.'

'Nope.' She gave that irresistible, timeless grin that made her face light up. 'Off to the washhouse with you now. And be happy it's winter and you can use the dryer. In the summer we'll do it all again, but with clotheslines.' She made shooing motions with her hands, and I stumbled outside into the cold, hardly able to see where I was going. At least I wasn't going to be boiling these suckers in huge cauldrons outside, I thought grimly. The washhouse was really just a big laundry room in one corner of the school building, where a row of seven industrial washers and as many big dryers waited for me.

Inside, I dropped the quilts, swearing, and started to separate colors.

Once, I'd had pneumonia really bad. My lungs were full of fluid, I was burning up with fever, and I was practically delirious. Any ordinary person would have died – many did, that winter. My friends had been on their way to Switzerland to celebrate the holidays, and I was too sick to go, so they dropped me off at a convent in Germany. They left the mother superior a sackful of money and said that would be enough to either keep me until I got well or bury me if I didn't make it. I can still remember their knowing laughter.

Anyway. I was there for two long months, and believe me, you don't know what a nun is until you've seen a late nineteenth-century German nun. Those women were scrubbers, and no nonsense, but, like, to an incomprehensible degree. If those nuns had been running things, Germany would have won World War II. Very serious nuns.

And that convent didn't have anything on River's house during the pre-Yule scrub-fest. That's how bad it was. Windows were washed, inside and out, walls wiped down, rooms vacuumed and swept and mopped. Every closet and cupboard was gone through, aired out, cleaned, and tidied. A growing pile of stuff was earmarked for a tag sale, once the weather warmed up. It was unbe-freaking-lievable. Nothing else had happened to me of late – Reyn stayed out of my way, though every once in a while I caught him looking at me. Nell flitted through everything with a sugary smile, and I saw her and Reyn working together several times. She looked happy as a clam. I'd had no more bad dreams, visions, or wormhole-type revelations. Life was feeling somewhat normal, or as normal as it could, considering that it had changed a hundred and eighty degrees from three months ago.

One night during the cleaning frenzy, I was literally *on my hands and knees* on the kitchen floor, scrubbing the flagstones. I mean, flagstones are *rocks*. Rocks are inherently *dirty*. That is their freaking *nature*. I was *going against their nature* in trying to make them be *clean*.

No one had bought that reasoning. So here I was.

A really gifted scrubber with years of experience in flagstone care might have finished the gargantuan kitchen's floor in about two hours. I was rolling into hour three, and had started swearing forty minutes ago. I'm still pretty fluent in about five languages, though every once in a while I use an old-fashioned grammar construction or idiom, and I can swear expressively in about three others.

And I was.

I was trying hard not to enjoy the lifting of months of grime, seeing the subtle colors of each individual stone reappear as I sopped up the dirty water with a rag.

'Stupid fricking hard fricking stupid stone,' I hissed quietly. 'Would linoleum have killed them? No. Damp fricking mop. But nooo. Have to scrub with a goddamn actual fricking scrub brush.' I was going along in this intellectual vein when I heard the back door open and shut. I was more wary nowadays, and I sat back on my heels and listened. There was a long mudroom between the back door and the kitchen, lined with closets and cubbies and storage for extra kitchen stuff that wasn't used too often. I heard feet stamping off snow, heard the rustle of coats.

And voices. A male and a female. Who?

Slowly and silently I stood up and took one of the long kitchen knives off the magnetic strip on the wall. It was a carver, a good twelve inches long and wicked sharp.

It wouldn't help if someone used magick on me, but it made me feel better. I crouched down again, slipped the knife under the lower shelf of the kitchen island, and listened.

I closed my eyes and let out my breath very slowly. My breath became slower and shallower. My hearing seemed to expand to fill the space.

'You can!' I heard a woman say. Her voice was full of emotion.

'No,' said the man.

'You can!' the woman said again. It came to me then, the knowledge, as if it were a scent carried on the air. It was Nell. And Reyn. She wanted something from him, wanted him to do something; he was saying no with stolid coldness. But he was torn, he was unsure. She could sense that, was pressing home her advantage.

I listened, head cocked like in movies. They were wrapped up in each other. This was about the two of them, not about any third party, such as yours grimly. As far as I could tell, she wasn't begging him to kill me.

Their voices hushed, but I could feel her longing, her pleading that was trying not to be pleading. She was close to the breaking point.

I am nothing if not sensitive. And who among us has not had a tortured, whispered conversation with an unrequited love that they didn't want someone to overhear?

I opened my eyes, dipped my scrub brush in the bucket

of soapy water, and tried to give a subtle, face-saving alert that someone was nearby.

'Swi-innng looow, sweeet chaaaar-i-ottttt,' I wailed, scrubbing my little black heart out. 'Comin' for to car-ry me hoooome . . .'

Silence.

'Swi-iiing looow,' I began again, and then Nell appeared in the doorway. Her lovely English-lass face was flushed; two high spots of fury pinkened her cheeks. She stared at me, saw what I was doing. She was dressed, adorably, in high, fur-topped boots, tight jeans, a chunky ivory sweater, and the pièce de résistance, a velvet headband.

I was in dirty jeans, a filthy, sopping-wet T-shirt (due to a little bucket-filling mishap), no makeup, with raggedy light hair streaked with sweat and tucked behind my ears. (And here's a big shout-out to River – you made me look this way!)

A mean, gratified smile twisted her face into a snarl, and I suddenly wondered again if she had been the one who'd spelled my room. I hadn't thought so; hadn't thought she was strong or knowledgeable enough. But she more than disliked me – that much now seemed obvious.

She saw the half of the floor I'd already done, and with a smirk strode quickly across it. Leaving a line of muddy, snowy boot prints across the pristine flagstones. She bashed her way through the swinging door and was gone in a cloud of some fresh, gardenlike perfume.

I sat back, looking at the stones in dismay, and then in anger. God*damn* it! I roared inside my mind. That *bitch*! First thing tomorrow, I was going to look up a spell to draw spiders to her room! Tons of 'em!

Reyn appeared in the doorway. I glared at him, jaws clenched, too angry to even think about feeling weird or wary.

'Go on,' I said tightly, gesturing at the ruined floor. 'She's already undone an hour's work. Go ahead.'

'I'm sure she didn't realize,' he said, with that faint crispness of consonants that said English wasn't his first language. Those were the first words he'd spoken directly to me in more than a week.

'Oh, no, of *course* not,' I said, dripping with sarcasm. 'I'm sure she didn't equate half a clean floor with *me*, scrubbing my ass off, on the other half! And I'm sure you *believe* that because you're a stupid, imbecilic *moron*!' My voice was rising, and I wanted to throw my brush at his head, because I couldn't throw it at Nell. After avoiding him and being avoided by him, something had broken loose in me and the words tumbled out. 'Just like you can pretend not to know that she's eating her heart out over you! It must be hard to be God's gift to women!' I went on, my mouth unfortunately working much faster than my brain. 'So gorgeous, so everyone's panting after you, *longing* for you, working things to be close to you – probably conjuring *love* spells!'

Reyn's golden-sherry eyes widened and he looked

at me more intently. I saw him weigh more measured responses, and then, to my surprise, saw him throw them all into the wind. Maybe he, too, was furious at Nell, and taking it out on me.

'Yes, just as hard as it is for *you* to be every man's fantasy!' he snapped back. 'Hair like snow, eyes like night, all tough words and soft—' He stopped abruptly, looking horrified. It was more emotion, more expression than I'd seen out of him in the more than six weeks I'd been here. I'd have to think about it later. But for now, we were locked in battle.

'Oh, yes,' I snarled. I took my wet, soapy hands, with their grimy, broken nails, the skin red from hot water and soap, and dragged them through my unwashed hair. As Reyn stared, I pulled them down over my dirt-spattered, wet T-shirt, two sizes too big. 'Who wouldn't want to get with *this*? I'm just what every guy dreams about.' For a split second, I could swear that I saw a sudden feral light in Reyn's eyes, saw actual hunger as he looked at me. I had a moment of *uh-oh*, then it was gone, and I wasn't sure I had seen it. I hardened my eyes and my voice. 'Oh, *wait* – no, I'm *not*. I'm difficult, demanding, unfaithful, prickly, and self-centered! So get out of here while you can, you *idiot*!' I was practically shouting now, and I hoped no one would come to investigate.

Reyn was breathing hard, and part of me wondered if he would start throwing things or come after me, but he controlled his temper. Face stiff, he walked carefully across the washed flagstones in his socks, one hand holding his boots, and pushed through the door without a word or a glance back.

I was practically shaking from adrenaline, completely unnerved. I had no idea what had just happened. I almost never got into screaming arguments with anyone – I didn't care about anything so much that it was worth screaming about. But Reyn had really, really gotten to me. And maybe I had really, really gotten to him. There was something unnamed between us, probably something bad. But I couldn't figure it out.

What I really, really *wanted* was a *drink*, a long draft of whiskey, maybe, over some cracked ice. I could practically taste it, could almost feel the fire as I swallowed it. That was what I did when I was upset. I got drunk, or whatever, went and found someone, distracted myself. So I wouldn't have to feel anything.

There was no hard liquor here that I had found. The idea of running out alone in the darkness made me feel afraid. There was no one here to distract myself with – everyone was probably already asleep, and no one wanted to distract themselves with me, anyway.

I was stuck with myself. Me, myself, and I. We were all in pain, all feeling it keenly, like an open wound.

Try not to think about it, I told myself over and over, and picked up the scrub brush again with a shaking hand.

* * *

That night I got back to my room so late that my traditional bedtime tea was long cold, with a thin film on top. I didn't drink it – just dropped my flannel shirt on the floor and fell into bed, too tired to even cry.

I had dreams that night, like I used to have. Bad dreams, dreams that were half memories. I also dreamed about things that weren't memories, things that seemed like I was looking down on them from above, watching from a distance.

I saw my crowd, Boz and Innocencio, Cicely and Katy. They were in a car, speeding down a dark, twisting highway. They were going way too fast – racing another car, one with regular people in it, teenagers, maybe. Boz was driving. Incy looked less crazy than he had, though he didn't exactly look like his old self. It was late; there was barely any moon. Both cars were taking turns so fast that they skidded out on every switchback. Boz's car was in the lead. Katy was in the front seat; Incy and Cicely were watching the other car through the back windshield. The four of them seemed grotesque to me – their so-familiar faces twisted with calculated daring. They seemed too loud, too wild, too reckless and irresponsible. Two months ago I had fit in perfectly.

This was going to end badly.

The driving was getting more and more reckless. Katy and Incy were yelling at the other car, taunting them, shooting the bird. There was a strange light in Incy's eyes that I didn't recognize. I saw the other driver's face tighten, saw his white-knuckled grip on the steering wheel. The friend next to him had given up his righteous anger for sincere fear – he was gripping the door handle and squinching back in his seat as if stomping on an imaginary brake. He spoke to his friend, but his friend ignored him, furious about Boz.

I didn't want to watch any more.

It happened toward the top of the road. Boz went screaming around a corner, skidding out so far that one of his wheels actually left the road, hanging over the cliff for a second. Incy and the girls shrieked with panicked excitement. Then Boz gunned the engine, and the front-wheel drive grabbed the road again and shot them forward.

The other car wasn't so lucky. The driver was risking everything to catch up to Boz. He knew this road well, had clearly raced here before. But he hadn't been racing it regularly in a hundred different cars over the last fifty years. He skidded out on the same turn, his back wheel left the road . . . and the car tipped backward, over the cliff. I saw their terrified eyes, their hands clenched like claws, their mouths open in screams. Then they tumbled end over end down the cliff, bouncing off a lower turn. On the next tumble, the engine hit a rock and the car exploded into flames, the ruptured gas tank spewing fiery fuel everywhere.

Far above, Boz stopped. My four friends peered over the edge of the cliff, watching the car. The girls had their hands over their mouths, their eyes lit with adrenaline. Boz and Incy looked shocked but forced nervous laughs. They had killed those boys. Boz and Incy and the others had actually killed those boys – murdered them. It made the paralyzed cabbie look like a schoolboy prank. Even in my dream, I felt a sick coldness in my stomach.

Incy turned to Boz. 'We have to find Nasty,' he said, the words not really audible to me, but clear nonetheless. 'Don't you see? She shouldn't be missing this.'

The idea of once being the Nasty who they thought shouldn't be missing that – it was sickening, repulsive.

'Okay, Incy,' said Cicely. 'Enough's enough! Let's find her.'

Boz nodded, still looking over the cliff, his face solemn. Then he looked straight ahead, it seemed directly into my eyes, as if he could see me, right then. 'Yes,' he said. 'It's time to find her.'

I bolted upright, gasping, and flicked my light on. I was alone in my room. I was in West Lowing. If that had been another vision, then it showed that they still didn't know where I was. But I had recognized those hills, that twisting road.

Boz and Incy and the girls were in California. They'd come to America.

Chapter 24

I could feel Solis's barely concealed impatience.

Which only made it worse, of course.

I tried again. Releasing a breath all the way out. Trying to calm my mind, to empty it of thoughts. To achieve a perfect, centered stillness – which was about as foreign to my life as growing wings and flying. When I felt ready, I looked once again into the large, flat bowl of water. Breathe in, breathe out.

'What is water?' Solis's voice was so quiet I could barely hear it.

I remembered his words and murmured, 'Water is life and death, light and dark, hard and soft. Water is past and present and future. It is liquid and solid and gas. It is gentle as rain and terrible in its force. It is all knowing; it holds the deepest secrets.' I breathed in and out, trying to move as little as possible. 'Water, reveal my truths to me.'

I waited. This was my third attempt. Scrying with water is, supposedly, easier than other methods of scrying, but it's still a skill. And I needed to master it. And I kept screwing up.

I waited, watching the still surface of the water. So far what I had seen was: Water. A wet bowl. I was kneeling and my feet were freezing and falling asleep. I was hungry. I realized my brain wasn't empty and my thoughts weren't still. And of course, there were so many things I didn't want to see. Solis was gonna kill me.

Suddenly I blinked. Shimmery images were forming in the bowl, as if reflected in a mirror. 'There's a picture in the water,' I whispered without moving my lips. Solis said nothing. I kept watching, focused now on this spell. The image shivered and resolved itself: It was me, looking happy, holding a baby I didn't recognize. I looked unnaturally normal, like a regular person. The image fogged up and faded, then changed. I drew back, my breaths shallow: It was a castle burning. Then I had a split-second image of someone dead, a girl, lying on a cold stone floor, her dark eyes open and unseeing, her fair hair soaked in blood. I could see the big empty space between her head and her neck, the dark pool of blood spreading out around her.

No, no, my mind shrieked. Time rewound more, and suddenly I was back in that night, that night of terror when my mother had woken us and gathered us in my father's study. We heard the raiders trying to break down the door with a battering ram. We smelled the smoke from the bailey, where they'd set fire to our servants' homes, to the stables. Animals were screaming in panic; men were shouting.

My mother was holding her amulet and singing. I'd never heard this song. I always loved it when she sang. She sang on the spring equinox, to welcome the earth's fertility in the coming months. She sang on the solstices, praising the balance of the wheel of the year. She sang over our villagers if they were injured or having trouble in childbirth. But this song was different – there was a thread of blackness in it, like a pulsing umbilical cord, and the thread thickened and grew. The blackness was all around us. The five of us watched her, our eyes wide. Sigmundur and Tinna looked solemn, but not shocked. The three of us younger ones were slack-jawed.

The main castle door crashed open below us. Acrid smoke seeped in through the arrow slits and burned our noses. My mother's voice was now haunting and terrible, huge and dark and powerful. The light in the room seemed to dim, and it was hard to breathe, hard to see anything else except my mother's face, drawn white, suddenly scary, almost unrecognizable.

They started trying to break down the study door. The door was two inches thick; the lock was forged iron. The beam across the door was another three inches thick.

My mother paused for just a moment and focused her gaze on my older brother. 'Remember, Sigmundur,' she said, and her voice didn't even sound like her. I was frightened, clinging to Eydís and crying, and Háakon was clinging to me and trying not to cry because he was a big seven-year-old boy. 'Remember what I told you, yes?'

My brother nodded grimly, both hands holding his sword. 'I will, Móðir,' he said.

The room shook with the crash of the battering ram at the door. Delicate glass globes fell off the stone mantel above the fireplace. The room's one torch was flickering; the fire in the hearth was dancing crazily.

Two things happened at once.

I saw the scene from a shorter height, the height of a ten-year-old. I felt the linen of Eydís's nightgown ripping under my hysterical grip. I was the daughter of Úlfur, the wolf, and I should be strong and brave. But my sword had dropped out of my numb hands, and all I could do was watch my mother.

The fire in the hearth leaped, then spit out toward the room, showering sparks onto the hearth rug. Something as big as a cabbage fell down the chimney, bounced on the fire, then rolled out into the room.

It was my father's head, cut off at the neck, with eyes and mouth partially open, still bloody.

The high-pitched sound that filled my ears was my own screaming.

At the same moment, the door finally burst in, the wood shattering, iron rivets popping. Two men stormed through, tall, broad, wearing chain mail, their faces painted in primitive streaks of black, white, and blue. One of them roared and raised his axe. My mother shouted harsh words, words that made me cringe, that hurt my ears to hear them, words of blackness and power and fury. She snapped her hands open at the man, and suddenly the room was sprayed with rings of metal chain mail and blood.

The other man stood thunderstruck, staring at his companion, who reeled a bit, dazed, looking down at his body of bloody meat. My mother had flayed him alive, with magick, and he had no skin, no hair, no clothes. Just round, bulging eyes and a muscled skeleton's head. He dropped forward onto his face, and my brother Sigmundur shouted a battle cry and leaped forward, swinging his sword. He lopped off the man's head with one blow, then kicked the head across the room.

I was going to faint. I peeled away from Eydís and Háakon and ran to my mother, standing behind her, grabbing on to her skirts. Out in the hall, other raiders were shouting, breaking things, setting fire to our home.

The other man bellowed, staring at my mother, and raised his heavy longsword.

Gasping, I jumped back, swallowing convulsively, my foot accidentally knocking into the scrying bowl. I was here again, the gray winter light slanting through the window. I looked around wildly, seeing Solis's face, the classroom, the bare treetops out the window. My stomach clenched and roiled. I was gulping breaths, fighting the tunnel vision that came before a faint. The spilled water seeped up the leg of my jeans and I clawed at my eyes as if to erase what they had seen.

'Nastasya, what's wrong?' Solis cried.

On my hands and knees I threw up, hitting the scrying bowl. I heard myself howling as if from a distance. Solis put a cool hand on me, but I shoved it away and clambered gracelessly to my feet. I was weaving, unable to walk straight, sick with nausea and horror. Somehow I staggered to the door, flung it open, and threw myself down the hall. I raced out into the cold afternoon air, not knowing where my jacket was, scarcely knowing where I was.

Way across the field, a tall, thick hedge of holly stretched, separating the field from the goat pen. I ran to it, going around the back, out of sight. I was breathless but still keening, my heart pounding in my ears like a drum. There my legs gave way and I dropped to my knees on the cold ground. I was shaking. I would never be warm again. Squeezing my eyes shut, I tried to unsee the images, as I had tried so many times before. They were burned into my memory — not just the pictures but the sharp crackling of fire popping in my ears, the coppery smell of blood, the awful smell of wool rugs burning, the shouting of men's voices, the screaming of servants. My father's sightless eyes. A man made of bloody meat.

I huddled next to the hedge, my fingers scrabbling in the dirt, drenched in such raw, burning pain that I felt as though I'd go crazy. My throat closed abruptly, my nose started running, my eyes burned, and suddenly I was wailing, tears flowing down my face, crying now as I had been unable to cry then. I felt I'd never be able to stop.

I don't know how long I was there. At some point I crumpled sideways and lay curled on my side, sobbing, my face wet and cold where the wind chilled my tears. I kept my eyes wide open so I wouldn't see anything but leaves and sky, the occasional hawk wheeling overhead, the heavy clouds moving in from the southwest. I sucked in heavy, painful breaths, wondering how I had gotten from that time to here, how I had survived, not just physically but emotionally.

I had turned off my emotions. Not all at once, not overnight, but slowly, over a matter of decades. By the time I was fifty, I was a hard shell.

Gradually my sobbing lessened, turned to quivering gasps.

Eventually I heard voices, and then two dark figures walked toward me.

'She's here,' one called, and they came quickly.

River knelt on the ground near me and pushed my hair away from my face.

'My poor child,' she said. 'My darling. I'm so sorry. Please come now – come in and get warm.'

Slowly my eyes shifted sideways to rest on her face. Could she know? She couldn't possibly know. No one could know. I was the only person alive who knew.

'Nastasya. You're *here* now; you're not there. Do you understand?' River looked intently into my eyes. She drew a soft white handkerchief from her pocket and dried my face.

Solis knelt also and draped my coat over me. The immediate warmth was shocking. They waited patiently, kneeling in the cold grass, River holding my hand, which felt like ice. I wanted to lie here forever, letting leaves cover me, being slowly buried by time. Then, I don't know why, I pictured Reyn, the Reyn of today, standing over me, the chilly wind tousling his hair as he frowned down, arms crossed.

Slowly, every breath painful, I sat up, then stood up on shaky legs. The adrenaline had leached out of my blood, leaving me exhausted and empty. River and Solis helped me push my arms into my coat, as if I were a child. I felt a thousand years old.

'My dear,' said River, stroking my hair. 'I can only imagine.'

'You can't,' I managed to croak.

'Nastasya,' said Solis sympathetically, 'I'm afraid no one gets to be our ages unscathed. Each of us here has a horrific story, or two, or five, or twenty. Each of us here has hit rock bottom in some way, endured the unendurable, seen things that no human should ever see. And we keep the memories forever, for centuries. You're not alone, and you're not the darkest aefrelyffen on the planet.'

His words trickled into my ears, into my brain.

'And how much worse it is for the people who actually

committed such atrocities,' River said, sounding almost distant, off in her own thoughts. 'As bad as it is to be a victim – and believe me, I know how bad it can be – the inescapable truth is that it's even worse to be the perpetrator. To have to live with that . . .' Her voice trailed off as my mind whirled.

We walked back to the house, the sun behind us snuffing out quickly. Inside, it smelled like cooking food and floor wax and the evergreen boughs that had been cut for Yule decorations. I wanted to lie down on my hard bed and never get up.

River and Solis walked me to my room and stood as I opened my door and went inside.

'Do come eat something,' said River, in her lovely, melodic voice. 'Or shall I bring you up a tray?'

I stared blankly at her as if she was speaking nonsense.

'I'll bring a tray,' she decided, and they left me, silently closing my door.

No one knows, I told myself again. I never had to tell anyone, and no one would ever know. I was the only person alive who had seen that, seen my mother and my brother kill a man, seen my father's head roll across the floor. I was the only person alive who knew that I was the last survivor of my father's house, that his magick was buried somewhere deep in me. As long as no one knew, no one would come after me, no one would try to take my power from me by force. It was my secret.

Chapter 25

Somehow I kept on with the daily rhythm of my new life. My chores gave me purpose and structure – I knew where I had to be and what I had to be doing at any given time. I could perform all my duties without much thought: Sweeping leaves off the porches, cleaning the stove, gathering firewood, sowing winter rye in the kitchen garden. I moved mechanically, and people seemed extra kind to me, except Nell and Reyn, who both avoided me.

'My mother had been sold three times before my father bought her,' Brynne said one day while we were beating rugs outside. We both wore scarves tied over our mouths; the fine, silty dust powdered the air all around us. Her voice was muffled, but I heard her. 'They split her apart from other children she'd had, not immortals. Some of them she never found, and one she found only when the child was very old and about to die.'

I took the story in.

'But now she's . . . content,' Brynne went on, looking off in the distance. 'Still in love with my dad. Loving

~ 289 ~

everything she does. Loving all of us so much. She really enjoys it, being an immortal.'

Everyone had stories, both horrific and beautiful. Each story was taken out, examined, told, and then put away. They were things that had happened; they weren't happening now.

As my brain began to wrap around all of these weighty concepts, my daily life got a few rocks in it. I forgot to move the sodden quilts and blankets from the washers into the dryers, so they got mildewy. I had to wash those suckers three more times, because the expensive, ecologically sound detergent that River bought worked like crap. I mean, the invention of bleach was a step forward for mankind, you know? It would have worked *immediately*. It was such a relief to be irritated and swearing about that, instead of roiling in misery over something else.

The next day, I was in one of the pantries, knee-deep in glass containers, tidying and dusting and trying to focus on being in the *now*, since as we've all seen, being in the past was clearly a freaking nightmare. Through a crack in the pantry door I saw Reyn and Nell, both washing the simple iron chandelier that hung over the dining table. Nell said something, and the side of Reyn's mouth quirked in a half smile, their earlier tension forgotten, forgiven. It made my heart burn.

We had turnips at three dinners in a row.

The devil-hen pecked my hand again, drawing blood. I almost throttled her.

Solis gently asked me to try scrying again. I guessed he was from the 'get back up on that horse' school of thought. Being from the 'hell no' school of thought, I said hell no. He assigned me extra chores.

After the floor-muddying incident with Nell, she avoided me, but pretty skillfully – I doubted anyone else noticed. But she did little things: My coat pockets were full of dirt, my boots soaked in water, my food covered with salt. I didn't see her do any of this, and some of it would be so hard to pull off that she must have done it with magick. But I knew it was her – her tiny, superior smile and knowing glance said as much. I wanted to throttle both her and the hen. Together. Maybe beat her *with* the hen.

My sleep was heavy and dreamless, thanks to River's nightly tea.

One night I was out cold, and someone grabbed my shoulder, shaking hard. I was awake in an instant, bolting upright and opening my mouth to scream – when Reyn said, 'Quiet! Don't wake anyone else!'

I grabbed his hand with both of mine and tried to bite it.

'Stop that!' he said, sounding annoyed and not, say, filled with battle-stoked bloodlust. I looked from him to the door, and realized that I had completely forgotten to do my lock-door spell. This was maybe the second or third time I'd forgotten. I was an idiot.

Pushing his hand away, I shrank back, remembering

the dark spells in my room, my memory of the raider, the feelings of someone being after me, someone hating me – but then I thought that if he'd wanted to hurt me, he would have done it while I was still sleeping, and not woken me up for it.

'What do you want?' I said, trying to sound strong and angry.

'You're on the board for haying the horses.' His voice was low.

I stared at him. 'So?'

'You didn't do it,' Reyn said.

The door to my room was still open – could I make it past him and out the door if I needed to? Probably not. What in the world was he doing?

'I guess I forgot,' I said. 'Solis assigned me extra chores. I'll do it in the morning.'

'You should have done it after dinner,' he pressed.

'Okay, Mr Chore Monitor.' I actually was angry now, and it was superseding any fear. 'I'll do it tomorrow. Get out.'

'You'll do it now,' he bit out. 'I have to feed and muck the horses at dawn, and the hay has to be down there, waiting. I'm not going to throw the hay down – doing your job as well as mine. Get up now and do it.'

He couldn't be serious. After everything I'd been through, he was harassing me in the middle of the night over a chore? Coming into my *room* for this? I mumbled something that started with 'fuh' and ended with 'ou.'

His eyes flared and he stood there, hands clenched. 'Get up now.'

'What the hell is the matter with you?' I snapped. 'Get out of here! I'll do it tomorrow!'

'You'll be milking tomorrow at dawn,' he said. 'Are you going to get up an hour earlier to do the hay?'

I stared at him with loathing. 'To hell with the hay! You do the effing hay! Now get out of my room, asshole!' He hadn't looked at me or talked to me in more than a week, and now he was in my *room*, yelling at me in the middle of the night? Had he had a total breakdown?

To my complete shock, he actually grabbed one of my ankles to literally pull me out of bed. Naturally, I kicked him hard with my other foot, catching him squarely in his broad, rock-hard chest and making him stagger back against my small wardrobe.

'What in the world is going on here?'

Our heads swiveled to see River standing in the doorway, tying the belt on her red flannel robe.

This scene suddenly seemed ridiculous.

'She didn't hay the horses,' Reyn said, trying to control his anger. 'I don't want to do her job for her tomorrow morning. I was trying to get her to do it now.'

River looked at him in astonishment, and it was then that recognition seemed to filter into his brain. He'd been literally trying to pull me out of bed to go do a chore. It was probably the weirdest and most out-of-character thing he'd ever done at River's Edge. He stared down at the floor, seeming surprised to find himself here. I just shook my head at River, holding my hands out. I had no explanation.

River looked at me.

'I was supposed to hay the horses,' I admitted. 'Solis gave it to me extra. I forgot. I thought I could do it tomorrow. But Reyn had a brain attack and it somehow made sense to him to actually come drag me out of bed. In the middle of the night. In my own private room.'

A muscle twitched in Reyn's cheek, and color flushed his face.

River looked back at him, a wrinkle between her brows, as if there were a puzzle here she was trying to figure out.

'Did you kick him?' she asked me.

'He was trying to *yank me out of bed*,' I pointed out.

'She refused to get up!' Reyn said.

'Did you call him an asshole?' She seemed more bemused than anything. Reyn was practically hyperventilating.

'Well, he was being . . . an asshole,' I said lamely.

'Hmm.' River looked from me to Reyn and back. Then she nodded, as if she'd made a decision. 'Both of you go now and hay the horses,' she said, in a tone that would not entertain any pleading for leniency.

'Me?' Reyn asked, incredulous.

'It seems very important to you,' River said solemnly.

'Right now?' I said.

'Right now,' she told me. I opened my mouth to argue,

but she just looked back at me steadily until I shut it. For once. Giving us one last look, she shook her head and headed back down the hall.

I glared at Reyn with narrow-eyed disgust, all fear gone. He stalked out of my room as I got out of bed and grabbed yesterday's jeans from a chair, and a couple of sweaters. Of course it was bone-chillingly cold at this hour of the night.

This just did not make sense.

I swore all the way to the barn, inhaling frigid air that burned my nose and mouth, hurrying as if the night were full of wraiths that could reach out, snatch me up, and pull me into their shadows. Inside the building, the air was full of the warm scent of horses and hay. It's a smell you never forget, once you know it. The very dim night lighting was on, and I had to pause a second in the darkness to get my bearings.

Whump! I shrieked as a dark shape fell heavily to the ground in front of me, scraping my face. I stumbled back, hand to cheek, my brain frantically registering that it had been a bale of hay, 130 pounds of it.

A silhouette leaned over the hayloft above.

'You tried to kill me!' I said, stunned, feeling the warm stickiness of blood on my cheek. Was that what this was about? Had he lured me out here to—

'No, I didn't!' Reyn said. 'I didn't know you were there.' Pause. 'Are you hurt?'

'You tried to kill me!' It wouldn't be the farthest-fetched thing that had happened lately.

'Of course I didn't try to kill you,' he said testily. 'I had no idea you were there. I was sure you'd dawdle for another twenty minutes. I repeat, did I hurt you, yes or no?'

'Yes!' I snapped. 'You threw that thing right down on top of me!'

'If it were on top of you, you wouldn't be standing there carping at me,' he pointed out.

This was the smaller barn, where River's six horses lived. Plus the mower and some other garden tools and supplies were kept in one corner. The bales of hay were loaded up into the loft by a winch on the outside of the building, and then one threw the bales down into the alley between the stalls, if it was one's turn to hay the horses. Usually the bales broke apart when they landed, making the hay easier to fork into the feed racks.

Horses *whoof*ed gently into the dim quiet as I stomped past their stalls to the ladderlike steps at the end of the barn. Some of them were dozing, so I stomped more quietly. Reluctantly I climbed up into the loft where Reyn waited, a small, battery-operated Coleman lamp hanging on a nail nearby.

'I've already gotten three down,' he said. 'You can do the rest.' He looked tall and powerful in the half light, and he still sounded angry. I didn't want to get close to him, but then being such a wuss felt unbearable and I strode forward as if he were nobody. He and I had rubbed each other the wrong way since the first moment we'd met, and the fact that he was my ideal of a perfect man only pissed me off more. And *I*'d suddenly looked familiar to *him*, with my light hair? How? Why?

Bravely, trying to channel Wonder Woman, I shrugged out of my coat and a sweater and tossed them onto a pile of bales. I still wore my long underwear top, one sweater, and of course a scarf wrapped around my neck. Ever since I'd overheard someone's thoughts during meditation – about someone kissing someone's neck – I'd had dangerous thoughts about Reyn kissing mine. When I wasn't furious or disgusted with him.

Anyway, the air up here was warm and almost sickly sweet with the scent of timothy hay – the good stuff. Hay dust tickled my nose and I rubbed my hand across it.

'Fine,' I said shortly. 'You go down and start putting it in the racks.' It was fun, giving him orders. I wanted to do a lot more of it.

He took a breath as if to start arguing with me, then pushed the lamp so it shone more on my face. Frowning, he took my chin in his hand and turned my cheek to the light. I flinched away from his touch, but he held my chin firmly.

'I did this with that bale?' he asked.

'No. I was attacked by a rogue bale waiting outside,' I said snidely, pulling away from him and *focusing* on the work cut out for me *now*. No doubt Reyn had lifted the 130-pound bales with one pinky and chucked them over, but not all of us were muscle-bound freaks of nature.

'I . . . apologize,' he said gruffly. 'I really didn't know you were there. I wouldn't have tried to deliberately hit you with a bale.' He hesitated. 'Probably,' he admitted.

I was taken aback by his apology, and shrugged one shoulder. My cheek stung, but it wasn't actually dripping blood. 'Whatever. Okay, so I should throw down another three bales?'

'Do you want to go downstairs and wash it off?' he said, sounding like having to be concerned was totally galling.

'Oh, like you care,' I said. 'You can't stand me. You can't even look at me. No. I want to do this and go back to bed.' I leaned over, wrapped my fingers around the thin twine holding a bale together, and tried to shove it toward the edge of the loft. I shifted it about an inch. Less than an inch. It weighed more than I did.

Reyn hadn't moved, and I looked up, hating for him to see me struggle.

'What?' I scowled at him.

He looked down and made a curt gesture toward his own cheek, as if to say again that he was sorry.

I scowled more. The scent of the hay and the horses, the quiet of the barn – it was all too reminiscent of past times. I hated being here. 'Forget it. I'm sure it only enhances my natural gamine charms. Now could you get out of my way, you big oaf?' I bent over the bale again, ready to give it a good shove.

His eyes, darkened to the color of whiskey in the dim

light, narrowed. Before I knew what was happening, he'd put out his foot and pushed me gently off balance. I fell over, landing clumsily on my butt, my mouth open in astonishment.

'What the hell is the *matter* with you?' I stared up at him from where I sprawled, and it occurred to me that maybe I should feel afraid, after all.

'I don't – want you here,' he said, looking angry and upset and confused. He turned to glare at me. 'Why did you have to come here?'

I didn't even know what to say. He wasn't the only immortal who needed rehab. I wondered not for the first time what he was being rehabbed from. He leaned over as if to help me up, and I flinched and put out my hand to ward him off. Moving with quick intent, he grabbed my hand and pushed it down, following it, and as I sucked in a shocked breath, he pressed me down into the hay, his body on top of mine, and kissed me.

I couldn't react, couldn't think. I'd had a thousand fantasies about having him at my mercy, had pointlessly lusted after him since the first moment I saw him, but I had never, ever expected to actually be with him.

Now he was kissing me, not in a scary way, not with hostility, but with warm, seductive intent. In a hayloft, in the barn, in the middle of the night. This scene brought to you by the letters *W*, *T*, and *F*.

He pulled back, his eyes glittering, and looked down into my stunned face. His dark blond hair fell across his forehead, and the high planes of his cheekbones were flushed. Right then, putting all of my hysterical neuroses aside, he was hotter than I'd believed any guy could ever be, and me stone-cold sober. I stared up at him, seeing that he was breathing harder, his lips tinged with color. Softly, as if giving me time to protest, he kissed my scraped cheek, making it sting. Still I stared up at him, struck dumb by the situation, by the humiliating realization that despite *everything*, I actually did want him, more than I'd ever wanted anyone in my entire loooong life. Winding a handful of my hair in his fist, he held my head in place and leaned down again. 'Kiss me,' he said, looking at my mouth. 'Kiss me.'

My nerves began to waken, from my feet up my body to my chest and my arms and my face. He dropped his head again, his mouth hard on mine, and slowly, as the impossibility of all this filtered into my brain, I began to kiss him back.

It had been months since I'd kissed anyone – and I barely remembered that guy in the warehouse in London. I couldn't recall the last time I'd been wide-awake and sober, kissing someone *on purpose*. I mean, really couldn't remember. Years? Decades? It was . . . lovely. I couldn't believe that this was Reyn. *Reyn*, with everything between us. My breath came faster.

Reyn wedged his leg between my knees, and I felt all of him pressed against me, a warm weight that felt completely new and unique. His other hand went to my waist and slid up my side under my sweater, as if gauging the span of my ribcage. He pulled back for a second, looked into my eyes, and then our mouths met equally, my arms around his neck, one leg curving around his.

This felt . . . incredibly, incredibly good. His weight, the scent of his skin, the feel of his hair in my fingers, his mouth on mine, our breaths coming together . . . it was the most astonishingly good feeling I'd had in I don't know how long. I felt a sharp burst of – happiness? – explode in my chest, and I pressed myself closer to him, feeling how our bodies fit together. My fingers reached up to where his shirt's buttons started, the smooth, tan skin of his chest. His skin felt like it was on fire.

Oh, if he were mine . . .

I squeezed my eyes shut and quit thinking, just let go and felt thrilled and giddy and almost – yes. I was happy.

He dragged his mouth away from mine and moved down to kiss my neck, under my jaw. 'You're beautiful,' he murmured while my head spun. 'You are beautiful.'

I looked into his slanted golden-sherry eyes. 'You don't like me.'

'I like you too much,' he said raggedly. 'I want you too much. I've tried to stay away.' He kissed my mouth again as those words swirled around my bemused brain. These moments were wiping out any memory I'd ever had of anyone else, four hundred years of faces and kisses. It all felt breathtakingly new and important, as if I really were a teenager all over again. He was everything I wanted, everything I'd ever wanted, everything I would ever want. My idea of the best man possible, the only man I wanted to be with. And as I watched, our breaths coming fast in the barn's quiet, my mouth half curved into a smile, I saw cold knowledge cross his face, saw it enter his eyes and extinguish the flame there.

No, no . . .

He blinked, as if waking from a dream, and a sharp dread pressed on my chest and curled in my stomach. He looked at the strands of my hair, caught in his fingers, and looked down into my eyes as if seeing me for the first time. My arms tightened around him even as his eyes widened and he pushed himself off me. *No, no, no – come back, come back . . .*

'Your eyes. Your hair. You've *grown up*.' Looking shocked, he stood quickly, whacking his head hard on the low sloping roof of the barn. He spit out a word I didn't recognize but was no doubt some translation of 'shit!'

'Yeah, of course,' I said. I swallowed, my arms feeling aching and empty, my body cold where he'd left me.

'You . . . you're . . .' he said, almost to himself. He looked horrified, appalled, staring at me, his hand over his hard, beautiful mouth. And right then, with the small lamp casting him in a silhouette, with the smells of the barn and the horses, the dark cold night, I had a horrible realization.

I froze, one memory shooting across my brain, then another. Oh, Jesus, oh my God, oh no . . .

He looked haunted, desperate. 'You're of the House of Úlfur.' His voice came out in a whisper, and my heart slammed to a halt against my ribs, my breath seizing in my throat. 'That hair, those eyes . . . your power. You're a survivor of the House of Úlfur. The only survivor.'

My throat closed. My eyes were locked on him as the blood drained from my face. I couldn't breathe. Everything around me faded except his face, outlined by the lamp.

'And . . . you're the winter raider.' My voice was cracked and thin, barely audible. 'The Butcher of Winter.'

Reyn staggered backward, putting out a hand to catch himself before he fell over the side of the hayloft. He looked green and sick, even in the pale light, and I heard him drawing in rough, shallow breaths.

I had been *kissing* him. Kissing *him*.

'You're not two hundred sixty-seven,' I said slowly. 'You're older than I am. Maybe five hundred? Six hundred? You came down from the north, over and over, every couple of years in the winter, and raided. You killed whole villages. You raped my neighbors. You almost raped me. You almost killed my *son*. You stole horses and cows and anything of value. You left behind people with nothing, people who then starved to death. The ones you didn't kill outright.'

Everything in me was shrieking, screaming, freaking, but my voice still came out, and some part of my mind kept clicking pieces together, bits of memory, snatches of rumor, pictures and sounds and scents. The barn seemed to fill with the blackness of my memories. I sat up, pushing my back against the hay bales.

'You're not Dutch.' I gave a short laugh. 'You're Icelandic and Viking and Mongol. I suffered under your hands at least four different times, all over Noregr and Svipjoi and Ìsland. Finally I escaped you – I moved down to Hesse in 1627. Even there I heard horror stories of what you were doing up north.'

Reyn looked like he wasn't even seeing me or anything around us.

And then I felt very powerful, coldly certain, and stood up, facing him. 'Right now I'm imagining you with your face painted. White, black, and blue.'

He made a choking sound, seeming ill.

'That was you, wasn't it? You who killed my whole family? You who destroyed my father's village? It was your horde who destroyed the house at Tarko-Sale, you who then came west, to Iceland.'

His head lifted, his eyes wild. 'Your mother skinned my brother alive. Your brother cut his head off. I was in the hall. I saw it.'

'Then who was it who killed everyone else? Who cut off *my* little brother's *head*?' My voice was rising as my outrage grew.

'My father.' It came out as a whisper.

'Where's your father now?' I felt like I could snap my

hand open and fling a fireball at him. I felt like a scary, powerful witch, ready to exact justice.

'Dead. He tried to use your mother's tarak-sin, the amulet. He wasn't strong enough. The spell went wrong, and he was consumed by a storm of fire, of lightning. There was naught but ashes left. Him, my two other brothers, seven of his men. They were . . . ashes.'

'What about you? Why didn't it consume you?'

Reyn shook his head. 'I don't know. It did this.' He pulled open his flannel shirt and ripped down the neck of his T-shirt. There, on the smooth golden skin of his chest, was a burn. Exactly like mine.

Chapter 26

A storm broke loose inside me. If I weren't so ignorant of magick, I would have skinned *him* alive with a word, flaying him to make him as bare and raw as my emotions. As it was, I had to rely on launching myself at him, taking him by surprise. My body hit his, hard, and we both went over the side of the hayloft, falling twelve feet below and landing heavily with an *oof* on the broken hay bales he'd tossed down.

I was flailing at him, shrieking and swearing at him in Old Icelandic, trying to claw him, punch him, smack his head. After a few moments of trying to catch his breath, Reyn easily clamped his hands around my wrists like iron vises, and then he flipped us both over, his weight pinning me to the ground.

He was murmuring things in Icelandic, the words reaching my ears being 'Sefa, calm down, stop, don't hurt yourself, shah,' words you would use on a horse or a child. I was kicking, trying to knee him, bucking with all my might, and of course he was like a rock, unmoving, holding me like a straitjacket.

'Reyn!' Solis's voice was loud and very close.

'Nastasya!' River said, bending down to be within my eyesight.

Reyn and I both went still. I stared up into his face and saw an immortal's lifetime of pain and guilt and regret and anger. I imagine he saw the same in mine.

'Both of you, stop!' said Solis. 'Reyn, get up.' He put a hand on Reyn's shoulder.

Cautiously Reyn got to his feet, letting go of my hands at the last minute and quickly stepping out of kicking distance.

River was looking at me. It occurred to me that her world had probably been pretty orderly before I got here.

She knelt down as I sat up, brushing hay off me. My emotions were too big to process, too unbelievable to face. Four hundred forty-nine years of avoidance had just exploded inside my head.

'I know who she is,' said Reyn. His chest was heaving, the burn covered up.

'I know who *he* is!' I said, scrambling to my feet.

'So,' said River, looking back and forth at us. 'Now you know.'

My head spun and I looked at her calm face. 'Do you know who he *is*?' I pointed an accusing finger.

'Yes,' said River. 'And wc know who you are, too.'

I couldn't even fathom that.

'We knew it was just a matter of time before the two of you figured it out,' said Solis, not looking worried.

'He has to leave!' I knew this was stupid as soon as I said it. I was the last one to come; I would be the first to go.

'No,' said River, picking bits of hay out of my hair.

My heart broke. 'Fine. Then I'll leave! Right now.' I started crying inside. I so didn't want to leave. I would be lost if I left here.

'No,' River said more gently, brushing off my sweater. 'You would be lost if you left here.'

'My face is not that expressive,' I said automatically.

'You should both stay,' said River. 'There's no point in leaving. You'll have to deal with this sooner or later. Stay and deal with it now, with our help.'

I gaped at her. 'He's killed *thousands* of people!'

'Not thousands! And not in hundreds of years!' Reyn said. 'I've left all that behind.'

I shook my head. How did one 'leave all that behind'? It was who he was. *What* he was.

And you kissed him, said my hateful subconscious. And you loved it.

'That was then,' said River intently, holding her hand out to the side. 'This is now.' She held her other hand out wide. 'He is no longer in that time. You are no longer in that time. You are *here*, now. This is who you are *now*.' She placed a gentle hand on my chest. I felt her warmth through my sweater.

She gestured to Reyn. 'This is who *he* is *now*.'

'An asshole!' I spat.

'But not a winter raider,' River said solemnly. 'Not the Butcher of Winter.'

I didn't know what to say to that. I looked at the three of them, and with shock I realized that they felt more familiar, more *whole* to me than any of my other friends, back home. I didn't know what to do with myself. I shook my head again, suddenly exhausted, the adrenaline seeping out of my veins, leaving me shaky and empty.

'I can't deal with this. It's too much. He should be dead. I can't stay. I'm going to bed,' I said dully, and walked past them to the barn door. 'I will *never* forgive you.' This I threw over my shoulder at the winter raider.

He said nothing; none of them did. I crunched through the icy grass, through the darkness to the house by myself. Inside I left my boots at the door and plodded upstairs. I went into my room and spelled my door twice to keep anyone out. Then I climbed into bed in all my clothes and lay there dry-eyed.

'Nastasya? Time to get up.'

Blearily I blinked. Someone was knocking on my door.

'Nastasya?' It was Asher.

'Yeah?' I said. My clock said 6:15. It was pitch-dark outside.

'Time to get up,' Asher repeated. 'If you hurry, you'll have time for breakfast, after milking and before you go to work.'

He could not be serious. My mouth dropped open.

I realized he couldn't see it, so I got up, padded to the door, and opened it. Asher stood outside, looking fresh as a daisy. I let my mouth drop open again.

He smiled, then patted my shoulder. 'I hear you had a rough night. Well, the cows are waiting. I think Anne's making cinnamon rolls for breakfast.'

I just stared at him. My *entire universe* had been blown apart last night. *Hundreds* of years of pain and death had gotten laid at Reyn's feet. And I had to go milk cows?

Asher waited, his eyes calm. I remembered what I'd heard about him, that his family had been from Poland. They'd been there during World War II.

'If I see Reyn, I will kill him,' I said.

'I think Reyn got up early. He's plowing the cabbage field.' Asher scratched his beard.

I blinked. My world was surreal. But this *was* reality. However painful, however awful, this was *reality*. I put on my shoes.

Amazingly, I drove myself to work that day – the big Fish-Fest was over. I headed into MacIntyre's, actually glad to have a place to go, something to do. Old Mac and I grunted at each other and then started our days. I focused on the *now*. Stocking shelves in MacIntyre's Drugs wasn't exactly like working in a ballistics factory, where I was leaping forward and power-drilling screws into place every twelve seconds. I forced myself to pay attention, to notice what I was doing, to keep my mind firmly on every second that passed here as I emptied cartons of Ace bandages and ice packs. Now that I knew where everything was (and the shelves were now arranged logically), it took much less time to stock stuff.

I started looking around the store, grimly hanging on to what I was experiencing right now. It was definitely better – cleaner, brighter, and like I said, arranged better. But let's face it, it still looked like crap. The walls were water-stained and full of old nail holes, the light fixtures were ancient, and the linoleum floor was so old that each aisle had a worn stripe in the middle.

'What are you doing?' Old Mac roared at me, making me jump. 'I don't pay you to stand around and daydream!' He stood ten feet away, bushy black eyebrows in an angry V over his hostile eyes.

'You need to order some homeopathic stuff,' I retorted. After last night, Old Mac would need to up his game considerably if he wanted to faze me. 'And, like, some mittens or something. A little stand of assorted mittens. Plus, you've got room over in that corner for some bags of salt, the stuff people put on sidewalks so they don't kill themselves.'

He stared at me as if I were speaking in tongues.

I picked up one of the thousands of drugstore-supply catalogs that came every week. 'Look at all this stuff! This is what people are buying nowadays, even people in this backwater hellhole. I had three people ask for homeopathic cold medicine this morning. And it's going to be totally snowy any day now. People need to run in to buy, like, ChapStick, and see the bags of salt right there, and think, Excellent! Gotta put one in my car.'

His mouth was slightly open, as if he didn't know how to talk to someone who wasn't cowering. 'What do you care?' he growled, finally. 'You're just passing through! This isn't your store! My great-grandfather started this store! My grandfather ran it, then my father, now me! And my son—' Suddenly his face looked devastated, horrified. Like he'd just remembered he had only a daughter. He swallowed and said, 'If I had a son, he'd run it after me.' But his fire was gone, and he looked haunted and suddenly old.

I finally got it. 'Did you used to have a son?'

Old Mac nodded, looking gray.

'And he died with your wife?'

A haunted look came over his face, and he nodded again.

'I'm sorry,' I said. 'It's hard to lose someone.' I'd lost so many people. I paused, wondering if I should go on. Yes. He had to leave the past behind and live in the now. I made my voice firm. 'But listen, old man, you've still got Meriwether.'

Old Mac's head snapped up and the usual fire entered his eyes.

'And despite the fact that you treat her like yesterday's crap, she's smart! She cares about this place, God knows why. And after you kick the bucket, she's going to make it what it should be, and make a ton of money, and laugh on your grave!'

Okay, maybe that was going a little far. Old Mac looked astounded, and I pretended to study the ingredient list of some pediatric Triaminic.

'She hates this place.' His voice was gruff and sour.

'She hates being treated like pond scum,' I retorted. 'She remembers when this place was hopping. It was her idea to start fixing it up.'

'It'll never be hopping again.' Old Mac tossed the catalog back down on the counter.

'Yeah, yeah, the mill closed, wah, wah, wah,' I said in my usual caring, sensitive way. 'There are still people here, and they still need the crap you sell. I mean, the nearest Walgreens is way out on the highway. *Or*, people could come here, support the local economy, and save gas!' It was such a brilliant new marketing angle that I couldn't believe it.

Excited, I turned to Old Mac, ready to brainstorm.

He narrowed his eyes at me. 'Forget it! Get back to work! I should dock you for the last ten minutes!'

'You know I'm riiiighhht,' I said under my breath in a singsong voice.

He grunted.

Our relationship was really blossoming. And my life was going on, despite everything. I was still here, I was still living my life, after everything that I had realized last night.

For some reason, Meriwether didn't show up at four, but Old Mac didn't seem surprised or worried. I clocked out as usual, already dreading driving back and possibly running into Reyn at home. As I headed to my car, I saw Dray loitering across the street, in front of an empty building that had once housed a Dunkin' Donuts. She saw me but didn't react. I got into my battered piece-of-crap car, started it, then swung a big U-ie and pulled up beside her. I rolled down the passenger side window.

'You want to get some coffee? My day has sucked,' I said, not even looking at her. 'Actually, the last several days have sucked.'

Dray hesitated, then came and opened the passenger door. I tried not to look triumphant. She got in and slammed the door, and I headed to a nearby diner called Auntie Lou's. I'd never been in there – had barely gotten over my Sylvia's experience – and when I walked in, it was like I'd stepped back about fifty years. Like MacIntyre's, it seemed frozen in time, though it was clean and nothing was obviously broken.

I looked at Dray. 'What is this place? The quaint town that time forgot? You guys ever hear of the wonders of modernization?'

Her darkly painted mouth quirked on one side, and we slid into a booth, the vinyl seat slick beneath my corduroys.

'Pretty much,' she said. 'But without the quaint part.'

The waitress came over, a well-scrubbed blonde who

looked about Dray's age and, in fact, seemed to recognize her. Dray gave her an appraising glance, which seemed to fluster the girl.

'Chocolate milkshake,' said Dray.

'How's the coffee here?' I asked. 'On a scale from one to ten. Be honest.'

The waitress looked surprised, then blushed. She glanced back at the cook, waiting in the kitchen, and lowered her voice. 'Don't order it,' she advised. 'I messed up and put in too many scoops of coffee. It's like sludge. Three people have sent it back.'

'Ooh – sounds like my idea of good coffee,' I said. 'Bring it on.'

'Really?'

'Yes. I desperately, desperately need some caffeine.'

The waitress – whose name tag said Kimmie (I am not making that up) – gave a brief smile and looked really pretty for a moment. 'Be right back.'

'You just spread sunshine wherever you go,' Dray said.

'That's me,' I agreed bleakly. 'I am a freaking Christmas elf.'

Dray sat sideways in the booth, her back against the wall, her feet up on the bench. She seemed even more distant than usual, looking pale and unhealthy beneath her heavy makeup.

'How come you're still in this town?' she asked.

I sighed. What a good question. Focus on the now. 'I'm trying to . . . get through a program.' Or at least I was.

Now I was just shell-shocked and didn't know where else to go.

'Like a twelve-step?'

'Yes. Only worse. My job is part of it.'

'Oh. I thought you just had a burning desire to answer people's pharmaceutical needs,' said Dray. Kimmie put down Dray's milkshake, which looked fabulous, and my cup of coffee, which also looked fabulous, in a thick, tarry sort of way.

'You don't have to drink it if you don't want to,' Kimmie whispered.

'Okay,' I whispered back. After she left, I asked, 'Does she go to your school?'

'There's only the one high school,' said Dray, taking a deep slurp of her milkshake. 'I don't go to it anymore.'

'So what do you do?' When everything in me was crying out to just curl up in a shell and pull a blanket over me, I was making myself be here, making myself interact with her. And it seemed . . . good. I was glad I was here.

Dray shrugged, her face closing. She sat up, holding her glass in both hands like a little kid.

'Do you work?' I asked.

She shrugged again, looking bored.

I thought, What Would River Do?

In the silence, the *now* retreated and Reyn burst into my mind. I'd *kissed* him. He'd kissed me. We'd made out like crazy up in the hayloft. I would have gone much farther. Except for the whole Butcher of Winter thing.

My parents. Oh, God.

'Why'd you bleach your hair?' Dray interrupted my thoughts.

It took me a moment to come back. 'I didn't. This is my natural color. I'm thinking about going red next.'

'You shouldn't,' she said, her eyes on my ragged, shoulder-length hair. 'It's a cool color. I don't even remember what color my hair is.'

'I know what that's like,' I said.

We were silent for several more minutes. I needed to get going soon. Usually I came straight home from work, but usually someone else drove me. I loved having the freedom and independence of driving my own gas-wasting self.

'Anyway,' Dray said, breaking the silence. 'There aren't any jobs around here. This place is dead.'

I snorted. 'You got that right.' I took a sip of my thick coffee, then stirred in two more sugars.

A flicker of surprise lit her eyes, as if she'd expected me to defend her hometown.

'People here – don't like me,' she said. 'They just think I'm gonna screw up like my . . . relatives.'

'People here don't like you?'

Dray nodded defiantly.

I stared at her. 'You give a crap about what some yokels from a nowhere town *think* about you?'

She blinked.

'Dray. This is just one little town. It's not the only

place to live in the world, or even in America. Or even in Massachusetts. The people here are just a few people, here on earth for just a blip on the screen. They're *nobodies*. What do you care what they think?'

'It's *every*body,' Dray said. 'Everyone at school. Everyone in town.'

'Everyone in this *one town*,' I pointed out. 'Not everyone *everywhere*. Go to California, or Mississippi, or France. No one there's ever heard of you, and more important, no one there's ever heard of the losers running the place *here*.'

Her mouth actually dropped open. Had this truly never occurred to her? Had she thought she was stuck here forever?

'Just go . . . somewhere else?' I could practically hear her brain whirring into action.

'Go *anywhere* else,' I said.

Her face closed. 'How? It takes money.'

I thought. 'Two ways. Either take whatever job you can find – go work at Home Depot. Mop floors. Go work in a funeral home – anything. And save enough for a one-way bus ticket somewhere, enough for a week's worth of food. Then get on the bus. Or—'

She waited.

'You can go be all you can be,' I said. 'Go be anyone you want to be. If you can hack the military, you get money, education, travel, and some useful skills with a rifle.'

Dray snorted a laugh. 'I only turned seventeen last month.'

'So you either have a year to work and save money, or you can get your folks to sign their permission for you to join the army,' I said, then glanced at the sky outside. 'You have options, Dray. You always have options. It's never so bad that you can't just leave town. Think about it. And now I gotta bounce. That pillow body in my bed will only fool them so long.'

Dray finished up her shake. She still looked thoughtful as I put on my Michelin Man down jacket.

'Can I drop you anywhere?' I offered.

'Nah.' She shook her head. 'I can walk. Thanks for the shake.'

'No prob. See you around.'

Dray headed off down the street, looking somewhat less forlorn than she had. I got into my car, and then she turned.

'How'd you get so smart and all?' she asked, her tone making it a possible joke, if needed.

Because I've made many thousands of stupider mistakes than you have, I thought. *I've been through much worse.*

I shrugged. 'I've been around the block a few times.'

She nodded, then turned and hunched her shoulders up into her jacket.

She was becoming important to me. Meriwether and even Old Mac were becoming important to me, after decades of having nothing be that important.

It was unusual.

It was scary.

I knew all too well how much it would hurt when I lost them.

I really didn't like it.

Chapter 27

Back at home, River, Asher, Solis, and Anne treated me incredibly normally. It was weird. I was expected to do chores. My name was on the board. Apparently all four teachers knew the whole sordid story, but none of the students seemed to treat or look at me any differently.

I saw Reyn for the first time at dinner.

He came through the kitchen door, holding a heavy tureen. My senses were exquisitely tuned to him and I examined him closely, trying to see him with long hair matted with blood, and a painted face. He saw me and his jaw tightened. My imagination pictured him standing, shocked and terrified, as a tower of lightning consumed his family and soldiers.

He and I both looked very solemn, and we deliberately didn't meet eyes again. Interestingly, when I glanced over to get some bread, I looked up and saw Nell's eyes locked on me like blue lasers. I ignored her. Reyn sat where I couldn't see him easily, and didn't say a word during dinner.

After dinner Anne stood and said, 'I'd like to work with some of you, exploring gems and crystals. Rachel?'

'Oh, I'd love to,' Rachel said.

'Charles?' Anne asked.

'Excellent, thanks,' said Charles, taking his plate to the busing table.

'Reyn?' Anne said. 'And Nastasya.'

Silence.

We each waited for the other to back out. And waited. And waaaiiiiited . . .

'Good,' said Anne. 'I'll see you all in the green room in ten minutes.'

'May I join you?' Nell sounded a little too eager. 'I've been dying to work more with gems.'

Anne hesitated a moment, then nodded. 'Yes, okay.'

Nell beamed.

Glumly I met River's eyes. She looked sympathetic, but also like she was daring me to back out. I got up and took my plate to the kitchen.

'You're not focusing.' Anne's voice was patient. Too patient.

I opened my eyes. I was in a class with someone whose family had murdered my family. Someone whose family had been killed by my family. We were in class together, trying to *bond* with stones. I was sitting as far away from Reyn as possible, and of course, Nell was stuck to him like glue. It still seemed surreal, who he was, what he had been in my life. The very memories and experiences I'd tried to block out of my mind for the last four hundred years were sitting six feet away from me, in living color. It was like confronting the monster under my bed, only amped up a thousand times. There he was: The monster. My worst nightmare was wearing a dark green plaid flannel shirt and jeans and smelled like laundry detergent and fresh autumn air.

We were sitting in a row at a long table. Anne had a black velvet bag of different stones and crystals, and we each had to close our eyes, put our hand in, and choose the one that seemed to want to be with us. Yes. That was the actual instruction. This was even more personal than the metalwork we'd done, and what stone we chose would influence how we made magick.

Charles had gone first and had chosen a tiger's eye. (Or was chosen by it.) 'Ah yes,' he said. 'Tiger's eyes are all the rage this season.' The rapidly dimming afternoon light shone on his red hair, and his green eyes glinted with humor. He wrote something in his leather-bound journal, his neat handwriting slanting to the right.

Rachel had picked out an amethyst, its deep purple color contrasting nicely with her olive skin and black hair. As usual, she didn't smile – she wasn't a smiley gal – but simply handled her stone, looking at it seriously.

'Reyn? Now you. Just set your mind free and concentrate, at the same time.' Anne held the bag open in front of him. Reyn's strong hand was almost too big to fit into the bag's narrow neck. Those same long fingers had slid under my sweater last night. And had also helped to break in my father's door so they could kill everyone in our house. My worlds, my past and present, were colliding with a horrible force, and I had to sit here, expressionless.

Moments went by. We all waited. Reyn closed his eyes, and I was able to gaze on his face without his knowing, trying to see bloodlust, trying to see desire. I looked away.

Slowly he pulled his hand out and opened it. In his palm was a dark green stone, flecked with red.

'A bloodstone,' Anne said, while I thought, How appropriate. 'And what are its qualities? Anyone?'

'It promotes . . . honesty,' said Reyn, and it occurred to me that Nell thought he was 267. She didn't know the truth about him, and I did. 'Integrity. It calms anxieties. People believe that holding a bloodstone against a wound will stop the bleeding. A long time ago, warriors wore bloodstone amulets to staunch blood in battle.' He sounded distant, thoughtful, turning the stone over and over in his hand.

'Very good,' said Anne. 'Nastasya? Your turn.' She held the bag open in front of me.

I put my hand in and felt around. Stone. Stone. Crystal. Possible stone. Crystal? Oh, who the eff knew? I just grabbed one and pulled it out – a rough emerald the size and shape of an almond.

'No, that's not it,' said Anne, quiet but definite.

I looked up at her. How could she tell?

'Close your eyes, concentrate, focus,' Anne said. 'There is a gemstone just for you. It wants to be with you. Try again.'

Feeling self-conscious, I closed my eyes and tried to clear my mind of any thoughts. Which didn't make sense – wasn't I supposed to be thinking about stones and crystals and stuff? Like, Here, stoney, stoney, stoney . . . come to mama . . .

I wanted to just take another stone out of the bag, but Anne would probably say it was the wrong one again. How did she *know*? How was *I* supposed to know? This was yet another example of the airy-fairy, witchy nonsen –

I felt vibrations. Tiny, quivering, subtle vibrations as my fingers only barely brushed over something. I touched another stone – it was cool and smooth but still, dead. My fingers drifted back, and there it was again, a stone trembling ever so slightly under my touch. Was Anne doing something? Was this a trick?

I opened my eyes and frowned at her. Her clear blue eyes were on my face, intently. Her hands, holding the velvet bag, were solid and unmoving. 'Yes?' she asked.

The stone now glowed with warmth under my touch. One side was polished and rounded; one side was broken and jagged. Its vibrations were almost imperceptible, like the beating of a hummingbird's heart. My fingers closed around it, and a surge of joy struck me like a splinter.

I pulled it out. It was about the size of a big cherry, and

seemed like . . . milky rain, solidified. It was the same as the stone in my mother's amulet. A moonstone. It was beautiful, mysterious. I loved it. And it loved me.

'Yes,' said Anne with satisfaction. 'That's it. You can feel it.'

I nodded without saying anything, kind of freaked out. I mean, I was here because I desperately wanted to believe in what they were selling, and yet part of me kept being surprised when what they were selling turned out to be true.

'Nell? Now you.'

Smiling, Nell immediately closed her eyes and put her hand into the bag. She made a couple of little 'hmm' sounds, as if to demonstrate how hard she was concentrating. I watched her, wondering what her story was. She was only in her eighties, from England, and so was born in the twenties sometime. So she'd been in her twenties during WWII. Why was she here? Why did she want Reyn so much? Wait till she found out he was a berserker, the Butcher of Winter. Would she even care?

Nell drew her hand out, holding up a marbled blue and white stone. 'Oh, it's pretty,' she said. 'And it goes with my eyes!' She held it up next to her face and batted her lashes. Charles smiled.

'Do you know what it is?' Anne asked.

'Yes, of course,' Nell said quickly. 'It's . . .'

Silence. More silence. Tick, tock . . .

'Sodalite?' I said, mostly guessing.

Nell looked at me with actual venom in the back of her eyes. 'Right, right, sodalite.'

'Yes,' said Anne. 'And what are its qualities?'

Nell paused again. I was still reeling from the lists of stones, crystals, gems, metals, oils, herbs, stars, elements, animals, plants, blah de blah blah that I'd been hit with since I came here. I had learned maybe one-half of one percent of what they wanted me to know. But Nell had been here for several years already. She had asked to be here tonight.

She smiled slightly, blushed prettily, obviously searching for an answer. She slanted her eyes at Reyn, as if hoping he would bail her out. He was turning his bloodstone over and over in his hand, not looking up. He had razed village after village. I'd seen the bodies of the people his horde had killed. His father had killed my father. My mother and brother had killed his brother. His father had killed everyone else, except me. And yet this man, sitting a few feet from me – I could still recall the way he tasted, how his weight had pressed me into the sweet-smelling hay, the feel of his warm skin beneath my fingers. Too many realities.

'Nastasya?' Anne turned to me. 'The moonstone chose you. What are its qualities?'

Nell was embarrassed and trying not to show it. I dragged my mind away from Reyn and tried to focus on the now, scrambling for every bit of moonstone lore I could recall. Um, it's smooth? Whitish? I looked at the stone in my hand. It felt heavy and warm. It was silly, how much I loved it. Had my mother felt the same way, about hers?

'It's always cut into cabochons, to display the cat's-eye,' I said slowly. 'Rather than faceted.'

'Yes. What else?'

My mind blanked on its chemical composition, or how it was formed, or even where it was from. Ceylon? Was that sapphires? Um, um . . .

'It's attracted to the moon,' I recalled, the words seeming to come to me out of nowhere. 'People believed its cat's-eye, or shiller, would wax and wane according to the moon's cycles.'

'What else?'

Crap. My mind was whirling with bits of facts and figures. I felt the stone in my hand and looked at it. *Tell me your secrets*, I thought. *Tell me why you are mine.*

'It's considered a more feminine stone than most.' I don't know where I pulled that from. 'It's used to connect and attract feminine energy – especially for dreams and intuitions.' I closed my eyes to let the thoughts settle down inside my mind. 'It's used to help balance feminine and masculine energy, and to aid in healing, especially women's ailments related to our cycles and childbirth. It aids intuition. And, um, prophecy. Like, if you're scrying, and you hold it, it will help clarify what you see.' Huh – that's interesting, I thought.

'And, um, it . . . reunites lovers who have parted in

anger.' Where the hell had I read that? I hoped it was true, and not, like, a movie quote or something. 'It protects those who travel by water. It helps clarify decision making.' Now I had no idea if I was talking about moonstone anymore. I shut up and opened my eyes.

Anne was smiling at me. 'Very good, Nastasya. Have you worked with moonstones before? It seems particularly well suited to you.'

'No. I mean, I haven't.'

'Sodalite,' said Nell, as if she couldn't bear to have the attention on me. She gave a light laugh. She was the one who should be working with moonstone, I thought – she was a thousand times more feminine than me. 'Is it – for attracting love?'

'No, not particularly,' said Anne mildly. 'Basically, it helps to clear your mind, so that you can identify your feelings. It helps clear out old patterns of anger, guilt, and fear, so that you can see your path more clearly.'

'It's grounding for people who tend to be overemotional,' said Charles helpfully.

Nell's face was becoming stiff. I kept a carefully neutral expression on, but inside I was cackling meanly.

'It cuts through clouded thinking and illusion,' Anne went on, 'to reveal truths, and to make the user more grounded and confident.'

Nell didn't say anything.

'Now, I'd like us to focus on charging our stones with our energies, our vibrations,' said Anne. 'Every crystal, stone, and gem has its own uses, its own character. Working with one can be very powerful. Working against one can be pointless at best, and dangerous at worst. So we're going to sit in a circle, bind ourselves to our stones, and see where that takes us.'

Anne got a small silver bowl and filled it with sea salt. 'Put your stones in here,' she instructed us. 'Stones retain the vibrations of energies around them, their former owners, and the residue of spells they've been used in. We'll purify them first.'

Next she drew a circle on the floor with salt, simply walking in a circle, holding a box of sea salt upside down. I guessed immortals and other magick-makers were keeping the salt industry alive and healthy. The circle was as perfect as if it had been drawn with a compass. We all went through its 'door' and sat down. I hoped we weren't going to do anything big. I felt fragile, on edge, and I really, truly, totally couldn't take any more memories or visions or reality right now. And yet part of me realized that, in fact, I'd already, and recently, seen most of the worst of it. The stuff I had suppressed for centuries – it had gotten dragged out into the sunlight. There weren't that many skeletons left in the closet. Still, I could use a break. What would happen if I simply stepped over the line of salt? Would my head explode? Would the room catch on fire? What?

I was careful to sit between Rachel and Charles, and Nell was equally careful to sit next to Reyn, bumping

Anne slightly to get the spot. I saw Anne glance at Nell. The circle was so small that our knees touched one another's.

Anne set a fat white pillar candle on the floor next to the stone bowl and murmured a few words. She seemed to snap her fingers on the candle's wick, and it sparked into flame. So cool.

'I don't need to borrow your energy for the purification – you guys can just watch,' said Anne. She closed her eyes and started chanting. The words sounded like old Gaelic to me – very fundamental and beautiful. Also kind of scary and unworldly. She gestured with her hands toward the candle flame, as though she was wafting its energy toward her face. Then she opened her hands again, spilling that energy onto the silver bowl.

I almost gasped as the salt in the bowl was licked with faint blue flames. Salt is completely nonflammable – Brynne had put out a kitchen fire with it. Yet there it was, burning, but not being consumed. After just a few minutes, Anne's chant wound down, and the salt flame flickered out. Immediately, Anne slipped her fingers into the salt and brought out Reyn's bloodstone.

'Careful,' said Anne. 'The salt is okay, but the stones are warm.'

We each got our stones back. To me, mine looked more beautiful, its colors more reflective, as if a tiny star were encased within it, glowing brightly. Hoo – listen to poetic me! Anyway, I wanted to hold it to my heart, cradle it in my hand. Like, no one has ever loved a stone the way I did this one. It was pretty . . . freakish.

'Now we'll bind our stones to us,' said Anne. She took out her own stone, a piece of jagged obsidian, half as big as her finger.

'Um – are we actually going to do a circle?' I asked unenthusiastically. I glanced around the room, wondering what I could barf in.

'Yes,' said Anne. She leaned over and quickly traced runes – maybe sigils? – on my forehead, my throat, and the backs of my hands.

Nell looked at me condescendingly – the newbie with the delicate stomach.

'I'll lead the binding,' said Anne. 'Hold your stone in your left palm, and cover it with your right palm, like this.' She showed us. 'Simply – get in touch with your power, and when you're ready, repeat the words I'm saying. Okay?'

Each circle I had attended in the last several weeks had been quite different, though their basic forms were the same. There had been the big group circle outside, the tiny, two-person circle I'd had with River, and a couple of small-group circles with classmates. Most of me still dreaded them, but a small part was now also starting to crave them – the rush of power, the beauty, the glimpses of cosmic truths that danced along the edges . . . and if the power-focusing spells held up, maybe it wouldn't be a big upchuck-fest.

'Close your eyes, hold your stones, and get in touch with your power,' said Anne.

I still didn't have a prescribed method of 'getting in touch with my power.' Mostly I just sat there, thought about things, and hoped it would show up. I listened to Anne's incredibly soothing voice, tried not to feel the acid in my stomach at the thought of Nell and Reyn together, reminded myself how – *ridiculous* wasn't a strong enough word – it was to even care about the Butcher of Winter, and felt the warm weight of my stone in my palm.

Eventually I started humming, an old tune that came to me, and I blended my humming with Anne's voice. It had a distinct melody, and the melody felt thick and dark and old, like an ancient tree root that reached down to the earth's core.

I didn't know where this stuff was coming from – all of a sudden I was a little magickal sprite, bonding with my stone, feeling my earth roots, la la la . . .

All I can do is describe the way it felt. And that was how it felt. So sue me.

Was I swaying? I felt like I might be swaying. I could no longer feel Charles's knee, or Rachel's, touching mine. No longer felt my bony ass going numb on the cold wooden floor. My stone was getting warmer and heavier, and the more I thought about it, the happier I felt. I opened my mouth now and actually sang my tune, letting it move up through the earth, through me, out into the air. It was thick and strong and filled my chest, flowing out of my mouth with ease. Without my even noticing, it had become quite beautiful and quite powerful. Now I felt like I knew it, recognized it, and with a blinding flash I suddenly saw my mother, singing the same song, performing some rite. My *mother*.

'Oh!' There was a cry and a crash, and my eyes popped open. My stone felt so heavy that my hand dropped to the ground, the moonstone hot in my palm.

I looked around and saw Nell, her eyes wide, her mouth open in an O. The silver bowl and the candle had both been knocked over. Salt spilled across the floor, mingling with the thin river of wax that flowed from the doused candle on its side.

'What happened?' Anne was concerned, looking at each of us.

'My stone!' Nell opened her hand, and I blinked as I saw the small pile of powder, white and blue. It had been crushed, pulverized. But surely sodalite was stronger than that?

'What happened?' Anne asked again.

Nell turned suddenly blazing eyes on me. 'You did it! You crushed my stone! I heard your song – it was evil! It was a black cloud, filling the room! You're evil! Dark!'

Two months ago I would have been able to shrug off an accusation like that, or even laugh about it. It would have been meaningless. Now, though . . .

'No, no I'm not,' I stammered. Inside, a small thought

whispered, *You hope.* 'I'm not,' I said more strongly. 'I wasn't doing anything with my song – just trying to bind my stone to me.' I looked down at my hand, held down by my stone. For an instant, it felt like it weighed about ten pounds, this little rock – but suddenly it lightened, and I picked my hand up easily. In my palm, my beautiful moonstone glowed, its shiller flashing.

Anne looked nonplussed. Without saying anything, she stood and dismantled the circle. She picked up the candle and the silver bowl and set them on the shelf.

Finally she turned to where we stood around, unsure of what to do. 'How do you feel?' she asked Rachel.

'Fine,' she said, shrugging in bewilderment. 'I felt like I bound my stone to me.'

She turned to Charles. 'You?'

'I feel fine, too,' said Charles. 'I definitely felt powerful magick, but I don't think it was Nastasya – and it didn't feel dark to me.'

Next Anne looked up at Reyn, who was about a head and a half taller.

'I felt powerful magick,' Reyn said slowly, not looking at me. 'It felt old. Strong. I also bound my stone to me.' He held out his bloodstone and looked at it appraisingly.

Had my song been bad? Had that been all me? Was I hopelessly dark, evil? I thought of Boz and Incy and almost winced. My cheeks burned as fear raced through my brain.

Then I remembered that River had welcomed me here.

She had said that I could learn to be – not dark. She'd said it was a choice. That I could learn to be Tähti. My chin raised.

'She crushed my stone!' Nell said, almost spitting. She held out her hand, the powdered evidence undeniable.

'Why would I do that?' I asked. 'I have my own stone!'

'That's not what you wan—' Nell began hotly, then stopped, biting her lip.

Charles and Rachel were now staring at the two of us as if this were a sordid soap opera. And of course, in a way, it was.

'Reyn, Charles, and Rachel,' said Anne mildly, 'you may go. It's getting late.'

They went out as fast as they could, Reyn glancing back over his shoulder.

I crossed my arms over my chest, holding my moonstone tightly.

Then Anne was looking at me and Nell, her hands clasped in front of her.

'Is there something here that I should know about?'

Yeah – Nell's a complete bitch.

Nell looked as if she wanted to spill her guts, and with a morbid fascination I kind of hoped she would. But with visible effort she tamped her emotions down and arranged her livid face into a more neutral, but concerned, expression. 'No – except – I haven't wanted to mention this, but I keep getting the feeling that Nastasya is jealous of me.' She gave a charming, humble smile.

'And – I thought I felt dark magick. I'm worried – her magick is unschooled, unpredictable. And really, what do we know about her? My stone got *crushed* inside my hand. I didn't do it – it was something dark. Didn't you feel it?' She gave an exaggerated shudder, actually looking around as if Death might be waiting in a corner. Because that's the kind of thing I would do – conjure Death, just to mess with someone. Sheesh.

Anne looked at her, then over at me.

'Did you crush Nell's stone?' she asked me.

I gaped. 'No! The magick I felt – it came to me, through me. I didn't take it from an outside source, like her stone. Why would I want to? All I was doing was calling on my power, trying to bind my stone to me.'

Anne nodded. 'All right. Nell, leave the powder here.' She held out a small cloth and Nell dumped the crushed stone into it. 'You may go. Nastasya, I'd like you to stay for a moment, please.'

Oh, come on, I thought. Nell gave a secretive smirk that only I could see, and I clamped my lips shut, incredibly pissed. As she hurried out the door, I realized her face was reflected in an old-fashioned candleholder on the wall. It was backed by a highly polished piece of metal, to double the reflected light. The metal acted as a mirror, and in the mirror I could see Anne watching Nell. So she had seen Nell smirk, too. Excellent. You know, I think it's important that we all pause and appreciate little moments like this that make life so much richer.

Nell made a big show of closing the door behind her, emphasizing that she was leaving and I was being asked to stay behind with a teacher.

When the door was shut I turned to Anne. 'I didn't crumble her dumb stone.' I crossed my arms over my chest. As much as I hoped I wasn't irrevocably dark, I was terrified that Anne would say I was, say I wasn't cut out to be here after all, that I should be the one to leave.

Instead she said, 'Is there any chance that Nell is the one who put the dark spells on your room?'

I was so surprised that it took me a minute to process her question. 'I don't know,' I said slowly, thinking. 'I didn't think she was powerful enough, but then, I don't really know how to judge that. And I didn't think she hated me that much. But now I'm starting to wonder.'

'Why would she hate you?' Anne's blue eyes were kind and curious.

'I actually . . . don't know,' I said awkwardly. 'If it's about anything, it's about Reyn – she's crazy about him, and he's oblivious to it. But clearly, Reyn and I will be avoiding each other – I mean, he's the devil. So if it's about Reyn, it's a waste of her time. Yet I can't deny that she does seem to be on the "hate Nastasya" bandwagon.'

'Hmm.' Anne brushed her fine dark hair off her face and looked at me.

'But I didn't crumble her rock,' I felt compelled to add. 'I haven't made magick the – old way.'

'No – I know,' she said. 'She did. Her stone essentially refused to bind with her.'

I blinked. 'Wha— It self-destructed?'

'Yes. Even though I'm pretty sure it was the right one for her,' Anne said. 'It's interesting. How did your power feel to you?'

I didn't want to brag, or gush. 'It felt . . . really good. It felt strong. It didn't feel dark to me, or scary, like something I wanted to shrink away from. I heard the words I was singing, and I thought they sounded . . . strong. Beautiful.' So much for not bragging or gushing.

'They were. They were incredibly strong. And incredibly beautiful. It's your legacy.' She looked at me again, as if she was trying to memorize my face. I started feeling anxious, and I stuck my moonstone in my pocket and headed for my coat. Outside, the night was as thick and comforting as a black mantle, and I could see snowflakes starting to drift down.

'How do you feel about your stone?'

I looked down and tried to work the stupid double zipper thing on my coat. Who would ever want to unzip their coat from the bottom *up*? Nobody! I looked up, into Anne's clear eyes. Nothing snappy or sarcastic came to me. 'I . . . love it,' I blurted, embarrassed at expressing so much. 'I love it. It's mine. It's – it's—'

'It's part of you,' she said calmly.

'Yes,' I muttered, giving up on the zipper.

'It's the perfect stone for you,' Anne said, tidying the room, getting into her own coat. 'You're going to make interesting magick with it. I'm looking forward to seeing that.'

I didn't know what to say.

'Do you remember learning the song you sang?' she asked, closing the door behind us. We walked down the hallway side by side. It was late and my eyelids were heavy, my emotions drained.

'No,' I said, holding my coat closed as we went out into the cold night air. The darkness surrounded us, lending a feeling of intimacy to our walk. Suddenly the truth started coming out of my mouth. Most unusual. 'At the time, it felt like it was just coming from, like, the ground, from the earth itself,' I said. 'I felt like I was a conduit for something that already existed and was just going through me, you know?'

'Yes,' said Anne. 'I know.'

'Then, right before Nell's stone exploded, I suddenly remembered my mother, singing the same song as she did something. I don't know what.' I'd never voluntarily mentioned anyone in my family, and braced myself for the barrage of questions.

Typically, Anne didn't do what I expected. 'It was a very ancient power, my dear,' she said. 'Very strong, as I said. You're the only person in the world who can access that line of power. It's a powerful, even frightening gift.' Her eyes shone in the night, and I held my breath, waiting for the horrible peeling off of more onion layers. I wasn't ready. Not yet.

Anne rubbed her hands together and blew on them. 'You know Reyn isn't really the devil, right?' A glimmer of a smile played around her mouth.

'No, I don't know that,' I said.

Anne laughed. 'For one thing, we don't believe in the devil. In evil, yes. It exists. We fight it every day. But the devil? No.'

'Okay, an agent of evil, then,' I acquiesced.

She took one of my hands in both of hers. 'I understand why you feel that way, Nastasya.' Her voice was serious now. 'I do. But you know, Reyn is just a man, though an immortal one. Who Reyn was, what he did — that was the culture he grew up in. Was he the only raider who ever attacked your father's castle?'

'He was the only one who got in,' I said stiffly. My heart was aching inside. I didn't want to talk about it.

'Was his horde the only army who wiped out villages?' Anne pressed gently. 'People have been conquering and enslaving each other for the whole history of mankind. In our current time, people see it, know about it, revile it. Back then — it was a part of life, like the plague, like plowing with horses, like having seven of your ten children die.'

I looked at her. 'You're making excuses for him?' My voice was cold, disbelieving.

'Not at all,' Anne said firmly. 'Not every man back then did what he did, chose his path. Many, many men wanted peace, wanted homes and families. No, Reyn was a violent, power-hungry warrior, born into a violent culture where subduing other cultures was the norm. He didn't rebel against it, didn't run away from it. He embraced it – the horror, the death, the darkness. But almost three hundred years ago, he chose a different path and left behind his weapons and his armor. He left his father's house and abdicated his leadership. His people banished him for choosing to reject darkness and death. Since then he's waged war of a different kind, within himself, against his own nature. He has tried consistently to choose good over dark, peace over violence, life over death.'

I remembered Reyn talking about how following darkness meant madness and unending pain.

'It's been a hard battle, every day of his life since then,' Anne went on. We were at the house, but standing outside, in the dark and the cold. 'He's backslid. He's made progress and lost it. He's descended into abysses and crawled back out again. But I know, and River knows, that he's a good man, beneath everything.' She looked at me thoughtfully. 'And I think you know that, too.'

My mouth dropped open – how could she possibly say that to me?

Anne clapped her hands and breathed in. 'Oh, I smell wood smoke! Nothing smells as cozy as wood smoke on a cold night, don't you agree?'

I said nothing.

Chapter 28

The next day I was on breakfast duty. I burned two pounds of bacon. One minute I was totally on top of it, turning strips like a pro, then I stopped to grab a pan of English muffins out of the oven, and when I turned back, the entire griddle was covered with blackened strips of pork. I stared at them in disbelief, and then out of the corner of my eye, I saw a flash of light brown hair bobbing under the kitchen window. I raced to the door, yanked it open, and ran out onto the kitchen steps. There was no one there. But I was sure it had been Nell, and that she had done something to the bacon. She was really starting to rattle my cage. I wanted to grab her and tell her she could have her very own berserker, that I didn't want him – but I didn't. River hadn't asked either of us to keep our histories to ourselves, but as far as I could tell Reyn hadn't told anyone I was heir to the House of Úlfur, and I hadn't told anyone he was the Butcher of Winter.

For the first time, I arrived at work at MacIntyre's Drugs five minutes late. I'd gotten a ride with Rachel, who was going to continue on to Boston. The streets were clogged with last night's snow, and the small amount of town traffic was slower than usual.

'Oh, now she strolls in!' Old Mac roared as the bell over the front door jingled. 'Glad you could join us today!'

I was *five* fricking minutes late. The best defense is a strong offense. 'You order that homeopathic stuff yet?' I demanded, heading to the back to clock in and hang up my coat.

'Get to work!' he answered.

Old Mac had gotten up on the wrong side of the bed that day. Meriwether was out of school for the winter holiday, but he kept us both hopping all morning and I barely had a chance to nod to her.

The Christmas and Hanukkah displays were already pretty picked through. I spent all morning straightening them, refilling shelves where I could. Yule was two days away – I had no idea what River had planned.

'Are you a complete *moron?*' Old Mac's overloud voice made me look up. He was a couple of aisles away, but Meriwether's quiet, desperate voice clarified who he was yelling at.

'I've told you a hundred times! Keep the medical receipts separate! Are you deliberately trying to destroy what's left of our business?'

Two local women were shopping in the recently expanded cosmetics section, and now they looked up, frowning.

Meriwether mumbled something I couldn't hear.

'I don't care what you thought!' Old Mac bellowed. 'I don't pay you to think! I'll do the thinking! You just do what I tell you!'

The women, lips pursed, put down their purchases and left the store with stiff backs and disapproving glances. I was sure Meriwether had seen them – she must be writhing with embarrassment.

'Just because I let you move some stock, don't get fancy ideas!' he ranted.

I stood up, hands clenched. Old Mac was always bad, but usually not this outright cruel, targeting Meriwether so directly.

'Dad—' I heard her soft voice, knew she was on the edge of tears. I thought about how often her dad yelled at her, about what her life must be like at home.

My hands started moving in the air, and words slipped from my lips, almost without my realizing it. All I thought was, he'd never bully her again.

'*Gib nat hathor*,' I whispered. '*Minn erlach nat haben . . .*'

The aisle mirror showed the store empty except for Old Mac waving his hands under Meriwether's nose. Then I caught sight of myself, my white-blonde hair, my dark eyes, burning patches of anger on my cheeks, my hands tracing sigils in the air. I was making a spell, making magick. How? Where had this come from, this knowledge? I had a split-second memory of Incy and the cabbie, and me wondering where he had learned that magick. Now I was doing the same thing, and unknown magick was welling up inside me – I didn't even need to think about it. Thinking about it only made it slip away like smoke. But here I was, my ancient heritage finally showing up—

To hurt Old Mac.

There was a pinpoint of heat in my jeans pocket. Now it was burning my thigh, burning me through the fabric. I stopped and fished it out, my moonstone. It was glowing brilliantly, and seeing that really made me realize what I was doing.

I wanted to hurt Old Mac, and goddess knew he deserved it. He deserved it more than other people I'd hurt over the years, intentionally and unintentionally. So what was stopping me? My moonstone shone in my hand, almost too hot to hold.

What was stopping me?

Incy had crippled that cabbie. Boz had killed those boys.

River would be so . . . disappointed? Mad? Disappointed. She might even kick me out of River's Edge. Then where would I go? Solis and Asher would be mad – maybe not disappointed. Maybe they expected me to do something like this. Nell would be so, so happy, so joyful and triumphant that I had screwed up so spectacularly.

And they would know, beyond a doubt. They'd be able

to detect the scent of magickal energy around me, feel the vibrations in my fingers. I wasn't at River's Edge, where magick was cloaked, more or less, invisible to anyone outside. This was right here in town.

If I did this, if I worked this magick, it would leave an imprint of my energy here. I'd never thought about that before – maybe I'd never have noticed it or thought about it before. But when I walked into a classroom at River's, I could feel if magick had recently been worked there. I could sometimes tell by whom. I would leave my imprint here in the store, in West Lowing, for anyone to find.

Abruptly I sat down on an upturned plastic bin. My heart started pounding, and my ears filled with a buzzing sound.

I had almost ruined everything. I had almost advertised my presence to anyone who would want to pick up on it, to find me. Like Boz. Like Incy. Yes, River and the others had worked spells throughout the town so that I was more or less hidden here. But if I worked magick . . . that thought was perhaps even more scary than the thought of River's disapproval.

I had stopped. I had stopped in time.

I felt clammy and cold. Old Mac and Meriwether were still duking it out, two aisles over. I stood up, feeling shaky with nerves, and picked up a box of Tampax Pearls. Heading over to their voices, I strode up as if I'd been in Timbuktu and hadn't heard the shouting.

'Hey, does anyone know—' I began, then feigned surprise as two heads turned to look at me. Meriwether's face was splotched, and she had tears running down her cheeks. Old Mac was so red that I wondered if he was having a heart attack. I guessed I'd find out if he suddenly keeled over.

'Oops, sorry. Didn't mean to interrupt,' I went on with fake cheer. 'But do either of you know' – I held up the box of Tampax, its effect on Old Mac being similar to the effect of a cross on a vampire – 'does this come in a larger size?'

Meriwether, whose head must have been spinning, pulled her wits a bit together. 'Like, a seventy-eight pack?'

'No,' I said, as Old Mac started to back away, his eyes on the ground, muttering to himself. 'Like, this is a junior size. Then there's regular. Does it come in a jumbo, or super size? Like, for overnight, or . . . maybe . . . bigger people?'

Meriwether could barely think straight, but she valiantly tried, which got me madder at her stupid-ass father. 'I think it does,' she said faintly. 'Have you looked in the back?'

'Ah,' I said, seizing this brilliant suggestion. 'I haven't. I'll go do that. Hey, it's almost noon. I'm not hungry – you go eat lunch, and then I'll go when you get back. Okay?'

Meriwether bit her lip, then grabbed her coat and fled the store.

Old Mac was back in the medicine area, slamming small boxes around, muttering. I'd bought Meriwether a half-hour reprieve. I wished I could just – fix her situation. Hers and Dray's.

I cared about them. I wanted them to feel better, to live better lives. And then it occurred to me – I cared about myself. I wanted me to live a better life, too. Caring about myself was allowing me to care about others. River had been right *again*.

How annoying.

And I also knew – I had stopped myself from making dark magick. I had chosen *not* to. That was progress. It definitely was.

That night I was on dish duty, and I was focusing on the now, which meant really feeling how much I was not loving dish duty.

'Have you thought about an industrial dishwasher?' I asked River as she brought me another stack of plates. 'They have 'em that do a whole load in two minutes.' I swished my little handled brush over a plate, dunking it in the hot, soapy water. I'd forgotten to wear rubber gloves (let's all say *Of course*, all together, okay?), and my hands were chapped and reddened. They were the hands of, like, a Swedish fisherman. A man. An old one. I thought about Nell's soft, white girly hands, her manicure always perfect, and felt bile rising in my gut.

River smiled and brushed her hand along my back. 'I know how important it is to you to save time. 'Cause you just never have enough of it.'

I groaned, and she laughed.

In all seriousness, this whole past week had sucked. Nell seemed to be upping her warfare. I couldn't get Reyn out of my mind, reliving the terror of my memories of him, both as he had destroyed my childhood and now as he currently destroyed my peace of mind. I remembered our fevered kisses, remembered how horrified he'd looked when he recognized me. He had been appalled both that I was a 'bad girl,' who might make him backslide again, and also about the part he and his family had played in my life. His worlds were colliding, too.

Old Mac had been insufferable. I felt bad for both Meriwether and Dray. It was winter, my least favorite season, with the sun rising late and setting early, the endless cold, the snow, the ice. Why couldn't River have settled in, like, the Bahamas? Couldn't she rehabilitate souls there? Yes. She could have. She chose not to.

'Maybe I just can't do this.' I didn't even realize I'd said it out loud until River turned and said, 'What?'

Now that it was out, it was out. I gave a plate an angry scrub. 'I'm washing dishes and getting pecked by hens and targeted by two-faced bitches and making friends with kids whose lives are more miserable than mine and, oh yes, I'm here partying with the psycho who killed my parents – I mean, could it suck more?'

River looked at me.

'I'm not cut out to be an immortal Girl Scout,' I said tiredly. 'All this studying and accepting the past and examining my innards and this friend-being and shelf-stocking – this isn't *me*.'

River didn't say anything, and after a minute I steeled myself for what I might see in her eyes – disappointment? I looked up and saw . . . I don't know. Compassion?

'What do you want?' she asked softly.

'I want to feel better,' I said, like I had before. 'To not be in pain.'

'No – what do you really want?'

I clenched my teeth and blew out a breath. 'I want to . . . feel like I'm not a total waste of a person.'

'No.' She seemed quite sure. 'What do you really *want*?'

I wanted to scream and break this plate on the stone sink. 'I want to not be dark.' I almost whispered the words – I'd never said them out loud before.

River didn't say anything, but I got the distinct impression that that *still* wasn't the right answer. After a couple of moments, she brushed her hand over my hair and then left.

If Nell had come into the kitchen just then, I would have broken a plate over her head.

Instead I remained alone and finished washing the freaking dishes. Then I went upstairs, did my door-lock spell, got into bed in all my clothes, drank my tea, and cried until I fell asleep.

Chapter 29

The next day was Saturday. I had to groom two horses. I'd been assigned to Sorrel and Titus. Sorrel was a trim, neat quarterhorse that was used only for riding; Titus was an Irish Draught horse that occasionally got hooked up to wagons or carts or whatever. They were both nice animals, in that they were patient and calm, unlike, say, the chicken from hell.

I put Sorrel in the crossties and started in with the rubber currycomb. She *whuff*ed into my hair as I went over her coat, loosening up dirt and hair.

Horses. I don't even want to talk about horses. It's impossible to overstate how crucial horses have always been to people, until literally the last hundred years. For *thousands* of years, horses and cows are what kept people alive, enabled people to travel, to cart heavy things, to farm enough land to support a family. I'd always been around them. One of the times I'd lived in England, like in the mid-eighteen hundreds or so, I'd been horse crazy, rode every day, owned horses, had custom saddles. But they were like everything else: They died eventually.

Anyway, I'd gotten over them. Now I mostly avoided them. Their knowing eyes, their sensitive natures – they can see through bullshit, just like dogs, cats, and little kids. I tried to avoid all of those. Plus, as soon as I smelled a horse, it brought back so many memories, so strongly – the way scents do. Sometimes I can be in the exact same building or airport or see the exact same view from a bridge and not even remember it, though I know I've been there. But if that memory is coupled with a smell, it all floods back with excruciating detail. The smell of roasting peanuts in Manhattan. The smell of the Mediterranean Sea in Menton. Newly mown hay in Kansas. Snow in Iceland. Crushed grapes in Italy. Fried beignets and coffee in New Orleans.

And horses.

Sorrel stamped her left foreleg gently while I tried hard not to think about the hayloft just twelve feet above me. For a couple of minutes, I had been happy up there.

First the currycomb, then the dandy brush, then the body brush, then the towel. Sorrel looked like a postcard when I'd finished with her coat. I got the hoof pick and cleaned under her shoes and I was done. As I unclipped her crossties, she nuzzled my hair, her breath warm and hay-scented.

'Okay, horsie,' I muttered, and put her back in her stall.

Titus was bigger and heavier, but nowhere near as big as, say, a Percheron or a Shire horse. I've seen Shire horses that are truly enormous. I clipped Titus into the crossties and picked up the rubber currycomb with an arm that was already aching.

Draft horses.

My father had had warhorses – not huge and heavy, like in Europe, designed to hold men and armor weighing four hundred pounds. But still, big, powerful horses bred for war. Not for children to go near. He'd also kept what they called lady horses – smaller, lighter, usually dams, for me and my mother and my siblings to ride. I was put on one when I was three. By the time I was six, I would ride my horse – I don't know how to spell the old Icelandic name, but it meant starfish, because of a funny marking she had. My sisters and older brother and I would ride our horses sedately out of the bailey and pick our way down the trails to the rocky beach. There we would practice standing on our horses' backs, holding the reins in one hand, the other hand thrown dramatically above our heads. We thought it looked incredibly dashing and daring.

After I lost everything and lived with my foster family, and they married me off to Àsmundur, his father gave us a small draft horse as a wedding present. It was a princely gift – our own horse! Her name was – the translation is Mossy, because of her mane and tail. She was small but very strong and brave, and a hard worker. I loved her, though I could never ride her – when she wasn't working, she had to rest. Then Àsmundur died, and it was Mossy who carried his coffin to the burial field. Little Mossy pulled the flat wagon with Àsmundur, and the rest of us walked behind.

I'd had to sell Mossy after that – I couldn't afford to feed her over the winter, and I couldn't run even a tiny farm by myself. Plus, if I stayed in that community, it wouldn't be long before they found me another husband. A young, healthy widow – I would be snapped up like gold. So I'd sold Mossy and packed what I could carry on my back, and said good-bye to Momer and Pabbi and to Àsmundur's family, who didn't want me to go. They had another son, only fourteen at the time, so I would have been convenient to marry him off to.

I rode in a neighbor's hay wagon to the next-largest town, Aelfding. It took all day and some of the night. I cried the whole way, partly for poor Àsmundur but mostly for lovely, brave, strong little Mossy, whom I never saw again and missed for more than fifty years.

In Aelfding, I looked up Mother Berglind, who lived in an attic above a stable and earned her keep by weaving rough linen cloth for aprons and the like. She was very old and almost blind, working her loom mainly by touch. I had to go very close for her to see me. When she saw me, she squinted and cocked her head. I had changed – I was now eighteen, a woman, a widow, and the last time she'd seen me I was ten years old. But when she recognized me, she looked afraid and drew back.

'What do you want, child?' she asked.

'You remember me? I was . . . an orphan, and you placed me with a family, farmers, in the valley. Gunnar Oddursson?'

She hesitated, squinting at me, as if weighing whether to deny it or not. 'Yes,' she finally said reluctantly.

'My family's home was near Heolfdavik,' I said. 'Do you know if anyone is still there?'

The old woman looked around, as if someone might be listening. She seemed unhappy and upset at my visit. I had wanted to thank her for arranging my foster family, but she seemed anxious to have me gone.

'No one is there,' she said.

'Are there still people in the village?' I persisted.

'No! No one lives there!' She seemed angry now, turning away from me, hobbling back to the bench before her loom.

I didn't know what to say and felt embarrassed by her discomfort. I turned without a word and hurried down the narrow, slanting steps and out into the cool air.

I guess it was natural to go back. It wasn't as far as I thought – when I was little, it seemed like an incredibly long distance from my father's hrókur to Aelfding and from there to the Oddurssons' farm in the valley. But I walked it in about six hours, the road narrow and rutted with mud.

I remembered this road, vaguely. I'd only been down it this far a couple of times, but I remembered it as being wider, smoother, much more trafficked. In some places I had to practically break a path through overgrown brush. It had once been a thoroughfare between Heolfdavik and Aelfding, passing right by my father's lands, our village. It was odd that no one had been using it.

I barely noticed the turnoff that led to my father's lands. Only some rocks, shattered and overgrown by steppe grass, made me realize that this had once been our village gate. I headed down that road, and after half an hour, when my feet were sore and my shoulders ached from carrying my few belongings, I saw my father's bailey.

When I was little, the bailey was enclosed by stone walls maybe eighteen feet high, and over twelve feet thick, at the bottom. Now all I saw were fragments of broken stones.

Back then, any city that was more than four or five huts clustered together had a wall around it, to make it harder for raiders. It wouldn't stop them – nothing stopped them – but it would slow them down a bit. In our village we had the village wall first, with the gate I'd gone through, and then inside the walled village we had houses and huts and little patches of ground where people had goats or pigs or sheep, the occasional horse. Little plots of vegetable gardens. At the top of the hill was my family's big – the translation is castle, but it was a small castle. It was the biggest and most elaborate building for a hundred miles, but it was still rough, made all of stone, instead of wood or daub-and-wattle.

My father had been the king of this land, like his father before him, and his father before him. I had been born into royalty, royalty on a smaller scale than European kings and queens, though royalty who wielded a lot of power – the magickal power of the Fourth House of the Immortals. The House of Úlfur. The wall around our house probably enclosed about five acres. It was taller and wider than the village wall, and had places for soldiers to run along the top. Enormous wooden gates, studded with iron spikes, opened outward, to make it harder for them to be broken in by a battering ram. Right inside the gate was a thick wooden platform, covered with packed dirt. If you didn't know it was there, you'd walk right over it. But it could be pulled out of the way, in case of an attack, and it led down to a deep, deep hole. At the bottom of the hole were hundreds of wooden spikes. I guessed some of Reyn's men had ended up down there, that night.

It wasn't a castle like Versailles or Windsor castle – it was much rougher and older – but castlelike, with narrow arrow slits in the walls, curving stone stairs, and so on. The bailey was the yard enclosed by our wall. Our servants lived there, in little houses lining the walls, and we had our own horses and goats and pigs and sheep. Our own gardens. If raiders were attacking, the village people would grab whatever they could and run for my father's hrókur. The tall wooden gates would shut after them, and then we'd all hunker down and wait out the attack. Raiders had never gotten through my father's walls. Until they had.

That day it was almost nine years after the attack. I didn't know what I'd find. I thought perhaps the village would have been rebuilt. Maybe even a new lord established in the repaired castle. But what I found that day was nothing.

I saw the rubble of the village gates, and more rubble at our bailey wall. My father's house had been built of huge stones, cut right from the ground at an inland quarry. But as I stared at the site where it had to have been, the biggest rock I saw was maybe the size of a gourd. As if the stones had been pulverized, like Nell's sodalite. Now I knew that Reyn's father had tried to use my mother's amulet, the tool that helped focus her magick. But he didn't have her knowledge, her spells, and he had apparently been vaporized by an explosion of some kind of power. Reyn had seen his father and brothers and their men turned to ash in front of him. And he bore a burn, as I did.

Raiders always destroyed towns – setting fire to everything, taking or killing the livestock, taking or killing the people. But there were usually skeletal remains of cottages, foundations, chimneys. Sometimes the damage wasn't complete, and people would rebuild, but not often. Back then everyone believed that dangerous trolls followed in the wake of the raiders. So the village would be abandoned to the trolls, and a new village set up somewhere close by.

But this – I'd never seen anything like this. There was nothing left, and it had been a big stone structure with at least fourteen rooms. And unlike the road leading here, where my family's hrókur had been, nothing had grown back; not even nature had reclaimed the spot. I walked the outline of the house – the ground itself was charred, scorched. But things always grew back after a fire, sometimes even better.

I had set down my sack and sat on the ground. I had come back for nothing. No one was here to help me learn what had happened. Secretly I'd hoped that I'd find some of Faðir's books, maybe a little singed, but hidden under the rubble. Or my mother's jewelry, whatever the raiders hadn't found. Instead it was as if no one had ever been here. I rubbed the back of my neck. This was where I had lived for the first ten years of my life, where I'd had a real family. We'd been rich; my father had been powerful. Important people had traveled great distances to see him. We'd had servants and teachers and books and musical instruments and horses and a little cart, drawn by goats, for my baby brother.

Now there was nothing. I had nothing. I had no one.

That night I'd seen my father's head drop down the chimney and roll across the floor. I'd seen my mother flay someone alive, seen Sigmundur cut his head off. I'd run to my mother, leaving my next-oldest sister and my little brother, and I'd clung to the back of my mother's skirt. The scene was all choppy images, roaring, broken sounds. There were men, so many men, out in the hallway. The castle was on fire, everything outside in the bailey was on fire. Horses and sheep were screaming. Children – the children of my father's men – were crying. Sometimes I heard their cries suddenly cut short.

The skinned raider's body lay on the floor, every raw inch of it oozing blood. In the next moment, the bigger man, with golden-red hair and a painted face, roared and reached over his shoulder to grab his battle-axe. It seemed to happen in endless slow motion, but I saw the honed metal blade swing, saw my brother jump nimbly to avoid it, saw the blade slice down through his shoulder, almost severing his arm.

Sigmundur cried out and then the room was filled with more berserkers. Some stood guard outside the door, cutting down my father's guards as they raced down the hall.

Sigmundur staggered, wailing, but was lifting his own sword in his other hand when the raider's axe swung again, and then my brother's head was dropping to the ground, followed by his slowly crumpling body.

From behind my mother's skirt I heard her harsh, dark, terrible song, saw lightning flash from her hands, striking raiders in their faces, their eyes. They would shriek and fall back, but there were always others.

Someone cut off Eydís's head and she went down like a mown flower in a field. Her head stayed very close to her neck, and her eyes continued to blink, her hands twitching. A heavy boot shoved her head several feet away, and after a few minutes she was still and her eyes closed.

Tinna was next. She'd always hated fighting and swords, had always tried to get out of practice. Now she stood in her nightgown, her face as white as the linen, and let her sword drop to the ground. A man came forward and grabbed her, throwing her over his shoulder. He started to wade through the bodies to leave the room, but some of my father's guards attacked him, slashing their swords through his belly so that his guts spilled out.

Another axe cut off Tinna's head. The biggest man, the oldest one, was shouting orders – he was still alive, though spattered with so much blood that it was making the paint on his face run. He spoke a different dialect from ours, but it was similar enough that I understood the words 'Kill them all! Leave none alive! Even the children! Even one alive will curse their magick!'

Háakon sank to his knees, his small hands still holding his dagger. A man ran at him and Háakon automatically slashed out with his dagger, catching the man's calf. In another second my little brother, too, was dead.

My mother was standing, tall and terrible and radiating power. I saw a lightning bolt shoot through the air and hit the biggest raider in the eye. It exploded and he screamed, dropping his axe and clapping one hand over the ruined socket. As my mother raised her hands again, holding the amulet, he swung his longsword one-handed, faster than I would have thought possible. I felt my mother's body jerk from the blow, and then very, very slowly, she began to fall backward. I clung to her skirts and squeezed my eyes shut, and she fell right on top of me. My head hit the stone floor so hard, I saw stars and the chaos of the room dimmed for a moment. My mother's weight was heavy on me, the thick wool of her robe suffocating. I couldn't see anything, couldn't move. The shouting was muffled. My nose filled with horrible burning scents, of hair, wool, skin.

I don't know how long I lay there. Eventually there was silence, and still I stayed, though I could barely breathe. Smoke was filling my nose, burning my throat. Finally I realized I truly couldn't breathe. I pushed experimentally on my mother's body, but I had to brace my feet and shove hard. She rolled away from me. I opened my eyes. The room was empty of living things. Around me lay the bodies of my brothers and sisters. My mother's face, still beautiful, rested peacefully several feet away. The hall outside was empty. I heard dim cries from outside. The castle was burning down around me, this room aflame, the heat almost unbearable.

Slowly I got to my feet. I was numb, not thinking, not feeling anything. I felt dead myself – perhaps they had killed me, and I was a spirit now. I had to step over

Eydís's body, had to step over Háakon. If I were a spirit I could have floated over them.

The door to the study was broken in, shattered, and I headed toward it, and then from the corner of my eye I saw a wall move. I looked at it and it moved again, a narrow strip of stone wall next to a cupboard. It swung sideways and I crouched down, my fingers accidentally brushing Sigmundur's hair, sodden with blood.

A woman's face peered out, looking terrified. She saw the room and its contents and raised her hand over her mouth to prevent herself screaming. I blinked and recognized her: Gildun Haraldsdottir. She was the wife of my father's stable steward. A man appeared next to her: Stepan, her husband. His face crumpled with sorrow and horror and he put a hand on her shoulder.

I stood up.

They jumped back in alarm, seeing me standing among the flames and the bodies. Mouth open in shock, Gildun motioned to me to come to her. I started slowly toward her, hardly knowing what I was doing. Something crunched under my foot — it was a heavy gold chain, the one that held my mother's amulet around her neck. The amulet was gone, my mother's neck severed. I took another step toward Gildun, leaving the chain where it was.

Urgently they beckoned me. I'd never seen this secret door, had no idea where it led. Now, looking back, I can see that's why my mother had herded us all in there. Somehow things had happened too fast for her to get us down the escape tunnel, or maybe it could only be opened from the other side. I don't know. I'll never know.

Flames flickered along the carpet where I stood. In another moment my nightgown would catch on fire. I didn't know I was immortal, had just seen my family killed. I knew dying in a fire would be bad. Another step farther and I stepped on something else. I feared it might be someone's hand – didn't want to look down. But I did. I was standing on smoldering wool – the stench was terrible. Beneath the flames was my mother's amulet – or at least, half of it. Half was missing, the half with the moonstone. I quickly glanced around and didn't see it. I bent down and picked it up, burning my hand, and immediately dropped it again.

'Lilja, hurry!' Gildun's voice was hushed and scared. 'The fire!'

I ripped the hem of my nightgown – it came off in a long strip. I wrapped my hand in it, picked up the amulet, and then kept my gaze focused on Gildun's face. In five steps I had reached her, and Stepan reached out, grabbed me, and pulled me into the black tunnel. Gildun closed the door behind us and picked up her torch. Stepan held my hand tightly and rushed me along the tunnel.

'Wait!' I needed my hands free. I wrapped the amulet in the strip of cloth and tied it closely around my neck. Then I took Stepan's hand again, and the three of us ran along this low-ceilinged tunnel, dirt-floored, narrow, smelling of damp and earth.

It felt like we ran for hours. I tripped on roots and stones, and once Gildun had to drag me upright again. Finally we came out right into a huge boulder. A very narrow natural fissure in the boulder was the exit, and it was hidden by dense brush. We fought our way through the brush and I found that we were on a narrow farm road, quite a distance away from the castle. Over my shoulder I saw that the entire structure was alight with flame.

I didn't know if we were going to run all the way to Aelfding or what, but about a quarter-mile down the road, a farmer, someone I didn't know, was waiting on his hay cart. Working quickly, Gildun and Stepan tore a hole in the hay, then Stepan picked me up and tossed me up there like a parcel. More hay was dumped on top of me, at least five feet thick, but so loosely that I could still breathe, though just barely.

The farmer clicked to his donkey, and the heavy cart started to move.

The next day the farmer took me to Mother Berglind, and she took me to Gunnar Oddursson's farm, and I became Sunna Gunnarsson. Lilja and her life were set aside, a closed book I'd never wanted to reopen. I lived there for six years, till I got married. I never saw Gildun or Stepan or the farmer again, had no idea what ever happened to them.

As time went on, I got used to being a farmer's daughter, and the only sign that I had ever been anything different was the round burn on the back of my neck, where the amulet had burned through the cloth and right into my skin. I hadn't even noticed it at the time.

The sun was high in the sky – I had to start now to get back to Aelfding before sunset. Suddenly the back of my neck prickled and I stood quickly, shading my eyes to search the edge of the woods quite some distance away. I saw no one and nothing, and it occurred to me that I hadn't seen or heard a single bird, seen a single wild animal in this place. I hadn't even seen any insects. This place was worse than dead – it seemed cursed.

I grabbed up my pack and set off for the road. My pack felt five times heavier, my sturdy clogs unbearably heavy and clumsy. Everything was weighted; an oppressive stillness pressed down on me, making my breath thick in my throat. I hurried on. It seemed to me that not even the sun shone as brightly here. There was darkness here, a shadow not cast by any living thing. This place was soaked with horror and blood and evil.

And then I was struck down with pain, doubled over, my pack spilling out of my hand.

I stroked the dandy brush lightly down Titus's legs, feeling the warm strength there. I wished I'd had all these fancy tools to take better care of Mossy. I'd done the best

I could, but she would have been so happy with this fine barn and these bales of timothy hay.

That had all been so long ago. That was then, this was now. I straightened, my hand on Titus's side. An idea cracked into my brain, like sharp white light, and with astonishment I realized what River had said to me. Then, I was *there*, in time and distance, a faraway other world, another me. Now I was *here*, right here, in reality, and this was me *now*. I was *no longer* there, no longer that girl. Somehow, I'd never gotten that before.

Maybe what River had meant was that time itself was like a river, moving steadily forward, and you got to be in a new river every day, every hour. All my life I'd felt like − a lake. A lake where everything was contained, forever. All my experiences, all the different people I'd been, everything I'd had, everything I'd lost . . . I carried them around with me, all the time. They'd made up layer after layer of hardened shell, like layers of shellac on a Japanese box. That shell had protected the withered, half-dead me that could no longer bear to interact with anything or anyone normally.

My time here − not even two months − was gradually stripping away one paper-thin layer of shell at a time. And the wretched, coiled-up me inside was sort of . . . inflating. Plumping up, like an almost-dead flower suddenly drenched with rain. Why was that happening? Why was I letting it, after so long?

On that day, over 440 years ago, I'd lain on the charred

ground of my father's stronghold, weeping in fear and pain. I'd had a miscarriage, my only tie to Àsmundur and my life with him. Then I truly felt that I'd lost everything – my family, my home, my foster family, my husband, my beloved horse, and now my only baby, who had lived without my knowing and had died before I realized it. I had nothing left, nowhere to go. No one to be – not daughter, not wife, not even friend.

When I could walk the next day, I had gathered my things and set off down the road, away from the place of horror and death and loss. I walked until I found a tall, leafy plant with pretty sprays of small purple flowers. I ate a bunch of it, choking down the flowers, the rough, coarse leaves, barely able to swallow them. Our washerwoman had told us that monkshood was fatally poisonous and that we children were never to touch it.

I ate as much as I could, feeling the poison start to burn my mouth. My hands grew numb, and I doubled over again with terrible stomach pains. I cried and screamed and retched for hours before I lost consciousness.

The irony being, of course, that I was immortal, but didn't know it. After my suicide attempt failed, and I couldn't even die properly, I had somehow made my way to the biggest town, Reykjavik. I was taken in as a servant by a housekeeper, and introduced to my new mistress, Helgar. That was when my life as an immortal began, and my old life ended, just as sharply and surely as if that monkshood had killed me. I'd grown my first shell.

'If you brush that horse any longer, he won't have any coat left.'

My head jerked up at the words, and I watched Reyn's hard, broad back as he carried several heavy saddles down the aisle. It had been Reyn, that night. He'd been one of the raiders out in the hall. He himself hadn't actually killed any of my family, which was a relief, because *I* would *have* to kill *him*, and it's actually pretty hard to cut someone's head off. But he'd been there that night. He was the only other person alive who had shared the horror of that experience with me. And here he was, in Levi's and work boots. No face paint, no sword at his side. Just a normal guy. A normal, grumpy, stuffed-shirt guy who had shared the experience of my family's decimation, four hundred years ago.

In fact, Titus had turned his head and was giving me an *okaaaay* look.

'Sorry,' I muttered to him, dumping my tools and unclipping him.

I led him to his stall, made sure he had hay, and then went back to my room, lost in thought.

Chapter 30

Just another smidgen . . .

I took another slow bite, looking down at my plate, but focusing all my attention on Nell's dinner roll. I breathed in and out very slowly, concentrating on moving her roll just slightly out of reach, again and again.

Once, twice, three times I saw her reach for it as she chatted with an unresponsive Reyn and a more animated Lorenz, who threw his head back and laughed. Each time Nell's hand went automatically for where she had left her roll, and each time her fingers closed on air. Frowning, she would take it, break off a piece, then set it closer to her plate.

Then I would edge it out of the way, very, very slowly. Using just my super-duper immortal brain waves. It was an incredible triumph.

I had come in earlier and worked the necessary spells of limitation so that not *everyone's* rolls would move, and Nell would have *only* her roll move, and not her fork or her glass. I had pored over spellcrafting books in the library, and practiced individual bits of the spell for the last two days in my room. I was making white magick: Nothing near me was dying, nothing having its life sucked out. This was me, now, Tähti, utilizing my heritage of incredible magickal power. Of course, I was using it to do something kind of mean. Did that make it not white magick? Did *intent* matter as much as method? There was probably a class about that in my future.

I was practically aglow with suppressed excitement, and the effort to restrain a cackling laugh was making my stomach hurt. But I was doing it. And Nell was getting a little flustered, a little bit confused. It was such a minor thing, to have one's roll not where one thinks it is, and yet it's *such* a minor thing that an inability to do it becomes very puzzling.

I took another slow spoonful of soup, controlling my breathing, keeping my face still and neutral. Two seats away, Nell's lovely manicured fingers clicked down on empty table, again. This time she actually stared at her roll, and went through a quick motion of where it should be.

I almost snorted soup through my nose. I felt her look up, glance around the table. As far as I could tell, no one here ever used/misused magick like this. Ever since the smushed stone incident, Nell had made a subtle-yet-obvious show of watching me, not sitting by me, avoiding me. She wanted to make sure everyone knew that dear, sweet Nell was suspicious and didn't trust me.

After all, she'd been here for years. They knew her. I was still a relative stranger.

'Oh, Nas, did you uncover the onion rows this morning in the garden?' Brynne asked. She had another colorful cloth wrapped around her head, contrasting oddly with her woolen Nordic sweater. Lately it seemed that the radiators weren't quite up to the task of keeping the rooms warm. It was already an unusually cold winter, people said.

'Yep,' I said, and dipped my bread into my soup.

'And did you cover them back up before the sun went down?' Asher asked.

'Yep,' I said, and reached for more sautéed greens.

'There'll be no more spinach this year, not even in the cold frames,' said Jess in his gravelly voice. I tried to look suitably disappointed.

Nell now had a death grip on her roll, keeping it in one hand while her smile became strained, her laughter a little too bright.

Keeping as innocent an expression on my face as possible, I ate slowly and listened as people talked about Yule, which was tomorrow.

'We have the Yule log,' said Charles. 'It's been curing in the back barn since last year.'

'We'll light it at sunset,' said Solis. 'How is the cooking team coming along with their plans?'

'It's me, Charles, and Lorenz,' said Anne. 'I think we have it all figured out.'

'All right,' said Solis. 'Yell if you need help.'

'I can make cookies, if you want,' said Jess, and Anne looked happy and nodded. The thought of weather-beaten Jess, who looked like he'd been dragged off the street for some social-work program, being a cookie master was funny, and I smiled.

Out of the very corner of my eye, I saw that Nell had finally let go of her roll, leaving it on the edge of her plate.

'The decorating is almost done,' she said, plastering a cheerful smile on her face. 'And we're going to be hanging mistletoe, so watch out!'

Around the table, people smiled and chuckled, including me – even as I gently, gently, shoved Nell's roll off her plate.

The slight movement caught her eye and she jerked her head to stare at it. Lorenz, across from me, asked me to pass the salt, and I did so smoothly, without losing concentration. I was even able to ask him if people exchanged gifts at Yule.

'We do a "secret elf" kind of thing,' he told me in his accented English. Lorenz seemed to meld generations of Italian notions of perfection all in one person, and I wondered why I didn't find him more attractive. 'We pass out names in a hat, and we each choose one. Then we must give a secret gift to our chosen one.'

I wondered how far Nell would go to make sure she chose Reyn, or he chose her, or both.

Idly I glanced up and saw that Nell was actually tearing her roll into tiny bits and dropping them into her soup, where she flattened them with her spoon. I almost burst out laughing, but the intent, deadly expression on her face stifled my amusement.

Had anyone else noticed? She actually seemed a little like she was going off the deep end. Reyn was watching her out of the side of his eye, no expression on his face.

Everyone was talking about Yule plans, and the mood was light, happy, and cozy. I glanced around, and everyone — except Nell and Reyn — seemed content. I had another one of those forehead-slapping insights: I couldn't remember the last time I'd been in a group of people who seemed, by and large, content. Certainly not any of my friends, who, with time and distance seemed like sociopaths to me. I'd been around rich and powerful and kind of limitless people for a long, long time, but when had any of them seemed actually content? Triumphant, yes. Victorious, yes. But content was a completely new phenomenon for me, and I was struck by it.

The people at this table were not changing the course of history, or running huge companies, or taking over territories. They weren't pushing anything to the limit and beyond. They weren't subjugating other people, weren't working to increase their control over anything except themselves, weren't doing anything to excess, weren't acquiring whatever they could. Each of them, I now knew, had horrific tales, and stories of triumph.

Each of them needed to be here for a short while or a long while.

And yet there was a deep level of contentment here. Even Jess, ravaged by time and experience, seemed content. No one thought he or she was perfect – everyone was working on skills, strengths, areas of knowledge. Everyone was a work in progress. They were important in no sphere except this one, were known to few besides each other. We all had relatively low-key jobs, and we all schlepped and cleaned and carried like serfs, every day.

Why were they so happy? It wasn't even like everyone was with his or her ultimate soul mate. Asher and River were a couple, but no one else was, that I knew about.

I felt astonishment. More: I felt a sudden awakening, a dawning, a clarity of thought. Maybe my moonstone was helping me – but I suddenly, finally knew what I wanted. It all seemed obvious, as if it had been in front of me the whole time, even before I'd arrived here.

I saw that River was looking right at me, her clear brown eyes alert. Raising her brows slightly, she cast her eyes at Nell's roll, now mashed to bits inside her soup bowl. Then she narrowed her eyes at me, as if to say, I know you caused that.

I bit my lip.

The meal was over. I had prepared only the roll spell, so once it was paste in Nell's soup, my fun was over. But it had been glorious.

Then I found out that Reyn and I were the cleanup crew

for dinner. We hadn't been scheduled together since we'd found each other out, and I could have sworn my name hadn't been there before dinner. But it was there now, and when I looked at River she gave me a no-nonsense look back. Perhaps this was my penance for the roll? She couldn't have known for sure. Maybe she could.

In the kitchen, Nell was standing very close to Reyn, who was filling the sink with soapy water. She was laughing up at him, murmuring in her sweet voice.

'Nell?' said River.

Nell looked around with a charming smile. When she saw me her smile faltered, but she quickly propped it up again. She waved a cheerful hand at me. 'Nastasya, you go on. I'll take your part tonight.'

I whipped around and was about to zip out of the kitchen when River said, 'I'd like Nastasya to do the kitchen with Reyn tonight, Nell.'

We were all surprised – people switched chores all the time. This was kind of unusual. Clearly I had some kind of life lesson to learn by being cooped up in the kitchen with my archnemesis. I felt distinctly unready to learn it.

I let out a breath and started organizing the leftovers to store in Tupperware containers. River waited until Nell had reluctantly left, then came closer to me.

'We've felt . . . someone scrying for you, Nastasya. Usually we wouldn't pick up on it, but we've put spells in place to conceal your presence here. Someone has been trying to find you, using magick.'

My heart kicked up a notch. 'Incy?'

'That would be my guess,' said River. She patted my back. 'I don't want to worry you, but I wanted to let you know. We teachers will take steps to assure that you're safe here. Unless you want to talk to Innocencio?'

'I don't. Not yet.' Maybe not ever.

'Okay, then. Everything's fine, but I thought you should know.'

I nodded, and River left.

The night outside the windows was black and cold. Yule was tomorrow; the house felt festive. But here in the kitchen, Incy was hanging over my head, and there was bad blood between Reyn and me. And here, 'bad blood' is a ridiculously lame euphemism.

'River says we need to talk.' Reyn was scraping dishes into the pigs' bucket – they loved leftovers. 'She's right. She usually is.'

'Not this time. I don't want to talk to you.' I dumped some salad into a baggie and put it in the big fridge.

'Neither of us wants to leave here.' His voice was low and controlled. 'But we have this thing between us. I don't want it to cause problems for us or anyone else.'

This thing between us? He made it sound like a bad date. 'Anyone else, like Nell?'

He slanted a glance at me. God, he was good-looking. So totally, cosmically, karmically unfair. 'I don't know why you keep harping about that. There's nothing between me and Nell.'

I snorted. 'Does Nell know that? 'Cause she's practically picking out your china.' He looked blank and I clarified, 'For your wedding.'

'Don't be ridiculous.' He looked horrified, and my heart gave a little skip. My heart is so stupid that way.

'Don't be an oblivious, insensitive moron,' I retorted. 'Oops, too late!' I went into the big pantry to get some containers, and startled when Reyn followed me in. This pantry was a narrow closet, essentially, and there wasn't enough room for both of us.

'Get out,' I said, my hands full of plastic.

'We could kill each other,' he said. He was tall and broad and smelled surprisingly good for someone who had massacred whole villages. My gaze was riveted on the vee of skin at his shirt's collar, and I remembered the burn he had. Then his words sank in.

'What?' A cold knot tightened in my stomach. As defensive weapons, Tupperware was grossly inadequate.

'You could kill me for the part I played in your worst experiences. I could kill you for the part you played in my worst experiences. We both lost siblings, parents, friends, in horrible deaths. Now there's only you, heir to the House of Úlfur, and me, heir to the House of Erik the Bloodletter. You and I are all that's left.'

'And you think we should kill each other and be done with it?' I frowned. 'I can't even figure out how.'

The side of his mouth quirked and I drew in a quick

breath. 'We could hold hands and jump into an industrial turbine.'

I stared at him. 'You think this is funny?'

He made an impatient gesture. 'I think this is four hundred years later, is what I think. If you wanted revenge, you should have come after me then.'

'I was *ten years old*!'

'I was barely twenty!'

We glared at each other for long moments.

'Barely twenty?' I said finally. 'Not, like, two hundred by then?'

Reyn shook his head. 'No. My father was five hundred then. I had three brothers. One was four hundred and sixty. One was two hundred and ninety-nine. One was a hundred and seventy four. I was twenty. Being immortal was incomprehensible to me then.'

'And they all died?'

'Yes,' he said grimly. 'One died – that night. The other two died with my father when he tried to use your mother's amulet.'

'Why didn't you die then, too?' It would have been so convenient.

'I don't know. Why didn't you die that night?'

'My mother fell on me – I was hidden under her skirts.'

We were silent then, revisiting memories that, hidden, were so much more painful. It was amazing to me that I had someone to talk to about that night, someone who had experienced it.

Reyn let out a breath. 'What now? Do we come to terms with it? Do we kill each other? Does one of us leave? I can tell you, it won't be me.'

'I don't want to leave.' The last two months had been the best of my entire life, the healthiest. I felt so different now; though I often experienced more pain, I could see that it was like lancing a blister. Once the memories were out, they were less destructive.

'So we both stay,' Reyn said.

I scowled. 'I guess. Until I can think of something awful to do to you. But if you were a gentleman, you'd leave.'

He gave a hard smile and the oxygen in my lungs evaporated. 'We both know I'm not a gentleman.'

'Yeah. Okay, let me out. I'm tired.'

'There's something else,' he said, and I groaned.

'What now?'

'This.' He stepped closer to me, so close that the containers were sandwiched between us. His eyes looked down into mine, intent and golden, like a lion.

'Oh, no, you don't!' I hissed, dropping everything. I pushed hard against his chest; it was like shoving a tree.

'Yes,' he said very softly, leaning down. 'Yes, I do.'

I did wriggle. I did push against him and try to turn my head. I really did. But you know, he's so much stronger . . . and I'm, of course, a *complete and total idiot*, and when he held me tightly and finally captured my mouth with his, every coherent thought flew out of my head and within seconds, I forgot to struggle.

Thoughts like *mortal enemy*, thoughts like *hate him*, thoughts like *Nell's a problem* – they all just slipped away like smoke blowing away in a breeze.

I pulled my mouth away, torn and confused and so full of longing that my chest hurt, and said, '*Why?*'

'I don't know,' he said. 'I don't know.' He sounded frustrated and uncertain and dismayed. I felt his heart thumping against my chest. 'I just – want you. I want you so bad, all the time. I know I shouldn't, I know I can't, I know it's wrong . . . but even when you're pissing me off, when you're reminding me of pain and despair and torture – it's there, the wanting. I'm tired of fighting it. I fight so many things, all the time, every day. I don't want to fight this. Not anymore.'

Our foreheads were pressed together. His hands were locked around my waist; mine were on his shoulders. He felt like rock beneath my fingers, and I traced on his shirt where his burn must be. I wanted to melt into him, wanted to drag him back to the hayloft – and at the same time knew it was stupid and crazy and that I should be psychoanalyzed immediately. Possibly given shock therapy. Perhaps put into a straitjacket.

It was like everything on the outside knew it was wrong and traitorous and stupid, but everything on the inside was going, oh my God this feels so good, so right, we fit, we're the same, we know each other down to our bones.

I don't know how much longer we were there, or what time we finally broke apart. Was it a tiny sound that filtered into my fevered brain? A hissing? A slight brushing sound on the flagstone floor outside the pantry?

But minutes later we heard yelling, and at almost the same instant we smelled smoke.

'Fire!' someone shouted, echoed by other people, and then an actual fire alarm sounded.

Reyn grabbed my hand and pulled me out through the back kitchen door, out into the frigid night air. We raced around to the front of the house, where people were gathering in the front yard. Everyone looked shocked and upset.

'Where's River?' I grabbed Brynne as she ran by.

'They're putting it out,' she said breathlessly. 'The teachers. I'm supposed to count heads.' She started pointing at everyone – a few had run out of the house, some had been outside, and Jess had been in the barn. She got all eight students, including me and Reyn, who had been making out in the pantry. I winced when I remembered it.

Within just a few minutes, the windows no longer showed the flickering light of flames.

'It looks like it was in the dorm wing,' Daisuke said, rubbing his arms. Most of us weren't wearing coats. I was taking care not to stand too close to Reyn – inside, my thoughts were sort of screaming in both horror and joy, but I needed to keep it all a secret until I figured out what the hell I was doing.

'Oh, Reyn! There you are!' Nell came over and linked her arm through his while I looked the other way and tried not to react. 'Goodness – what's happening? I smell smoke.' She glanced around at the others and then caught sight of me. She did an obvious double take when she saw me – blinking, mouth open, looking at me as if to make sure I was there.

'There was a fire,' Rachel said. 'You're right, Daisuke, it was in the dorm wing. I had to use the fire stairs on the other side of the house.'

A minute later River, Anne, Asher, and Solis came outside.

'The fire is out,' Solis said, and a couple students clapped.

'What happened?' asked Charles. 'How did it start?'

'We're still figuring that out,' said River. She looked very serious and tired. I wondered if they had used magick to put out the fire.

'Exactly where was it?' Nell asked. Out of the corner of my eye I saw Reyn disengage her hand and step away from her. She looked at him longingly but tried to keep her face calm.

'It was by Nastasya's room,' said Anne, looking at me. 'All around her door.'

My mouth fell open.

Nell shook her head. 'Some people have to be the

center of attention,' she murmured under her breath, just loud enough for a few people to hear.

I turned to face Nell, but before I could speak, River said, 'Yes. I know what you mean.'

Nell looked as if she hadn't meant for River to hear her, and flushed.

'I didn't set it,' I said angrily. 'Is my room okay?'

'Yes, we think so,' said River. 'You can go in and check.'

'Well, where were you?' Nell gave me a concerned look. 'You weren't in the kitchen. You weren't in the barn. You weren't on a walk with the others. You must have been in your room. How did you get out? How do we know you didn't set it?'

I put my hands on my hips, wanting to smack that smug look right off her face.

'That's enough, Nell,' said Asher. 'Nastasya, let's go check your room.'

'But – why is anyone believing her?' Nell looked dumbfounded. The other students circled around us and I got the feeling they didn't witness stuff like this too often. I had brought excitement to River's Edge! In a totally bad way, of course.

'Nastasya was with me,' Reyn said shortly.

Nell's eyes were round. 'No – she was in her room. Where were you? You weren't in the kitchen. I – needed to ask you something, and you weren't there.'

'Nastasya was with me the whole time, after dinner till

now. Not in her room.' A muscle was twitching in Reyn's jaw – he was angry.

The possibility of Reyn's standing up for me did not seem to have occurred to Nell, and it flustered her. 'She might have taken a moment, run off, set the fire, then come back,' she tried. 'Where were you?'

'She didn't,' said Reyn.

'Nell – it's like you have it in for Nastasya,' Rachel said.

'I don't!' Nell insisted. 'But why does everyone trust her? Why does everyone believe *her*? Ever since she came, things have been awful! It's been dark – evil! She's ruined everything!'

Suddenly River and Solis were standing on either side of her. 'It's over, Nell,' Solis said gently.

'What's *happening*?' Charles asked.

'Nell,' said River, putting a hand on Nell's shoulder. 'You know what I'm going to say. We talked about this. You've gone too far, and I have to ask you to leave River's Edge.'

Jaw after jaw dropped, including mine.

Nell looked astonished. 'No! What are you talking about? Not me, *her*! *She* has to leave! She's evil, violent! She's tried to hurt me! I didn't want to tell you, didn't want to make trouble. But she's put spells on me! She's tried to hurt me! You have to get rid of her!'

'Nell,' River said, and waited till Nell focused on her face. 'We've talked to you about this, about the spells you put on Nastasya's room, the other things you've done. You're working dark magick, and we won't have it. We've given you several chances to choose a different path, but you seem unable to get past your hatred. Now, as we discussed, I've arranged for you to go spend time with my aunt,' said River. 'In Canada. Asher will go with you, get you settled in, if you like.'

'I do not understand what's happening,' I said.

'What's happening is that you're *winning*!' Suddenly Nell's face transformed into rage. 'You stupid bitch! You've been trying to get rid of me since the beginning! Reyn loves *me*! He wants to be with *me*! But you've cast a spell on him, made him want you! I saw you kissing!'

Please, ground, just open up and let me fall into an endless crevasse till I hit the center of the earth and combust. Please. Is that too much to ask?

Nell lunged at me while I was rooted with embarrassment, but River and Solis held her arms. River started murmuring things, tracing symbols onto Nell's back, her arms. Nell started screaming, writhing, kicking. 'No! Stop it! You've got it all wrong! It's her! She's the one! She's dark! We've all felt it! *Get rid of her!*' Her last words ended in a shriek.

It was horrible and painful and mortifying, even though I pretty much hated her. It was still bad.

A couple moments later Nell slumped, sobbing tiredly, and Solis put his arm around her, leading her to the van. Anne followed them, speaking softly, saying that they would send Nell's things up to her. Nell was still mumbling, tears streaming down her face, and to tell you the truth, she looked like a crazy witch.

I was trying to absorb the fact that River did seem to believe me, be taking my side, despite everything. Reyn was standing close to me, though he wasn't touching me. I saw his hands clenching and unclenching, and was aware that everyone was looking back and forth between us like they were watching a Ping-Pong match.

River came over to me. I felt like I'd been put in a blender and put on Shred. All my emotions were raw, my nerves stretched tight.

'Are you okay?' she asked.

I thought about it. 'No. Not really.'

She gave me the barest of smiles and rubbed my arm, then looked over at Reyn. Tilting her head to one side, River turned back to me, as if she was sensing some sea change inside my soul, had sensed it even before I had.

I let out a deep breath. Her eyes were still on me. 'What do you want?' she asked softly.

I swallowed. 'I want to belong here,' I said, telling her what I'd realized during dinner. 'To be content and at peace, needing nothing except to learn. I want to feel safe, and not like an outsider. I want . . . to *belong*, here. To be worthy of being here. As long as I can.' Stupidly, I was near tears, like a child, like someone who had her heart on her sleeve. Panic throbbed in my chest, but I ignored it.

Her gaze sharpened, and I thought I could see more than a thousand years of emotion behind her eyes.

'Yes?' she asked.

'Yes. But . . . most of all – I want to be myself. I want to be Lilja, of the House of Úlfur.' I rubbed my hand across my face, very tired. 'I know that now, and I under-stand everything that that means. I want my power back. I want my heritage. I want to be my mother's daughter, my father's heir.' My voice choked up, and I got that hot, pre-cry feeling behind my eyes. It all seemed so clear to me now, so inevitable.

A new light flared in River's eyes, a new wonder on her face. I thought I saw relief, gladness, anticipation in her expression. She put her arm around me. 'Yes,' she said simply. 'Yes. I want that for you.'

'Wait,' Brynne said, her voice seeming unnaturally loud in the silent night. 'You guys were *kissing*?'

I groaned and covered my face. Reyn shifted from foot to foot, looking anywhere but at me. Things weren't over between us – not the bad things, and now I knew, not the good things, either. I wanted to see how it came out. I was done running.

SNEAK PEEK!

DARKNESS FALLS

The second book in the IMMORTAL BELOVED series.

Available January 2012

I heard a voice. Was it . . . singing? It was singing. I pushed my way through some stabbing holly branches and then I was in a tiny clearing, and there was a fire flickering wildly inside a circle of rocks.

"Nas." My head jerked at the voice. I looked over to see Innocencio, my best friend for a hundred years, stepping out of the darkness of the woods.

"Incy! What are you doing here?"

He smiled, looking unearthly beautiful. His eyes were so dark that I saw tiny fires reflected in them. I stared at him, feeling alarmed even as I held my hands out to the fire's warmth.

"I've been waiting for you, darling," Incy said in a voice as sweet and seductive as wine. "Come, sit down, be warm." He gestured to a big fallen log at the edge of the clearing. I didn't want to – everything in me was screaming, Run! But my feet took me over to the log and I sat on it. I didn't want to be here, didn't want to be with him, but then again, the fire was so comforting, so cozy.

"You've been gone too long, Nasty," Incy said. "I've missed you so much. We all have." Still smiling, he gestured around, and I scanned the place for my old gang. No one was there except me and Incy, and I started to ask why.

Then I saw. The fire . . . there was a skull in the fire, the flames blackening and devouring bits of its peeling flesh . . . My mouth opened in a horrified gasp. The fire was *full* of bones, *made* of bones. I knew in a split second that this was Boz and Katy – maybe Stratton and Cicely, too. Incy had killed them all and was burning their bodies. I jumped to my feet, only to have Incy smile at me again; he had me. There was no escape. Suddenly the wretched, acrid stench of burning hair and flesh filled my nose and mouth, gagging me, making me retch. I couldn't breathe. I tried to scream, but no sound came out. I tried to run, but my feet were literally rooted to the ground – thick, dark, vining roots covered my feet, locking me into place, and started to climb my legs.

Knock knock.

I gagged again and in the next instant bolted straight up and opened my eyes. I was gasping, wild-eyed, covered with icy sweat – in my room at River's Edge.

Knock knock.

Be sure to read

DARKNESS
FALLS

the next book in the
Immortal Beloved trilogy

available
January 2012